ZELUCO

VALANCOURT CLASSICS

ZELUCO.

VARIOUS VIEWS

OF

HUMAN NATURE,

TAKEN

From LIFE and MANNERS,

Foreign and Domestic.

John Moore

Edited with an introduction and notes by Pam Perkins

——— Cur tamen hos tu
Evasisse putes, quod diri conscia facti
Mens habet attonitos, et surdo verbere cædit,
Occultum quatiente animo tortore flagellum?
Pœna autem vehemens, ac multo sævior illis,
Quas et Cæditius gravis invenit aut Rhadamanthus,
Nocte dieque suum gestare in pectore testem. Juv.

Kansas City:
VALANCOURT BOOKS
2008

Zeluco by John Moore
First published in 1789
First Valancourt Books edition 2008

Library of Congress Cataloging-in-Publication Data

Moore, John, 1729-1802.
Zeluco : various views of human nature, taken from life and manners, foreign and domestic / John Moore ; edited with an introduction and notes by Pam Perkins. – 1st Valancourt Books ed.
p. cm. – (Valancourt classics)
ISBN 1-934555-51-7 (alk. paper)
I. Perkins, Pamela Ann. II. Title.
PR3605.M5Z3 2008
823'.6–dc22
2008030389

Design and typography by James D. Jenkins
Published by Valancourt Books
Kansas City, Missouri
http://www.valancourtbooks.com

CONTENTS

INTRODUCTION

In September 1812, the poet Joanna Baillie reported to Walter Scott that she had just been out to a performance by a friend of his, the actor Daniel Terry. "The Play," she wrote "was a new Melo Drama taken from Dr Moore's *Zeluco*, and he [Terry] represented the jealous morose villain of a husband, with some power indeed, but with the heaviness & monotony that such an uninteresting, unmixed character is so apt to inspire."[1] Baillie's dismissal of the character of Zeluco might be seen as marking the beginning of a critical reaction against Moore's novel, a huge popular success that had also been celebrated as a modern classic by the generation that came of age aesthetically in the radical 1790s. Indeed, Baillie notwithstanding, the novel continued to have its admirers well into the nineteenth century, as the stage production itself makes clear. 1812 was also the year that the young Byron caused a literary sensation with his creation of what he described as "a poetical Zeluco" in his *Childe Harold*,[2] and only two years before, in her editions of what she identified as the standard English novels, the poet and critic Anna Laetitia Barbauld had taken for granted the continuing cultural pre-eminence of Moore's work. "The young," she wrote, "may melt into tears at *Julia Mandeville* and *The Man of Feeling*; the romantic will love to shudder at *Udolpho*; but those of mature age, who know what human nature is, will take up again and again Dr. Moore's *Zeluco*."[3]

Literary history, however, has tended to side with Baillie rather than Byron or Barbauld on the merits of *Zeluco*. Throughout the twentieth century, even specialists in the period tended to overlook the book—with a few notable exceptions, including J.M.S. Tompkins in the 1930s and, more recently, Henry L. Fulton, David Punter, and Gary

[1] *The Collected Letters of Joanna Baillie.* 2 vols. Edited by Judith Bailey Slagle. London: Associated University Presses, 1999, I: 308.

[2] Lord Byron, "Addition to the Preface," *Childe Harold's Pilgrimage*. 1813. In *Poetical Works* (London: Oxford University Press, 1966), 180.

[3] Anna Laetitia Barbauld, ed. *Zeluco*. London, 1810; reprinted 1820. (*The British Novelists*, vol. 34); see Appendix A.

Kelly[1]—while many of those who did read it tended to be markedly less enthusiastic than Moore's contemporaries. Patricia Meyers Spacks, author of one of the most recent detailed commentaries on *Zeluco*, echoes Baillie in her grounds for dissatisfaction: "Zeluco's monotonous emotional range [...] cannot long compel the reader,"[2] Spacks argues, suggesting that where Moore fails as a novelist is in his apparent inability to create a villain whose evildoing is marked by sublimity and grandeur. Yet if Zeluco fails to embody the sublime heights of evil that mark the now more familiar gothic villains imagined by Moore's contemporaries, that might well be in part because Moore was attempting a rather different sort of work. Despite its Gothic trappings and melodramatic plot, *Zeluco* is very much a novel of the Enlightenment, and in it Moore is attempting not—or not just—to offer the thrills and chills of stage Gothic villainy, but also to provide a serious analysis of the ways in which apparently unmotivated malignancy is in fact the product of acceptable and more or less untroubling social and cultural conditions.

Indeed, while Moore's contemporaries apparently had no trouble in reading the character Zeluco in the context of the then-emerging literary fashion for explorations of glamourous, gothic evil, the novel itself might just as easily be read as a slightly belated and very much elaborated literary exploration of the ideas driving William Hogarth's famous 1751 series of engravings, *The Four Stages of Cruelty*. Like Hogarth, Moore offers a tidily elaborated illustration of a central thesis—cruelty begets self-destruction—in which the stages of the protagonist's fall are mapped out with both artistic verve and didactic efficiency. The action of *Zeluco* is framed by two stranglings: in the first few pages, the child Zeluco wrings the neck of a sparrow that fails to

---

[1] See, for example, Gary Kelly, "Enlightenment and Revolution: The Philosophical Novels of Dr. John Moore" in *Eighteenth-Century Fiction* 1: 3 [April 1989], 219-237. J.M.S. Tompkins links Moore with other novelists of ideas such as Robert Bage in her classic study of the late eighteenth-century novel (*The Popular Novel in England 1770-1800*. 1932. Lincoln: University of Nebraska Press, 1961); more recently, David Punter and Henry L. Fulton have provided studies of Moore as a Revolutionary novelist; see Punter, "1789: The Sex of Revolution," in *Criticism: A Quarterly for Literature and the Arts* 24: 3 (Summer, 1982), 201-217; and Fulton, "Disillusionment with the French Revolution: The Case of the Scottish Physician John Moore," in *Studies in Scottish Literature* 23 (1988) 46-63.

[2] *Desire and Truth: Functions of Plot in Eighteenth-Century English Novels*. Chicago: University of Chicago Press, 1990, 194.

sing for him on demand, while a lifetime later, as the climax of all his wrongdoings, Zeluco strangles his own infant child, whose terrified shrieks enrage him as he confronts his maligned but innocent wife in a frenzy of jealousy. In case the reader is too caught up in the excitement of the plot to catch the significance of these mirrored deaths, Zeluco himself points to the moral. Moved to a brief, uncharacteristic pang of guilt following the death of his son, he recalls, penitently, the remonstrances of his tutor on the occasion that "he himself, yet a child, had in a fit of groundless passion squeezed his sparrow to death" and briefly wishes that he had learned to control his temper at the time. As with Hogarth, unchecked cruelty, exercised first on animals, leads naturally and inexorably to murder and violent, undignified death. Zeluco might not suffer the full didactic indignities that Hogarth inflicts on his protagonist—who ends the series spread open on a dissection table, dogs lapping up his entrails—but his lingering, painful death, after being betrayed and abandoned by the one person by whom he believed himself loved, is sufficiently unpleasant to make Moore's point.[1]

In *Zeluco*, Enlightenment rationality meets Gothic excess, a point that might help explain its success and influence during the troubled decades at the end of the eighteenth and beginning of the nineteenth century. Yet Moore's novel is more than just a curious artefact of a late eighteenth-century taste for Gothic violence filtered through impeccably moral commentary, as its melodramatic representation of more or less unfettered villainy is only one aspect of the book. Even if the character of Zeluco himself dominated—perhaps inevitably—discussion of the book in its own day, the episodic structure of the novel allows Moore to bring in numerous minor characters and to explore a wide range of issues, while the mainly Italian setting provides him with an excuse for narrative digressions on an array of historical and cultural subjects. What *Zeluco* offers its readers, no less today than in the eighteenth century, is not just the plot-driven narrative of its title character's self-destructive villainy, but also, and just as importantly, a survey of late-eighteenth century life and society from the perspective of an intelligent, sophisticated, and dryly amused observer.

---

[1] For a detailed reading of the moral lessons that Moore is inculcating through the deathbed scene, see Henry L. Fulton, "What Would Hospice Do? The Wretched Death of the Villain Zeluco," in *1650-1850: Ideas, Aesthetics, and Inquiries in the Early Modern Era*, vol. 7 (2002), 223-237.

John Moore's Life and Works

John Moore (1729-1802) was a somewhat unlikely figure to emerge as one of the most popular novelists of the 1790s: he was sixty years old in the year that *Zeluco* was published and had already had a distinguished and varied career. He was born in Stirling, Scotland, the eldest son and second child of a clergyman, but he spent much of his childhood and adolescence in Glasgow, where his mother, the daughter of a wealthy Glasgow merchant, settled with her seven children after being widowed in 1737. Moore studied at the University of Glasgow, continuing to attend lectures on medicine even after he apprenticed himself to the surgeon John Gordon, who had previously trained Tobias Smollett (1721-1771), a friend and distant cousin of Moore's. At nineteen, Moore left Scotland for the continent, serving in military hospitals in Flanders during the concluding years of the War of the Austrian Succession. After the end of the war, he studied briefly in London before going back to the continent, where he took up residence in Paris, continuing his studies and serving as the household surgeon for Lord Albemarle, at that time the British ambassador to France. After two more years, he returned to settle into marriage and professional practice in Glasgow; his wife, Jean Simson, was the daughter of Glasgow's Professor of Divinity, reinforcing his connections with the intellectual society of his home city. The marriage was by all accounts happy and successful. There were six surviving children—a daughter and five sons—and Moore's eldest son and namesake eventually became one of the most famous commanders of the Peninsular War.[1] By 1769, Moore himself was sufficiently well known to be called in to attend the dying Duke of Hamilton, the head of one of the two most powerful aristocratic families in the southwest of Scotland.[2] It was this association with the Hamiltons that led Moore to shift the direction of his life and career,

---

[1] Sir John Moore (1761-1809), who died after leading his forces to (relative) safety during the British army's retreat through Portugal to Coruna.

[2] This also reinforced a connection with the Dukes of Argyll, the other great landowners in the area, as Elizabeth Gunning, the widowed Duchess of Hamilton who became Moore's employer, subsequently became Duchess of Argyll by her second marriage. It had been the then Duke of Argyll whose patronage Moore's family had sought to find him a place in the military service when he first went to the continent.

as the duchess was apparently sufficiently impressed to hire him to attend the new duke, her younger son, when in 1772 he set out on what was one of the grandest of eighteenth-century Grand Tours, a five-year excursion through France, Germany, and Italy.

The purpose and effect of the Grand Tour were the subject of hot debate by the 1770s: there was a perception that it was, on the one hand, an excuse for casual debauchery by the more or less uncultivated sons of the wealthy, or, on the other, that it encouraged a deracinated cosmopolitanism among the youth who would make up Britain's future ruling class.[1] Moore's role as tutor was to guard against both pitfalls, ensuring that the young duke returned both uncorrupted by continental excess and impressed with a proper appreciation of what Moore, a firmly progressive Whig, saw as the clear superiority of Protestantism and the British political system. Yet at the same, the point of study abroad was to ensure that the duke was able to mix comfortably in all societies, a goal perhaps most famously set out and defended in the Earl of Chesterfield's letters to his son about the sorts of advantages that he might expect to gain from his own Grand Tour in the 1740s. Although Chesterfield's letters were not published until after Moore's tour, the assumptions underlying them were part of the aristocratic commonplaces of the day and it was taken for granted by both the duchess and the duke's guardian, Baron Mure, that the duke would come back to Scotland with the all the social polish that could be gained by meeting and mingling with the social elite of Europe. As tutor, Moore was thus responsible not only for providing the duke with intellectual training, a task for which he was unquestionably well prepared, but also for guiding him through his debut in continental high society, potentially a more tricky proposition for a provincial doctor. Unlike Chesterfield, who hired a clergyman to attend his son, the Duchess of Hamilton was apparently sufficiently concerned about

[1] For a thorough and very helpful overview of the debates about the Grand Tour, see Jeremy Black, *The British and the Grand Tour*. London: Croom Helm, 1985; a later essay by Black, ("Tourism and Cultural Challenge: The Changing Scene of the Eighteenth Century," in John McVeagh, ed. *All Before Them*. 3 vols. London: Ashfield, 1990) provides a more concise discussion of some of these issues. See also Gerald Newman's *The Rise of English Nationalism: A Cultural History 1740-1830* (New York: St. Martin's Press, 1987) for a very useful discussion of later eighteenth-century suspicion of the cosmopolitan, well-travelled aristocracy.

the state of her son's health to decide to send the duke abroad with a practicing surgeon and physician.

In doing so, the duchess provided Moore with access to a world that would not necessarily have been open to a man of his profession in other circumstances; indeed, there is some evidence that despite his experience two decades before in an ambassadorial household, Moore had to confront a degree of social anxiety on his own part and of social prejudice on that of others. In a letter to Baron Mure, for example, written from Geneva in October 1772, Moore reported, with what might be read either as mild self-deprecation or as a gentle hit at the duke's sense of his own social superiority, that when they had no other visitors, "the Duke can be tolerably amused with my company; many an afternoon we pass in riding or walking together, and he tells me that these are not the least agreeable."[1] A more explicit sense of the social divide that Moore had to negotiate is suggested by a 1773 letter from the Duchess of Hamilton to Mure, in response to a report that had reached her that Moore had assisted two Englishwomen in childbirth while in Geneva. "In many places abroad, if he was known to be a doctor he could not be received in the best company," she writes, "and his having publish'd it makes it almost impossible for him to go with the Duke to other places [...] he would not like, nor should I, that the person who travelled with the Duke of Hamilton was not upon a footing to go into all companys."[2] Moore's response to the duchess's reservations was twofold, as in a letter to the duchess herself, he focused on both his original respectability as a gentleman and on the social cachet gained from his association with her son. Having "supported the character" of a gentleman all his life, he writes, "there is very little danger of my forfeiting it while I attend the Duke of Hamilton."[3] Rather more interestingly, however, in his letter to Mure, Moore implies both pride in and some anxiety about his standing as a professional man. His reputation as a doctor, he writes, is "higher here than I could wish," with the result that English travellers seek him out for medical attention, something that seems "disobliging to Refuse. All I could do to prevent this," he continues,

---

[1] William Mure, *Selections from the Family Papers Preserved at Caldwell*. 3 vols. Glasgow, 1854. 2: 204.

[2] Mure, 2: 222.

[3] John Campbell, Duke of Argyll, ed. *Intimate Society Letters of the Eighteenth Century*. 2 vols. London, 1910. 2: 368-369.

> and which I have most sacredly observed, was absolutely to Refuse every offer of money, and to let it be known that every piece of trouble which I take of this kind is merely out of favour to my country men. This makes it indelicate on their part to consult me, which accordingly is never done but upon very particular occasions.[1]

In blurring the line between professional business and the conduct demanded by gentlemanly politeness, Moore suggests both the difficulty of the line he had to walk and the tact with which he was able to manage new social circumstances.

Notwithstanding whatever anxiety the duchess might initially have felt about the reception of a Scottish doctor in the courts and salons of the continent, or any defensiveness on his own part about his professional standing, the experience that Moore gained during his five years' travel provided the grounding of the assured urbanity with which the Italian upper classes would be depicted in *Zeluco*. Of course, Moore was already fluent in French—a major advantage as a tutor—and he had had experience of continental society while still a young man. While his private letters from abroad make clear that he made good use of the opportunities opened to him by his position in the household of a duke, it is also clear that, on balance, he was disinclined to be over-awed by the company to which he was given access through this connection. In a 1772 letter to Mure, for example, Moore notes that they were able to visit Voltaire,

> a privilege granted to very few. He was particularly attentive to the Duke, and, speaking of Mr. Hume, he said to me in English, 'you mos write him that I am hees great admeerer; he is a very great onor to Ingland, and abofe all to Ecosse.' The Duke, Mr. Mallet, and I am to sup and stay all night sometime this week with Voltaire; his vivacity and spirit is amazing; he is writing and publishing every day; and I do believe he is not without hopes that the Christian religion will die before him.[2]

Indeed, one might suspect that Moore himself benefited considerably more than the Duke from the intellectual opportunities granted by

[1] *Intimate Society Letters* 2: 371-372.

[2] Mure, 2: 203.

the Tour. In her brief account of Moore's life, Barbauld implicitly makes that very point as she notes that "[s]uch a tour, in the maturity of life, and with Dr. Moore's genius [...] might be supposed to afford ample materials for entertaining and informing the public."[1] Rather more poignantly, a painting of Moore and his pupil made in Rome by the Duke's distant connection Gavin Hamilton, in which the elegantly languid Duke stares off into space while Moore, looking out at the viewer, gestures towards the classical ruins behind them, might be taken as implying a certain lack of engagement on the part of the Duke with the educational aspects of his residence in Italy.[2]

Whatever the Duke learned (or failed to learn) on his travels, it is clear that Moore's engagement with European culture was both deep and lasting. The intellectual and social confidence implied by his amused verbal snapshot of Voltaire is mirrored and extended in the narrative voice of the two collections of travel letters that resulted from the tour: *A View of Society and Manners in France, Switzerland, and Germany* (2 vols, 1779), and *A View of Society and Manners in Italy* (2 vols, 1781). The first book was originally published anonymously, with a quasi-fictional framework, in which the narrator presents himself as a gambler travelling abroad in an attempt to break himself of the habit. Subsequent editions—the book was, from the beginning, a major

---

1 Barbauld, *The British Novelists*, vol. 34, ii.

2 The painting now hangs in the National Gallery of Scotland and also features Moore's son and namesake, the future Sir John Moore, who joined them on the continent while still a child. Perhaps inevitably, the published letters suggest that the Duke was an eager, receptive pupil and that relations between Moore and the Duke were always warmly cordial. The latter point, at least, is a view borne out in general by surviving private letters, although some of Moore's correspondence with the Duchess, (included in the second volume of *Intimate Society Letters*) suggests that the Duke's tastes didn't always incline him towards the cultivated life of the intellect that Moore recommends in his books. "He has not much Curiosity nor Ambition," Moore regretfully informs the Duchess in a 1775 letter (2: 391). The Duke's half-sister, Lady Charlotte Bury, was even more harsh, later commenting on her brother, who was then long dead: "My Mother from recommendations of Sensible Persons had chosen Him a Tutor in a private Scotch Gentleman that was at that Period Studying in Glasgow—with this Doctor Moor [*sic*] The Duke went Abroad and the Publications of the former have since that time proved Him a Man of Ability, but not all the Abilities in the World could Save the Duke, who inherited the fatal propensities of His Father Viz A Love of Low Company and Drinking" (National Library of Scotland, Acc. 8110, f. 29–f. 30v).

success—were printed with Moore's name on the title page and an Advertisement explaining that the "slight veil" of fiction had been the mark of the "diffidence" of a beginning author but that worries about "giv[ing] an air of fiction to the real incidents" had made him decide to print the letters "in their original form."[1]

How close the letters are to any sort of "original form" is of course open to dispute. Moore makes effective use of the informality and digressiveness permitted by the epistolary mode, and his relaxed, assured style reinforces the sense of immediacy ideally conveyed by the personal letter. That said, the letters that appear in the published volumes are still literary performances; they are, in effect, brief, interconnected essays on literary, social, and historical topics and are far more decorous and polished than any strictly private letters—including Moore's own—tend to be. One can illustrate this point by turning to the published comments on Voltaire, which unsurprisingly differ dramatically from the private observations to Baron Mure: in the book, the narrator confines himself to a cool evaluation of the impact of Voltaire's atheism on his literary achievements and reputation and to regretting that Voltaire ever "allowed the shafts of his ridicule to glance upon the Christian religion."[2] Yet this gap between the published and unpublished commentary on continental society merely emphasizes Moore's ability, from the very beginning of his literary career, to construct the knowing, sophisticated narrative persona that links his travel writing and his fiction.

Nor, according to Robert Anderson, Moore's first biographer, did the shift from physician to man of letters necessarily mark a sharp turn in Moore's intellectual life. Despite the doubts of the Duchess of Hamilton that the character of a medical man was compatible with aristocratic sociability, Anderson insisted that it was precisely through his work as a physician that Moore was able to lay the groundwork for the sophisticated moral and social observations that later marked all of his writing. In Anderson's words, Moore "found ample opportunity, in the course of his profession, of forming a just estimate of human life, of appreciating the weakness and the worth of human nature, for the use of his moral contrasts." Although Anderson is careful to go on to note that "with his professional accomplishments [Moore] united the

[1] John Moore, "Advertisement," *A View of Society and Manners in France, Switzerland, and Germany*. 1779. 2 vols. London, 1780.

[2] Moore, *France, Switzerland, and Germany* I: 194.

elegant attainments which adorn the character of the man of letters, an intimate acquaintance with classical and polite literature, and the various branches of modern learning,"[1] this insistence that Moore's professional life was a vital component in shaping his literary practice is worth emphasizing. Moore might have been very late in making his literary debut, but he compensated for that delayed start by bringing to his published work, from the beginning, a degree of cultural and intellectual confidence and a broad acquaintance with the world (in both the social and the geographical sense of the term) unusual in a novice writer.

After returning to Britain, Moore settled in London and inaugurated his publishing career. By the mid-1780s, he had established himself as one of the most successful and admired writers of the day, entirely on the strength of his two travel books. (Although he had published a work called *Medical Sketches* in 1785, he remained known for his work in *belles lettres* rather than in medical literature.) The success of the books is borne out by comments of individual readers as well as by contemporary sales and reviews. The Edinburgh literary hostess Eliza Fletcher, for example, commented in 1822 that Moore's "'View of Society and Manners' was the first book of travels I ever read, and it excited my youthful curiosity more than any work I had then met with."[2] She made this comment in the context of a congratulatory letter to her friend Robert Anderson on his biography of Moore, in which she also recalled her one meeting with the author: in 1786, as a schoolgirl of sixteen, she had visited the gallery at Hamilton Palace and Moore (whom she recognized from the Hamilton portrait) interrupted some work to give her party a guided tour, delighting them with his "vivacity and intelligence." "You will," she concludes, addressing Anderson, "be pleased with this instance of [Moore's] benevolent attentions to perfect Strangers." Nor was this warmth about Moore a matter of rosy nostalgia; in the journal that she kept at the time, Fletcher—or Eliza Dawson, as she then was—had been even more enthusiastic about the encounter:

---

[1] *The Life of John Moore, M.D.*, in *The Works of John Moore, M.D., with Memoirs of his Life and Writings*, by Robert Anderson, M.D. 7 vols. Edinburgh, 1820. 1: xliv.

[2] Eliza Fletcher, Unpublished letter to Robert Anderson, 10 November 1822. National Library of Scotland, Adv.Ms. 22.4.11, f. 256; the quotations in the next two sentences appear on f. 157v.

> I was scarce able to contain the delight I felt in being with a man whose works I had so much admired, I communicated it to my Uncle, who I wished to partake of my pleasure, to have a proper idea of this man, it is only necessary to read his works, as they are an exact type of himself very entertaining, interesting, and elegant—but I must withhold my rapsody [*sic*], and go on with an account of the paintings [....] There were many others the subjects of which I have forgot I was so attentive to our charming conductor.—he told us the Duke was in Ireland and the Dutchess not being well he came down about a fortnight ago to keep her company in the Dukes absence.—Ay! thought I, I envy her, her companion, more than any thing she possesses.[1]

This journal entry might read more like schoolgirl excitement than a reflection of serious literary tastes, but Fletcher's youthful enthusiasm for Moore's travel writing was shared by older and far more sophisticated readers. In January 1787, six months after Robert Burns launched his own career, he proclaimed to his friend Mrs. Dunlop that

> the wish to write him [Moore], has constantly pressed on my thoughts, yet I could not for my soul set about it. I knew his fame and character, and I am one of 'the sons of little men.' To write him a mere matter-of-fact affair, like a merchant's order, would be disgracing the little character I have; and to write to the author of *The View of Society and Manners* a letter of sentiment, I declare every artery runs cold at the thought.[2]

When Moore and Burns did begin corresponding later in that month, Moore was warm and admiring about Burns's work, but he also clearly demonstrated the literary confidence of an established author in the substantive literary advice that he offered his younger contemporary, including an earnest exhortation to use Scots as little as possible in his poetry in order to avoid limiting his audience.

However misguided such advice might appear to a twenty-first century audience, it is both a measure of the status that Moore had already achieved in the literary world and an indication of the literary

---

[1] Eliza Fletcher, *A Tour through Part of England and Scotland by Eliza Dawson in the Year 1786*, National Library of Scotland, Acc. 12017, 63-64.

[2] Robert Burns to Mrs. Dunlop, 15 January 1787; quoted in Anderson 1: xvii.

principles that guided his own writing when, two years later, he made his debut as a novelist. Scottish by birth and education, Moore was nonetheless disinclined to attempt any sort of regionalist writing; the Scottish content in *Zeluco* is strictly limited and is presented with hardly more local colour than are the pictures of Neapolitan society (which Moore knew first-hand, although merely as a privileged visitor) or of life on Cuban plantations (which were based entirely on other literature). *Zeluco* is unapologetically cosmopolitan in both tone and content, reflecting Moore's conviction that an author ought to write for "all persons of taste who understand the English language."[1] Fascinated though he is by local custom and culture—a fascination revealed in all of his writing—his interest is that of benignly detached observer, a stance that anchors his own work in the values and tastes of an era very different from that emerging with the work of Burns and his followers.

Moore followed up *Zeluco* with two more novels, which were reasonably popular and respectfully received, although neither achieved anything approaching the impact of *Zeluco*. *Edward* (1796) was an attempt to represent a thoroughly virtuous hero, a notoriously difficult task, while *Mordaunt* (1800) provoked some critical bemusement and unease because of its remarkably non-judgmental treatment of the title character, a young man of unapologetically easy-going morals who makes his way in the world almost entirely on looks and charm. As Hugh Murray, an early nineteenth-century critic noted severely, "*Mordaunt* is exceptionable in the character of its hero," who, though "entirely devoid of principle [...] becomes the complete fine gentleman. [...] This is evidently holding out a very dangerous and seductive example."[2] Although both novels have many of the strengths of *Zeluco*—sharp-eyed observations about the world, amusing vignettes and minor characters, and, particularly in the case of *Mordaunt*, evocative writing about foreign societies—the most interesting of Moore's post-*Zeluco* literary works was probably his final travel book, his 1793 *Journal During a Residence in France, from the Beginning of August to the Middle of December 1792*. A lifelong Francophile and an ardent believer in rational progressivism, Moore was initially

[1] Anderson xxii; the phrase is from the letter to Burns in which Moore advises against the use of Scots.

[2] Hugh Murray, *Morality of Fiction; or, An Inquiry into the Tendency of Fictitious Narratives*. London and Edinburgh, 1805, 112.

a supporter of the Revolution, so much so that, as he explained in the preface to the revised 1794 edition of the *Journal*, he determined to take the first opportunity that offered to visit "the same people in a state of freedom, whose complicated oppressions I had so often lamented."[1] Like his younger contemporary William Wordsworth, however, who made a similar journey at more or less the same time, Moore found his experience of revolutionary France deeply disillusioning. While he retained his sceptical open-mindedness, aware that "Nothing is more difficult than the discovery of truth regarding recent events of an important and complicated nature" (1: 140), he was nonetheless deeply shaken by the violence that he witnessed or that he heard about from trusted sources. The book as a whole is thus far more deeply pessimistic than his earlier travelogues, but it also offers a glimpse of an important moment in world history from the perspective of a sophisticated, thoughtful observer, and one, moreover, who had a long-term interest in the question of what happens when violent impulses are unfettered by any social restraints. While it would be considerably stretching the point to read *Zeluco* as an anticipation of revolutionary violence, the novel's latent pessimism about the limits of the rationality that it upholds as an ideal underpins, in important ways, Moore's disenchanted final view of the continental societies that had fascinated him throughout his writing life.

Zeluco *and its Eighteenth-Century Contexts*

When Moore switched from writing travel literature to fiction, he was taking something of a risk with his literary reputation. The value of the novel as a genre had been hotly debated at least since the days of Defoe's *Moll Flanders* (1722) or Eliza Haywood's *Love in Excess* (1719), and by the last decades of the century, worries about the effects of reading fiction had been thoroughly entrenched in critical discourse. As late as the second decade of the nineteenth century, at least one critic was dismissing speculation that Sir Walter Scott was the author of the anonymous *Waverley* novels on the grounds that a poet of Scott's stature would have no reason to "dwindle into a scribbler of novels."[2] One might not want to take this hostility to fiction too

[1] John Moore, *A Journal During a Residence in France*. A New Edition, Corrected. 2 vols. London, 1794. 1: 2-3.

[2] Anonymous review of *Waverley. The Critical Review*, vol 1 (s.5), p. 288.

seriously, given that there were unquestionably novelists who were prepared to be cheerily flippant about such critical disapproval of their literary efforts; Moore's almost exact contemporary Robert Bage (1730-1801), for example, marked his own 1782 debut as a novelist with a playful defiance of the reviewers, insisting that their hostility was utterly irrelevant to the success or failure of the works that they were criticizing. "Books of this class are printed, published, bought, read, and deposited in the lumber garret, three months before the Reviewers say a syllable of the matter," Bage proclaimed in the demurely provocative preface to *Mount Henneth*, his first novel.[1] As a declaration of artistic independence, this observation is obviously double-edged, but its ostensibly good-natured assumption about the inherent disposability of fiction is nonetheless of interest, pointing as it does to one of the central problems that commentators at the time had with the novel as a genre: that of determining what purpose might be served by entertaining, fictitious narratives.

The main moral worries about fiction were centred on the perception that novels offered distorted pictures of life, and as such were potentially dangerously misleading to the young or unsophisticated readers who were presumed to be their main audience. In the influential and troubled judgement of Samuel Johnson, the power of literature was so great that "the best examples only should be exhibited" in fiction, as the pleasure given by flawed characters could lead young readers to "lose abhorrence of their faults."[2] Much of these moral concerns were focused on the extravagant tales of romance and adventure that were so popular throughout the century, but even novels that, like Moore's, had an impeccably and overtly moral agenda were subject to critical suspicion. In an essay written four years before the publication of *Zeluco*, Moore's fellow Scot Henry Mackenzie (1745-1835) worried about the "mistaken and pernicious system of morality" inculcated by fiction in which "the virtues of justice, of prudence, of economy, are put in competition with the exertions of generosity, of benevolence, and of compassion."[3] Hugh Murray, though writing some fifteen years after the publication of *Zeluco*, was also fairly representative of such late eighteenth-century critical commonplaces as he attacked fiction that attempted either to provide a representation of

[1] Robert Bage, *Mount Henneth*, 2 vols. London, 1782. 1: vii.

[2] Samuel Johnson, *The Rambler*, no. 4 (Saturday 31 March, 1750).

[3] Henry Mackenzie, *The Lounger*, no. 20 (Saturday, June 18, 1785).

the world as it is or to offer any form of moral instruction through the depiction of actions and consequences. In the former case, the writer is simply providing a bad example (as at least some contemporary critics feared that Moore himself was doing in his sympathetic account of the sexual temptation of his virtuous heroine Laura), while in the latter, writers are attempting to "draw inferences from imaginary events,"[1] something that Murray believes to be self-evidently pointless. (He insists that biography offers a much less pernicious alternative to fiction for the provision of such lessons.) According to Murray, in an argument derived from both Samuel Johnson and the Scottish man of letters Lord Kames, the only justification of fiction is that it is able to present an aspirational vision of human nature, in which characters behave far better than any person is likely to do in real life—a point that explains why Murray was perhaps the only critic ever to prefer *Edward* to *Zeluco*.

This was a view that Moore himself vigorously disputed in an essay that he published on fiction in 1797, in which he also provides an implicit justification of his decision to move from the travel writing that had brought him so much success to the rather déclassé genre of the novel. While taking for granted that there are grounds for condemning many, even perhaps a large majority of, novels, Moore argues that critics have carelessly and destructively confounded the good and the bad:

> There were, for a considerable time, so many novels written of this description [frivolous romances], and with so few exceptions, that the very words Romance and Novel conveyed the idea of a frivolous or pernicious book. Even this, however, did not diminish the number, though it made many people at pains to declare, that for their part they never read novels; a declaration sometimes made by persons of both sexes, who never read any thing else. This is being by much too cautious. They might, with equal prudence, declare, that they never would read any book, because many books are silly or pernicious. The truth is, that the best romances always have been, and always will be, read with delight by men of genius;

[1] Murray, 10. Compare the arguments made by Elizabeth Hamilton for the moral superiority of biography to fiction in the preface of her speculative biography, *Memoirs of the Life of Agrippina, Wife of Germanicus* (3 vols, 1804).

> and with the more delight, the more taste and genius the reader happens to have. Nothing can be so interesting to men as man.[1]

Anticipating Jane Austen's famous defence of the genre in *Northanger Abbey* (1818), Moore insists that despite the intellectual fashion for treating fiction with scorn, novels are capable of offering a valuable insight into human behaviour. The ultimate basis of his defence of fiction is, however, practical and utilitarian: however much moralists might insist that readers should seek out history, sermons, or moral essays for their reading material, Moore points out that most readers who do not already possess a taste for the pursuit of self-improvement simply will not pick up such valuable but relatively dry works:

> Persons of dissipated minds, incapable of attention, who stand most in need of instruction, are the least willing to receive it; they throw such books down the moment they perceive their drift. But a romance in the highest degree entertaining, may be written with as moral an intention, and contain as many excellent rules for the conduct of life, as any book with a more solemn and scientific title. This, however, not being suspected by the persons above alluded to, they continue to read in the confidence of meeting with amusement only, and fearless of any plot or plan for their instruction or improvement; and they find folly ridiculed in a pleasant manner, vice placed in a degrading light, and a variety of instructive lessons so interwoven with an interesting story, that they cannot satisfy their curiosity until they have received impressions of a useful or virtuous nature, and thus acquire something infinitely more valuable than what they were in pursuit of.[2]

If not quite saying that novels are in fact the most useful form of literature (cultural prejudices against them notwithstanding), Moore is making a vigorous implicit defence of his own move from the undoubtedly respectable genre of travel writing to the more murky world of fiction.

There is no question that in writing *Zeluco*, Moore had a clear moral agenda, something that his contemporaries both recognized

---

[1] John Moore, *A View of the Commencement and Progress of Romance*. In *The Works of John Moore, M.D., with Memoirs of his Life and Writings*, by Robert Anderson, M.D. 7 vols. Edinburgh, 1820. 5: 62.

[2] Moore, *Progress of Romance* 5: 62-63.

and applauded. "This is not a common novel," *The Monthly Review* proclaimed approvingly; rather, the reviewer argues, Moore is providing "a series of moral essays [...] in which the dryness of reasoning is enlivened by the charms of narration, and the weakness of precept enforced by the power of example."[1] Likewise, Mary Wollstonecraft admired the book for inculcating "the purest morality [...] enforced by familiar arguments and forcible examples."[2] The novel in fact opens with an uncompromising statement of didactic purpose: the narrative is intended, readers are told, to prove that vice leads to misery, that "her ways are the ways of wretchedness, and that all her paths are woe." Admittedly, writing a two-volume novel to "prove" that crime doesn't pay might strike a reader today as naïve, at the very least; indeed, Hugh Murray might seem rather closer to twenty-first century assumptions than Moore in his assumption that a "philosophical" novel is more or less an impossibility, since no moral principle can be established or inculcated by fictional events. Not all of Moore's contemporaries would have been so sceptical, however; the Scottish educational writer Elizabeth Hamilton cited the character Zeluco as an admirable illustration of the dangers of being excessively indulgent with one's children.[3] Yet the point is perhaps not so much that Zeluco himself illustrates inevitable and invariable consequences of vice as that the reader is persuaded into sympathy with the virtuous characters and detestation of Zeluco's villainy. Moore, whose intellectual views were formed around the same time and in much the same cultural milieu as Adam Smith's—like Smith, Moore had been a student of Francis Hutcheson, whose concept of an innate "moral sense" shaped Scottish moral philosophy for the second half of the eighteenth century—seemed to take for granted, with Hutcheson and with Smith (in *The Theory of Moral Sentiments* [1759]), that morality was at least in part a matter of proper feeling.[4] What *Zeluco* offers is thus perhaps less a dramatization of a relatively trite idea about vice being

---

[1] Unsigned review of *Zeluco*. *The Monthly Review*, vol. 80, no. 6 (June 1789), 511-512.

[2] [Mary Wollstonecraft], Review of *Zeluco*. *The Analytical Review*, vol. 5, no. 2 (October 1789), 103. See Appendix A.

[3] Elizabeth Hamilton, *Letters on the Elementary Principles of Education*. 2 vols. London, 1801.

[4] See Fulton, "What Would Hospice Do?", 227, for further comments on the novel's indebtedness to Hutcheson.

its own punishment than a complex fictional exploration of virtuous sentiment and an attempt to evoke or reinforce such sentiments in the reader through both example and rational argument.

Perhaps because Zeluco himself was such an influential and obvious proto-Gothic villain, the novel has more frequently been read as looking forward to the Gothic novel rather than back to the literature of sensibility. Yet the book's affinities with works by writers such as Smollett and Henry Mackenzie are at least as important as its anticipations of Ann Radcliffe's *The Mysteries of Udolpho* (1794) or *The Italian* (1797). Moore's debts to Smollett have been noted; Robert Anderson, for example, observed in passing that "The principal personage of [*Zeluco*], utterly devoid of principle, perfidious, and profligate, is unrivalled by any character that has been invented by the writers of prosaic or poetical fiction, except Dr. Smollett's Ferdinand Count Fathom, his legitimate predecessor, and Lord Byron's Childe Harold, of whom he is the confessed prototype."[1] Anderson might have been overstating his case a little in seeing only one forebear of Zeluco; it is possible to see at least some aspects of him in other novels of the later eighteenth-century. He is, for example, in some ways a darker reworking of Sir Thomas Sindall, the titular anti-hero of Mackenzie's second novel, *The Man of the World* (1773). Like Zeluco, Sindall is raised by an adoring, widowed mother who ignores her parental responsibilities with the result that Sindall grows up doing "what he liked, at first because his spirit should not be confined too early, and afterwards [...] because it was past being confined at all.[2] He also, like Zeluco, comes to a violent and more or less unmourned end, dying as the result of wounds received in a scuffle as he attempts to rape his own long-lost and unrecognized daughter. The difference in the novels is not so much that Mackenzie, as in his earlier and more famous *The Man of Feeling* (1771), tends to be less interested in action and even character than in the presentation of sentimental tableaux (Moore has his share of such tableaux as well) but rather that Moore is at least as interested in the philosophies driving his plot as in the plot itself.

This point is particularly in evidence in the ways in which Moore presents some of the standard sentimental plots that reappeared

---

1 Anderson, 1: xv.

2 Henry Mackenzie, *The Man of the World*. 2 vols. London, 1773. 1: 77-78.

consistently in the fiction of the day. In *Zeluco's* inset story of the noble-minded but tragic slave Hanno, for example, Moore is presenting his readers with a tale that they would have encountered over and over in other literature. (When Anna Laetitia Barbauld comments that nothing in Sterne surpasses the pathos of the dying Hanno, her praise might be read as rather back-handedly implying Moore's dependence on familiar tropes.) Of course, few if any of the writers who used slavery episodes did so just for their sentimental impact; the abolitionist message in such writing is usually clear and unambiguous. Mackenzie, again, who features an episode on a West Indian plantation in his third novel, *Julia de Roubigné* (1777), has the virtuous hero proclaim explicitly that "the master of slaves has seldom the soul of a man."[1] Yet Mackenzie's novel also illustrates the tendency of much of this writing to use the representation of slavery as a measure of the worth and virtue of the European heroes, as the focus of the episode is less on Yambu, the initially sullen but then grateful and virtuous slave prince, but rather on the sentimental Savillon. Determining to run his property on free labour, with Yambu left in charge of his own people, Savillon thereby demonstrates not just his own good heart but his good sense as (at least in the world of the novel) such amelioration of slaves' conditions leads to happier, more efficient labour. Robert Bage's *Man As He Is* (1792) uses a similar plot for slightly different ends, as he relates the backstory of his heroine's black servant, a former West Indian slave. Unambiguously named Fidel, the ex-slave reflects the heroine's virtue through his loyalty to her; no less importantly, in the tragic story of the young slave owner who rapes Fidel's fiancée and drives her to her death, Bage also reinforces the argument made by both Moore and Mackenzie, that slave-owning dehumanizes the master even more than the slave. Fidel and Hanno are more or less interchangeable figures of saintly forbearance, while they and Yambu all function less as characters than as occasions for sentiment. Where Moore differs from his contemporaries is that he is less interested than they are in using that sentiment as a device to characterize his heroes. The unnamed Irish soldier who attempts to befriend Hanno and who intercedes for him with the reluctant priest is as much a "type" as Hanno himself, while the physician who lectures Zeluco on the evils of slavery is moved by an abstract opposition to slavery in

[1] Henry Mackenzie, *Julia de Roubigné*. 2 vols. London and Edinburgh, 1777. 2: 43

general, not by the sentimental particulars of Hanno's situation. No less importantly, Moore juxtaposes Hanno's tragic story not only with the reasoned anti-slavery arguments of the physician but also with a passionate attack on slavery made by the narrator himself. The result is a focus on the argument underlying the novel's emancipationist sentiment, rather than on the ways—as in Mackenzie or Bage—that such sentiment reflects favourably on the character of the hero.

This is an important point, as good feeling, on its own, is never enough in Moore's world; emotion undisciplined by reason leads to weakness or error, no matter how seemingly benign or even admirable the emotion might be. The good-hearted but foolish and superstitious Irish soldier achieves nothing except a degree of comfort for himself, while other characters motivated only by strong feeling cause very real harm. Zeluco's mother produces a monster while believing herself motivated only by maternal love; the hapless Rosolia and Zeluco's unfortunate first wife are misled to near, or fatal, disaster by giving in unquestioningly to what they believe to be love. Madame de Seidlits, good-hearted and loving as she is, nearly destroys her beloved daughter by pushing her, with the best possible intentions, into a disastrous marriage. On a very different and considerably lighter level, the comic servants Targe and Buchanan illustrate another sort of danger produced by substituting feeling for reason, as their opposed but equally emotive responses to the bare mention of the name of Mary, Queen of Scots lead not to reasoned debate but to an absurd and nearly fatal duel. On the other hand, Bertram, the character who might seem to approach most closely to the conventional figure of the man of feeling (he insists that he is amply repaid for considerable personal sacrifice and privation by the gratitude and affection of those he helps), is less of a sentimentalist than he might initially appear. He emphasizes repeatedly in his long conversation with Zeluco the effort and intellectual discipline that underpin his ability to renounce his youthful predilection for gambling and easy pleasures and to accept misfortune and difficulty. Even more importantly, he declares forcefully that benevolence is not and should not be evoked simply by involuntary effusions of emotion. When, for example, Zeluco takes for granted that a female cousin whom Bertram stints himself to help must be beautiful, virtuous, and charming, Bertram replies that she is in fact elderly, bad-tempered, and has a questionable reputation and therefore needs his help all the more. Humanity and benevolence are, for Bertram, the product of sympathy inflected by reason and moral imagination, as he attempts to see beyond his own pleasure—whether that pleasure is the immediate one of spending his own money or the more refined one of playing benefactor to an appropriately picturesque sufferer. Indeed, what the conversation between the two characters emphasizes is that it is Zeluco who is in a more real sense a "man of feeling," as he is driven only by his emotions, and, as a result is left in turmoil and anguish despite being in far more apparently happy circumstances than Bertram.

The obvious moral lesson of the novel—that Zeluco's crimes lead inexorably to misery and death—is thus rather more complex than it might initially appear. Despite Byron's enthusiasm for the novel, Zeluco is anything but a brooding, proto-Byronic anti-hero; his downfall is less the result of his violence than it is of the failures of moral imagination that lead to that violence. In some respects, Zeluco is a figure out of the philosophy of Bernard Mandeville wandering through Francis Hutcheson's or Adam Smith's world of moral sentiments. Believing absolutely and unwaveringly that everybody is motivated by selfishness and that only fools and hypocrites fail to recognize that point, Zeluco is nonetheless repeatedly thwarted or frustrated by virtuous characters such as Bertram or Laura, or even by imperfect but benevolent figures such as Signora Sporza. Nor is this a case of innocents blindly defeating or escaping evil they cannot understand; what Moore makes plain is that it is Zeluco who is in important respects the blind and naïve character, so convinced of his own superior insight that he is incapable not just of comprehending goodness but even of recognizing that he is being victimized by other figures around him, many of whom are hardly less unscrupulous and selfish than he is himself. Indeed, Moore uses incidents such as the blackly comic attempted murder of Signora Sporza (Sporza is untouched, but Zeluco ends up injured and thoroughly terrorized by his casually mercenary doctors) to emphasize the ineptitude of his anti-hero's villainy. Perhaps even more to the point, the fact that Zeluco's fall is set in motion by exactly the same lie as he used to revenge himself on the Portuguese merchant—that he is not the father of his wife's child—underscores the ways in which he is blinkered and limited by his deep conviction that humans are basically selfish and corrupt. The lesson that Bertram absorbs from his father—"never, O never, be such a fool as to be a knave"—encapsulates the argument that Moore implies through his portrayal of Zeluco.

Whatever affinities Zeluco has with later Gothic villains, in other words, Moore's eponymous anti-hero is much more than a prototype for figures such as the villains of Ann Radcliffe's best-selling novels of the following decade. There might be obvious connections in terms of plot—like Montoni in *The Mysteries of Udolpho*, Zeluco marries an older woman for her money and then torments her till she dies; like Schedoni in *The Italian*, he single-mindedly pursues a beautiful young woman who despises him and then becomes dangerously obsessed with the idea that she is unfaithful—but the tone and style of the books are very different. That is in part because unlike Radcliffe and other Gothic novelists, Moore is not particularly interested in the creation of terror, something that has perhaps contributed to the tendency of critics, from Joanna Baillie in the early nineteenth century to Patricia Meyer Spacks in the 1990s, to fault the character of Zeluco for falling far short of Gothic sublimity. Yet even if one accepts the argument that Zeluco's villainy cannot in itself sustain readers' interest, that point may well be a reflection not of Moore's failure as a writer but rather of his interest in doing something very different from what we find in the work of the Gothic novelists who followed him. As J.M.S. Tompkins writes, in what has remained one of the finest twentieth-century commentaries on the novel, "[t]here is no Titanic force about [...] Zeluco; he is a thoroughly wicked man who becomes wicked by natural means [....] He is mean, base and dangerous, and quite untouched by grandeur."[1] Unlike Baillie or Spacks, however, Tompkins reads this failure of "grandeur" in Zeluco as evidence of Moore's literary originality: far from being a proto-romantic exponent of the powers of terror, Moore is an Enlightenment rationalist who sees evil as an all too human, all too natural phenomenon and who presents villainy as the mark of a knave, not of a fascinating anti-hero. Wollstonecraft, writing in 1789, took for granted that the "deformity and want of order" in Zeluco's mind meant that it was impossible for him to dominate the novel and that reader interest would be concentrated elsewhere; by way of contrast, Barbauld, writing thirty years later, placed *Zeluco* firmly in the world of the Gothic by praising Moore for portraying a Satanic "sublime of guilt" in his titular anti-

[1] Tompkins, *The Popular Novel in England, 1770-1800*, 179.

hero.[1] Barbauld's reading of Zeluco might seem more comprehensible to a generation steeped in the Gothic, but Wollstonecraft's response to him is supported in important ways by the novel itself. Not only, as already mentioned, is Zeluco easily outflanked by both good and bad characters, but even more importantly, Moore shows him as evoking contempt, not fear, in of most of the other characters, particularly in the second half of the book. Seidlits deliberately manipulates him into a murderous rage by scribbling on a picture; Nerina strings him along for his money while maintaining her affair with the rope-dancer; even the passive, virtuous Laura—who comes closest to filling the role of the threatened Gothic heroine—is initially insulted and annoyed, rather than terrified, by Zeluco's pursuit. While it is true that readers are given no reason at all to doubt Zeluco's evil intentions (he fantasizes about abduction and rape when Laura remains stubbornly indifferent to what he is convinced is his irresistible charm), Laura herself remains entirely unmoved by and immune to his villainy until she is, against her better judgment, manœuvred into marriage by her mother and her confessor. If Zeluco lacks the "Titanic force" and charisma of the more typical Gothic villain, the novel itself makes clear that that is an attribute of his character, not a failure of Moore's literary skills.

Such an argument can be reinforced by the fact that it is possible to argue that Zeluco himself is not the only or even the main focus of interest in the novel. Although he is the driving force behind the action, and none of the many minor characters come near to becoming a major focus of attention, the sheer number of secondary characters and the range of subplots mean that Zeluco himself frequently disappears for large sections of the book and that interest in the central plot is diffused by an increasing focus on comic secondary characters. At times—as with the account of Bertram—these subplots become essential to the development of some of the novel's central themes; at others, as with the tale of the sleepily good-natured Mr. Steele and his eccentrically selfish uncle, Moore seems simply to be providing the reader with amusing comic interludes of the sort that he repeatedly provides in his travel books. In doing so, he is again aligning himself with the digressive, episodic literary practice of contemporaries such as Tobias

[1] Wollstonecraft, review of *Zeluco*, 98; Barbauld, *The British Novelists* vol. 34, v. (See Appendix A.)

Smollett or Robert Bage, the latter of whom writes novels that are so unstructured that it can be difficult to determine exactly what is plot and what is subplot. By the end of *Zeluco*, the melodramatic tale of Zeluco's villainy and Laura's increasing danger is subordinated to an almost dizzying range of secondary narratives, ranging from the tear-jerking tales of Bertram and of Miss Warren and her brother to a series of comic letters in which English and Scottish servants give their impressions of life in France and Italy.

Indeed, if there is a unifying force underlying the novel as a whole, it is not the proto- or quasi-Gothic figure of Zeluco but rather the urbanely amused voice of the narrator, a voice that at times becomes indistinguishable from that of the sophisticated man of the world who narrates Moore's earlier travel books. Parts of *Zeluco*, such as Buchanan's chauvinistic refusal to admit that Italian scenery can compare with that of Scotland are, indeed, little more than reworked versions of episodes in the travel books (see Appendix B, pp. 416-417). As the reviewer for *The Monthly Review* rather dryly noted, the lack of a name on the title page of the first edition of the novel did not mean that it was in any real sense an anonymous publication, since "internal evidence" made amply clear that the book might be "safely ascribe[d ...] to Dr. Moore, author of the well-known travels through France, Germany, and Italy."[1] The narrator's tendency to allow his voice to fade into that of characters who challenge perspectives associated with Zeluco or the other flawed characters further underscores the way in which Moore ensures that the Enlightenment voice of the narrator, rather than the self-absorbed villainy of Zeluco, dominates the novel. The emancipationist physician who lectures Zeluco on slavery and the Portuguese merchant on Christian charity offer perspectives that are more or less indistinguishable from those of the narrator; likewise, Colonel Seidlits' unswerving defence of religious tolerance or the Earl of —'s attempt to moderate the naïve self-absorption of Mr. Transfer provide clear, if comic, endorsements of the sort of good-humoured moderation that the narrator embodies. The result is that readers are never entirely permitted to lose themselves in the melodrama of the central plot; rather, what they are given is a vision of irrational passion filtered through the perspective of a sophisticated, humanely rationalist observer.

---

1 Unsigned review of *Zeluco*. *The Monthly Review*, vol. 80, no. 6 (June 1789), 515.

The difference between Zeluco's world and that of the narrator is further emphasized by the novel's firm grounding in a context of eighteenth-century and classical literature. Zeluco himself is more or less culturally empty; his wealth buys him art and when courting Laura he affects interest in her music, but his real pleasures, as the narrator makes very clear, are those of the body, not of the mind. Yet the novel itself takes for granted a reader who is able to share the narrator's easy cosmopolitanism, as it celebrates intellectual curiosity and quietly mocks those who are unable or unwilling to move beyond their own narrow perspectives on the world around them. The comic servants Targe, Buchanan, and Dawson are of course obvious targets of this mockery; Dawson's more or less illiterate resentment of the "d—d parlivoos" whom he fears will steal his sweetheart's affection represent one extreme of insularity, while Buchanan's insistence that Naples cannot equal Glasgow in beauty nor Caserta measure up to Holyrood in splendour exemplifies another. Nor is this failure of intellectual breadth simply a matter of class; the bewilderment of the *nouveau riche* Transfer about the classical statues that have been installed on his country estate links him with the artistically illiterate Squander, who makes himself a target for unscrupulous hucksters when he decides to mark his Grand Tour by making expensive purchases, despite having "no more taste in painting than his pointer."[1] By way of contrast, the novel assumes a reader who will not only get such quiet jokes as Squander's vain attempt to remember whether a painting he admired was by Guido or Reni, but who can also share the narrator's amused interest in matters ranging from European political manœuvres in the Mediterranean to the extreme views taken on the conduct of a long-dead Scottish queen.

The intellectually expansive world of the narrator is further suggested by the epigraphs with which Moore begins most of his chapters and which firmly situate the book in the context of late eighteenth-century literary high culture. Taken together, the epigraphs reinforce the divide between the world of the narrator

[1] Moore was impatient with self-proclaimed connoisseurs of art who ostensibly guided the tastes—and purchases—of less assured tourists, and in his tour books he repeatedly mocks the sort of obligatory raptures with which viewers greeted the artworks that it was fashionable to admire. Nor was he alone in doing so: Bage makes much the same point in *Man As He Is*—in which his hero, like Squander, allows himself to be robbed in his attempts to purchase art.

and the world of Zeluco and emphasize the ways in which readers are being guided by the narrator in their approach to the material. Unsurprisingly Moore chooses more epigraphs from English authors than from writers of any other nationality; the mainly Italian setting notwithstanding, the epigraphs make clear the very British tastes that shape the intellectual world of the book. (This is a point further emphasized in the fact that several of the normative voices—the emancipationist physician, Mr N— and his uncle the Earl—are either British or cite British thought.) Nor are the tastes implied by the epigraphs all that unpredictable: Pope, with eight epigraphs, and Shakespeare with four, are the British authors who get cited most, an entirely unexceptionable choice in the context of late eighteenth-century Britain. Yet there are also slightly less predictable voices; a selection from Helen Maria Williams's 1788 attack on the slave trade implies a ready familiarity with the contemporary as well as established literary taste.[1] Moreover, the author who is quoted more than any other is not British at all: the French moralist La Rochefoucauld gets eleven epigraphs, while classical authors—notably Ovid and Virgil—get eight each, as many as Pope and twice as many as Shakespeare. It is also worth noting that the fourteen epigraphs from French authors are all given in the original language, as are the twenty-five from Latin sources. The implication is, clearly enough, that the reader is expected to share the narrator's easy and multi-lingual comfort with the canonical and classical literature of the day. More generally, the prevailing tone of the epigraphs also invites attention, suggesting as it does both the strong satiric bent of Moore's rationalist vision and the place of the novel in an established intellectual tradition. The work by Pope to which Moore turns to most frequently is the "Epistle to a Lady," an unsurprising choice given that the opening of the novel functions as something of a more sympathetic prose elaboration of Pope's satiric vision of female frivolity and folly; likewise, his fondness for the famously disenchanted epigrams of La Rochefoucauld and for the English satirist Samuel Butler (who is cited three times) implies a degree of cynicism and a world-weary acceptance of the human capacity for hypocrisy and self-deception. Indeed, if taken on their own, the epigraphs might be read as implying a considerably harder-

[1] Moore's inclusion of Williams's poetry might also owe something to their personal friendship; she became his amanuensis when he began having trouble with his eyesight. I am indebted to Henry L. Fulton for this information.

edged perspective on human failings than is actually present in much of the book. The aphoristic detachment of La Rochefoucauld—or even of some of Pope's harsher observations—clashes with the amused warmth with which the narrator presents the follies of a Buchanan or a Transfer. Yet the effect is not any incongruity but rather of a balance between the rational disapproval of human folly encapsulated in the epigraphs and the more nuanced exploration of such failings elaborated in Moore's prose. Granted, this balance vanishes more or less entirely in the treatment of Zeluco himself, who lives selfishly and dies painfully and squalidly, but even there, the effect is to position Zeluco as an extreme example of ordinary human failings rather than as a terrifyingly inhuman monster. Grounding himself firmly in his literary context, Moore invites his readers to see the novel as an elaboration and reinterpretation of a particular strand of philosophical and literary thought and, in doing so, positions it as a contribution to an ongoing literary debate rather than as either a piece of escapist romance of the sort attacked in late eighteenth-century polemics, or as an early example of the sort of terror fiction that enthralled the following generation.

Challenges to and debates about the literary canon from the 1980s onward have added immeasurably to the scholarly understanding of late eighteenth-century fiction. Women writers have been the main beneficiaries of this historical revisionism, and authors such as Ann Radcliffe and Frances Burney have been accorded in recent years a degree of critical and aesthetic respect that they had not received since shortly after their initial publication. John Moore, though at least as successful as them in his own day, has not yet received that sort of renewed interest and attention, a rather surprising oversight. Despite an intense late twentieth- and early twenty-first century interest in the literature of revolution, Moore's compelling eye-witness account of revolutionary France remains relatively little-known and even less discussed; a vibrant secondary literature on the theory and practice of travel writing has continued to neglect his lively, outspoken accounts of his own Grand Tour. The fiction has, if anything, fared even worse. Oxford University Press published an edition of *Mordaunt* in 1965, but aside from that, any readers interested in Moore at any time since the nineteenth century would have had to rely on out-of-print and increasingly rare editions of his novels, even *Zeluco*, notwithstanding its undeniable historical importance.

It is pointless to speculate about why Moore failed to sustain the critical interest and respect that he generated in his own lifetime; the more important matter is that his work has a great deal to offer scholars and readers today. In some respects, Moore's travel writing might be a fairly uncomplicated example of what Jeremy Black has called the Whiggish tendencies of later eighteenth-century British travel;[1] even so, its relaxed, amused cosmopolitanism makes it anything but a literary museum piece. This is also very much the case with *Zeluco*. Moore's intellectual curiosity and lively prose make *Zeluco* into something far more than either the melodramatic tale of villainy and excess that inspired the young Byron in his creation of Childe Harold or the rational exploration of moral lessons that won the approval of *The Monthly Review*. Simultaneously a plot-driven melodrama and a digressive, stimulating novel of ideas, *Zeluco* is a work of fiction that resists easy categorization. If it has a place in the pre-history of Romantic-era Gothic literature, it deserves at least as much attention for its comic vignettes and its reinterpretation of a number of the standard motifs of sentimental fiction. Although clearly very much a product of its time, *Zeluco* is a novel that also demonstrates the skill and sophistication of a writer who was able to use, without ever becoming trapped by, some of the dominant literary concerns and practices of his day.

PAM PERKINS
Winnipeg

July 2008

PAM PERKINS teaches in the Department of English at the University of Manitoba, specializing in eighteenth-century and Romantic fiction.

---

[1] Black discusses British travel and Whiggish political philosophy (mentioning Moore among many others) in *The British and the Grand Tour*, 162-188.

Note on the Text

This edition follows the first edition of 1789, and I have retained Moore's inconsistencies in spelling and punctuation. Moore made few substantive changes to the novel; I have, however, included in the endnotes a later revision of a repeated passage and an added paragraph in which Moore emphasizes the connection between Zeluco's attempt to deceive the Portuguese merchant and Nerina's lie to Zeluco. In both cases, the text of the changes is taken from Anna Laetitia Barbauld's 1810 edition.

Acknowledgements

I am very grateful to James D. Jenkins for all of his help in preparing this edition, particularly for providing me with an electronic version of the 1810 edition and for his willingness to accommodate several unexpected delays in the completion of the project. Henry L. Fulton, whose work on Moore has shaped my own interest in and approaches to *Zeluco*, very kindly agreed to read a draft of the introduction and provided helpful comments and corrections (remaining errors are of course entirely my own). I would also like to thank Ryan McBride for taking the time to read and comment on the introduction and to thank, as always, Cliff Eyland for his unflagging fascination with the lesser-known fiction of the eighteenth century.

Z E L U C O.

VARIOUS VIEWS
OF
HUMAN NATURE,
TAKEN
From LIFE and MANNERS,
Foreign and Domeſtic.

——— Cur tamen hos tu
Evaſiſſe putes, quod diri conſcia facti
Mens habet attonitos, et ſurdo verbere cædit,
Occultum quatiente animo tortore flagellum?
Pœna autem vehemens, ac multo ſævior illis,
Quas et Cæditius gravis invenit aut Rhadamanthus,
Nocte dieque ſuum geſtare in pectore teſtem. JUV.

IN TWO VOLUMES.

VOL. I.

LONDON:

Printed for A. STRAHAN; and T. CADELL, in the Strand.

M DCC LXXXIX.

Title page of the first edition (1789)

ZELUCO.

VARIOUS VIEWS

OF

HUMAN NATURE,

TAKEN

From LIFE and MANNERS,

Foreign and Domestic.

John Moore

——— Cur tamen hos tu
Evasisse putes, quod diri conscia facti
Mens habet attonitos, et surdo verbere cædit,
Occultum quatiente animo tortore flagellum?
Pœna autem vehemens, ac multo sævior illis,
Quas et Cæditius gravis invenit aut Rhadamanthus,
Nocte dieque suum gestare in pectore testem. JUV.[1]

IN TWO VOLUMES.

ZELUCO.

CHAPTER I.

Strong Indications of a vicious Disposition.

Religion teaches, that Vice leads to endless misery in a future state; and experience proves, that in spite of the gayest and most prosperous appearances, inward misery accompanies her; for, even in this life, her ways are ways of wretchedness, and all her paths are woe.

This observation has been so often made, that it must be known to all, and its truth is seldom formally denied by any; yet the conduct of men would sometimes lead us to suspect, either that they had never heard it, or that they think it false. To recal a truth of such importance to the recollection of mankind, and to illustrate it by example, may therefore be of use.

Tracing the windings of Vice, however, and delineating the disgusting features of Villany, are unpleasant tasks; and some people cannot bear to contemplate such a picture. It is fair, therefore, to warn Readers of this turn of mind, not to peruse the story of Zeluco.

This person, sprung from a noble family in Sicily, was a native of Palermo, where he passed the years of early childhood, without being distinguished by any thing very remarkable in his disposition, unless it was a tendency to insolence, and an inclination to domineer over boys of inferior rank and circumstances. The bad tendency of this, however, was so strongly remonstrated against by his father, and others who superintended his education, that it was in a great degree checked, and in a fair way of being entirely overcome.

In the tenth year of his age he lost his father, and was left under the guidance of a mother, whose darling he had ever been, and who had often blamed her husband for too great severity to a son, whom, in her fond opinion, nature had endowed with every good quality.

A short time after the death of his father, Zeluco began to betray strong symptoms of that violent and overbearing disposition to which he had always had a propensity, though he had hitherto been obliged to restrain it. Had that gentleman lived a few years longer, the violence of Zeluco's temper would, it is probable, have been weakened, or entirely annihilated, by the continued influence of this habit of restraint, and his future life might have exhibited a very different character; for he shewed sufficient command of himself as long as his father lived: but very soon after his death, he indulged, without control, every humour and caprice; and his mistaken mother applauding the blusterings of petulance and pride as indications of spirit, his temper became more and more ungovernable, and at length seemed as inflammable as gunpowder, bursting into flashes of rage at the slightest touch of provocation.

It may be proper to mention one instance of this violence of temper, from which the reader will be enabled to form a juster notion than his mother did, of what kind of spirit it was an indication.

He had a favourite sparrow, so tame that it picked crumbs from his hand, and hopped familiarly on the table. One day it did not perform certain tricks which he had taught it, to his satisfaction. This put the boy into a passion: the bird being frightened, attempted to fly off the table. He suddenly seized it with his hand, and while it struggled to get free, with a curse he squeezed the little animal to death. His tutor, who was present, was so shocked at this instance of absurd and brutal rage, that he punished him as he deserved, saying, "I hope this will cure you of giving vent to such odious gusts of passion. If it does not, remember what I tell you, Sir; they will render you hateful to others, wretched to yourself, and may bring you one day to open shame and endless remorse." Zeluco complained to his mother; and she dismissed the tutor, declaring, that she would not have her son's *vivacity* repressed by the rigid maxims of a narrow-minded pedant.

CHAPTER II.

> See how the world its veterans rewards!
> A youth of frolicks—an old age of cards.
>
> POPE.[1]

BEING now freed from that authority which had hitherto stimulated him to occasional exertions, Zeluco renounced all application to letters. This was partly owing to the love of dissipation and amusement natural to boys, but principally to the influence of a maxim very generally adopted by servants, and by them and other profound observers instilled into the minds of the young heirs of great fortunes, whose faculties it too often benumbs, like the touch of the torpedo,[2] and renders them incapable through life of every praise-worthy exertion. The maxim is this—That learning, although it is sometimes of service to those who are intended for certain professions, or are in any way to gain a livelihood by it, is entirely useless to men whose fortunes are already made.—It is hardly to be conceived how many young minds have been checked in the progress of improvement by the secret operation of this malignant doctrine.

The neglect of letters was compensated, in his mother's opinion, by his assiduous application to dancing, fencing, and other accomplishments of the same class. Indeed, she imagined he bestowed superfluous pains even on these, being persuaded that nature had done so much for her son, that there was no need of the ornaments of art.

Being captivated with the uniform of some Neapolitan officers, Zeluco, at an early period of his life, announced a decided taste for the profession of arms. This heroic resolution was highly approved of by all those to whom he communicated it; which, indeed, was generally the case whatever he communicated, because he associated only with those who were ready to approve of all he did or proposed; for it was another miserable trait in this young man's character, to prefer the company of obsequious dependants, who on no occasion withhold their assent, to that of men of a liberal spirit or of equal rank with himself; a feature which infallibly puts an end to improvement, and renders a man at length as disagreeable to society as society is to him.—The tender affection of his mother was not greatly alarmed at the martial resolution of her son, because, in the Neapolitan dominions,[3] the profession of a soldier having no connection with fighting, this indulgent parent knew that her son's military ardour would subject him to no other danger than is attendant on reviews: to this she submitted, being aware that glory could not be obtained for nothing.

The pacific situation of the Neapolitan army, however, was not Zeluco's reason for preferring it; for he was naturally of a daring spirit. He, like many other idle young men, was attracted to the profession of arms by a relish for the dress of an officer, and by the vanity of command over a few soldiers. At this time he thought no deeper on the subject. An application was therefore made by this indulgent mother for a commission for her son; between which period and the time of its being granted, Zeluco counted the moments with the most fretful impatience; for although he had already ordered his regimentals, and often indulged himself in the pleasure of strutting in them before a mirror, yet he experienced the agonies of Tantalus[4] till he could appear with them abroad. As the exigencies of the service did not require the immediate presence of Zeluco, he was permitted to remain at Palermo,[5] and was introduced by his mother into a select circle of her own acquaintance, which, she informed him, consisted of *the very best company* of Palermo, where he would acquire the most useful of all knowledge—the knowledge of the world—and this too in the most agreeable and most effectual manner.

This society was principally composed of a set of ladies of quality—maidens, wives, and widows—respectable undoubtedly on account of their sex and age; and a few gentlemen, who bore a wonderful resemblance in character to the ladies. Whatever business or avocation the members of this society had, besides those of cards and sleep, it must be confessed that such avocations occupied but a moderate share of their time, as all of them spent six or seven hours of the four-and-twenty in the former, and none of them allowed less than nine to the latter.

Zeluco's bloom, vivacity, and aptitude in learning the different games, procured him many flattering marks of attention from the female members. These for some time pleased the youth himself, while his mother was highly gratified with the congratulations poured out on all sides on the promising talents and charming appearance of her son; she reflected with pleasure also on the vast advantage which he enjoyed in being, at such an early period of his life, removed from the contagion of frivolous company, and introduced into so polished a circle.

What degree of improvement a steady and persevering cultivation of this society might have produced in Zeluco, was not fairly tried; for the flattery and blandishments of the old ladies soon became insipid, and he strayed in search of pleasure to those haunts where she appears with less decorum and more zest; soon after he joined his regiment at Naples, where he passed most of his time with a few young officers, who, with an equal passion for pleasure, had not equal means of indulging it, and were therefore too apt to flatter his vanity and bear his humours.—The love of pleasure seemed to increase upon him by indulgence, and was greatly cherished by the ill-judged prodigality of his mother, whose fondness could not resist his unrelenting importunity for money. The means with which this furnished him of indulging all his humours, in a country where rank claims an almost despotic sway over the lower orders of mankind, joined to his keeping company only with dependants, cherished and invigorated the seeds of caprice, selfishness, pride, and injustice, which had been early sown in the breast of Zeluco, and perhaps generated those which did not originally exist. With no pursuit but pleasure, and with superfluous means of attaining it, he enjoyed very little, being the constant slave of humour and caprice; and, besides, he looked forward with such fretful impatience to the period when the law allowed him the uncontrolled command of his fortune, as was sufficient of itself to embitter all his present enjoyments.

The original source of his wretchedness, and what had augmented, or perhaps generated, this miserable impatience of temper, was the indulgence of his humours and his being too liberally supplied in the means of gratification; but he himself imputed all his misery to the scanty allowance granted by his tutors, and to his not being of age.

Previous to this period he returned to Palermo; and although he did not attend his mother's assemblies with all the punctuality that she wished, yet he could not *always* resist the importunity of a mother who was ready to make every sacrifice for his gratification, and who exacted nothing in return but that he should give her the pleasure of seeing him admired in public, and condescend to bestow a little of his company on her in private.

The happy moment he had so anxiously sighed for arrived; and his guardians devolved into his own hands the intire conduct of his fortune. But while he remained in Sicily on account of certain arrangements, for which his presence was thought indispensibly necessary, an incident occurred which detained him longer than he intended.

CHAPTER III.

Virtue she finds too painful an endeavour;
Content to dwell in decencies for ever.

POPE.[1]

ONE of the most important personages of the society into which Zeluco had been introduced, was the Countess Brunella, a lady who took every opportunity of insinuating that she had been in her youth greatly distinguished for her beauty. Nothing, however, remained to justify her pretensions, except this single consideration, that as she had no fortune, and possessed no amiable quality, it was impossible to account for the marriage which raised her both to rank and fortune, but by supposing that, at the time it took place, she had been handsome. Her charms, however, whatever they had once been, were now entirely fled: but she still retained all the vanity, insolence, and caprice, which ever attended the bloom of beauty, with the addition of that peevishness and ill-humour which often accompany its decay. Her insolence, however, was only displayed to the unprotected, and her ill-humour to her servants; for, to her superiors she was always obsequious, and to her equals she wore an everlasting simper of approbation. This woman's benevolence was regulated by decorum; her friendship by conveniency; and all her affections by etiquette. Her heart had no concern in any of these matters.

She was chaste, without being virtuous; because in *her* it proceeded from constitution, not sentiment. Guarded by the breast-plate of frigidity, which, like the Ægis of Minerva, repels the shafts of love,[2] she walked through life erect, and steady to the dictates of decorum and self-interest, without a slip or a false step.

Inexorable to all helpless females who, from the frailty of nature, or the perfidy of man, were observed to totter, or even to stoop, in their progress, she insisted that they should be for ever excluded from the society of the upright: and if any person shewed a disposition to palliate their errors, this vulture of chastity quitted, for a moment, the frail bird on whom she had pounced, and turned her envenomed beak against those who were for shewing the smallest degree of mercy; and being freed by nature from any propensity to one particular frailty, she indulged, without bounds, in the gratification of envy, hatred, slander, haughtiness, and other vices of the same class, for which, from her childhood, she had discovered a decided taste.

This lady had a niece who lived with her. The young lady had little or no fortune in her own possession, and as little in expectation from her aunt, who was too vain and ostentatious to save any of her income, ample as it was. But the Countess flattered herself that she should procure her niece such a marriage as would instantly supply all deficiencies, and raise her to wealth and grandeur. She made several unsuccessful attempts for that purpose; the failure proceeded more from the general dislike in which the aunt was held, than from the want of attractions in the young lady.

A little after Zeluco came of age, the aunt fixed her eyes on him as a commodious match for her niece.—She was not unacquainted with his irregularities, but as she considered rank and fortune as the great essentials in a husband, these being secured, she thought the rest of small importance. On former occasions she had proved, that she looked upon age and infirmity as no obstacles to the honour of being a husband to her niece, and by the pains she now took to draw in Zeluco to a marriage, she made it clear that she considered profligacy as an objection equally frivolous.

She began by paying uncommon attention to the mother of Zeluco; as the Countess Brunella was her superior by nuptial rank, this attention greatly flattered the vanity of that weak woman.—She had for some time observed that Zeluco seemed to pay more particular regard to her niece than to any other young lady at Palermo; and she carefully instructed her in the arts of cherishing a moderate degree of liking into a violent passion. But this young lady, with less prudence, had much more sensibility than her aunt. The genteel figure and alluring manners of Zeluco seduced her into all the unsuspecting confidence of love; but he, amidst affected passion, preserved all the circumspection of determined perfidy.

Whilst the aunt, therefore, was artfully planning what she considered as an advantageous match for her niece, the unwary young woman granted, without marriage, what her aunt in similar circumstances had carefully preserved; not from any value she put upon the thing, but merely because she knew that by that means alone she could secure the husband who then paid his court to her.

Zeluco soon became tired of his conquest, and disgusted with the tears of the unhappy girl. He neglected her with an unfeeling indifference more unpardonable than the crime he had committed. This being observed by the aunt, she questioned her niece, who candidly confessed what her situation would in a short time have revealed.

The Countess expostulated with Zeluco, attempting to obtain by threats, what integrity and a sense of honour ought to have inclined him to perform. He treated her threats with derision, and with all the coolness of a veteran in iniquity he told her, that if *she* chose to keep her niece's secret, *he* should; in which case, by the industry of her aunt, she might still be provided with a husband: "in the mean time," added he sarcastically, "it is to be hoped you will make your own niece an exception from your favourite maxim, that all who have made a single false step should be for ever excluded from respectable society."

The young lady retired to a relation's in the country, and the adventure might have remained unknown to the public, had not the aunt, in the madness of her resentment, prompted a Neapolitan officer, who depended on her interest for his promotion, to call Zeluco to an account for his conduct on this occasion. Zeluco, who was constitutionally intrepid, had, for some time, wished for an opportunity of fighting a duel, the eclat[3] of which was wanting to his reputation. He went out at the first hint with the Neapolitan, and, being an admirable swordsman, wounded and disarmed him; and thus became an object of greater admiration in the eyes of many ladies than ever, both on account of this duel, and the occasion of it.

The rage, disappointment, and wounded pride of the aunt, when she knew the event of the duel, rendered her exceedingly miserable; but as in her prosperity she had no feeling for the unfortunate, her own misfortunes excited no compassion. Some of her most intimate acquaintance, who passed for her friends, involving the niece in their hatred of the aunt, betrayed a malicious satisfaction at the fate of the unhappy young woman. And what was equally unjust, the public indignation at the base conduct of Zeluco, was not so great as it ought to have been, merely because the person he had ruined was the niece of this odious dowager.

This woman might have gone through life with as few enemies as friends, had she remained passively selfish; but she was making continual professions of friendship; she affected to be the dearest friend of all her acquaintance, and to take a most extraordinary share of interest in all their concerns. Each of them in their turns discovered that her professions were false—from her acquaintance they became her enemies, and beheld her misfortunes with joy, which otherwise they would have regarded only with indifference.

CHAPTER IV.

The Gratitude of a Son to an indulgent Mother.

A SHORT time after this adventure, Zeluco passed over to Italy, and in the different states of that luxurious country he spent two years, in every voluptuous and expensive gratification that his own imagination or that of the profligate company he kept could suggest. His mother had parted from him with reluctance, her fond partiality remained strong as ever, in spite of all the proofs of a vicious disposition he had displayed: she viewed his character in a manner precisely the reverse of that in which Desdemona contemplated Othello's; she saw Zeluco's *mind in his visage*;[1] and as this was fair and regular, she fondly believed it to be a faithful index of the other, imputing all that part of his conduct which she could not justify, to the warmth of youth, which a little time and reflection would soon correct. She extracted a promise from him, before they parted, that he should write to her regularly twice every month till his return. And as she had observed on many occasions that he was by no means exact in fulfilling his engagements, she took this promise with some solemnity, and made him renew it oftener than once; adding, that if he neglected, she should certainly imagine that something very terrible had happened: she therefore intreated him very earnestly, by a punctual correspondence to save her from such a painful idea.

The manner in which Zeluco fulfilled this engagement will set his filial affection in a clear point of view.

In a very short space after his arrival on the continent, he began to think the writing a few lines every fortnight to his mother a piece of intolerable slavery.—And being, while at Rome, confined to his chamber, on account of a complaint which debarred him equally from pleasure and amusement,[2] he thought this a commodious opportunity of anticipating the trouble of a correspondence which was apt to break in upon him at less convenient seasons. He therefore wrote a number of letters to his mother, a little varied in the expression, and properly dated; these he arranged according to their dates, and then calling his valet de chambre,—"There," said he, "carry one of these letters to the post-house every fortnight, and when they are exhausted let me know, that I may prepare some more for the old lady."

It would be equally superfluous and disagreeable to follow Zeluco through the scenes of extravagance, folly, and vice, in which he acted a principal part for two or three years in the various towns of Italy. Although he had been happy during the whole of that short period, it would have been happiness rather too dearly bought at the expence of the misery and remorse he felt on finding his credit exhausted, and his fortune involved to such a degree, that nothing but a long and steady course of œconomy could possibly extricate it:—but he had not even the recollection of happiness to comfort him for the ruin of his affairs;—his fortune had been dissipated in debauchery, without pleasure; in magnificence, which conferred not respect; and in gaming, which sometimes drove him to the brink of desperation. Let this general account save us from entering into a detail of adventures which bear the strongest resemblance to those of so many profligate young men who have acted the same parts on the same theatre.

When his money and credit were nearly exhausted, he joined his regiment at Naples; where, after having remained a decent time to intitle him to ask a new leave of absence, he made application for permission to pass over to Sicily for the arrangement of his domestic affairs.

On his return to Palermo he had no immediate resource but in what his mother could spare him from her own jointure; and these supplies were not granted without strong remonstrances against his extravagance. Those, however, he heard with apparent patience, and repeated assurances of amendment, as long as she had either money or credit remaining; but when both were exhausted, he shewed the same impatient and overbearing temper to her he had always given proofs of to the rest of the world; but what in the one case she had palliated as the ebullitions of youthful spirit and vivacity, in the other she considered as the most unheard-of cruelty and ingratitude.—In the bitterness of her heart, she enumerated every instance of indulgence, generosity, and affection she had shewn him, and upbraided him for the returns he had made, in terms dictated by rage and disappointment. He answered with the most insulting coolness and the most stinging indifference. The unhappy woman was wounded to the soul.—She had looked forward with parental impatience to the hour of her son's return.—Her spirits had risen or fallen as that happy epoch seemed to advance or to recede.—Her daily prayer, and nightly dream, was this darling son's return, improved by experience, accomplished by travel, the object of universal admiration, while she imagined that she herself should be envied by every mother in Palermo.

Her disappointment was as severe as her hopes had been sanguine.—She felt

> How sharper than a serpent's tooth it is
> To have a thankless child.——[3]

She retired to the house of a poor relation who lived in the neighbourhood of Palermo;—one whom she had neglected in the pride of her prosperity; a circumstance which made her misery more acute, and her misfortune less pitied in this retreat. After languishing a few months, she died heart-broken.

The emotions of remorse which took place on this event, in the conscious mind of Zeluco, were not of long duration;—his embarrassed circumstances gave him more lasting uneasiness; for, notwithstanding his estate was now disburdened of his mother's jointure, he was still under the necessity of confining himself to a very scanty revenue.

Being mortified with the idea of remaining either in Sicily or the kingdom of Naples while his affairs were in this embarrassed situation, he applied to a brother of his father, an officer of rank in the Spanish service who was then at Madrid, declaring a desire of entering into that service, on conditions of obtaining the same rank in the Spanish service with the which he had in the Neapolitan, with the hope of future promotion. He had already got leave from the Neapolitan court for this step, with a recommendation from the minister. His plan was to put his estate under management till such time as the most pressing debts were cleared, and he thought, with the remainder of his fortune added to his pay, he should pass his time more to his mind in the character of a soldier, than he could by observing a languid system of œconomy in Sicily.

CHAPTER V.

The Love of a very young Lady.

Fallere credentem non est operosa puellam
Gloria. Ovid Epist.[1]

While Zeluco waited the result of this application, a young lady of Palermo became, by the sudden death of her brother, heiress of a very considerable fortune; for although her father was still alive, and her mother only forty years of age, yet as she had not proved pregnant for many years, the daughter's succeeding to her father's whole fortune was considered as next to infallible. This certainly was the opinion of Zeluco, and he immediately applied every art of insinuation he was possessed of, to gain the affections of this young lady.

Zeluco was of a very elegant as well as vigorous make, his person was finely proportioned, and although some people who pretended to skill in physiognomy asserted, that they could detect the indications of ill-nature and of a vicious disposition in his countenance; yet, in the general opinion, and particularly in that of Signora Rosolia (the young lady in question), he was a very handsome man. Rosolia was one of those young ladies who, when they greatly approve of a man's face and figure, are inclined to believe that every other good quality is added thereunto.

A gentleman superior to Zeluco in all respects but external figure had for some time, with the approbation of her parents, paid his addresses to her. But no sooner had the new lover made a declaration of his passion, than he appeared in her eyes preferable to the old. On what this preference was founded appeared afterwards, when Zeluco lamented his hard fate in having a rival who was countenanced by both her parents; for Rosolia then assured him, that this could proceed solely from their not being informed of Zeluco's sentiments; "But as soon as they are," added she, "they will certainly prefer you as a son-in-law to Signor Michelo."

"I am extremely happy to know that you are of that opinion," cried Zeluco.

"I am quite certain of it," said she.

"You have heard them speak upon the subject then," said he.

"No, never;" replied she.

"Idol of my soul," cried Zeluco, "how then are you certain that they would prefer me to Signor Michelo?"

"Because," replied this judicious young lady, "there is no comparison between you. Every body that has eyes must see that you are a far handsomer man."

However flattering it may seem, Zeluco was a good deal disappointed when he was informed of the circumstance on which she founded her hopes, and he thought his surest course was to get possession of the young lady's fortune and person in the first place, and to solicit the father and mother's consent afterwards.

Having expressed his gratitude on account of the favourable sentiments she entertained of him, he told her, "That parents often viewed things of this nature in a different light from their children—That his rival had probably secured the favour of her father and mother, by applying to them in the first instance; because her fortune, not her heart, was that gentleman's sole object.—That he, on the contrary, had given no hint of his passion to *them*, but had applied directly to *her*, because it was her heart alone that he was solicitous about. As for fortune, it was what he had always despised, and had not the least weight with him in his present suit—of which disinterested way of thinking he was ready to give her an immediate proof, by marrying her secretly without any person's consent but her own, and without the certainty of a single sequin."[2]

The young lady, in answer to this, told him, "That she could not comply with his proposal without impiety; for that her mother had been alarmed on a former occasion with the assiduities of a person she did not approve, had conducted her to the *Madre Chiesa*, and in the chapel of St. Rosolia,[3] in the presence of the saint herself, had made her pledge her solemn promise, never to give her hand in marriage without the consent of her father and mother; assuring her, at the same time, that they, on their part, should never exact of her to marry any man contrary to her inclination."

"It is impossible for me therefore," added this pious young lady, "to break the engagement, without incurring the displeasure not only of my parents but also of my patroness, who hitherto hath always displayed great kindness to me, and will certainly not easily forgive the breach of an engagement to which she herself was an eye-witness."

Zeluco, perceiving that the idea of provoking St. Rosolia filled the lady's mind with horror, did not think it prudent to insist at that time on the point he wished to carry;—he took her promise, however, that she would not mention what had passed to her parents, till he had time to reflect on what were the properest measures to adopt.

This injunction she punctually observed.—At their next interview, he told Rosolia, that he had been considering what she had said, regarding the promise she had given to her mother in the chapel of her patroness; "That he was not surprised to find this made great impression on one of her piety and understanding. This, and similar instances of the goodness of her disposition," he said, "endeared her to him more and more; for although the graces of her face and person had made the first impression on his heart, yet it was the beauties of her mind, the amiable sweetness of her disposition, her piety, and above all her admirable good sense, that rivetted his chains." Zeluco had an opinion, that people in general are most gratified when praised for those qualities in which they are most deficient. On this principle, he never failed to praise this young lady on the superior excellency of her understanding.

He then proceeded to observe, that with respect to the engagement which she imagined she had entered into at the Madre Chiesa, she had evidently been surprised into it, and it was not to be supposed that St. Rosolia could, *in her heart*, approve of so rash a vow, especially as it had been made without her previous consent; adding, that as for himself, he was certain that he should not survive the refusal he was sure of receiving from her mother:—he therefore left it to the young lady to consider whether it was probable that St. Rosolia, her patroness, and without a doubt, the most compassionate of all the saints, would approve of a measure which would infallibly occasion the death of a person who was, and had ever been, her faithful votary. And all for what? to gratify hard-hearted parents, who only consulted their own avarice, and disregarded true love.

As the tenderness of this young lady's heart was equal to the weakness of her understanding, and both infinitely surpassed those graces and beauties which Zeluco had so liberally imputed to her, she began to be convinced by his reasoning, and melted by his intreaties; but having, in the course of their conversation, said, that she was quite certain of prevailing on her father at least to give *his* consent,—for he had always been in the highest degree indulgent to her, and never had, in any one instance, withstood her persevering solicitation; Zeluco, contrary to his first opinion, thought it would be most prudent to allow her to try to move her father; and if, in spite of her sanguine hope, she should fail, he still would have it in his power to persuade her into a secret marriage.

CHAPTER VI.

The Reasoning of a young Lady in Love.—The Weakness of a Father.

The impatience of the lady's love made her seize the very earliest opportunity of acquainting her father with the state of her heart, which she did in very pathetic terms.

The astonished father at first insisted on the encouragement which had been given to her first lover, the real worth of his character, and the advantages of such a connexion. To these arguments the lady opposed her love for Zeluco, and her indifference for the other.

The father hinted at the embarrassed situation of Zeluco's circumstances.

The lady declared, that this gave her peculiar satisfaction, because it afforded a proof to the whole world, that in so material a point as the choice of a husband, she was superior to all low and sordid considerations, which could not fail of raising her in the esteem of the judicious, and would for ever insure to her the gratitude, as well as the love, of her husband.

The father suggested, that while she thus proved the disinterested purity of her own conduct; she could not be certain that her lover was actuated by the same noble and disinterested motives.

To this the daughter, with equal readiness and warmth, replied, that Zeluco had already given the most undoubted proofs of the generous turn of his mind; his superiority to all mercenary views and sordid considerations, by the magnificent manner in which he had spent the greatest part of his own fortune.

The father shook his head with an air of dissatisfaction, and then mentioned the libertine character of Zeluco, the number of women he had seduced, and his neglect of them afterwards; dwelling, with emphasis, on the cruel treatment of the countess Brunella's niece.

This was an unlucky argument, and produced an effect directly contrary to what was intended. The young lady acknowledged, that "Zeluco had been wild and rakish;—most young men of spirit were;—that he had turned the heads of many young women—no wonder, he was so very genteel and handsome;—that he had afterwards neglected them because he found them unworthy of his esteem, and they, of course, accused him of inconstancy;—that Signora Brunella's niece was a *very weak young woman;* it was not to be supposed a man of Zeluco's good sense would ever dream of taking such a person for his wife;—that, for her own part, she was aware, that by entirely possessing a man so greatly admired by all other women, she must be exposed to the envy of her own sex;—but that internal tranquillity, and domestic happiness, would enable her to despise their disappointment and malice; for she knew that Zeluco had fixed his heart upon her, and her alone; was now determined to reform, and to be constant; and all the world allowed that reformed rakes made the very best of husbands."

The young lady's last arguments seeming rather to alarm than convince her father, she had recourse to a method of reasoning which she had often found successful when all others failed.—She burst into a flood of tears, sobbed as if she had been ready to expire; and, when she recovered her voice, declared that her heart was fixed upon Signor Zeluco, who had given her the surest proofs of the sincerity of his love, and of his noble and generous character;—that happiness in marriage depended on mutual affection and endless passion, and not at all upon fortune;—that she would wander over the wide world with her lover, blest in his fidelity, and depending on St. Rosolia for protection and sustenance, rather than live in the greatest affluence with any other man, although he were the first monarch on earth, or even the king of Naples, Jerusalem, and the Two Sicilies[1] himself:—that these were her unalterable sentiments, or if any alteration could happen, it would be that of an increase, not a diminution, of her love, for she felt it augmenting every hour; and finally, she intreated on her knees, that he would prove himself an affectionate father to a daughter who had always loved and honoured him, and would obey him in every thing but in this one point, which, she was sorry to say, was out of her power; and which, if he insisted upon, he would soon behold her laid in the same grave with her dearest brother, whom he had so long and so bitterly lamented.

Before the daughter had finished this affecting address, the good-natured father was also in tears, and as soon as he was able to speak, he raised her up, with an assurance that her happiness was his chief object in life, and he would do every thing she could desire to promote it.

Having thus melted her father to compliance, she begged, in the next place, that he would use his influence with her mother, that she might likewise consent to the only measure that could make her truly happy, which the good-natured man engaged to do.

CHAPTER VII.

The Prudence of a Mother;—and Termination of everlasting Love.

THE father speedily had an opportunity of breaking the subject to his Lady, assuring her at the same time that he was convinced their daughter would never marry any man but Zeluco; so that she had best save herself the trouble of endeavouring to prevent it, as he had already said every thing that could be said, and without effect.

He was then proceeding to give her an account of the scene which had passed between them, when she saved him the trouble, informing him she had overheard the whole in an adjoining room, where she happened to be when his daughter had made the pathetic attack upon him above described. Perceiving that her husband's heart was quite melted by the daughter's tears, and his resolution moulded to her views, she declined all discussion with him; and thought it not prudent to let him into the plan which she had already formed in her mind, to disentangle her daughter from a connexion fraught with ruin and remorse. She contented herself therefore with saying coolly, "That although she did not much relish the match, yet, as she could not think of crossing her daughter's inclinations, she certainly would not persist in opposition, if, on full deliberation, the young lady continued in the same mind; and at all events she would take no step without the concurrence of her husband, who, she was pleased to add, was a much better judge in a matter of such importance than she could pretend to be."

In reply to this the husband said, "That he candidly acknowledged that he was *a far better judge*; adding, that it was impossible for him ever to change his mind."

"Not quite, my dear," said the wife meekly; "you were under the necessity of changing your mind before you could relinquish the *unalterable* resolution you told me yesterday you had formed of giving your daughter to Signor Michelo, whom we then equally approved of."

"I did not know *yesterday*," said he, a little disconcerted, "that Zeluco was the *only* man who could make our daughter happy."

He then went and acquainted his daughter that he had prevailed on her mother to consent to her marriage with Zeluco.

The young lady flew in a transport of joy to her mother, asked her forgiveness for having disposed of her heart without consulting so indulgent a parent;—informed her, that she was now absolutely certain of St. Rosolia's being pleased with her choice; and assured her, that for the future she would be the most obedient and dutiful of all daughters.

The mother thanked her for her good intentions, and asked her how she came to be so certain of the Saint's acquiescence.

"Because," replied the pious young lady, "as I have been able to think or even to dream of nothing for some time, but my marriage with Signor Zeluco, after attending mass this very morning, I retired to the chapel of the Saint, and looking her devoutly in the face, and watching her eyes, I humbly entreated to know whether she approved of my passion or not?—On which the sweet image of Rosolia looked in the most propitious manner; and at length, with a gracious smile, nodded assent."

"Nay," said the mother, "after such a testimony of approbation there can be no doubt.—And have you equal proofs, my dear, of Signor Zeluco's love?"

"Stronger, if possible," answered the daughter;—"he has sworn it to me an hundred times; and, besides, I have it under his hand."

"These are proofs indeed," said the mother; "and," continued she, "you have no reason to doubt that all this love is for you alone, independent of your fortune!"

"Santa Maria!" exclaimed the daughter, "Signor Zeluco is not only the most loving, but also the most disinterested of mankind.—He has often assured me, that he would be still happier if my fortune were less, that he might prove to the world how far he is above all mean and mercenary views."

"Then it is highly probable," said the mother, "that he will enjoy the felicity he so earnestly desires; for I shall now inform you, my dear, of what I did not chuse to hint till I was quite certain of it; I am several months gone with child, which, at any rate, will reduce your fortune one half; and in case of a son, will leave you a very moderate portion."

"I wish with all my heart you may have a son, my dear mother; for I should like a little brother of all things," cried Rosolia.

"Very well, my dear," said the mother; "you will very probably obtain your wish. But," continued she, "I suppose you would not wish that your marriage should take place till I am recovered of my lying-in, that I may join in the pleasure of such an occasion."

"Good Heaven! certainly not," answered the daughter; and immediately went, in raptures, to communicate these glad tidings to Zeluco, whose joy at the parents acquiescence was prodigiously damped on hearing of the situation of the mother. His chagrin was evident on his countenance.

"I perceive," said the young lady tenderly, "that the postponing of our happiness till my mother shall be delivered grieves you."

"Very severely indeed," said Zeluco.

"Be not afflicted, my dear Zeluco," said this love-sick maiden, "I will endeavour to prevail on her to consent to our union before she is delivered."

Zeluco begged she would not attempt it, as it might give offence, and render her mother averse to the match altogether.

She then, in the most endearing manner, assured him, that the delay gave her very near as much uneasiness as it could him; but he, on the other hand, protested, that he felt the disappointment with greater poignancy than she could possibly do, which, however, he would endeavour to bear, rather than risk disobliging her mother, especially in her present condition, when the smallest importunity might injure her precious health.

"But, good God," added he, "did you never before suspect that she was in this condition?"

"Never," said this penetrating young lady; "though I am not surprised at it; for the moment she mentioned it, I plainly perceived that her waist was uncommonly large."

Zeluco retired, in all the agonies of disappointment; but determined to be more fully informed before he gave up a pursuit on which he had founded the re-establishment of his fortune.

He called the following morning on a certain monk, who occasionally exercised the function of a physician, and was known to be employed in that capacity by the mother of Signora Rosolia.

After an affected consultation on his own health, he turned the conversation on her's.

The wary mother, having thought it probable that Zeluco might question this man, had prepared him in what manner to answer his inquiries: the medical monk, therefore, assured Zeluco that she was in the way that he, and the best friends of her family, could wish.

"What, is it true then," replied Zeluco, "*what I have with so much pleasure heard*, Signora Maria is really with child?"

"Nothing of that nature can be more certain," replied the physician, "than that she is pregnant of one child; some think from her appearance that she will have twins."

"Twins!" cried Zeluco.

"Yes, Signor," continued the Doctor; "that is the opinion of some who are thought judges in such matters; but, in my own mind, no indications however strong can ascertain the point with such precision as those people pretend;—that she has one lively child seems beyond a doubt; that she will have two, I will not positively assert."

"Why, Doctor," said Zeluco, "it is a very long time since she was in the same situation."

"If she has twins," replied the monk gravely, "she never was precisely in the same situation; it is true, indeed, that when a woman has once had twins, she will afterwards be more likely to have them again."

"Pray, how long is it since she had her last child?" said Zeluco.

"About nine or ten years," replied the physician.

"Is it not uncommon, after such an interval, for a woman to recommence bearing children?" said Zeluco.

"It *is* a little singular," replied the monk; "but when a woman does recommence, she generally proceeds with more spirit and perseverance than if no such interruption had taken place:—therefore, as Signora Maria is only forty years of age, I should not be surprised if, by the favour of the Blessed Virgin, who is her patroness, she should have several children before she leaves off child-bearing entirely."

"Several children!" repeated Zeluco with an accent of anger;—"you must imagine her patroness has prodigious powers in such matters."

"Do you call the powers of the Blessed Virgin in question?" replied the monk, in a threatening tone.

"Heavens forbid, father," said Zeluco, with an expiatory look.

"Let me tell you, Signor," continued the monk in an authoritative style, "that the powers of the Virgin are unlimited; it were impiety to doubt it."

"I have not the least doubt," cried Zeluco; taking the monk in an affectionate manner by the hand:—"so far from calling her power in question, I am convinced, my dear father," added he, with a hypocritical accent, "that she could bring it about without the assistance of the husband."

"Unquestionably she could," said the monk.

Zeluco being now persuaded of the reality of Signora Maria's pregnancy, took his leave of the monk; and having two days before received a letter from his uncle at Madrid, assuring him of promotion in the Spanish service, he resolved to set out for that city as soon as possible. When he received the letter, his determination had been to secure his marriage with Signora Rosolia in the first place, and then deliberate what answer he should make to his uncle's letter; but having now resolved to have nothing more to do with the fair object of his disinterested and unalterable affection, he seized the opportunity of a vessel ready to sail for Barcelona; embarked with a single servant, and a very moderate quantity of baggage; and after a prosperous voyage arrived at that city. Being very impatient to get quickly to Madrid, he ordered his servant to have every thing prepared for the journey as soon as possible. While these arrangements were making, he intended to have amused himself by sauntering through the town, but was prevented by a heavy shower of rain.—"I do not know what in the devil's name to do with myself," said Zeluco.—"You had as well take this opportunity of writing to Signora Rosolia," said his valet;—"she may perhaps be surprised at our sudden departure."—"Ay, so I will; bring me pen, ink, and paper," said Zeluco, yawning.

The servant supplied him with the materials for writing; and this ardent lover renewing his fits of yawning very frequently during the performance, at last finished the epistle.

Signora Rosolia, when she heard of Zeluco's having sailed for Spain, immediately fainted, as is usual with young ladies when they are abandoned by men who pretend to be dying for them, and whom they consider as the only men who can make them happy:—she continued for some weeks subject to hysterical affections: these, however, gradually disappeared; and her old lover, by the mediation of her mother, renewing his courtship; she was in due time prevailed on to give him her hand. Her mother then informed her, that she was mistaken in the notion of her being with child. And the day after her marriage, the daughter in return declared to her mother, that she herself had undoubtedly mistaken the image of St. Rosolia, being now convinced, that her present husband was the only man who could make her completely happy.

"I hope, my dear," said the mother, "he is the only man who ever will attempt it."

CHAPTER VIII.

His Generosity gets Credit for what was due to his Resentment.

ZELUCO was received in the kindest manner by his uncle at Madrid, who viewed his past extravagances in the most favourable light, considering them as entirely proceeding from youthful vivacity and imprudence. He therefore treated him with all the respect due to the head of his own family; introduced him to every house of distinction; flattering himself, that the ardent spirit of his nephew might excite him to the same impetuous pursuit of military glory with which he had followed pleasure, and fondly hoping that he would one day arrive at higher distinction than he would have attained by an unambitious prudence of conduct in the Neapolitan service, which afforded no opportunity of displaying military genius. After pointing out the advantages he would derive from his birth, he inculcated the necessity of distinguishing himself by activity as an officer, that he might give an early impression in his favour, and smooth the way to that rapid promotion he had reason to expect, from his exertions in an army where discipline was greatly relaxed, and in which few men of rank distinguished themselves.

Zeluco was appointed to a regiment then on its march to one of the sea-port towns, but with permission to remain at Madrid till the troops should arrive at the place of their destination, and were completed. He spent this interval in those societies to which he had been introduced by his uncle, and being sufficiently sensible of the graces of his own person, he was not without hopes of engaging the affections of some female as wealthy as Signora Rosolia, and whose mother was less liable to pregnancy.

At some of those assemblies, gaming, to a considerable depth, was permitted. Zeluco had always been fond of play, and had acquired, at the usual expence, a very great knowledge in most games; yet he by no means possessed that degree of coolness and command of temper which is requisite for a gamester: he was sensible of this himself, but he could not always resist the temptation of gaming; and sometimes, not satisfied with the play at the assemblies, he went in search of deeper stakes at less creditable houses.

At first he was fortunate, which encouraged him to attend those houses more constantly. One unlucky evening, however, he lost all the money he had about him, amounting to a considerable sum; most part of it was won by a person who had lately appeared at Madrid, assuming the character of an Hungarian gentleman, with the rank of a lieutenant-colonel of Hussars in the Emperor's service.[1] As the company played for ready money only, when Zeluco had lost his, he sat in very ill-humour, looking over those who continued to play: in this disposition it was not unnatural in him to suspect that the person who had won his money had, by other means besides superior skill in the game, assisted his own good fortune. Zeluco watched him with the most malignant attention, wishing to detect him in some unfair trick, and ready to quarrel with him even if he should not.

The game was pass-dice. A young stranger held the dice, and had already won four times; and as his whole money had been covered each time, the sum before him was now sixteen times larger than what he had originally staked. But while he seemed preparing to throw a fifth time, there was only about a third part of the money which he now had on the table taken by the company.

On observing this, the stranger said, "Does nobody choose to take more?" Every body declined, on which he put the residue of the money into his pocket; but as he shook the box, being about to throw, the Hussar officer cried, Banco; and the others took up what they had staked.

The rule of the game is, that if any one person offers to take the whole, the rest of the company, who have taken smaller sums, immediately withdraw their money in favour of the person who offers to stand against the entire bank; that is to say, the whole sum which the person who holds the dice has on the table.

The Hussar meant to avail himself of the equivocal situation of the case: if the dice should prove fortunate to the thrower, he intended to pay the exact sum on the table; but in case the dice turned against the stranger, he resolved to claim not only that, but also what the young gentleman had just put into his pocket.

The stranger threw and lost. "Take your money," said he; shoving the whole parcel to the Hungarian.

The latter insisted on having that also which he had put into his pocket, saying, it belonged to the bank as much as what remained on the table, since there had been no intervening throw.

The young gentleman was astonished at this demand, asserting, that the money he had pocketed was entirely out of the question, having been withdrawn before the Hungarian had spoken. That if the officer meant both sums, he ought to have declared that meaning when he called Banco; adding, that in case he had done so, or if the company had set against the whole of his winning, he himself had determined to pass the box, and not have risked so great a sum on one throw.

This pretended colonel, however, who was a stout man, with a long sabre and a formidable pair of whiskers, was loud and boisterous in asserting his right to the whole. The stranger defended his cause but faintly; the company in general, whatever they thought of the justice of the case, did not seem disposed to assert the stranger's claim against this ferocious Hussar.

In this state of affairs, Zeluco, who burned with resentment against the person who had won his money, said, "It was a clear case, and that the Hungarian had a right to nothing but the sum on the table when he first spoke;" adding, "he was convinced if he had lost he would have paid no more." "How, Sir!—what do you mean?" cried the Hungarian, turning fiercely round to Zeluco. "I mean precisely what I said," replied the latter. "What, Sir!" repeated the Hussar, in a loud tone of voice, and putting his hand to his sword. "Yes, Sir," cried Zeluco, "and further, I mean to cut the throat of any rascally adventurer who dares be insolent to me:" saying this, he half drew his sword, when the company interposed. The Hussar affected not to have heard Zeluco's last words, but said, in a softened tone, "That if the company were of opinion that his claim was not strictly just, he was willing to yield it."—"Willing or unwilling, you shall yield it," cried Zeluco; and the company being *now* unanimous in favour of the stranger, the pretended Hungarian officer withdrew from the assembly, and next morning early he left Madrid, afraid that this incident would produce an investigation exceedingly prejudicial to him, being conscious that he had no title to the character he assumed.

This adventure was much talked of, and did a great deal of honour to Zeluco. It was peculiarly agreeable to his generous uncle, who having heard that his nephew had been unfortunate on the night in which he had behaved with such spirit, he presented him with a sum sufficient for clearing all his expences at Madrid, and equipping him in the genteelest manner for his expedition to the West Indies. Zeluco himself, having no immediate prospect of meeting with another Rosolia, grew tired of the formality of Madrid, and impatient to join his regiment, which he understood had now arrived at the head-quarters.

This resolution being communicated to the uncle, was imputed by him to a laudable zeal for the service. The worthy veteran assured him, that he would take particular care of his interest, and assist his promotion with all his influence at court, making no doubt but his efforts for that purpose would be rendered successful by the rising reputation of Zeluco.

The regiment was in a very short time completed, and soon after embarked for the island of Cuba, where it arrived in safety.

CHAPTER IX.

La férocité naturelle fait moins de cruels que l'amour-propre.

Duc de la Rochefoucault.[1]

The Remonstrance of an old Officer.

Zeluco possessed not the generous ardour of a soldier; his impatience for promotion was excited by the hopes of emolument more than a thirst for military glory; and if he was willing to suffer fatigue and incur danger, it was because in his present situation they were necessary for his obtaining some lucrative command, that might speedily furnish him with the means of pleasure and luxurious enjoyment, which he considered as the only sensible pursuits in life.

Having heard that the commander in chief was a very strict and attentive officer, and Zeluco's views being now centered in military promotion, he was impatient to acquire favour and recommendation by distinguishing himself as a disciplinarian; naturally selfish and unfeeling, he was not checked in the prosecution of this plan by any sentiment of justice or compassion; provided he could make the men under his command more dexterous in their exercise, or more smart in their appearance, than others, he regarded not the inconveniency or torture he occasioned to them; nor did he care whether this was of use to the service or not; he was convinced it might be of use to himself, and that was sufficient. Without temper to make allowance for the awkwardness of recruits, or equity in proportioning punishments to crimes, his orders were often dictated by caprice and enforced by cruelty; he exacted from the private men such a degree of precision in the manual exercise, and in the minutiæ of their dress, as was almost out of the power of the most dexterous and best disposed to observe.

Provoked and irritated on finding that the soldiers did not arrive at that degree of perfection which his vanity required, and becoming daily more unreasonable and unrelenting by the exercise of power, he exhibited many instances of cruelty on a detachment from the garrison of Havannah, of which he had for some time the command.

His conduct on that and other occasions came to the knowledge of the commander in chief by the following incident:

A soldier having committed some slight mistake in the exercise, Zeluco treated him with great severity, which the man endured with all the passiveness which military discipline exacts;—till Zeluco, swelling with the insolence of power, expressed himself in this barbarous and absurd manner: "If you are not more alert for the future, you scoundrel, I will cut you to pieces, and send your soul to hell."

To this the man replied with tranquillity—"Your honour may cut me to pieces if you please; but I thank God it is not in your power to send my soul to hell."

This very sedate answer, while it raised a smile in others who heard it, augmented the rage of Zeluco.

"Do you mutiny, villain?" cried Zeluco.

"I do not, indeed," said the soldier.

"I'll let you know in due time," said Zeluco, "whether you do or not."

He ordered the man to be carried to the guard prison, and put in irons.

Zeluco had been long disliked by all his fellow-officers.—On talking over this matter with some of them, in order to prepossess them with the opinion that what the soldier had said amounted to mutiny, he found them little disposed to consider it in that light; he was in no haste, therefore, to bring the man to a court-martial, being convinced he would be acquitted: but he had it insinuated to the soldier himself, that if he would acknowledge a mutinous intention, and implore mercy, he should be liberated without a trial; whereas, if he were tried, he would certainly be severely punished.

But the soldier, secretly encouraged by those of the officers who most detested Zeluco, refused to make any such avowal, and remained in irons.

Meanwhile the chaplain of the regiment having visited the soldier, approved of his conduct, declaring he could not justly be punished for an answer so orthodox. He next day informed the commander in chief of the whole transaction.

This gentleman, unwilling to rely intirely on the account he had received, sent for some of the officers belonging to the detachment, and obtained from them the same information which he had already received from the chaplain.

In the mean time Zeluco, having got a hint of what was going on, freed the soldier from confinement. But the indignation of the commanding officer being roused by what he had heard, he made inquiries into Zeluco's conduct to the soldiers on other occasions; and soon discovered, with astonishment, and some degree of self-condemnation, that many acts of unnecessary severity and oppression had been committed by Zeluco. Having blamed some officers, whose duty he thought it was to have informed him of those transactions sooner, he sent for Zeluco, and in the presence of all the officers of the battalion to which he belonged, he addressed him to the following effect:

"Signor Zeluco,

"I think it my duty to deliver my sentiments to you before these gentlemen, on a subject that ought to be well understood by every officer; but of which it appears by your conduct you have formed very erroneous notions.

"Strict discipline is essentially requisite for the well-being of an army; without which it degenerates into a lawless mob, more formidable to their friends than enemies; the ravagers, not the defenders, of their country.

"But it is equally essential that discipline be exercised with temper and with justice; a capricious and cruel exertion of power in officers depresses the spirits of the private men, and extinguishes that daring ardour which glows in the breast of a real soldier.

"Is it possible that a man of a generous mind can treat with wanton cruelty those who are not permitted to resist, or even to expostulate, however brave they may be.

"I believe, Sir, you have not as yet served in time of war; but I will inform you, that in the course of my services I have seen common soldiers gallantly face the enemy, when some officers, who had been in the habit of using them with insult and cruelty, shrunk from the danger.

"You are sufficiently acquainted with the condition of private soldiers, to know, that when they are treated with all the lenity consistent with proper discipline, still their condition is surrounded with such a variety of hardships, that every person of humanity must wish it were possible to alleviate it.

"Only reflect, Sir, on the smallness of their pay; how inadequate to the duty required of them, and how far beneath the intrinsic value it bore when it was first fixed; yet this grievance remains unremedied in some of the wealthiest countries of Europe, even in those where the greatest attention is paid in other particulars to the rights of mankind. But weak as the impression may be which the soldier's hardships make on the cold heart of the politician, one would naturally expect they should meet with sympathy in the breasts of their own officers; the men best acquainted with their situation, whom they are constantly serving and obeying, who are acting in the same cause, and exposed to the same dangers though not to the same hardships with themselves. It is natural to imagine that, independent of more generous motives, their own interest, and the idea of self-preservation, would prompt officers to behave with mildness, at least with equity, to the soldiers under their command. How many officers have been rescued from death or captivity by the grateful attachment and intrepidity of the soldiers? I myself, Sir, once lay on the field severely wounded, when, in the midst of general confusion, officers and men flying promiscuously, I was carried to a place of security by two soldiers, at the infinite hazard of their own lives. From one of those, indeed, I might naturally have expected some exertion in my favour; he was a Castilian, born on my own estate: but I had no claim on the other, except as an officer who had always behaved equitably to him in common with the rest of my company;—he was an Irishman.

"Had I treated him with caprice or ill-nature, would this foreigner, or even would my own countryman have made such a generous exertion to preserve my life? No, Sir; if they had refrained from giving me a fresh wound as they fled past me, which soldiers are not unapt to do to cruel officers, they certainly would at least have consulted their own safety by continuing their flight, and left me to be trampled to death by the enemy's cavalry, as I certainly must have been, had not these two soldiers removed me from the spot on which I lay.

"But waving every consideration derived from the ideas of personal safety, there is another kind of selfishness which might induce officers to behave well to soldiers; that is, the pleasure of alleviating, in many respects, the unavoidable hardships of our fellow-creatures, and the consciousness of being loved by those around us."

At this part of the general's remonstrance, Zeluco raised his eyes mechanically with that kind of stare which a man gives when he hears what he thinks a very extraordinary proposition.

"It is true, Sir, I assure you," continued the Castilian; "next to the approbation of his own conscience, nothing is so grateful to the heart of man as the love and esteem of mankind. In my mind, he is an object of compassion, in whatever situation of life he may be placed, who is not sensible of this from his own experience; and surely no man can be tolerably happy, who thinks himself the object of their hatred.

"We all know, gentlemen," continued he, turning a moment from Zeluco to the other officers, "that the love of soldiers, important as it is to those who command them, may be acquired on easier terms than that of any other set of men; because the habit of obedience, in which *they* are bred, inclines them to *respect* their officers; unbiassed equity in the midst of the strictest discipline commands their *esteem*, and the smallest mark of kindness secures their *gratitude* and attachment. I have ever endeavoured to preserve a steady and regular discipline among the troops I have had the honour of commanding; yet I have the happiness to believe, that I am more loved than feared by those among them who have had the best opportunity of knowing me.—One of the greatest pleasures I ever enjoyed (I see some here who were with me on that occasion) was, in over-hearing an advanced guard of soldiers talk affectionately of me, when they knew not I was near them: I will own to you, Sir, it came over my heart like the sweetest music: and if I thought myself the object of the secret execrations of the men under my command, it would spoil the harmony of my life, and jar my whole soul out of tune.

"Signor Zeluco, what I have heard of your behaviour to the soldiers, I am willing to impute to a misplaced zeal for the service. It is difficult to believe, that a man of birth and education could have been prompted to the severities you have exercised by other motives.

"This consideration, joined to the regard I have for the recommendation of my old friend your uncle, have weighed with me, in not subjecting certain parts of your conduct to the judgment of a court martial.

"With respect to the soldier whom you confined so long and so improperly in irons, you certainly treated him from the beginning with too much severity. The natural awkwardness of a recruit is to be corrected gradually, and with gentleness; severity confounds him, and increases the evil that is to be remedied. To give way to anger and passion on such an occasion is inconsistent with the dignity which an officer ought to preserve before the men, and is always attended with injustice. As for this man's answer to your very intemperate menace, although a soldier under arms ought not to make any reply to an officer, yet, all the circumstances being weighed, what he said was excusable; to endeavour to torture it into mutiny would be absurd.

"You ought to remember, gentlemen, that as military discipline looks to the general tendency and remote consequences of things, more than to their intrinsic criminality, many actions are treated as crimes by the military laws which in themselves are innocent or frivolous. And when a soldier, irritated by undeserved insult, overleaps subordination, and repels the wanton tyranny of an officer, however he may be condemned by the unrelenting laws of discipline, he will be absolved by the natural feelings of the human heart, which revolts at oppression; nor will he appear, even in the eyes of those who think his punishment expedient, an object either of contempt or aversion. But when an officer, armed with the power, and intrenched within the lines of discipline, indulges unmanly passion, or private hatred, against an unprotected and unresisting soldier, in what light can this officer appear, either in his own eyes, or in those of others?

"Signor Zeluco, I have thought proper to explain my sentiments to you thus fully before these gentlemen, who have been witnesses to your conduct since you first joined the regiment, and who I do not think intirely free from blame for not making me acquainted with it. I have only to add, that the considerations which prevent my laying the whole before a court-martial, cannot operate a second time. I hope, Sir, that for your own sake you will keep this in your remembrance, that while I insist upon all the troops under my command performing their duty with punctuality, I will not permit the poorest centinel to be treated with injustice.

"The soldier whom you used so harshly may still appeal, if he pleases, to a court-martial; it will be prudent in you to find means to prevent him."

Having said this, the general dismissed the company. Zeluco made a present to the soldier more than sufficient to satisfy him. And his expectation of sudden promotion in the army being greatly damped by the general's harangue, he formed the resolution of quitting the road to military renown, and of turning into a path more agreeable to his talents, and from which he hoped to reap greater advantage.

CHAPTER X.

Gratitude to a Friend.—Curiosity in a Maid.

ZELUCO had formed an acquaintance with a Spanish gentleman, to whom he had brought a recommendatory letter from his uncle at Madrid; and from whom he received daily marks of attention and civility. As this gentleman, though of but a moderate fortune, lived in a most hospitable style, and was of a character less reserved than the Spaniards in general are, Zeluco found him a very convenient acquaintance, and cultivated his good opinion with such assiduity, that he gained at last his entire confidence. In the course of their intimacy, the Spaniard informed Zeluco that he had long paid his addresses to a widow lady possessed of a very valuable estate of her own, and a large sum of money secured in mortgages on some of the best estates in the islands of Cuba and Hispaniola:[1] that she had, on his first making proposals, protested in positive terms, according to the established custom of widows, against ever entering into a second matrimonial engagement; but that of late he had observed with much satisfaction, that her objections became gradually weaker, both in their nature and in the manner in which they were urged; and that he now had good hopes of their being soon removed altogether: that as her great fortune was entirely in her own power, as she had no children, and was in herself a woman of good disposition and of a cheerful temper, he expected many advantages and much domestic happiness from the union.

Zeluco was introduced to this lady's acquaintance by her lover; and having made a cautious and minute inquiry into the state of her finances, he was satisfied that they rather surpassed than fell short of the account he had received of them; and from that moment formed the design of supplanting his unsuspicious friend.

But he did not think it prudent to pay his court avowedly to a woman who was almost betrothed to another; and that other, a person from whom he received hourly civilities, and whom he acknowledged to be his friend.

He assailed her, however, with the eloquence of glances and sighs; which, while he *affected* to conceal them from her, he took particular care should not escape her observation; and as often as they seemed to be discovered he endeavoured to blush, and then assumed an air of uneasiness and confusion.

When he was in her company, which happened as often as he decently could, he added to this the most obsequious approbation of whatever she said; and the general tendency of his discourse, though often addressed to others, was to adopt and illustrate those sentiments and opinions which he knew to be hers.

By these means, aided by the graces of his person, he gradually made advances on the heart of the widow; and in a short time gained a decided preference over the old lover. But although this skilful engineer was fully sensible of the impression which he made, he declined sending an open summons, trusting that his masked battery of sighs and glances would extort from the fortress itself a proposal of surrender. To hasten which, he took care to engage the widow's confidential maid in his interest, by ordering his own valet to make assiduous love to her, and instructing him in what manner to proceed after he had gained her heart.[2]

The attentive valet began his operations without loss of time; having spent a few days in general courtship, he told her that he had something of an important and very secret nature to communicate to her private ear.

"To my private ear!" cried the maid.

"Assuredly, my dear," said the valet, "to your's, and to no other person's."

This so mightily raised the curiosity of the maid, that, she gave him a rendezvous in a grove of her mistress's garden; merely, as she herself repeatedly assured him, to know what this important matter was; for she owned it was beyond the compass of her power to divine what it could be.

The valet gained her heart as he had been ordered; and in the intervals of his own successful passion he observed the other instructions of his master.

CHAPTER XI.

Rien ne pese tant qu'un secret;
Le porter loin est difficile aux dames;
Et je sais meme sur ce fait
Bon nombre d'hommes qui sont femmes.

LA FONTAINE.[1]

AFTER having lived for some time together in a state of mutual happiness, the valet presented himself one day to his mistress with every appearance of sorrow; this tender-hearted maiden (for she had never been married) affectionately inquired into the cause of his grief. The valet answered, "That it was all on account of his unhappy master, who, from being the most cheerful of mankind, was of late become the most dejected and heart-broken."

"Have you no notion," said the maid, "what has occasioned such a melancholy change?"

"No notion!" replied the valet; "I know but too well what has brought it about."

"And pray, for goodness sake, what can it be?" said the maid impatiently.

"That," replied the valet, "is what no earthly consideration will make me ever divulge."

"No!" cried the maid, "and for what reason?"

"Because," said the valet, "I have promised never to mention it to any human creature."

"I insist upon knowing it immediately," said the maid.

"I beg you will not," cried the valet, "it would be horrid in me to divulge a secret with which I have been intrusted—my master never would forgive me."

"Your *mistress* never will forgive you, if you do not," said the maid.

"Only consider what you require of me," rejoined the valet; "to break my trust! To press such a thing is an attack on my honour."

"Well," exclaimed the maid, "have you not made an attack on *my honour*? Is all your pretended love come to this? To refuse the *first* favour she ever asked, to her who has granted you the *last*.[2] Was there ever such ingratitude. O! I shall burst with vexation.—Yes," continued she, weeping, "if you do not immediately tell me the cause of your master's misery, you will render me ten thousand times more miserable than he."

There was no resisting such a rational and pathetic remonstrance. The valet unfolded the whole mystery. "His poor master was desperately and hopelessly in love with her mistress; for knowing that she was in some measure engaged to a friend of his own, he was a man of such delicate honour that he would pine away his very soul in secret, rather than interfere with a friend; that he ate little or no food, never slept a wink, sighed from morning to night: and as for my own part," continued the valet, "how shall I be able to support the loss of such a generous master! for he is the most liberal of men; one who thinks he never can sufficiently recompense those who do him even the smallest service."

The maid expressed her admiration at the account he gave of his master, particularly at his neither eating nor sleeping; she likewise approved very much of his sighing night and day for love. She knew that such things were common formerly, for in the course of her studies she had read of them in books. "But I fear," said she, "they are not much the fashion among lovers of the present age. Yet I must confess," continued she, "that your master is to blame for not acquainting my mistress with his passion."

"He never will," replied the valet; "nothing will ever prevail on him to come in competition with his friend; he will rather pine away his very soul in secret."

"He is very much to blame," said the maid; "for allow me to put a case which has this moment come into my head.—If so be that many men were to act in the same manner, it would be a great hardship on the fair sex; for many of them might accept a man who was not very agreeable to them, while others, whom they would have preferred, are pining away their souls in secret; for if they always pine in secret, how is a woman to know that they are pining at all? And a prudent woman," continued the maid, "will secure what she can get, rather than run the risk of getting nothing. It is therefore a clear case, that your master should speak out, and acquaint my mistress with his love, and who knows," added she, with a significant nod to the valet, "what may happen, since your master is so generous a man?"

"Generous!" cried the valet, "you can have no notion how generous he is; nobody ever did him a service without being rewarded far beyond their expectations; but as for speaking of his passion to your mistress, it is what he never will do;—but no doubt it might be happy for both, that she knew how much he loves her; for I confess I tremble for his life; for rather than offer himself in competition with his friend, he will conceal the flame which consumes him within his own breast."

"Jesu Maria!" cried the maid, "conceal a flame within his breast!"

"Yes," continued the valet, "and sigh his soul to the last puff unobserved, like the dying flame in a dark lanthorn."[3]

The maid burst into tears at this affecting image; and after endeavouring to comfort her, he begged of her never to mention, to any of the human race, what he had told her,—but particularly not to her mistress.

"I am sure," replied the maid, "my mistress would not deserve to be numbered among the human race, if she allowed so faithful a lover to expire in any such manner."

"It would, indeed, be ten thousand pities," said the valet; "but you will never give a hint of what I have told you."

"I give a hint!" exclaimed the maid; "I will be cut into ten thousand pieces first."

So saying, she left him, and went with all possible speed, and informed her mistress, as the valet expected, of all he had said; ending the narrative, which the lady listened to with evident satisfaction, by declaring, "That in the whole course of her life, she had never heard of such an ardent lover as Signor Zeluco."

"Ardent!" said the mistress; "what can you know of his ardour?"

"All that I know," replied the maid, "is, that he carries a flame in his breast; and is, besides, a much handsomer man than Don Lopes."

"Thy head," said the mistress, "is always running on beauty—a prudent woman will think of more essential qualities."

"To be sure, every prudent woman, like your ladyship, will do so," replied the maid; "but there is no judging for certain but by experience;—though in all appearance, Signor Zeluco has every essential quality as perfect as Don Lopes, and is a handsomer man into the bargain."

"Well, but," said the widow, smiling, "you would not have me go and court this handsome man of your's—would you?"

"No; assuredly," said the maid; "I am always for supporting the dignity of our own sex;—but I would have you to dismiss Don Lopes."

"What, before Signor Zeluco makes any proposal?" cried the widow.

"Yes," said the maid, "he will not dip an oar into the water till Don Lopes is dismissed;—this I know from good authority, that till you have given a final answer to Don Lopes, Signor Zeluco, rather than speak, will expire."

"Expire!" cried the widow.

"Yes, indeed, madam, I am assured that Signor Zeluco is that kind of man."

"He is a very extraordinary kind of man indeed then," resumed she.

"That I am informed for certain he is," said the maid; "for although he is languishing for love of your ladyship, yet rather than open his mouth to you on the subject, he will certainly die."

"Die! nonsense," cried the widow.

"Yes, die," cried the maid, "and, what is worse, die in a dark lanthorn; at least, I am told that is what he is in danger of."

CHAPTER XII.

Heroic Love.

ALTHOUGH the widow affected to laugh at the maid, and despise her advice; yet she had for some time been in expectation of a declaration of love from Zeluco; and having gathered from her maid's discourse what the obstacle was which prevented it, after consulting her pillow, she determined to overleap the barriers of female delicacy, and encourage him to a declaration of sentiments which were highly agreeable to her.

Zeluco paid her a visit at a time when she was disengaged from all other company, and she had previously given orders that none should be admitted while he remained with her.

When they met, the lady's countenance was dressed in smiles, and her whole manner announced the most encouraging frankness. But on the brow of Zeluco, care and solicitude seemed to sit brooding, and the sighs of despondency burst, as it were, involuntarily from his bosom.

They conversed for some time on indifferent subjects, but Zeluco displayed such absence of mind, and made so many pauses of melancholy import, that the conversation was continually interrupted.

"I fear," said the lady tenderly, "that some secret care preys upon your mind."

Zeluco, heaving as profound a sigh as ever was hove in any theatre, threw up his eyes and was silent.

"Why will you not disclose the cause of your affliction?" said the widow.

"Alas! madam, the cause of my misery cannot be removed; my complaint is past remedy; why, therefore, should I disquiet others with sorrows which are peculiar to myself; especially, why should I disquiet those whose happiness it is my ardent wish, and would be my greatest pride, to promote?"

"I know not who have the honour to be of that number," said the widow with diffidence.

"My most fervent desire, madam, would be to promote the happiness of——" here he hesitated, and seemed in a state of trembling confusion.

"The happiness of whom?" cried the impatient widow.

"Alas! madam, do not insist upon my disclosing sentiments which I have so long strove to suppress, and still wish to conceal; sentiments condemned by the voice of friendship, though inspired by the purest love; sentiments which, if known, might render me odious and criminal in your eyes."

"I am convinced you labour under a mistake, Sir," said the widow; "pray tell me therefore whose happiness it is you wish so earnestly to promote."

"The happiness of the most deserving and most amiable of her sex," cried Zeluco, fixing his eyes ardently on the widow;—"but this blessing never will be in my power."

"If I am the person you allude to," said the lady, throwing her eyes modestly on the ground, and blushing with all her might, "I must acknowledge that it is in *your* power more than in that of any man alive."

There was no resisting a hint so directly favourable as this. "Angels and saints of heaven," cried Zeluco, "am I awake, or am I deluded by a dream of felicity!"——And so he poured out a rhapsody extremely insipid in itself, but mightily relished by the hearer. This was followed by a long conversation, in which the lady removed all the scruples of Zeluco, by assuring him of what he was convinced was not strictly true, that she never had any intention of giving her hand to Don Lopes; and that although he, Zeluco, were entirely out of the question, she never would: that the gentleman was much mistaken if he had entertained any such hopes; and she would seize the first opportunity that offered to inform him of this.—Zeluco begged that if she was resolved on that measure, that she would execute it in the least offensive manner possible. An advice which she promised to follow.

In the next conversation which Don Lopes had with the widow, while, inspired by the most flattering hopes, he began to urge his suit, and was endeavouring to remove those objections which the lady had formerly stated against a woman's engaging in a second marriage; an expression fell from her which did not so much imply a reluctance to marriage as to chusing him for her husband. On his appearing surprised, and humbly requiring an explanation; the lady acknowledged, that the prejudice she had so strongly entertained against a second marriage was now effaced by his very judicious arguments, many of which would never have occurred to her uninstructed judgment, and she should always retain a grateful sense of the pains he had taken to free her mind from an error so prejudicial to society. But, at the same time, after a thousand apologies, she confessed, that, although she was convinced of the propriety of her marrying, yet she had not that degree of love for him which, in her opinion, was necessary to constitute happiness in the marriage state. That she should be extremely glad to remain on a footing of friendship with him (for she really had a high esteem for his character), but unfortunately not that *passionate ardour of love,* which alone could ensure mutual felicity to a married couple; and therefore, on his own account, as well as her's, she begged he would desist from his suit.

The gentleman thanked her for her esteem, and the obliging

attention she displayed for his felicity; hinted, that if she had been equally explicit sooner, it would have saved both herself and him some trouble, and begged to know whether he might be permitted to ask, if the sentiments she expressed proceeded intirely from her indifference to *him*, or were in part owing to a *passionate ardour of love* for some other man?

After throwing her eyes on the ground, and covering her face with her handkerchief, the lady declared, that, contrary to her wishes, and without any design on his part, she felt such an attachment to his friend Zeluco, as rendered it highly improper for her to give her hand to another; particularly, she was incapable of such injustice to a person for whom she had so high a regard as the gentleman to whom she then spoke.

"You are certain that Zeluco is unacquainted with the preference which you give him?" said the gentleman.

"I know not what he may suspect," answered the blushing widow; "I only know that he never explained himself to me, nor, I am convinced, ever will, whatever his sentiments may be, while it is believed that you continue your pursuit."

"My pursuit terminates here, madam; and I will, myself, inform Zeluco of his good fortune," continued the generous Spaniard; "since I cannot have the happiness I expected myself, I will not stand in the way of another whom you prefer, and who very possibly may render you happier than I could."

This well meaning and candid man acquainted Zeluco, according to his declaration, of the widow's sentiments. The consummate hypocrite expressed great surprise and concern at the intelligence, and affected infinite reluctance, in accepting of a piece of good fortune, however desirable in itself, which had befallen him, at the expence of so dear a friend. All this affectation and mummery[1] was in due time overcome, and Zeluco's nuptials with the widow were celebrated in form.

CHAPTER XIII.

On ne trouve guère d'ingrats, tant qu'on est en état de faire du bien.

ROCHEFOUCAULT.[1]

As the gentleman who so generously had quitted his claim had never, during his courtship, shewn any anxiety on the subject of settlements, Zeluco also waved all discussion of that kind, that he might appear equally disinterested. He knew, however, that by the lady's will, as it then stood, her fortune, independent of children, would devolve to one of her relations. This destination he thought he would prevail upon her at his leisure to alter, and as the lady was near fifty years of age, and never had a child by her former husband, or, as far as he knew, by any other person, Zeluco thought there was little danger of his being shoved out of her fortune, either by her relations, or his own offspring. The lady herself, indeed, did not look upon her having a pretty numerous posterity in such a desperate light as it appeared to others; for in her latest settlement, which was not of an old date, she had specified the provision of her second begotten son or daughter, her third, her fourth, and so on, and with the most laudable and truly maternal solicitude she had amply provided for a dozen of her expected progeny.

Zeluco appeared equally obsequious after marriage as before, making every effort in his power to engross and secure the affections of his spouse, who, on her part, became every day more doatingly fond of him; and at length, all the regard, kindness, and friendship, she formerly felt for other relations and connections, were totally effaced, and the whole affections of her heart centered in her beloved husband.

One idea however intruded into her mind, and disturbed her happiness; this arose from her husband's profession, which she dreaded might occasion a separation between them, and expose him to the hardships and dangers of war. She often conjured him, therefore, with all the eloquence of love, to abandon a situation which kept her in perpetual alarm, and embittered the sweetest enjoyments of her life.

Zeluco disliked the profession as much as his lady, and was fully resolved to quit it, but he was equally resolved to make his yielding to her entreaties subservient to another plan which now occupied his thoughts.

He always replied to her endearing solicitations on that head with every appearance of grateful acknowledgement, expressing at the same time the greatest reluctance to give up a profession of which he was passionately fond, and in which he expected to obtain glory and preferment.

This affecting contest was often renewed; on one occasion, Zeluco, exaggerating the advantages he might derive from continuing in the service, said, that if he should be as fortunate as some other officers, he might be enabled one day to redeem the estate of his ancestors, and appear with splendour and reputation in his native country. He probably expected, that in consequence of this hint she would have put it in his power immediately, by making over her fortune to him;—but whether from not fully comprehending the import of what he said, or from some remains of prudence, she made no direct answer; and her fears respecting her husband's profession seemed to relapse into a slumber, when they were suddenly roused by her receiving an anonymous letter from one who pretended great anxiety for her happiness, at the same informing her, that war would very soon be declared; that her husband's regiment was destined for immediate service, in a secret expedition, of which he himself had already received intimation, though out of tenderness he concealed it from her.

This alarming news at once awakened her apprehensions, and lulled her prudence. She tenderly expostulated with her husband for concealing intelligence of such infinite importance to her peace of mind. Without absolutely admitting the truth of her information, he used it as a fresh argument against the propriety of his quitting the army. "If he had hesitated, even in the time of peace, how could he in honour agree to it on the eve of a war?" This convinced her of the truth of the intelligence.

"But you have not heard," cried the half distracted woman, "that war is yet declared."

"With whatever certainty it may be expected, it assuredly is not actually declared," replied Zeluco; "if that were the case, even you, my dearest love, could no longer wish that I should leave the army; nor could I after that allow of any intreaty on the subject."

"Well, thank heaven, it is not yet too late," cried she; and immediately leaving Zeluco, she ordered an irrevocable deed to be made out, by which her whole fortune, real and personal, was transferred to her husband. This she shewed him, telling him at the same time, that she would deliver it into his possession the moment that he resigned his commission. After the highest expression of admiration, at what he termed her generosity of soul, and some very heroic sentiments denoting the reluctance with which he had sacrificed the hopes of military glory, he concluded, by repeating a line from a Spanish poet, equivalent to this from Pope's Eloisa:

> Fame, wealth, and honour, what are ye to love?[2]

This scrap of poetry, though not very applicable on such an occasion, was heard with rapture, and considered by the enamoured lady as exceedingly in point.

Having obtained liberty to resign, he quitted the army, to the great joy of his lady, and of the regiment to which he belonged.

CHAPTER XIV.

> Proprium humani ingenii est, odisse quem læseris
>
> TACIT.[1]

THE heroic mark of love above mentioned was the last that Zeluco was solicitous of receiving from his lady; for he seemed ever after very willing to dispense with all indications of her passion, and his expressions of affection towards her diminished in their energy from this period. She, at first with gentleness, and afterwards with a mixture of acrimony, remonstrated with him on this alteration. But it has been observed, that complaints and remonstrances seldom prove restoratives to a languid love. In the best and mildest dispositions they do no good, in acrimonious dispositions they exasperate the disease.

Zeluco bore the murmurings of his wife from the beginning with but an ill-dissembled patience, became more and more morose and sulky as they were continued, and his behaviour terminated in avowed contempt and open abuse.

The unhappy woman, finding herself thus neglected, insulted, and despised by the person on whom she had fixed her affections and bestowed her whole fortune, gradually sunk into despondency, and after enduring all the bitterness of self-reproach, she died at the end of two years.

Disappointment and disquietude had attended Zeluco through

the whole of his life, notwithstanding the great acquisition of fortune he derived from his marriage; even his matrimonial state had been embittered with continual chagrin. This was the natural effect of his own vicious conduct; yet by a partiality of self-deceit, which is very common, he always imputed his missing of happiness to other causes: few people blame themselves, while it is in the power of self-love to twist the charge against others. All the discontent and fretfulness which Zeluco experienced during the lifetime of his wife, he thought originated in the ill-humour and bad temper of that unhappy woman.

When he was freed therefore from what he considered as the only obstruction to his happiness, he expected that what he had hitherto pursued without attaining was at last within his reach.

But to render his felicity more certain and permanent, he thought it necessary to bring his estate to the highest pitch of improvement; after which he proposed to return to Europe, and there in splendour and magnificence enjoy every pleasure that his heart could desire.

In the prosecution of this plan he laboured with such assiduity and impatience as kept himself in everlasting fretfulness, and proved fatal to several of his slaves, some of whom expired under the exertions he forced them to make, and others under the punishments he inflicted for the smallest remissness or neglect.

Zeluco was now in that situation in which the understanding cannot improve, and the disposition is the most likely to degenerate; avoiding and being avoided by every person of a liberal and independent mind; living almost constantly on his own estate with a set of people over whom he had unlimited power; seeing no person whose character he much respected, or whose censure he so much dreaded as to put him on his guard against the overflowings of passion, or make him check the impulses of caprice, of course he became every day more unreasonable, passionate, and cruel; and at length was unable to hear with patience the most candid and rational remonstrance, flying into violent fits of rage on the most trivial occasions; and when his domestics had the good fortune to execute his orders with such precision and rapidity as left him not the least pretence for blame, he then turned his rancour on the climate and soil, the vicissitudes of the weather, bursting into ridiculous fits of passion at the commonest and most inevitable occurrences.

The daily habit which this odious man thus acquired of tormenting himself, would have afforded satisfaction to all who were witnesses to it, had it not been accompanied with the diabolical propensity to harass and torment all those unfortunate creatures whom Providence, for reasons we cannot penetrate, subjected to his power.

When a man of a good disposition is of a peevish, fretful, and capricious temper, which unfortunately is sometimes the case, the uneasiness which he needlessly gives himself is lamented by those who are acquainted with his entire character. But when a villain is the slave of caprice, and of course a self-tormentor, his misery affords satisfaction and amusement to all who know him. And although they durst not display it openly, yet it undoubtedly gave secret satisfaction to every one of this wretched man's slaves, to be witnesses to the disquietude and misery of their persecutor.

Zeluco having been represented as avaricious as well as cruel, it may be said that the first of those dispositions would prove a restraint upon the last; and that the suggestions of self-interest would prevent his pushing cruelty the length of endangering the lives of his slaves.

It is a common argument against the necessity of new laws for the protection of slaves, that they need no protection from a just and humane master, because he will never injure them; nor from a master of an opposite character, because his own interest will be their protection: but let it be remembered, that men who are not naturally compassionate, who are devoid of religious impressions, and in the habit of giving vent to every gust of ill-humour, are apt, in the violence of rage, to become deaf to the voice of common sense and interest, as well as of justice and mercy. An unfortunate gamester throws the cards into the fire, and regrets that they have not feeling; a choleric man breaks and destroys the furniture of his house, however valuable; and how often do we see men in an absurd rage abuse their most serviceable cattle? But a thousand causes, which must occur to every one, expose *human creatures* to the vindictive rage of ill-tempered proprietors, in a much greater degree than inanimate things or the brute creation ever can be. And we find in fact, that cruel and passionate masters, however interested in other respects, do gratify their ill-humour against their most valuable slaves at the expence of their interest.

It will be alleged, that in all the Christian colonies the slaves are so far protected from the injustice of their master, that none of them can be condemned capitally, but after a trial in a court of justice. Long experience has made it clear, however, that the proprietors of land in those colonies, Christians as they are, shew little disposition to listen to the complaints of slaves, or interfere with each other respecting the manner in which slaves are treated; and when it is whispered about, that a slave has expired under the lash, or has died in consequence of the arbitrary punishment of his master, people in general are not fond of the trouble of collecting proofs, or appearing in the character of accusers; particularly when the delinquent is a white man, of interest perhaps in the colony, and the sufferer a black slave. Besides, there may in many instances be a full conviction of the crime, and yet the criminal may not be deemed within the grasp of those vague laws which the policy of Europe has thought sufficient for the protection of slaves from the cruelty of their masters. The law may direct, that a master shall not order more than a limited number of stripes to be inflicted for any fault that his slave commits. But if the law requires no proof of the fault, except the allegation of the master, what security has the slave that he shall not be punished unjustly, or that his master shall not, as often as he pleases, repeat the punishment at such intervals as keep him out of the reach of the law? it must be owned that the slave has no security from such abuses, which is tantamount to putting it in the master's power to torture his slaves to death with impunity. Such laws are no safeguard, but rather a mockery of the unhappy race of men they pretend to protect.

This unlimited power, which is left in the hand of the masters, has a bad effect both on the slave and the master. It tends at once to render the first more wretched, and the second more wicked. How many men have, for a great part of their lives, supported the character of well-disposed good-natured people; and on going from Europe to the West Indies, and becoming proprietors of slaves, have gradually grown ill-tempered, capricious, haughty, and cruel. Even Zeluco, though of a capricious, violent, and selfish disposition, was not naturally cruel; this last grew upon him in consequence of unlimited power. His severity to the soldiers arose from a desire of gaining the favour of the commander, by rendering the men under his immediate command more expert than others. In pushing this point he disregarded, indeed, the sufferings of the men; because his excessive selfishness engrossed all his feelings, and left him quite indifferent to the feelings of others; he still was not positively cruel. Independent of passion or rage, he had no satisfaction in giving pain; he was only unconcerned whether they suffered or not. And afterwards, when he became the absolute master of a great number of unfortunate creatures, whom he considered as his property, he thought he had a right to make the most of them. And he was informed by those who have heads for such a calculation, and hearts to act in consequence of it, that to force slaves to their utmost exertions, and purchase new ones as the old expire, is, upon the whole, more œconomical than to treat them with a certain degree of gentleness, and oblige them to no more labour than is proportioned to their strength, although, by this means, the expence of new purchases would be less considerable, and less frequent. A person who passed for a very sensible man, who formerly kept an inn on one of the great posting roads in England, and was at this time a considerable proprietor of land in one of the West India islands, had assured him, that he had found this to hold with regard to post-horses; and the argument was equally just when applied to slaves. Zeluco therefore had originally no direct intention of injuring his slaves; his view was simply to improve his estates to the utmost; but in the execution of this plan, as *their* exertions did not keep pace with *his* impatience, he found it necessary to quicken them by an unremitting use of the whip. This produced discontent, murmurs, sulkiness, sometimes upbraidings, on their parts; rage, threats, and every kind of abuse on his: he saw hatred in all their looks, he presumed revenge in all their hearts; he became more and more severe, and treated them as he imagined they wished to treat him, and as he was conscious he deserved to be treated by them; at length he arrived at that shocking point of depravity, to have a gratification in punishing, independent of any idea of utility or advantage to himself.

This, unfortunately for a large proportion of mankind, is often the progress of unlimited power, and the effect which it too frequently produces on the human character.

If the reign of many European proprietors of estates in the West Indies were faithfully recorded, it is much to be feared, that the capricious cruelties which disgrace those of Caligula and Nero[2] would not seem so incredible as they now do. And perhaps no memoirs could be more affecting to a candid and humane mind, than those of many negroes, from the time of their being brought from the coast of Guinea, till their death in the West Indies. The fate of one of Zeluco's slaves, called Hanno, being connected with our purpose, may, without impropriety, be mentioned here.

CHAPTER XV.

——Merciful Heaven!
Thou, rather, with thy sharp and sulphurous bolt,
Split'st th' unwedgable and gnarled oak,
Than the soft myrtle! O, but man! proud man!
Drest in a little brief authority;
Most ignorant of what is most assured,
His glassy essence—like an angry ape,
Plays such fantastick tricks before high Heaven,
As make the angels weep.—— SHAKESPEARE.[1]

HANNO the slave, mentioned at the end of the foregoing chapter, allowed symptoms of compassion, perhaps of indignation, to escape from him, on hearing one of his brother slaves ordered to be punished unjustly. Zeluco having observed this, swore that Hanno should be the executioner, otherwise he would order him to be punished in his stead.

Hanno said, he might do as he pleased; but as for himself he never had been accustomed to that office, and he would not begin by exercising it on his friend. Zeluco, in a transport of rage, ordered him to be lashed severely, and renewed the punishment at *legal* intervals so often, that the poor man was thrown into a languishing disease, which confined him constantly to his bed.

Hanno had been a favourite servant of his lady's before her marriage with Zeluco; he was known to people of all ranks on the island, and esteemed by all who knew him. The Irish soldier who had carried the commanding officer from the field, as was related above, was taken into that gentleman's service some time after, and remained constantly in his family from that time; this soldier had long been acquainted with Hanno, and had a particular esteem for him. As soon as he heard of his dangerous situation, he hastened to see him, carried him wine and other refreshments, and continued to visit and comfort him during his languishing illness. Perceiving at last that there was no hope of his recovery, he thought the last and best good office he could do him was to carry a priest to give him absolution and extreme unction.

As they went together, "I should be very sorry, father," said the soldier, "if this poor fellow missed going to heaven; for, by Jesus, I do not believe there is a worthier soul there, be the other who he pleases."

"He is a Black," said the priest, who was of the order of St. Francis.

"His soul is whiter than a skinned potatoe," said the soldier.

"Do you know whether he believes in all the tenets of our holy faith?" said the priest.

"He is a man who was always ready to do as he would be done by," replied the soldier.

"That is something," said the capuchin,[2] "but not the most essential. Are you certain that he is a Christian?"

"O, I'll be damned if he is not as pretty a Christian as your heart can desire," said the soldier; "and I'll give you a proof that will rejoice your soul to hear.—A soldier of our regiment was seized with the cramp in his leg when he was bathing; so he halloed for assistance, and then went plump to the bottom like a stone. Those who were near him, Christians and all, swum away as fast as their legs could carry them, for they were afraid of his catching hold of them. But honest Hanno pushed directly to the place where the soldier had sunk, dived after him, and, without more ado, or so much as saying by your leave, seized him by the hair of the head, and hauled him ashore; where, after a little rubbing and rolling, he was quite recovered, and is alive and merry at this blessed moment. Now, my dear father, I think this was behaving like a good Christian, and what is much more, like a brave Irishman too."

"Has he been properly instructed in all the doctrines of the catholic church?" said the priest.

"That he has," replied the soldier; "for I was after instructing him yesterday myself; and as you had told me very often, that believing was the great point, I pressed that home. 'By Jesus,' says I, 'Hanno it does not signify making wry faces, but you must believe, my dear Honny,[3] as fast as ever you can, for you have no time to lose;'—and, poor fellow, he entreated me to say no more about it, and he would believe whatever I pleased."

This satisfied the father; when they arrived at the dying man's cabbin, "Now, my dear fellow," said the soldier, "I have brought a holy man to give you absolution for your sins, and to shew your soul the road to heaven; take this glass of wine to comfort you, for it is a hellish long journey."

They raised poor Hanno, and he swallowed the wine with difficulty.

"Be not dismayed, my honest lad," continued the soldier, "for although it is a long march to heaven, you will be sure of glorious quarters when you get there. I cannot tell you exactly how people pass their time indeed; but by all accounts there is no very hard duty, unless it is that you will be obliged to sing psalms and hymns pretty constantly; that to be sure you must bear with: but then the devil a scoundrel who delights in tormenting his fellow-creatures will be allowed to thrust his nose into that sweet plantation; and so, my dear Hanno, God bless you; all your sufferings are now pretty well over, and I am convinced you will be as happy as the day is long, in the other world, all the rest of your life."

The priest then began to perform his office;—Hanno heard him in silence,—he seemed unable to speak.

"You see, my good father," said the soldier, "he believes in all you say. You may now, without any further delay, give him absolution and extreme unction, and every thing needful to secure him a snug birth[4] in paradise."

"You are fully convinced, friend," said the priest, addressing the dying man in a solemn manner, "that it is only by a firm belief in all the tenets of the holy catholic church, that——" "God love your soul, my dear father," interrupted the soldier, "give him absolution in the first place, and convince him afterwards; for, upon my conscience, if you bother him much longer, the poor creature's soul will slip through your fingers."

The priest, who was a good-natured man, did as the soldier requested.

"Now," said the soldier, when the ceremony was over, "now, my honest fellow, you may bid the devil kiss your b——de,[5] for you are as sure of heaven as your master is of hell; where, as this reverend father will assure you, he must suffer to all eternity."

"I hope he will not suffer so long," said Hanno, in a faint voice; and speaking for the first time since the arrival of the priest.

"Have a care of what you say, friend," said the priest, in a severe tone of voice; "you must not doubt of the eternity of hell torments.—If your master goes once there, he must remain for ever."

"Then I'll be bound for him," said the soldier, "he is sure enough of going there."

"But I hope in God he will not remain for ever," said Hanno—and expired.

"That was not spoken like a true believer," said the priest; "if I had thought that he harboured any doubts on such an essential article, I should not have given him absolution."

"It is lucky then that the poor fellow made his escape to heaven before you knew any thing of the matter," said the soldier.

As the soldier returned home from Hanno's cabbin, he met Zeluco, who, knowing where he had been, said to him, "How is the d—d scoundrel now?"

"The d—d scoundrel is in better health than all who know him could wish," replied the soldier.

"Why, they told me he was dying," said Zeluco.

"If you mean poor Hanno, he is already dead, and on his way to heaven," said the soldier; "but as for the scoundrel who murdered him, he'll be d—d before he get there."

CHAPTER XVI.

The Portuguese.

Sometime after this an occurrence took place which contributed more to render Zeluco less cruel to his slaves, than all the occasional attacks of compunction he felt for the death of Hanno, or than all the laws existing for the protection of Negro slaves.

A rich Portuguese merchant, who had been settled for several years in the town of Havannah, had lately purchased an estate contiguous to that of Zeluco, who displayed a great inclination to cultivate his acquaintance by every kind of polite attention.

He frequently visited this merchant at his house in town, and offered him every kind of accommodation which his estate afforded, while the Portuguese was repairing a house on his new purchase for the reception of his family.

This very obliging behaviour of Zeluco seemed extraordinary to all those who knew him, and did not know that the merchant had a very handsome wife, who was fond of admiration, and not entirely free from coquetry.

Zeluco was much struck with her beauty, and used all his art to seduce her. She, on her part, although not entirely insensible to the charms of his face and person, was still more pleased with the eclat of having a man of his rank and fortune among the number of her admirers, and probably had no idea of ever making any other use of him. This lady was one of that class of women, who, being kept out of the way of temptation, and not vigorously attacked, will preserve the citadel of their virtue inviolate through life. She was apt, however, through vanity, to expose some of the outworks a little too much, which invited the attacks of the enemy; and although she had no serious intention of ever formally surrendering the fort, she might possibly, through inattention, have allowed it to be surprised by a *coup de main*.[1]

This lady was allured into a literary correspondence with Zeluco; at first on the most trifling subjects, and with the knowledge of her husband, to whom she shewed the billets: by degrees, however, it happened that she received some which she thought it unnecessary to communicate.

When the Portuguese brought his family to the house which he had repaired for their reception, Zeluco's intercourse with them was more frequent; and he often walked with the husband and wife in a sequestered field situated between his own house and that of her husband.

With some difficulty Zeluco at length prevailed on her to promise to meet him at this place towards the close of an evening, when he knew that her husband was engaged on business, which would necessarily detain him very late at the house of a gentleman who lived at a considerable distance.

From the time that Zeluco's correspondence with the lady became of a nature that she was rather shy of communicating, he always employed one particular slave, who, he imagined, was very cordially attached to him on account of a few indulgences which were granted to him previous to his being entrusted as an agent in this business.

In this conjecture, however, Zeluco was greatly mistaken; those slight favours had not eradicated from the man's mind that hatred and thirst for revenge which his master's former treatment had planted there.

Having come to the knowledge of the intended interview, he actually went and communicated all he knew to the husband, and returned rejoicing in the hope that his detested master would be assassinated that very night.

The lady however had accidentally seen this slave with her husband, and remarked, that from the time the slave had spoken to him he was uncommonly thoughtful, morose, and agitated.

This led her to suspect that her husband was informed of the appointment, which she herself had already begun to repent of, and to hesitate about keeping.

After maturely weighing every circumstance, she determined to reveal to her husband what she thought he knew already.

She approached him therefore with an air of sincerity and contrition, saying, she was about to acquaint him with something which lay like a load upon her mind; that she had without scruple indulged an acquaintance with Signor Zeluco on account of the friendship he expressed for her husband, and his polite and obliging behaviour to herself; but that of late she had been surprised at a change in his manner of addressing her, which had terminated in a declaration of love; that she had been restrained from mentioning this to him sooner, being unwilling to give him uneasiness, and in hopes that from the manner in which she had received his declaration, he would not venture to renew it: but finding he persisted in his criminal assiduities, and had even gone the length of proposing that she should meet him privately and unknown to her husband, she thought herself bound in duty to conceal this behaviour of Zeluco's no longer; but to inform her husband of the whole.

Here she made a full stop;—and the husband perceiving that she meant to add nothing further, said,—"Have you then informed me of the whole?"

She took heaven and earth to witness that she had.

"I did not hear you mention that you had promised to meet him," said the husband.

The lady having recovered from a short embarrassment which this observation occasioned, replied, that she had been so much shocked with the proposal, and in such confusion, that she could not now recollect every word of what she had said; but that she had immediately left him; "and whatever," added she, "has fallen from me, which he may construe into a promise, I am conscious that I never should have gone near the place: of the truth of this, the information I have just given you is a sufficient proof; and if I have erred in concealing this matter so long, my error proceeded from a desire of preventing mischievous consequences, and out of tenderness to you."

The eloquence and fair pretences of the wife at length lulled the suspicions, and soothed the rage of her spouse with respect to herself; but his rancour against Zeluco remained in full force; and he threw out some threats of determined revenge. The wife was alarmed at this; for, although she was now resolved never to renew the intrigue, yet being conscious that she was in some degree to blame herself, she would willingly have prevented any mischief from befalling Zeluco; with this view she begged of her husband to overlook and despise the vain attempt which had been made, and leave the man to be punished by the mortification of disappointment, and the thoughts of the ridiculous light in which he must be conscious that he stood in the sight of both. The husband seemed to acquiesce in his wife's reasoning, but was determined to satisfy his revenge, a plan for which had already occurred to him.

Having persuaded his wife to go to bed earlier than usual, he dressed himself in her clothes, and throwing a white mantle over his head and shoulders, he slipt secretly out of his house, and with vindictive impatience walked to the place of rendezvous, where Zeluco had been waiting ever since the appointed moment.

With reviving joy, and by the glimmering light of the stars, he perceived a person in female attire approaching; and never doubting but it was the object of his wishes, he sprung forward with bounding velocity to meet her embrace; but at that instant his boiling blood was frozen on hearing the following words pronounced in an unnatural voice,—"The spirit of thy wife, she who fell a victim to thy perfidious cruelty, sends thee this." On which the Portuguese plunged his stiletto into the breast of Zeluco, who immediately fell to the ground. The blow was given with good-will, the weapon rushed to the hilt, and the husband, convinced he had killed him, returned quietly to his own house, without his wife or any of the family having suspected that he had gone abroad.

CHAPTER XVII.

The Reward of Inhumanity.

Zeluco lay for some time on the ground, before he could recollect his terrified and scattered senses, and when he had in some degree recovered them, he was still unable to account for what had happened; sometimes he believed he had, in reality, seen the ghost of his deceased wife; and every circumstance of his ungrateful and perfidious conduct to her rushing on his memory, at a moment when he thought himself on the point of entering into a state of retribution, filled his mind with horror, and drove him to the brink of madness, from which perhaps he was saved by the quantity of blood he lost as he lay on the ground.[1]

After passing several hours in a state of terror and remorse, the day beginning to dawn, he felt himself, though in a very weak condition, able to move; and at length, by the aid of a tree, at whose root he had fallen, he got upon his legs, and then attempted to move towards his own house, but soon, through faintness, sunk again to the ground, where he lay a considerable time longer in anguish, and despairing of relief. At length he saw some of his own slaves going to their morning labour.

In a tone very different from that in which he had been accustomed to address them, with whining humility he implored their succour, and begged they would have the goodness to carry him home.

At the sound of a human voice, expressive of distress, the slaves sprung eagerly to give their assistance; but the instant they perceived it was their master, they stopped short with looks of abhorrence, as if it had not been a man but a wounded serpent, which they saw writhing on the ground. Some turned aside, willing to be thought not to have observed him; others looked as if they enjoyed his agony; none offered him assistance; and it is not probable he would ever have reached his own house alive, had not one of his managers joined them. By his authority, he was at last carried thither, and the best medical and surgical aid was immediately sent for. The wound, upon the first examination, was thought mortal, and the universal satisfaction that this occasioned, as soon as it circulated among this detested man's slaves, was very evident, in spite of all their endeavours to control their features and gestures. After languishing many weeks, however, the symptoms at last became favourable. During all the time in which it was doubtful whether he was to die or to live, the mind of the patient himself was hardly more cruelly agitated between fear and hope, than that of every slave, male and female, that belonged to him. And when he was pronounced to be out of danger, so fully was he loaded with their hatred, that the news produced a shock like that of electricity over his whole family. A number of slaves who happened to be at work in the garden, under the window of Zeluco's bed-chamber, burst into a loud and uncontrollable howl of sorrow when his recovery was first announced to them.

The patient, alarmed at the sound, asked the physician, then sitting by his bed-side, what it meant. The physician, who understood it no more than Zeluco, went to enquire, and having discovered the true source of the outcry, returned to the patient.

"What is the meaning of that howl?" said Zeluco; "it seemed prompted by sorrow."

"It proceeded from your slaves," answered the physician; "they are enquiring after your health."

"Well, what then?" cried Zeluco.

"Why then," answered the Doctor, "I suppose they must have been told, by *mistake*, that you are worse, and likely to die. I have frequently known slaves express their grief in the same manner, when they were in danger of losing a good and humane master."

The irony of this reply was wormwood[2] to Zeluco; he fell into a gloomy fit of musing, and made no farther inquiry, neither did he, during his illness, or after his recovery, give any satisfactory account of the manner in which he had received the wound. Whatever his opinion might be, his fears were dissipated, and when he was able to weigh circumstances, he abstained from suggesting any suspicion against particular persons, or from making any investigation of the subject.

CHAPTER XVIII.

Ye, who one bitter drop have drain'd
From slav'ry's cup, with horror stain'd;
Oh, let no fatal dregs be found,
But dash her chalice to the ground.

HELEN MARIA WILLIAMS.[1]

FOR a considerable time after Zeluco was out of danger from his wound, and even after he began to walk abroad and resume the management of his affairs, he appeared more pensive than formerly; and although his thoughts seemed of a gloomy nature, yet he did not burst out into those violent fits of rage that had been customary with him before that accident. But the impression which it had made on his mind gradually diminished, and the sentiments of dread and remorse, which influenced his conduct for a time, wearing quite away, his former dispositions returned with his bodily health.

One day, as he was walking around his estate, with the physician already mentioned, who had called upon him on his return from visiting a patient, Zeluco gave pretty strong indications of a relapse into his former cruelty. The physician, who was a man of sense and humanity, checked him, and expressed sentiments of compassion for the deplorable condition of the poor slaves.

"They are," said Zeluco, "the most villanous race alive."

"They certainly are the most unfortunate," said the physician.

"Let them perform their task as they ought," replied the other, "and they will not be unfortunate."

"Why, it is not a slight misfortune," said the Doctor, "to have *such* tasks to perform."

"They are in a better situation than when they were in their own country."

"That would be difficult to prove," said the physician; "but were it certain, I should think it a bad reason for treating them ill *here*, merely because they had been very ill treated *there*."

"Negro slaves in general, all over the West Indies," said Zeluco, "are in a better condition than the common people in most countries in Europe. I have heard this asserted a thousand times."

"If it were so," said the physician, "it would convey a dreadful idea of the condition of Europeans; but the thing is impossible, Signor."

"How impossible?" said Zeluco.

"Because, even if slaves were in general fed and clothed as well as you are yourself, yet while it is in the power of their master to impose what task he pleases, and punish their faults according to his humour, their condition must be infinitely worse than that of the cottager whom nobody can abuse with impunity, and on whom the cheering spirit of liberty smiles as he reaps the fruit of his own industry."

"You have certainly," said Zeluco, "borrowed that sentiment from an Englishman; some of those enthusiastic fools who are pleased to bear the insolence of mobs, and to sacrifice many of the conveniences of life to the empty shade of freedom. Yet I have heard some, even of *their* West India proprietors, assert, that the negroes of those islands were happier than the common labourers in England."[2]

"There is nothing too absurd for some men to assert," said the physician, "when they imagine their interest is concerned, or when it tends to justify their conduct. And were a law to be proposed now against the slave trade, or to render the condition of slaves more tolerable than it is at present, which is more likely to happen among the generous enthusiasts you mention than in any other country, it would perhaps be opposed by those very proprietors; but would you impute such opposition to tenderness to the slaves, and a humane wish to prevent their becoming as miserable as the common labourers in England?"

"I am told, however," replied Zeluco, "that your English in general are a most lugubrious race, and that there is much melancholy and discontent in their country with all their liberty."[3]

"I am told," answered the physician, "that there is much frost and cold in their country with all their sunshine, yet it has not been as yet clearly proved that the sun is the cause of either."

"Well, but to return to the slaves," said Zeluco; "I do not perfectly understand what is your drift. Are they not my property? Have I not therefore a right to oblige them to labour for my profit?"

"With regard to the right which any man has to make a property of other men, and force them to labour as slaves solely for his benefit, I suspect it would be difficult for the greatest casuist that ever lived to make it out."

"Why so?" replied Zeluco; "I am assured that the slave trade is authorized by the Bible.[4] You are too sound a Christian, my good Doctor, to controvert such authority."

"Without considering whether those who furnished you with that argument did it with friendly or unfriendly intentions to the Bible, Signor, and without touching any controvertible point in the Scriptures, I will just observe, that charity, benevolence, and mercy, to our fellow-creatures, are not only authorised, but in the plainest unequivocal terms repeatedly ordained, in those writings. Let therefore the proprietors of slaves begin, by conforming their conduct to those injunctions, and then they may be allowed to quote Scripture authority in support of such property.—*Blessed are the merciful, for they shall obtain mercy.—Whatsoever ye would that men should do to you, do ye so to them.—Come unto me, all ye that labour and are heavy laden, and I will give you rest.*[5]—These are the words of the Author of Christianity, whose whole life was a representation by action of his own precepts. Let the proprietors of estates in America and the West India islands consider how far their treatment of the negroes is agreeable to his doctrine and conduct; and their time will be better employed than in perverting detached passages of the Bible, and endeavouring to press that which is proclaimed peace on earth, and good-will to men, into the service of cruelty and oppression."

"After all this fine sermon," said Zeluco; "you do not pretend to assert, that negroes are originally on a footing with white people; you will allow, I hope, that they are an inferior race of men."

"I will allow," replied the Doctor, "that their hair is short and ours is long, that their noses are flat and ours raised, and their skin is black and ours white; yet after all those concessions, I still have my doubts respecting our right to make them slaves."

"Well, Doctor," said Zeluco, "if you are determined to dispute our *right*, you must admit that we have the *power*, which is of much more importance."

"While I admit *that*, Signor, I most sincerely wish it were otherwise exercised."

"How the devil would you have it exercised?"

"We should, in my opinion, exercise it with more moderation and lenity than some of us do," said the physician.

"Lenity," cried Zeluco, "to a parcel of rascals, a gang of pilfering dogs, downright thieves! why, as often as they can, they steal the very provisions intended for my own table!"

"You cannot be much surprised at that, Signor, when they are pinched with hunger."

"You would have them pampered with delicacies forsooth, and never punished for any crime?"

"No, Sir, but I would certainly allow them a sufficient quantity of wholesome food; and perceiving that all my neighbours are liable to commit faults, and being conscious of many failings in myself, I should not expect that poor untutored slaves were to be exempted from them, nor would I be relentless or unforgiving when they were discovered."

"Po, poh—that is not the way to deal with negroes; nothing is to be made of them by lenity; they are the laziest dogs in the world; it is with the greatest difficulty sometimes that my manager can get them roused to their morning work."

"Consider, Signor, how natural it is after hard labour to wish to prolong the intervals of rest."

"Rest!" cried Zeluco, angrily; "they will have rest enough in their graves."

"Well, Signor," replied the physician, shocked at this brutal remark, "it would be fortunate for some people that they could promise themselves the same."

"But, Doctor," said Zeluco, taking no notice of the last observation, "can you really imagine that such treatment as you seem to recommend, would render slaves of equal benefit to the proprietors of West India estates?"

"Ay, Signor," replied the physician, "that is coming directly to the point, which a man of sense would wish to investigate, leaving all the foreign matter concerning *religion* and *humanity*, which embarrass the argument, out of the question.

"Well, considering the business with a view to a man's interest or profit only; long observation on the conduct of others, with my own experience, which has been considerable, convinces me that the master who treats his slaves with humanity and well-directed kindness, reaps more benefit from their labour, than he who behaves in a contrary manner. There are many instances of ingratitude to be sure, but it is not natural to the human heart; we naturally endear ourselves to those to whom we impart pleasure, and men in general serve with more alacrity and perseverance from love than fear. The instant that the eye of the manager is turned from the slave who serves from fear alone, his efforts relax; but the industry of him who serves from attachment, is continually prompted by the gratitude, and the regard for his master's interest, which he carries in his breast.

"Besides, Signor, how infinitely more pleasing is it to be considered as the distributor of happiness, than the inflictor of pain? What man, who has it in his power to be loved as a benefactor, would choose to be detested as an executioner, and see sorrow, terror, and abhorrence, in the countenances he daily beholds? Come, Signor," continued the physician, "having, during the course of your illness, given you many advices for which you have paid me; pray accept of one from me gratis; you will reap much satisfaction from it, and it may prevent your being exposed to new dangers, similar to that from which you have with such difficulty escaped.—My advice is this: Alter intirely your conduct towards your slaves; scorn not those who demand justice and mercy; treat them with much more indulgence, and sometimes with kindness; for certainly that man is in a most miserable as well as dangerous situation, who lives among those who rejoice in his sickness, howl with despair at his recovery, and whose only hope of tranquillity lies in their own death or in his."

The physician having made this remonstrance, took his leave. Zeluco remained musing for a considerable time after he was gone; the result of his reflections was a determination to behave with more indulgence to his slaves, being alarmed by what was suggested, and convinced that such conduct in future was highly expedient for his own personal security. Those resolutions were however very imperfectly kept. Indeed, Zeluco had already given so very bad an impression of his character, that a much more thorough reformation must have been continued a long time before it could answer the purpose of recovering the good opinion of the public.

Perceiving, therefore, that all intimacy with him was rather avoided, he gave over every attempt of cultivating new acquaintance; and, as it frequently happens to those who have deservedly forfeited the public esteem, he endeavoured to indemnify himself for the loss of character and the want of respectable society, by an unbounded indulgence in sensual pleasure, and the company of a few dependents; to which he added, the contemplation of accumulating wealth, which indeed was the only *mental* enjoyment he had, as well as the only cause of his remaining out of Europe; for, according to the custom of money-makers, he had set his heart on a particular sum, and was resolved not to quit the superintendence of his own affairs till he had acquired it, after which he proposed to pass the rest of his life in uninterrupted enjoyment.

In this manner, therefore, Zeluco spent a few more miserable years in the West Indies; miserable surely they must have been, for what bodily gratifications, what accumulation of riches, could prevent that man from being wretched, whom no one approached that could avoid it, whom no one served but through fear, and who was conscious of being the object of the hatred and execration of all who knew him?

Fatigued and jaded by a life of comfortless voluptuousness, and finding a favourable opportunity of disposing of an estate he had purchased to great advantage in the island of Hispaniola, as well as a considerable part of his estate in Cuba, he granted a lease of the remainder, settled his affairs, remitted his money to Europe, and prepared to return to his native country, in expectation that his wealth would procure him there that happiness which he found it unable to produce in the West Indies. But before he finally left this part of the world, he resolved to settle an account, which, in his own vengeful heart, he thought he justly owed to his neighbour, the Portuguese merchant.

CHAPTER XIX.

Perfidy and Revenge.

In giving an account of Zeluco's adventure with the Portuguese merchant, it was remarked, that he slipped out of his own house, and returned, unobserved by his wife, or any other person. With like caution, he ever after abstained from mentioning what had happened.

When it became publicly known that Zeluco had been stabbed, the Portuguese expressed equal surprise, and rather more concern than other people, and was exceedingly attentive in sending messages of enquiry about his health.

One of Zeluco's slaves having run away the same evening on which his master was stabbed, it was generally believed that this slave had done the deed; Zeluco himself encouraged that report, and for obvious reasons discouraged all pursuit or search for the fugitive. He had no doubt, however, that the real perpetrator of the fact was the Portuguese; and strongly suspected that the wife was an accomplice. On his recovery, however, he thanked his Portuguese neighbour with the most satisfied air imaginable, for his obliging inquiries, and descanted with every appearance of conviction on the treachery and ingratitude of the fugitive slave who had so basely attempted to murder him.

No man was ever more ready to forget a good office done to him than Zeluco, and none ever more tenaciously remembered an injury: these opposite turns of disposition generally go together.

While Zeluco carefully concealed his suspicions within his own breast, he determined to act as if these suspicions amounted to certainty, and to be fully revenged of both the husband and wife. He saw, however, that it behoved him to act with great circumspection, and it was not easy to form what he considered as a suitable plan of revenge, for whatever concern the Portuguese had seemed to take in the health of Zeluco, he did not carry his dissimulation the length of renewing their intimacy; his wife likewise observed the utmost reserve towards Zeluco, giving him no opportunity of demanding an explanation of what was past, or of renewing the intrigue.

She had not proved with child during the first two years of her marriage, but in the course of that in which her adventure with Zeluco took place she bore a son. As the husband had been uncommonly anxious to have children, his impatience on that head had made him almost despair of ever having any. His joy on the happy event was equal to his former uneasiness, and his fondness for his wife was redoubled by his satisfaction in being a father; while the augmented attention which he paid her, joined to the natural affection she felt for her child, operated a favourable alteration in her character, and confirmed her virtuous resolutions.

Zeluco understood, with redoubled wrath and malignity, that two people he mortally hated lived with mutual confidence and in the happiest union; sometimes he had the mortification of hearing them quoted as a striking example of parental affection and conjugal felicity. He at length founded his scheme of revenge on a knowledge of these circumstances, and resolved to attack their happiness in its source.

By a few presents, and the intervention of his valet, he gained the maid of the Portuguese, and without exactly explaining what his views were, he prevailed on her to be subservient to them.

He was informed by the girl, that the nurse sometimes carried the child to a shady seat, at a small distance from her master's house; Zeluco passed that way one day, when he knew of the Portuguese and his lady being elsewhere; he expressed the greatest joy at the sight of the child, took it in his arms, and fondled it with every appearance of the tenderest affection; he earnestly and repeatedly begged of the nurse to be exceedingly careful of the sweet infant, presented her with a purse of gold as a reward for her past care, and promised her another in due time, provided she persevered in her tenderness; he earnestly entreated the woman not to mention what had passed to her master; and taking his leave with seeming reluctance, entreated her to return to the same place with the child, as often as she should know that her master was absent, or engaged with company. He had several interviews of the same kind, in the same place, within the space of a month.

Whatever reflections occurred to the nurse on these secret visits, and his extraordinary affections for the child, she kept a prudent silence, and hoarded them carefully up within her breast, as a precious fund to be expended among her particular friends and gossips on future occasions.

Zeluco at length arranged matters so that the lady and her maid approached the place while he was caressing the child; and as soon as he was satisfied that they observed him, he delivered the infant with precipitation into the nurse's arms and retired.

The lady, greatly surprised at what she had seen, questioned the nurse, who, with some hesitation (as the maid was present), told her all that passed, without suppressing a circumstance, except that of her having received the purse.

The lady was more and more at a loss what construction to put on so strange and unlooked-for an incident.—She asked the nurse, "Whether she had ever mentioned this matter to her master?"

"No, never; I do assure your ladyship I never did," replied the nurse with earnestness.

"I do not know why you should not," said the mistress, with affected unconcern; "as there seems something a little extraordinary in this man's taking so much notice of the child; I think it would be proper that my husband should be informed of it."

"Lord, madam," said the maid, who was instructed to prevent this, "if the nurse were to inform my master of all those who caress and seem fond of the child, she could do nothing else;—every mortal is struck with his beauty, and Signor Zeluco, in admiring and caressing him, does no more than others. To mention him in particular to my master would seem exceedingly odd." The mistress seeming still to balance whether it would not be her safest course to acquaint her husband;—the maid continued, "I will refer it to the nurse, if any body could ever look on the child without admiration."—The nurse declared, that nobody ever could.—"Only look at him yourself, madam," continued the maid; "observe how like an angel he smiles. Can you be uneasy, or think it extraordinary, that all the world should admire and wish to caress such a delightful creature?"

The mother, whose eyes were fixed on the child during this harangue, thought, as she gazed, that the incident which had given her uneasiness was less extraordinary than she had at first imagined, and at length allowed herself to believe, that it was very natural for Zeluco, or any other person, to behave as he had done.

Let those who are ready to accuse this poor woman of excessive weakness, remember that she was a mother, and that the infant, though far from being handsome, was her first born and only child.

Yet as she is represented as not deficient in quickness of thought and clearness of understanding, she may be thought to have acted inconsistently with this character, in attempting to conceal from her husband what he was so likely to come to the knowledge of, from the babbling propensity natural to nurses and maids. If I am not mistaken, however, the sex in general are apt to shrink from present inconveniences, even when sensible that by encountering them they would obviate the risk of future misfortunes. The lady was certain, that the knowledge of Zeluco's secret visits to the child would throw her husband into immediate ill-humour, and awake very disagreeable reflections in his mind. She flattered herself, that he might never hear a word of the matter, and she could not bear to disturb the present calm to secure herself from a future storm, which possibly might never occur. In behaving as she did in this particular, she will be kept in countenance by many who act on the same principles in matters of far greater importance; but she seems to have been intirely forsaken by her natural sagacity, when she anxiously enjoined the nurse and her own maid to conceal what had happened from her husband. For it required but a superficial glance of their dispositions to perceive, that this was giving them an additional incitement to reveal it.

She was probably tempted to this inconsiderate step, by the knowledge she had, that Zeluco was soon to return to Europe; and she lost no time in persuading her husband to remove with his family to his house in town, that Zeluco might not be tempted to seek another interview; and she resolved to keep herself and the child sequestered from any chance of meeting him before his departure from the island.

Zeluco being informed of these circumstances by the maid, who, on the pretence of some necessary arrangements, remained one day after the departure of her master and mistress; he, in prosecution of his base scheme, gave her a letter, which he desired her to place in such a situation as to be observed by the former, and seem to have dropped from the latter. When the maid joined the family in town, she executed these orders with but too much dexterity. While she stood behind her mistress, who was writing, the husband entered the room a little abruptly, and told his wife that somebody wished to speak to her in the parlour. She immediately locked up her papers into a small writing desk, and withdrew.—As she rose, the maid took that opportunity of dropping the letter she had received from Zeluco, beneath the seat her mistress was quitting, and immediately followed her out of the room. The husband picked up the letter which was unsealed, rumpled, addressed to his wife, and conceived in the following terms:

"It is impossible for me, my dearest soul, to express the happiness I have enjoyed in seeing and caressing the sweet pledge of our mutual love; I shall never forget your kind attention, in directing the nurse to the spot where I had that delicious enjoyment. I must, however, acquiesce in the prudence of your determination, to persuade your tyrant to move for some time to his house in town, where an interview may be arranged with less danger, and I shall wait with as much patience as I am able for that happy moment.

"*P. S.* I continue to disguise my writing, and earnestly recommend to you the same precaution."

The astonishment and rage of the Portuguese on reading this may be easier imagined than described; seizing his wife's writing-desk, which stood upon a table, he carried it into his own apartment, and there read over and over the fatal scroll which filled his heart with anguish. Notwithstanding the disguise of the writing he easily distinguished it to be that of Zeluco,—which left him no doubt of his wife's infidelity. The first violence of his wrath and indignation might have proved fatal to her, had it not been damped and counteracted, in some measure, by the grief and dejection he felt, that the child he so dearly loved, and had been so proud of, might not be his own, but the offspring of his detested enemy.

The impression of sorrow, from whatever cause it is derived, mollifies the violence of rage, and the conflict of those opposite sentiments in the present instance, repressed a little the madness of the husband's fury. However convinced he was of his wife's guilt, he could not be certain that the child was *not* his own; and all his rage against the mother could not unloose the bonds of affection which nature and the child's infantine endearments had twined around his heart.

Hearing the voice of the nurse and the maid in the passage, he called them into his apartment, and shutting the door, he, with as much serenity as he could assume, questioned the nurse, whether any man was in the use of accosting her at a particular place which he named, and of caressing the child.

The woman denied that any such thing had ever happened.

"Be sure, woman, that you speak truth," said the Portuguese.

"I would not depart from the truth," said the nurse, "for all the gold in Mexico."

The Portuguese repeated the question, and the nurse gave the same answer.

"Thou abominable wretch," cried he, "I have certain information of the contrary; and nothing but an avowal of the truth shall save thee from punishment here, and a long expiation in purgatory hereafter!"

"I have told the truth," said the woman, hesitating with conscious falsehood.

The Portuguese, with augmented rage and repeated threats, continued to question her.

She at length acknowledged, that Signor Zeluco had several times met her at the place he mentioned, and had shewed great fondness for the child.

"Wretch!" cried the enraged Portuguese; "Why did you deny this?"

The nurse was silent.

"What harm did you imagine there was in that man's seeing and caressing the child?"

"No harm in the wide world," said the nurse, "for if there had been any harm I should never have permitted it."

"Wherefore then did you conceal it from me? and wherefore did you so solemnly deny it just now?"

The confounded woman finding herself so hard beset, and quite unable to extricate herself by prevarication, acknowledged, that she had concealed it from him at the request of her mistress.

"I suspected as much," cried the husband.

"But my mistress," interrupted the maid, "desired her to conceal it for no other reason but merely that your Honour might be saved the uneasiness of hearing that another man was in the practice of caressing, and shewing such paternal affection to your child."

The wrath of the Portuguese, which had been for some time glowing, was so instantaneously kindled by this suggestion, that he struck the maid an unmanly blow on the face, so that the blood gushed from her nose and mouth, in which condition she ran to her mistress, who was just returned to her own apartment.

The poor woman was exceedingly terrified at her husband's violence, and her fear was not diminished when she understood the cause of it. She was now sensible of her imprudence, in concealing from her husband, Zeluco's treacherous visits to her child, and in depending on the discretion or fidelity of servants. She knew nothing however of the letter, and imagined that her husband's ill-humour proceeded solely from his hearing of Zeluco's behaviour. She thought her best course was to explain the whole to him without farther delay.

She flew into his apartment, assured him that the information which displeased *him* had given still more vexation to *her*, and that when the nurse acquainted her with it, her own first impulse had been to mention it directly to him; that she sincerely repented her not having done so, for she was now convinced that a virtuous woman should have no secrets concealed from her husband.

The Portuguese, who had listened hitherto with a stern countenance, burst into a laugh, which forcing its way through features distorted with anger, and the thoughts of vengeance, chilled his wife with horror. She proceeded in a confused manner to assure him, that however improper it was not to acquaint him with what the nurse told him, she had refrained for no other reason than to save him uneasiness.

"Your faithful confident and you adhere I find to the same story, and are both equally tender of giving me uneasiness," said the Portuguese, renewing his frightful laugh; "but be assured, faithless woman, that you shall not deceive me twice, and that your punishment, if possible, shall equal your guilt."

"What guilt? alas! I know no guilt," cried the trembling woman; "I am innocent as the babe newly born."

"Before you have the effrontery to speak of innocence, you should learn to be more careful of your letters—look at this," cried he, holding the letter open before her eyes.

"Holy virgin!" cried the astonished woman, as she perused the letter; "I never saw this paper before,—it is a forgery of the villain's to deceive you, and ruin me."

"How came this forgery of the villain's to drop out of your pocket?" said the husband.

"It assuredly dropped not out of my pocket," replied she; "for as I hope for mercy from Heaven I never saw the paper before."

"No, never; to be sure," said the husband, with a ghastly sneer; "You—you are innocent as the babe newly born."

"I am indeed," exclaimed the wife, "and when you have patience and coolness to examine the whole matter, you will find so."

"What examination is necessary?" cried he; "what confirmation can be added to such a letter as this?—this infallible evidence of your shame!"

"That letter is an evidence of nothing, but of the mean revenge of a disappointed villain. I beseech you therefore," added she, laying hold of his arm; "I earnestly beseech you, for the sake of your child, for your——" "Think not," interrupted he, shaking off her hand, "to deceive me again;—be gone to your chamber, and repent, for be assured that I will have ample revenge." So saying, he thrust her rudely out of the room, and shut the door with violence. She was put to bed, and passed the rest of the day and the whole night in anxiety and terror.

CHAPTER XX.

Unjust accusations seldom affect us much, but from some *justice in them.*

As soon as he was alone, the husband broke open her writing-desk; but after a very strict scrutiny he found nothing to justify the insinuations of the letter, or in the smallest degree to confirm his suspicions:—"But what confirmation is needed," said he, "of her criminal connexion with this man?—why should he wish to see the child in a clandestine manner?—why did she order the nurse to conceal this from me?—And above all, this letter, on which he has in vain attempted to disguise his handwriting, *must* have fallen from her pocket!—O! her guilt is manifest!"

In reflections of this nature, and in forming plans of vengeance, the Portuguese passed as sleepless a night as his lady.

The following day she was so ill that she kept her bed; the husband went not once to enquire for her, nor did he send any message: he also kept his apartment, and was heard walking backwards and forwards with a hurried pace the whole of that day. The next forenoon the physician who had formerly attended Zeluco called accidentally, and was taken immediately to see the lady, one of the servants having informed him she was indisposed.

As she had the greatest confidence in the Doctor's good sense and prudence, and knew also that her husband had a very high opinion of him, she informed him of the true cause of her illness; Zeluco's visits to the child; her own imprudence in ordering the nurse to conceal them; of his hearing of them; his jealousy thereupon, and of the horrid anonymous letter.

The first thing that struck the physician in her narrative was, That no motive was assigned for the base scheme the lady imputed to Zeluco: he hinted this to her.

She said, it must have proceeded from the natural malice of the man's wicked heart; she knew of no other motive.

The physician observed, that it was hardly credible that any man would form such a shocking scheme without some more particular cause.

The lady perceiving the force of this remark, thought herself obliged to mention her first connexion with Zeluco; although that was a subject on which she never thought without pain. She could not help however giving as favourable a gloss to her story as possible, by declaring, that Zeluco had formerly had the insolence to make love to her; that no woman was safe from an insult of this nature; yet, as it is generally imagined that men seldom make such declarations but where they have reason to hope they will be well received, she had naturally wished to conceal this incident, though she had heard his wicked proposal with equal surprise and horror; and had, in consequence of his persevering, been obliged to acquaint her husband; and, finally, she now suspected that the pride of the man, hurt by her resistance, so different from what he was accustomed to, had prompted him to this diabolical scheme on purpose to ruin her.

It is evident that in this narrative the lady did not adhere exactly to the truth, but thought proper to sink the circumstance of her having at first agreed to meet Zeluco. If all those forgive her for this part of her conduct, who, in relating facts in which themselves are concerned, are apt to leave out what makes against them, and put in the most conspicuous point of view whatever is in their favour, it is to be presumed, that the Portuguese lady will not be censured by a vast number of our readers.

The physician, it is probable, made allowance for a bias so very general among men, and from which the fair sex themselves are not entirely free.

After inquiring very minutely into every circumstance, his suspicion fixed strongly on the maid as an agent of Zeluco's. On his hinting this to the lady, she declared, that of all her family this girl was the last she could suspect; because she had always displayed the most unbounded attachment to herself, and often expressed, particularly of late, an aversion to Zeluco.

This did not weaken the physician's suspicions.—"Poor girl," continued the mistress, "she is of a delicate constitution, and subject to hysterical fits; she was much terrified by my husband's treatment of herself, but still more on seeing me so ill. I happened to say, that I feared it would kill me; on which she was seized with a violent trembling, and has kept her bed ever since."

The physician asked, whether the lady had ever intrusted this maid, who seemed to be a great favourite, with any secret which it would give her uneasiness to have revealed.

The lady answered, with some warmth, that she had no such secret; that she cared not if all the actions of her life were made public; that she defied the power of malice;—and thus she ran on with a zeal and fluency natural to people who are endeavouring to justify themselves, and are conscious of not being entirely innocent; she concluded by asserting, that there was no part of her conduct she wished hid from the world.

The physician having waited till being out of breath she stopt, he then calmly observed, that his question was not of so extensive a nature as she seemed to imagine; that he was not so impertinent as to inquire whether she had ever done what she wished to conceal from the world, but only whether *her maid was acquainted* with any thing of that nature.

"Certainly not," said the lady; "since I am not myself conscious of any such secret, how is it possible that my maid could be acquainted with it?" "I admire the acuteness and logical precision with which you reason, Madam," said the Doctor; "but I would be glad to know, whether this maid was in your service at the time you mention when Signor Zeluco paid his addresses to you?"

"If she had, she could have known nothing of that nature," said she. "Certainly not," said the Doctor; "but I wish to know the fact, Was she or was she not?" "She was not," answered the lady. "So much the better," resumed the Doctor. "I ask pardon, madam, for being so inquisitive; but I thought it of importance to have this point cleared up before I visit the maid, which I now mean to do with a view to discover, if possible, by whose means the letter was thrown in your husband's way; if that can be traced to the person you suspect, your justification follows of course."

So saying, he left the lady, and was conducted into the maid's chamber, and left with her alone. The maid immediately inquired how her mistress was?

"Your mistress is very ill indeed," replied the physician, looking at her with a penetrating eye; "some monster of wickedness has been bribed to ruin that worthy woman: you know of the forged letter which was thrown in your master's way—do you not?"

"I have heard of such a thing," said the maid, changing colour.

"Have you any notion who has been guilty of such a perfidious action?" said the physician, still fixing her.

"Lord, Sir! how can I have any notion?" replied the maid.

"Could you have believed," resumed the Doctor, "that such a viper crawled upon the earth?"

"I could hardly have thought it," replied the maid, with a languid voice.

"Do you not think that the vengeance of Heaven will pursue the vile wretch?" said the physician.

"Perhaps *she* will repent before she dies," said the maid, trembling.

"*She!*" repeated the physician—"how do you know she is a woman?"

"Me!—I,—I know nothing;—no, nothing in the least," said the maid, in confusion; "only if she *is* a woman, I hope she will repent before she dies."

"If she is a woman," cried the physician, "she is a disgrace to her sex, and the vengeance of Heaven will overtake her in this life, and hell awaits her in the next, unless she confesses her crime, and prevents the ruin of an innocent lady:—But how are you yourself? you seem very ill."

"I am indeed not well," replied the maid. The physician, feeling her pulse, cried with a voice of surprise, "Good God, you are very ill indeed;—let me see your tongue.—Gracious Heaven! what is this!—why, I had no idea of your being in this way."

"O, dear doctor," cried the maid, "do not frighten me; you do not imagine I am in danger of dying."

"Danger!" said the doctor; "yes, assuredly: yet, perhaps,—at least, I hope you still may recover;—that is, provided you—in short I will do all I can for you;—but if you have any spiritual or worldly affairs to settle, you had best set about it directly."

The Doctor having ordered her some medicines, went into the apartment of the Portuguese, whom he found alone and in a very gloomy mood. He expressed satisfaction, however, at seeing the physician, who immediately told him that his lady had informed him of what had happened. "Her assurance must equal her guilt," cried the Portuguese, "to enable her to mention it." He then poured out a torrent of abuse against his wife. The physician did not think proper to interrupt him; but when he had done, he coolly asked what proofs he had of her guilt?

The Portuguese enumerated the circumstances of Zeluco's behaviour towards the child, his wife's having instructed the nurse and maid to conceal it, and then shewed him the letter.

The physician having heard him patiently, endeavoured to make him sensible that all these circumstances were not sufficient to justify the inferences which he drew against a lady who had always behaved with affection to him, and the greatest tenderness to his child. "Besides," added he, "these circumstances, inconclusive as they are, lose much of their weight, if they can all be accounted for on the very probable supposition of their being contrived by an enemy."

"The letter!—the letter!" cried the Portuguese: "Well," said the Doctor, "the letter is of a piece with the clandestine visits; it was no difficult matter to bribe some person to throw a letter in your way in such a manner as that it would appear to have dropt from your lady. Recollect if there was any person in the room with her immediately before you observed the letter."

"Nobody but her own confidential maid," said the husband.

"And if an enemy had formed the scheme of ruining you both in this manner, who would he think of seducing as an assistant so likely as the domestic who attended her person. Consider also," continued the Doctor, "how very improbable it is, that she would keep such a letter in her pocket."

"If guilty people were always cautious, they would not be so often detected as they are," said the Portuguese.

"But is it not natural to think," rejoined the Doctor, "that the same want of caution which made her wear a letter of this importance carelessly in her pocket, would have appeared when you examined her papers: Did you find among them any other letters to the same purpose with this?"

He answered, that he had not.

"This, therefore, is a fair presumption," said the Doctor, "that there never was any; that the letter you found was purposely thrown in your way by the direction of some person equally the enemy of you and your lady."

CHAPTER XXI.

Comfortable Hints to married Men.

WHILE they were conversing, the Capuchin, who had attended Hanno in his dying moments, was introduced. This venerable person was spiritual director to all the Christians white and black in the family. The Portuguese immediately ordered, as was his custom, some cold victuals and a large flask of wine to be set before the Father, who had only time to drink a few glasses when a message came from the sick maid, who earnestly wished to see him. He was rising with reluctance from his repast, when the Physician begged his delay for a moment; and taking the Portuguese to a corner of the room, he, in a few words, explained his intention, which the other, on whom the Doctor's arguments had already made some impression, having approved, they turned to the Father, who in this interval had finished his flask of wine. The Doctor then informed him, that a very unfortunate affair had happened, in which he might be of service; that in short a discovery had been made, that the lady of the house had been unfaithful to her husband, as was proved by a letter from her lover, which she had dropt; that a plan was already formed for punishing her in an exemplary manner; that in the mean time she was kept in confinement till endeavours were made to discover those who had assisted in carrying on the correspondence with her lover, as there was reason to think she had been assisted by some person in the family.

The Capuchin, who was a little warmed with wine, and who valued himself greatly on his eloquence, and on the happy talent he thought he possessed of consoling the afflicted, could not allow so fair an occasion of displaying it to slip unimproved; addressing himself, therefore, to the Portuguese, he expressed his concern for the misfortune which had happened to him, observing at the same time, that however painful it might be, his case was by no means uncommon; for that a large proportion of husbands laboured under the same calamity. "Not," continued he, "that I mean to insinuate that any number being in the same predicament renders you, my worthy friend, less a cuckold than if you were the only one upon earth. I only mention this circumstance, because, although not much to the honour of human nature, yet there is reason to think that mankind in general derive consolation from the thoughts of others being in the same disagreeable situation with themselves. I therefore assure you, that even among my acquaintance there are many, some of them very respectable gentlemen, to whom the same accident has happened that there is so much reason to think has befallen you, notwithstanding which they live as easy and comfortably as they did before; this depends entirely on people's way of thinking. Things of this kind are undoubtedly rather unpleasant at first; but when we are accustomed to them, they give little or no uneasiness; for habit reconciles us to any thing."

The Capuchin was a man of influence in the island; and the Portuguese, who had been, although unjustly, accused of Judaism, had more reasons than one for wishing to keep on good terms with him;[1] yet he could not help betraying his impatience at the reverend

Father's manner of comforting him, by a most agonizing contortion of countenance at the last observation, which the other observing, he added, "I perceive, Sir, that you do not bear this dispensation with the resignation you ought; I must therefore desire that you will keep in your remembrance, that it has been undoubtedly permitted for some wise purpose; it will therefore be as impious as unavailing for you to murmur, for what has happened admits of no remedy. Now that the thing is done, it cannot be undone, at least I never yet heard of any method by which a man can be uncuckolded: this, my valuable friend, is the peculiar cruelty of your case; another person commits the crime, and you who are innocent suffer the shame. And what is still more vexatious, although one wicked woman can place her husband in this opprobrious state, all the virtuous women on earth cannot take him out of it. I beg you will further observe——" Here the eloquent Father was interrupted in the middle of his harangue by another message from the maid; and was with some difficulty prevailed on by the Physician to go directly, without waiting to finish his discourse.

When he was gone the Physician remarked to the Portuguese, that in the present state of the maid's mind, she would probably confess every thing she knew to the Father, and was impatient to see him for that very purpose; that although the Capuchin was bound not to mention what was revealed to him in confession, yet there would be no great difficulty in gathering from him, particularly in his present trim, the import of all the maid should say, without his intending to inform them of a tittle.

The Physician was right in his conjecture. The maid, terrified with the idea of immediate death, made a confession of her sins to the priest, and particularly acknowledged that she had been prevailed on by Zeluco's valet, to throw under the chair of her mistress a paper which he gave her, and which she now, to her great affliction, understood had produced the most mischievous consequences to her mistress; but the import of which she did not fully understand at the time; otherwise, she added, in alleviation of her conduct, she would not have been accessary to so great a crime.

The Priest, although not the clearest-headed of his profession, had understanding enough to tell her, that the best reparation she could make was by a full avowal of this to her master, and he refused to give her absolution on any other conditions. On the maid's consenting to this, the Father returned to the Portuguese, whom he found in his apartment with the Doctor; and addressing himself to the former, he begged that he would attend him to the maid, who had something of the last importance to communicate.

They went accordingly, accompanied by the physician. The maid, with a flood of tears, and the most earnest supplications to her master for his forgiveness, made an avowal of what she had told the Priest; confessing at the same time, that she had prevented her mistress from informing him of Zeluco's interviews with the child, which was her intention the moment she was informed of them; and this the maid owned she had done at the desire of the same valet who had given her the paper.

The Portuguese with difficulty restrained his indignation against the woman; at length, however, he was prevailed on to say, he forgave her, and immediately desired to see the nurse. When she appeared, he asked in what manner his wife had expressed herself when first she was informed of Zeluco's behaviour to the child. The nurse naturally, and without hesitation, declared, that her mistress had insisted on her husband's being informed directly, but was persuaded from that measure by the maid.

After a few more questions, being fully convinced of his wife's innocence, he repaired along with the Priest and the Physician to the apartment in which she was confined;—apologized in the most earnest manner for the ill-treatment she had received; begged her forgiveness for the suspicions he had harboured; declared his perfect confidence in her virtue, which, he added, it should never again be in the power of villany or malice to shake.

CHAPTER XXII.

> ———He
> Compounds for sins he was inclin'd to,
> By damning those he had no mind to. BUTLER.[1]

THE lady behaved with the utmost propriety on the occasion; throwing the whole blame on the villain who had wove such an artful net of circumstances as might have caught the belief of the least suspicious of husbands.

"Dearly shall he pay for his villany," said the Portuguese.

"Leave him to the torments of his own conscience," rejoined his wife.

"In case his conscience should not torment him sufficiently," said the Father, "the deficiency will be amply made up to him before he gets out of purgatory."

The Physician then drew the Father out of the room, thinking the husband and wife would complete their reconciliation in the most satisfactory manner by themselves. He told them, however, as he retired, that he would have the pleasure of dining with them, and then walked with the Priest into the garden, where he remained till dinner was announced.

His view in remaining was to endeavour to turn the Portuguese from thoughts of revenge, which he suspected to be brooding in his breast.

Being left alone with him after they had dined, he observed, that however strongly he was convinced of Zeluco's being the writer of the letter, yet as he had had the precaution to disguise his handwriting, it would be fruitless to found any legal prosecution upon that circumstance.

"I despise all legal prosecution," cried the Portuguese; "but I will find means of doing myself justice without any such tedious and uncertain process." The Physician apprehending that he meant to challenge him, represented that as a most absurd and uncertain method of repairing an injury; and the Portuguese, who had no such plan in his head, listened calmly to his arguments, and at length seemed to be convinced by their force, on purpose to deceive the Physician, and prevent his suspecting the real design he had in view.

In a short time Zeluco was informed that the base train he had laid for the ruin of the Portuguese and his lady, with every circumstance of his perfidious conduct, was discovered by the husband; and although the particular cause of their misunderstanding was not publicly known; yet he was told that it had been whispered about, that he was hurrying out of the island to avoid the resentment of the merchant.

This rumour determined him to postpone his voyage for some time, that he might give his enemy an opportunity of calling him to the field if he chose it; or in case he did not, that the world might be convinced that Zeluco himself was not afraid to give him that species of satisfaction.

It appears in the course of this narrative that Zeluco, however defective he was in other virtues, possessed a considerable share of constitutional intrepidity; in the early part of his life, from sheer vanity, he had oftener than once courted opportunities of distinguishing himself by a duel; and through the whole of his life he shewed, that whatever injustice or wickedness he was tempted to commit, he had also sufficient firmness to justify, if he thought that measure expedient; or to fight any person who accused him when he thought proper to deny it. Courage was indeed the sole virtue he admired in others, and the only one he possessed himself. It has been often said, that cowards only are cruel; but although it is natural to think, and observation will justify the opinion, that they are more apt to be so than the intrepid; yet there are but too many proofs that one of the most respectable and brilliant qualities which can adorn the character of man, is sometimes united to the most odious that can disgrace humanity, and that courage is not incompatible with cruelty.

Of this Zeluco was a striking example; and the same person who with little regret had forfeited the good opinion of every virtuous mind, could not brook to have it thought that he feared the resentment of the man he was conscious of having injured, or that he would make any apology to him, rather than run the risk of injuring him in a more violent manner.

In the mean time the suspicions of the Physician were not intirely removed by the dissimulation of the Portuguese. Notwithstanding the latter's declining to seek legal or honourable redress from Zeluco, the Doctor perceived something in his manner, which gave him the impression that the Portuguese meditated a less justifiable measure than either; his benevolence inclined him to prevent what his sagacity and knowledge of the man's character led him to suspect. His suspicion was confirmed a very short time after by the merchant's wife, who, under pretence of being indisposed, sent him a very urgent message to come and see her.—With perturbation of mind she told him, That she had reason to dread that her husband had formed a very criminal project of being revenged on Zeluco, and watched an opportunity of putting it in execution. She was prompted to this step by no regard for Zeluco, but from a horror at the intended deed, and from anxiety for her husband;—adding, that she was afraid of displaying much concern, partly because she did not wish that he should know of her being suspicious of what he intended, and partly that she might not awaken the jealous disposition of her husband;—with tears in her eyes, therefore, she intreated the doctor to exert all his influence to turn her husband from such an unjustifiable design; or if he failed, to use such means as his own prudence could suggest to render it ineffectual.

The good Doctor applauded her conduct, and seized the earliest proper opportunity of renewing the subject, which he had once before touched on to the Portuguese; adding, That he feared he still harboured vindictive intentions against Zeluco; representing the danger of such a scheme: that however cautiously it might be executed, he would infallibly be considered as the perpetrator. "I know no other reason which you can have for suspecting that I harbour such intentions," said the Portuguese, "but your thinking it impossible, after what you know of this man's behaviour, that it should be otherwise."

"You are mistaken," replied the Physician; "I think it *ought* to be otherwise; and this is not my reason for harbouring suspicions."

"I do not tell you," said the Portuguese, "that your suspicions are well or ill founded; but could you be surprised if *it* were as you suspect?"

"Neither shall I be surprised," rejoined the Doctor, "if you are convicted and executed for gratifying your revenge in such an unjustifiable manner. Come, come, Sir," added he, "allow yourself to be guided by reason, and not impelled by passion in this matter: consider what a dreadful situation your wife and child will be in, should any misfortune befall you in consequence of such an attempt. The wisest plan you can follow, since this man is on the point of leaving the island, is to let him go in safety, and it is probable you will never see him more."—Here the Portuguese shook his head.—"Then, Sir," resumed the Doctor, "your next best measure is to challenge him honourably."[2]—"What right has a man who has acted so perfidiously to expect that he is to be so dealt with?" said the Portuguese. "None," replied the Doctor; "but were I in your place, I should be more solicitous about what was reputable for myself, than about what my enemy had a right to expect. I only hinted this as being of two evils the least; and the best argument that can be made use of to one who despises the Christian religion."

"I do not understand you! what do you mean?" said the Portuguese.

"Why, that you are in that predicament," answered the Physician.

"Who! I despise the Christian religion!" cried the Portuguese, in terror and amazement.

"You seem at least to despise one of its most important precepts," said the Physician; "from which it may naturally be concluded, that you have no great respect for the rest."

"I have not the smallest comprehension of what you mean," rejoined the Portuguese.

"Yet I have expressed my meaning very plainly," said the Physician; "I really do not think you can with propriety be called a Christian."

"Jesus Maria!" exclaimed the Portuguese, "you fill me with horror. Why, Sir, I take the Holy Trinity, the Blessed Virgin, with St. Joseph her husband, St. James, and all the host of heaven to witness, that I attend mass regularly, and have always from my infancy believed in every article of faith which our holy mother church requires; and I am ready to believe twice as much whenever she is pleased to exact it; if this is not being a Christian, I should be glad to know what is."

"Nay, my good friend," resumed the Physician, "it is a matter of indifference to me what you do or do not believe; I am not, I thank God, your or any man's father confessor: but if you understood the *spirit* of the Christian religion half as well as you believe what the church exacts, you would find that your attending mass, and all your faith into the bargain, will not make you a Christian, while you indulge such a violent spirit of revenge."

"As for that," replied the Portuguese, "neither the church nor the Christian religion have any thing to do with it; that is my affair, and depends on my private feelings; and it is impossible for me ever to forgive a villain who attempted to injure me."

"It is because he attempted to injure you, that it is in your power as a man, and your duty as a Christian, to forgive him. Had he never injured you, nor even attempted it," continued the Doctor, "it would indeed be impossible for you to have the merit of forgiving him."

It will naturally be imagined, from the vindictive character of this Portuguese, that he was a hypocrite, and pretended to more faith than he really had; but this was not the case. It never had occurred to his mind that there could be any doubt of the truth of those tenets in which his father and mother had instructed him, and which he heard venerable-looking men in sacred habits proclaim from all the pulpits of Lisbon. He was decidedly of opinion, that none but monsters of wickedness, who ought to be burnt in this world by way of preparing them for the next, could harbour any doubts on such important points; he had indeed occasionally heard it hinted, that some of those doctrines were incomprehensible, and others contradictory; but this did not convey to his judgment any reason for doubting of their truth. He never omitted, therefore, any of the ceremonies prescribed by the church; he confessed his sins regularly, performed penance faithfully, would not eat a morsel of meat on a Friday on any consideration; and with the most punctual perseverance repeated daily his Pater Noster, Ave Maria, and Credo, to the last bead of his Rosary.[3] A person who thought that the whole of Christianity consisted in these and other ceremonies, could not but be surprised and shocked to hear his claim to the name of a Christian disputed. As to that thirst for revenge on every real or imaginary injury, which he had indulged from his childhood, and some other culpable propensities to which he was addicted, he considered all of these as venial foibles, which were more than expiated by his obedience to mother church in more essential points; and when his indulging in those culpable practices to which he was by temper or constitution prone came in question, he shrugged his shoulders, and said, "Well, I thank God, they are neither heresy nor schism."

The Physician, however, endeavoured to give him a different notion of these matters, founding most of his arguments on passages of a sermon to be found in the gospel of St. Matthew;[4] for this happened to be a Physician who sometimes read the Bible: there are, it would appear, some of that kind in America. The Portuguese, at first, thought the passages in question of a very singular nature; and as they were plain and intelligible, and nothing mysterious in them, he could hardly believe that they were quite orthodox: besides, he was a good deal surprised that certain articles which he thought of great importance were not touched upon; yet on being informed who the person was who had preached this sermon, he could not deny that it had a fair chance of being sound Christianity. The Physician having brought him so far, found little difficulty in persuading him that it was his duty as well as interest to leave Zeluco to his own wicked heart, which carried its punishment within itself; hinting also the probability of his falling sooner or later within the grasp of the laws of society, which his passions continually tempted him to violate.

It was probably owing to the remonstrances of this extraordinary Physician that Zeluco left the island in safety, and the Portuguese merchant was indebted to him for being freed from the two most tormenting dæmons that can possess the human heart, Jealousy and the spirit of Revenge.

CHAPTER XXIII.

To whom can riches give repute and trust,
Content or pleasure, but the good and just?
Judges and senates have been bought for gold;
Esteem and love were never to be sold.

Pope.[1]

When it was evident that the Portuguese had no intention of calling Zeluco to account for his base behaviour, he publicly announced the time of his departure from the Havannah, and having freighted a vessel entirely for his own use, after a prosperous voyage he arrived at Cadiz, where he was detained for some time, but as soon as he had transacted his business he proceeded to Sicily.

Soon after his arrival at Palermo, Zeluco furnished a house expensively, and began to live in a most magnificent style; inviting every person of distinction to his table, and entertaining in the most sumptuous manner. This way of living, with the idea universally entertained of his great riches, soon acquired him a numerous acquaintance, and the warmest professions of attachment.

Zeluco, who had never known any motive of action but self-interest, was not deceived by such professions; but while he plumed himself on account of his superior penetration, he was the dupe of his own maxims, which being drawn from the feelings of a corrupted heart, were often erroneous.

Insensible himself to the ardour of friendship, he thought there was no such sentiment, and most certainly never had a friend. What the world calls friendship, in his opinion was merely a compact of conveniency or interest between a class of people, in which it was tacitly agreed, that when, by the loss of fortune, health, or otherwise, any individual of the association became useless to the rest, all farther connexion with that person terminated of course.

Had Zeluco been satisfied with thinking this was *often* the case, he would have been in the right, but he was convinced it was *always* so, and there he was wrong; all declarations of attachment and friendship, therefore, he viewed as indirect attacks upon his purse; the punctual attention paid to his invitations, he *rightly* considered as nothing else than a proof of the excellency of his cook, and of the superior flavour of his wine.

The favourable notion which he entertained of the symmetry and beauty of his own person and face, inclined him however to believe, that the partiality which several of the ladies displayed towards him was void of hypocrisy, and proceeded from sincere personal attachment. For Zeluco had no sooner returned to Palermo than he became an object of great attention, and sometimes a subject of controversy among the ladies.

The elegant turn of his person and the graces of his countenance were universally admired, and even his character and disposition were favourably thought of, from that common trick of the fancy which gives the head and heart as much sense and virtue as the face has beauty. But he had not remained long at Palermo till his real character began to develope itself, and then the graces of his countenance were called in question, and his features were said to convey an idea of malevolence, or even atrocity:—this happened from another play of fancy which transfers the deformity of the mind into the face.

Pleased with the attention paid him by the men, and the favour of some of the women, he passed his time less disagreeably than he had done in the West Indies. But that degree of popularity which he had obtained at his arrival gradually diminished; his temper, naturally insolent and overbearing, detached the most respectable of the men from his society; and the intolerable caprice of his disposition, joined to a continual jealousy of temper, rendered him at last odious to the women. He therefore, with great satisfaction, embraced a proposal made by a Sicilian nobleman, more distinguished by rank than character, of accompanying him to Naples.

In that gay city he immediately set up a still more splendid domestic establishment than he had at Palermo, and as he played deep, and with apparent inattention, he was considered as a valuable acquisition by some very fashionable societies.

CHAPTER XXIV.

The frail one's advocate, the weak one's friend.

POPE.[1]

SOON after his arrival, he was presented to Signora Sporza. This lady was the widow of a Neapolitan nobleman, one of the poorest of a class of men in which few are rich. He had lived for two years after his marriage in a degree of magnificence more suitable to his rank than fortune, and died very opportunely when he had nothing left to live upon.

As, contrary to the advice of her friends, she had relinquished great part of the funds appropriated for the security of her own jointure, to relieve her husband's difficulties, she had nothing to support her after his death, but the revenue arising from the small part which remained, and a very moderate pension granted to her by the court.

She lived however in a decent, not to say a genteel style, which was the more surprising, because, although her husband had left no money to maintain her, yet he contrived to leave a child by another woman for her to maintain.

Signora Sporza was not acquainted with this circumstance till several months after her husband's death, when she was informed of it by the mother, who was then in a starving condition, and who, as the wretched woman herself expressed it, would not have appealed to her for relief, had she not been driven by compassion for her infant more than for herself.

Those same relations who had advised Signora Sporza not to relinquish any part of what was secured by marriage articles to herself, for the sake of an extravagant husband, exclaimed against the indecency and folly of her supporting an adulterous bastard, and its wicked mother; they insisted upon it, that she, of all women, had the least call to take such a load upon her. All the answer which Signora Sporza made to these exclamations and arguments, was desiring them to find out some other woman, or man, if they pleased, who would maintain the unhappy woman and her child, in which event she was willing to yield up her claim. "Till that is done," added she, "however indecent it may seem, I must be indulged in this folly."

She accordingly took both the mother and child into her house, where, contrary to the prediction of her relations, that the two serpents she was taking into her bosom would certainly sting her, they greatly contributed to her happiness; for the wicked woman became a most grateful and serviceable domestic, and Signora Sporza grew as fond of the child, who was a very sprightly boy, as if he had been her own.

This lady was of a character which rendered her universally agreeable; she supported the inconveniences of very narrow circumstances with so much gaiety and good humour, understood the art of arranging her parties so judiciously, and animated them with such pleasantry, that her assemblies were thought the most agreeable, though the least splendid in Naples. As she was well received everywhere, and her house frequented by the most fashionable company, Zeluco thought it worth his while to cultivate her acquaintance, and he was for some time a pretty constant attendant at her assemblies. One circumstance, however, made him less so than otherwise he would have been; the play in general was not so deep as in many other assemblies, owing to Signora Sporza's discouraging it as much as she easily could. Independent of more permanent ill consequences, she declared an aversion to deep play on account of the immediate gloom with which it overspread every countenance engaged in it, to the entire destruction of all good-humour and pleasantry. But Zeluco had a greater relish for deep play than for either good-humour or pleasantry; and as he sometimes met at Signora Sporza's with people of the same turn of mind, they were apt to indulge their humour in spite of her remonstrances, which indeed, however seriously *meant*, were always jocularly made.

Among the British subjects at this time at Naples, there were two young Englishmen, Mr. N—— and Mr. Steele, who lodged in the same house, although of very different characters. The honourable Mr. N—— had already made the tour of Europe, and returned to his native country more free from narrow prejudices, less infected with foreign fopperies, and more improved both in knowledge and in manner, than the generality of his countrymen who have made the same tour. After remaining a few years at home, he was seized with a complaint in his breast threatening a consumption, for which he was advised to return to Italy, and resided for the most part at Naples, where he intended to remain a year longer, although at this time he seemed to have in a great measure regained his health.

Mr. N—— had been well acquainted with Signora Sporza, during his first residence at Naples, and was now on the most friendly footing with that lady. Besides his companion Mr. Steele, he had introduced to her acquaintance another countryman of his own—Mr. Squander. This gentleman was distinguished by spending more money with less enjoyment than any English traveller in Italy; without any knowledge of horses, or any love for the animal, he kept a stable of English horses at Naples. His incitement to this was his having heard a certain peer who had a violent passion for the turf mentioned with admiration for having established a horse-race in the English stile. Mr. Squander matched one of his horses with one of his lordship's, and had the renown of losing a greater sum than ever was lost at a horse-race at Naples; what rendered this the more memorable though the less surprising was, that he rode himself. He gave frequent entertainments, to which he invited his own countrymen only; they generally ended in drunkenness, noise, and riot. He bought pictures, statues, and seals, because they were highly praised by the venders; and afterwards gave them away in presents, because they were despised by the rest of the world. Without any inclination for gaming, this young man was ready on the slightest invitation to join any party at deep play, and had sometimes been drawn into that above-mentioned at Signora Sporza's. As he was the only one of this party devoid of skill, and who played without attention, he generally lost the most, and sometimes was the only person who lost at all.

How Mr. Steele came to be connected with Mr. N—— will appear hereafter, but as he and Squander had been presented by him to Signora Sporza, she was particularly uneasy to see them throw away their money. She was uncommonly attentive to strangers, and rather partial to the English;—by her frank and engaging manners, she gradually overcame their natural reserve, and dissipated their timidity; and some of that nation who, from the time of their crossing the channel, had never dined but with a club of their own countrymen,[2] and had never gone twice to any other assembly at Naples, were insensibly prevailed upon to attend those of Signora Sporza, and at length they went with pleasure instead of reluctance.

At her assembly one evening, Signora Sporza perceived the same party forming with which Mr. Squander had lost so much money. "Why do you not advise your countryman," said she, in a whisper to Mr. N——, "to avoid these people, they will pillage him of all his money."

"Because," replied Mr. N——, "my countryman hates advice more than he loves money."

"You Englishmen," resumed she, "perhaps consider advice as an encroachment on that liberty you are so fond of."

"Certainly," said Mr. N——, smiling; "the Cherokees, and other refined nations in America, think in the same manner."

"Will you not try then to keep him out of those people's hands?" said she.

"I should try in vain," said Mr. N——; "but if you please to draw him off to a safer party, whatever he may wish, he is too awkward, and will be too much embarrassed, when a lady speaks to him, to be able to excuse himself."

"Basta!"[3] cried she; and immediately accosting Squander; "we have need of you here, Signor," said she; and so she engaged him for the evening with a party who played at a very small stake.

Signora Sporza thus using all her address to prevent deep play at her assemblies, and to save the unwary from being preyed upon, the gamesters gradually paid her less attention, and at last entirely forsook her house, for that of another lady with whom Signora Sporza was on ill terms, and who, out of mere spite, established an assembly at her own house on the evenings which Signora Sporza had fixed upon.

Zeluco, although he now possessed far more wealth than he could enjoy, required the agitation of gaming to ward off the intolerable languor which is apt to invade unoccupied minds, and also to preclude reflection, or retrospect on past conduct, which in him was always attended with self-condemnation. He therefore became a constant attendant at the rival assembly, and a considerable time had passed since he had waited on Signora Sporza, when he observed her one evening at the opera, accompanied by two ladies, neither of whom he had ever before seen. The elder a genteel-looking woman, between forty and fifty years of age;—the other about twenty: he gazed on the latter, and thought her by far the most beautiful woman he had ever beheld; the longer he looked he was the more confirmed in that opinion: he now regretted the coldness subsisting between him and Signora Sporza, and resolved to use all means for removing it, as the most easy way of being introduced to the lady whom he so much admired. Impatient as he was to address Signora Sporza, he hesitated about doing it that night, lest she should impute it to the real cause. A glance from the young lady brought him at once to decision; he could no longer command his impatience, but leaving Signora Sporza to put what construction she pleased on his behaviour, he suddenly darted from his own box, and entered that in which she and the two strangers were. With eagerness, and in the most obsequious language, he apologized to the former for not having paid his duty to her of late, imputed it to indispensable business, and begged to be permitted that honour the next morning, alleging he had something of importance to acquaint her with. Having finished his apology, he bowed very respectfully to the strangers, and then looked with significance at Signora Sporza, who heard him with the reserve of offended pride, taking no notice of his significant look, but after a grave bend of her head to him, resumed her conversation with the strangers as if no other person had been in the box. In spite of this very cool reception, Zeluco kept his place in the box, and his eyes almost constantly rivetted on the young lady, till the opera was finished, and then attended them to their carriage; after which he went home and ruminated all the rest of the night on the charms of the fair stranger.

He waited next morning on Signora Sporza, who had not been an inattentive spectator of the impression which her young friend's beauty had made on Zeluco; she allowed him with the most cruel tranquillity to go through the ceremony of explaining his pretended affair of importance, without interrupting him, or assisting him in his way to the real business which she well knew was the object of his visit.

She heard him without seeming to take any interest in what he said;—the important affair did not draw from her a single observation; he was so much disconcerted by the coldness of her behaviour, that he was unable to introduce any discourse regarding the strangers. He wished to do this in an indirect manner, as a thing in which he took little concern, and waited for a favourable opportunity.

"Do you know," said Signora Sporza, interrupting the silence, "how many birds his majesty killed yesterday? I heard he went early a shooting."

"*A-propos*," replied Zeluco; "Pray, Signora, who is that lady I had the honour of seeing with you yesterday at the opera?"

"Very *à-propos* indeed," said she; "may I ask which lady you mean; there were two in the box with me last night."

"Two!" cried Zeluco: "O yes; I now recollect there were two;—but I mean—I mean the *elder*."

"She is a very near relation of mine," replied she, suppressing a smile; and then turned the conversation to a different subject, which, with the awkward manner in which he had introduced his favourite topic, increased his embarrassment. Yet before he took his leave, he recovered his presence of mind so far as to let a china snuff-box he had taken off the table, fall on the hearth, where it instantly shivered in pieces. After making becoming apologies, he took his leave, and the same day sent a gold snuff-box, enriched with diamonds, with a letter to Signora Sporza, intreating her to accept of the one as an atonement for having destroyed the other.

CHAPTER XXV.

Digna minùs misero, non meliore viro. OVID.[1]

SOME few days after this, Zeluco again waited on Signora Sporza. She received him with more frankness than at his last visit; he imputed this to the benign influence of the snuff-box: as soon as he was seated, she whispered her maid, who instantly withdrew.

They talked for a while on the common incidents of the place; of a new singer that was expected; of a violent explosion which had happened the preceding night from Mount Vesuvius; of the queen's having seemed out of humour at the last gala; of a man who had stabbed his rival in the street at mid-day, and then had taken refuge in a church; of a religious procession that was to take place next morning, and of a ball in the evening.

Zeluco endeavoured to turn the conversation from those topics, so as that it might seem to fall undesignedly on that which was the object of his visit. Signora Sporza observing this said, "I will give you the history of the ladies by and by, Signor; but I expect two people immediately, to whom you have rendered a most essential service; and you must permit them to thank you in the first place."

He could not possibly comprehend her meaning: but soon after the maid introduced a very handsome young woman, plainly dressed, with a child in her arms, followed by a genteel-looking man, who seemed to be a tradesman, and a few years older than the woman.

Zeluco was greatly surprised at their appearance.

"This is your benefactor, Camillo," said Signora Sporza, addressing herself to the man, "the generous person who enabled me to free you from prison."

"I am greatly indebted to you, Signor," said the man, in a most respectful yet manly manner; "and although I do not absolutely despair of being one day enabled to repay what you have so humanely advanced to liberate me, yet I shall never be free from the strong sense of obligation I feel towards you."

"Ah, Signor!" cried the woman, unable to contain herself, "you do not know what a worthy and noble-hearted man you have relieved; you do not know the extent of the blessed deed you have done; you have preserved my sweet infants from death; you have ransomed my beloved husband from prison, and you have saved my poor brain from madness. O Signor! Had you but seen——" Here the tears obscured her sight; the recollection of her husband's condition when in prison, with the keen sensations of gratitude, suppressed her voice;—she was ready to faint;—her husband snatched the child from her arms, and the poor woman sunk down on a chair, which Signora Sporza suddenly placed to receive her.

Camillo, with his child in one arm, supported his wife with the other; while Signora Sporza chafed her temples with aromatic spirits.—"Margherita will be well immediately, Camillo," said Signora Sporza; "see, she recovers already."—"Thank Heaven," cried Camillo with fervour; then begged leave to conduct his wife home. Signora Sporza attended her with Camillo and the child into another room, ordered them some refreshment, and desired they might not leave the house till she came back.

All this was as great a mystery to Zeluco as it is to the reader.—"If I had suspected," said Signora Sporza to him, as she returned to the room in which he had remained, "that this poor woman would have been so much affected, I should have spared you the scene, which I will now endeavour to explain:—I have known this young woman from her childhood; she was always the most cheerful sweet-tempered creature I ever knew. By my recommendation, on the death of her mother, she was taken into the service of the Marchesa de B——; and in a short time she became her favourite maid. The Marchesa is liberal, and the girl was as happy as a maid could be whose mistress has the misfortune of being put out of humour every day as soon as she rises: the cause of her ill-humour was without remedy, and grew daily more inveterate; it proceeded from her observing more gray hairs on her head, and more wrinkles in her face every morning than she had seen the day before; but although her peevishness was diurnal, it did not last long at a time, for Margherita powdered her hair with wonderful expedition; and as soon as her face was varnished, and her toilet finished, she contemplated herself in the mirror with complacency, recovered her cheerfulness, and Margherita was happy for the rest of the day. Meanwhile, the man who has just left us fell in love with her, and she fell in love with him; and from that moment the girl's mind was more occupied with her lover than her mistress; whose head, after this incident, was neither so expeditiously nor so neatly dressed as formerly. When the Marchesa found out the cause of this alteration, she was very much out of humour indeed, and told Margherita, that she must either give up all communication with the lover or with her;—"so you will consider the difference between me and him," continued she, "and then decide." Margherita accordingly did consider the difference; and decided in favour of the man.—After leaving the Marchesa, she passed more of her time than ever with her lover; and their mutual love increased to a very alarming height. Neither of them however ever thought of any other remedy than marriage; and notwithstanding the numbers who have found it a radical cure for love, to this couple it has hitherto proved ineffectual; in the opinion of the poor people themselves, the disease rather gains ground, although they have now been married two complete years, and have two children.

"The husband, who was at first employed in the coarse preparatory work for sculptors, has himself become a tolerable artist; he redoubled his industry as his family increased, and saved a little money.—Margherita on her part cheered him under his labour, by the most active attention to family œconomy, by everlasting good-humour, and undiminished affection. The bloom and growing vigour of their children was a source of joyful foreboding to both.—It was delightful to contemplate the happiness of this little family. I often called on Margherita, purely to enjoy that happiness; health, content, and mutual love resided under their humble roof: obtaining with difficulty the superfluities, or even necessaries of life, they tasted pleasure with a relish unknown to those who have the overflowing cup of enjoyment constantly pressed to their lips. The gloom of their poverty was cheered by some of the brightest stars of pleasure, and by the hope of permanent sun-shine. But all this fair and serene prospect was suddenly obscured by a terrible storm. The imprudent husband, impatient to become rapidly rich, was persuaded to raise all the little money which he had saved, to accept of a larger sum on credit, and to risk the whole in a commercial adventure:—the whole was lost;—and the obdurate creditor immediately seized on all the furniture and effects of this little family, and threw Camillo into jail.—Margherita, half-distracted, came and told me her story. It happened by a superabundance of ill luck that I was very low in cash myself, and had overdrawn my credit with my banker; I gave her what I had, but it was not sufficient to procure her husband's liberty, which happened to be what poor Margherita was most solicitous about. I begged of her to call on me the following morning, determining then to go in search of the necessary sum; but before I set out, the snuff-box, of which you desired my acceptance, arrived: instead of going to borrow money, Signor, which, if you ever had the experience of it, you must know to be the most disagreeable thing on earth, I went and sold the snuff-box, and in my opinion to very great advantage; for the sum I received has not only freed the poor fellow from prison and redeemed his effects, but also makes him a little richer than he was before his unfortunate attempt in commerce. I informed the joyful couple that I had received the money from you, which in effect I did; they know no more of the matter; and now that you have heard the whole, and have seen the family whom your bounty has saved, I am convinced you will approve of what has been done."

Zeluco expressed great admiration of the benevolence of Signora Sporza, but insisted on redeeming the snuff-box, and restoring it to her. This she absolutely refused, saying, That the circumstances which she had related formed the only consideration which could have prevailed on her to accept of a present of that value; but she was willing to receive from him a snuff-box of the same kind with that he had so fortunately broken, which she would wear as a memorial of that happy event. Zeluco, finding her obstinate, was obliged to agree to this compromise of the matter.

But although Signora Sporza had informed him of all she knew, Zeluco himself knew certain particulars relative to this same affair, that he did not think proper to mention to Signora Sporza; but which it is now necessary to impart to the reader.

It was already observed, that Zeluco was greatly surprised when Margherita was presented to him: he had, however, frequently seen her before; and this was one reason of his being a little confounded at her appearance at Signora Sporza's; but on recollecting, that although he knew her yet she did not know him, he re-assumed his composure.

In going to church, Margherita usually had passed the windows of Zeluco's apartment, and he had often remarked her as she went and returned to and from mass.

Being somewhat captivated by her face and person, he employed an agent to find out where she lived and what she was; and afterwards commissioned the same person to engage her to meet a *very honourable gentleman*, who was greatly captivated with her beauty, at a house appropriated for a rendezvous of this nature. Margherita rejected the offers of the agent, baffled the arts employed to seduce her, and would have nothing to do with the very honourable gentleman.

This unexpected resistance increased Zeluco's ardour. His valet was acquainted with the man who had lent Camillo the money which the imprudent fellow had sunk in the ill-judged commercial adventure. This man, who thought his money in little or no danger when he first advanced it, was now exceedingly uneasy, and had already begun to press Camillo for payment. The valet acquainted Zeluco with those circumstances, who instructed the valet to persuade the creditor, that it was vain for him to expect that ever Camillo could pay the money; and that as long as he was left at large, none of his friends would think of advancing it for him; but that if he were thrown into prison for the debt, some of his or his wife's friends would then certainly step forth for his relief. The man scrupled to use so violent an expedient; but having mentioned it to his wife, by whom Margherita was envied on account of her superior beauty, and hated on account of her unblemished character, she pressed her husband to adopt this harsh expedient, as the only means of recovering his money. The creditor, however, still hesitated, till the valet assured him, under the obligation of an oath of secrecy, that he knew a person who would advance a sum sufficient to pay all Camillo's debts, rather than allow him to remain long in prison; and he became bound himself to do this if Camillo was not released by the other within a month.

Zeluco, who took care not to appear in all this infamous transaction, imagined, that when Margherita was once separated from her husband, and humbled by distress, she would then listen to the secret proposals he intended to renew through his former agent.

The creditor having given orders to his attorney to proceed to extremities against Camillo, went himself into the country, that he might avoid a scene which his heart was not hard enough to support. But his orders were executed very punctually on the very day in which Zeluco was so much struck with the beauty of the young lady at the opera. She had engrossed his mind so entirely, that from that moment he never once thought of Margherita, till he saw her introduced with her husband at Signora Sporza's, and found that the present he had sent to that lady with a very different view, had been the means of relieving a family brought to the brink of ruin by his insidious arts.

CHAPTER XXVI.

On aime à deviner les autres, mais on n'aime pas à être deviné.
ROCHEFOUCAULT.[1]

WHATEVER shame or compunction Zeluco felt on receiving praises he so little deserved, for conferring benefits which he never intended, he certainly supported the character he had to act with great assurance.

After the compromise already mentioned, Signora Sporza gave him the following account of the ladies whose history he was so impatient to know. The elder, she said, was her cousin-german,[2] and widow of Colonel Seidlits, an officer lately deceased in the king of Prussia's service. She was a Neapolitan by birth, who finding it disagreeable after her husband's death to remain at Berlin, where she could not afford to live in the same style she had formerly done, had lately returned to her native country, with her daughter Laura; that she inherited from her father a small estate in the Campagna Felice,[3] and her inclination for removing from Berlin to Naples had been strengthened by the hopes of making good a claim she had in right of an uncle, which, although of no great value in itself, was of great importance to her in her very circumscribed circumstances; and which, however just, did not the less depend on the favour of the minister.

Zeluco expressed much concern that two ladies of their merit should labour under difficulties, adding, that on account of their connection with her, he should think himself very happy in having it in his power to be of service to them.

Signora Sporza penetrated into the motive of Zeluco's proffered services; but she also knew that he was on an intimate footing with the minister, and might be of essential service to her cousin in the affair of her claim, the decision of which had been hitherto protracted on the most frivolous pretexts in the most litigious manner. It must be confessed, that, in the warmth of Signora Sporza's zeal to serve her friends, she was often regardless of the motive from which those who served them acted: could she have induced Zeluco to serve Madame de Seidlits from pure and honourable motives, no doubt she would have preferred it; but that not being in her power, she thought the next best was to secure the same effect whatever produced it. After thanking Zeluco therefore for his obliging offer, she added, That if he would do her the pleasure of calling in the evening, she would present him to her two relations; and that Madame de Seidlits would herself explain to him the grounds of her claim.

Being introduced accordingly to the two ladies as a friend of Signora Sporza, he became intoxicated with the elegant sweetness of Laura's manner, which he found equal to her beauty, and listened with much seeming attention and apparent solicitude to the history of her mother's suit, expressing great zeal to serve her on that or any other occasion.

The nobleman with whom Zeluco came to Naples had considerable influence with the minister: Zeluco himself had more; both were employed in giving him a favourable idea of Madame de Seidlits's case, or rather in inspiring him with a desire of promoting it, independent of the right on which it was founded. It is probable that Zeluco was thinking on something else during that part of Madame de Seidlits's narrative, for the foundation of her claim was what he was unable to explain, but it was also what the minister shewed no anxiety to understand. Soon after, however, he publicly hinted, that having taken much pains to get a clear idea of Madame de Seidlits's claim, he was led to believe that the judges would decide in her favour. As the minister's prophecies of this kind were generally accomplished, Madame de Seidlits was congratulated on this happy omen, as if she had already gained her cause; and she imputed this fair prospect to the interposition of Zeluco.

From this time he had frequent opportunities of seeing and conversing with Laura, and he exhausted all his power of insinuation to ingratiate himself into her good opinion, but without success. This young lady had more penetration into character, and a far juster way of thinking than any of her sex with whom he had hitherto been acquainted; the same arts which had rendered him agreeable to many of them, had a contrary effect on her: she was not pleased when she observed, that, as often as he found her alone, his conversation was much interspersed with compliments on her beauty. She had been sufficiently accustomed to sweeteners of this kind, not to value them above their worth; and she had remarked, that they proceeded as often from a contempt of the understanding as from an admiration of the beauty of the person to whom they were addressed. But whatever doubts Laura might have of Zeluco's sincerity when he expressed a high opinion of *her* merit, there was something in his air and manner which convinced her he had a very high opinion of his own. In this, however, Laura was in some degree mistaken; for notwithstanding the loftiness of his manner, Zeluco's self-conceit was confined to his external figure, to his address, and his natural talents; he was conscious of having neglected the opportunities of improvement, and lamented the want of certain accomplishments which he with envy saw others possess; for with whatever plausible varnish he concealed his foibles or vices from the sight of others, he found it impossible to hide them from his own; so that when flattery poured the honey of adulation into his cup, the unconquerable power of conscience often turned it into gall, and rendered him unable to swallow the nauseous draught; yet by a singular effect of selfish caprice, though sensible of his own failings and vices, he detested all whom he suspected of having sufficient penetration to see into his real character, and of harbouring the same sentiments with himself. He could support the company of those only upon whose understandings he imagined he imposed, by giving them a much better idea of his character than it deserved. This accounts for his constant preference of ignorant society, and for the gloom and dissatisfaction which attended him as often as he was not engaged in such pursuits as bury thought and kill reflection. Yet this dissatisfied miserable man, on whose mind repentance and remorse were often obtruding themselves, was, on account of his wealth and the splendid style in which he lived, considered by many as remarkably fortunate and happy.

We are never more apt to be mistaken than in our estimate of the happiness of grandeur. The grove overlooking the precipice has a fine effect at a distance; we admire the sublimity of its situation, and the brightness of its verdure when gilded by the rays of the sun; we grudge no labour in scrambling up to this seat of pleasure, which, when attained, we often find cold and comfortless, overgrown with moss, pierced by the winds of every quarter, and far less genial than the sheltered bank from whence we set out. In like manner many men, who are viewed with admiration and envy at a distance, become the object of pity or contempt when nearly approached. Of this we may be most assured, that all the decorations of rank and the smiles of fortune cannot prevent the intrusions of remorse and self-condemnation upon a mind sensible of having abused talents, and neglected through life the opportunities of improvement; far less can they convey happiness, or even tranquillity, to one conscious of perfidy, cruelty, and ingratitude. But Laura did not at this time know that the peace of Zeluco's mind was disturbed by intruders of this nature; and the vain satisfaction which he frequently enjoyed from the contemplation of his face and figure, she imagined extended to his whole character, and rendered him, in her opinion, by much too well satisfied with himself.

However profuse of panegyric Zeluco was, as often as he happened to find Laura by herself, yet he always stopt short, and abruptly changed the tenor of his discourse when her mother joined them.

This did not escape the observation of Laura; and one day on his making this sudden transition as Madame de Seidlits entered the room, Laura said to him gravely, "There is no need, Signor, for you to fly from the subject on which you have dwelt so long; I do assure you, the praises of my beauty are to the full as agreeable to my mother as they are to myself."

At this unexpected remark, Zeluco's countenance suddenly displayed strong marks of displeasure, and even rage; but recollecting himself, he instantly smoothed it over with the smile of good-humour; and having bowed, and enquired after the health of Madame de Seidlits, he turned to Laura, saying, "I fly not from the subject, Madam; the praise of your good qualities is the most delightful of all subjects to me; but a sudden thought struck me immediately before your mother entered the room."

"A sudden thought seemed to strike you also *after* she entered," said Laura, "if one may judge from the alterations in your countenance."

"I know nothing of my countenance," said Zeluco, with a careless air; "but I have great satisfaction at my heart in informing you, Madam," continued he, and turning to Madame de Seidlits, "that your claim is admitted to its fullest extent, of which you will have more formal notice this very day from the court."

Madame de Seidlits expressed a strong sense of obligation to Zeluco, imputing her success to his influence and exertions; he on his part affected to place it wholly to the justice of her cause; expressing astonishment, however, at its having been delayed so very long, and with an ostentatious air of modesty disclaiming any kind of merit from *his poor feeble* efforts.

When Zeluco withdrew, Madame de Seidlits spoke of him with

all the partiality of gratitude. Laura assented with coolness and moderation; she had observed something in his looks and conduct which displeased her, and conveyed some faint suspicion of his motives. Madame de Seidlits did not refine on looks or language; she founded her idea of Zeluco's general character on the personal obligation she lay under to him. On occasions of this nature the mother is generally more prone to be suspicious than the daughter; in this particular instance it was otherwise: Laura had as much sensibility to the impressions of gratitude as her mother; but having doubts respecting Zeluco's disposition and motives, she would have been more pleased if the favour had come from another hand.

CHAPTER XXVII.

> La physionomie n'est pas une règle qui nous soit donnée pour juger des hommes; elle nous peut servir de conjecture.
>
> La Bruyere.[1]

Madame de Seidlits felt great satisfaction in the thoughts of her having at length obtained justice; and the good and friendly character of Zeluco was the frequent theme of her panegyric. When she was dwelling one day on this favourite topic, "It is unfortunate," said Laura, "that the expression of his countenance corresponds so ill with the qualities of his heart."

"I do not know what you mean, my dear," said the mother; "few men are so handsome as Signor Zeluco."

"It is, I believe, generally thought so," said Laura; "but I confess I am not of the general opinion."

"No! that a little surprises me."

"When I speak of the expression of the countenance," resumed Laura, "I mean something different from beauty or ugliness; there are many men whom I think plainer than Signor Zeluco, whose countenance has nothing of that expression, which I think rather disagreeable in his."

"Am I to understand, child," said Madame de Seidlits, smiling, "that a man may be too handsome to be agreeable to you?"

"You would laugh at me if I said so," replied Laura; "yet if a man seems too sensible of his being handsome, you must admit that he is the less agreeable on that account."

"When a man happens to be handsome," replied Madame de Seidlits, "people are apt to conclude, without any other reason, that he is vain of his looks."

"I am not, however, so unjust," said Laura; "for example, I agree with the general opinion in thinking Mr. N——, the Englishman who is so often at our cousin's, very handsome; yet he is so free from airs and all appearance of conceit, that it is impossible to think him vain. *His* features express goodness of heart, but I have seen features which, considered separately, seem as good, and yet the countenance on the whole to which they belong, conveys the idea of the reverse."

"I do not admit," replied Madame de Seidlits, "that this is the case with Signor Zeluco's."

"Perhaps I am whimsical in this point," said Laura; "but I am convinced a man may be ill-looking, and yet give no idea of his being a bad man. And with respect to Signor Zeluco, I do think that those who do not know from experience that he is of a good character, might be apt to suspect him of a bad."

"Nothing depends more on whim, or is more uncertain, than the pretended art of physiognomy," said Madame de Seidlits.

"Yet it never fails to have some influence on our opinion," replied Laura.

"It ought not," replied Madame de Seidlits; "it may mislead us greatly: Did you ever, for example, behold a more lovely face than that of the wretched woman we saw the other night at the opera? yet her profligate life is well known. You may recollect also, how very harsh and unpleasant the countenance of your father's friend Colonel Sleiffen was; yet there never existed a worthier man. You ought therefore, my dear Laura, to beware of imagining that vice is connected with deformity, or virtue with external beauty."

"I beg pardon, my dear Madam," replied Laura, "but I might use the two instances you have given in support of my argument; for the opera woman you mention, in spite of her beauty, I should never have thought a person of a virtuous disposition; and I always imagined I saw benevolence shining through the harsh features of Colonel Sleiffen."

"I suspect," replied Madame de Seidlits, "that a previous knowledge of their character led your opinion in both cases, and I am sure that candour and charity ought to prevent our suspecting any person of being bad, till we have reason to believe so from their conduct."

"I do assure you, my dear mother," said Laura, "that it always gives me pain to think ill of any body, and it affords me sincere pleasure to find them better than I expected."

"Have you ever reason to think ill of Signor Zeluco?" said Madame de Seidlits with some emotion; "I remember you said something that seemed unpleasant to him as I entered."

"Why, no,—no," replied Laura, with a little hesitation; "he was paying me a few compliments, and stopped short as you entered. I only hinted to him that I liked no conversation when you were *not* present, that he judged improper when you were. But as to thinking ill of him,—I have—I have no reason;—we were talking of his looks."

"*They* afford no reason indeed," said Madame de Seidlits; "I hope experience, my dear, will teach you to judge of worth by some more certain criterion than the features of the face."

"I hope it will, my dearest madam," replied Laura, taking her mother's hand affectionately in both hers, "and till then, my opinions shall be directed by your judgment; of this you may rest assured, that nothing can ever influence me to think ill of those whom you *continue* to think well of."

CHAPTER XXVIII.

Illa quidem primò nullos intelligit ignes.
Ovid Metamorph. Lib. 9.[2]

Zeluco had been disconcerted, as has been mentioned, and was a little piqued at the manner in which Laura received the compliments that he paid her, and what she said in his hearing to her mother; but he was still more mortified to perceive the indifference which she displayed towards him on all occasions, notwithstanding his peculiar attention to her, and the pains he took to gain her regard. Had Laura been thoroughly acquainted with Zeluco's character, the distaste she had to him would not have been surprising, but she had not had sufficient opportunity of knowing him; she saw something in his manner indeed, and in the expression of his countenance, which she did not like, yet it might have been expected that the elegance of his person, and the splendor of his wealth, would have inclined her to get the better of this prejudice, as perhaps they would, had not her imagination been prepossessed in a manner which will appear singular.

Laura's father had a son by a former marriage, who was now a captain of dragoons in the Prussian service. This gentleman's most intimate friend was the Baron Carlostein, a man of family and very considerable fortune. They served together under the great Frederic,[2] in the short war concerning the Bavarian succession.

After one unfortunate skirmish, a small detachment which Carlostein commanded, formed the rear of the retreating party, and defended a particular post with great obstinacy, that the main body might have time to make good their retreat; as he was falling back at last, his detachment was surrounded by a numerous party of Austrian Hussars, and notwithstanding a very steady resistance, would have been cut to pieces, or made prisoners, had not Captain Seidlits, at the head of a few dragoons, made a desperate charge, by which the Hussars were dispersed, and Carlostein, with the survivors of his detachment, brought off.

This was the commencement of a very intimate friendship between these two officers. At the termination of the war, Captain Seidlits prevailed on his friend to pass a few days at a little villa belonging to his father, in the neighbourhood of Berlin; Laura was then a child between ten and eleven years of age. She had often heard her father, and other officers, mention Carlostein as a young man of the greatest hopes; she had heard many ladies talk of him as remarkably genteel and amiable. Her brother had written in terms of high admiration of Carlostein's conduct in the action above-mentioned, and she had heard his letters read to the company at her father's table. When Laura understood, therefore, that the person whom she had heard so much applauded was coming to her father's house, she expected to see a hero. The appearance and manners of Carlostein did not belie her expectation: during the short stay which he made at the villa, he was treated by Colonel Seidlits and his lady with that distinguished hospitality which it was natural they should pay to a man of his character and rank, the intimate friend of their son. What Laura had heard of this young officer, the respect paid him by her parents, the affectionate attachment of her brother, his own figure and elegant manners, tended to fire her fancy, and render him, in her mind, the first of human beings. He had received a wound with a sabre on one side of his brow, which reached beneath his temple; the scar was covered with a slip of black plaster, appearing peculiarly graceful in the child's eyes, and a confirmation of the heroic character of Carlostein. Colonel Seidlits and his lady perceived Laura's admiration of their guest, and were amused with the earnest manner in which she sometimes looked at him, and the pleased attention with which she listened when he spoke.

The Colonel one day observed her examining a print of Le Brun's picture of the family of Darius;[3]—"What has caught your fancy here," said he, coming behind and tapping her on the shoulder. The child imagined that she saw a likeness to Carlostein's in the countenance which Le Brun gives to Alexander.—"Do you not think," replied she, "that this face," pointing to Hæphestion, "has a resemblance of my brother?"

The Colonel having looked attentively at the print, and observing the resemblance which *really* had attracted Laura's attention, fell a laughing, and replied, "No, my dear, I cannot say I do,—but I own I am somewhat surprised that the resemblance between *this* face," pointing to Alexander, "and your friend Baron Carlostein, seems entirely to have escaped so accurate an observer as you are."

The child seemed a little out of countenance, and when Colonel Seidlits recounted the circumstance to his lady, he added, "I should be glad to know at what age a young lady begins to disguise her sentiments?"—"At the same age that young gentlemen begin to disguise theirs," replied Madame de Seidlits, "when they suspect, from the behaviour of those around, that there is something wrong or ridiculous in their sentiments. We first taught Laura," continued she, "to admire the Baron, and afterwards, by laughing at the child for the marks of admiration which she shews, we give her a notion that there is something ridiculous in it, of course she wishes to conceal what exposes her to raillery. A boy would have done the same."

"I imagine not exactly in the same way," replied the Colonel.

Carlostein went soon after to his estate in a distant part of the Prussian dominions; he afterwards past some time in France; on his return to his own country, his duty as a soldier kept him with his regiment, and he had never after seen Laura, or thought of her more, than as an agreeable child, the sister of his friend.

The impression which he made on *her* imagination was certainly stronger, and more permanent; although her parents considered this partiality of Laura's to Carlostein as

> A violet in the youth of primy nature,
> Forward, not permanent; sweet, but not lasting,
> The perfume and suppliance of a minute.[4]

Laura herself endeavoured to conceal it to prevent the raillery to which it exposed her; yet it had some influence in making her reject the addresses of more than one lover before she left Germany; all of whom were thought advantageous matches, considering the smallness of her fortune. She found them to fall so far beneath the accomplished Carlostein, that she did not hesitate a moment. The same impression, though now considerably weakened by time, tended to make her view Zeluco with indifference, and often with dislike: so much did he fall below that model of which she still carried the traces in her memory. In this preference, Laura proved that her judgment was not directed by external appearance, for in the general opinion, Zeluco would have passed for a handsomer man than Carlostein.

CHAPTER XXIX.

Non te Penelopen difficilem procis,
Tyrrhenus genuit parens.
HORAT.[1]

HOWEVER much Zeluco was mortified and piqued at the indifference of Laura, his passion for her rather seemed to augment than to cool. As the house where he had the most convenient opportunities of meeting with her was that of Signora Sporza, he thought it indispensably necessary to keep that lady in constant good humour with him; with this view he cultivated her favour with the most respectful assiduity. He attempted in vain, however, to prevail on her to accept of any present of value: she always declined his offers with good-humour and gaiety, saying, nobody in whom she was particularly interested, was at that time in *prison for debt*; but when any such case occurred, she would apply to him for a ring or snuff-box proper for their relief. Zeluco considered all this as mere affectation and grimace, and was convinced that she would, in due time, unfold the particular mode in which she wished to be indemnified; for he took it for granted, that indemnified in one shape or other she intended to be, for whatever civility she shewed, or whatever trouble she took on his account. In the meantime, he plainly perceived that she would not stoop to be directly assisting to his views on Laura. He imagined she had come to a resolution to observe a neutrality, till such time, at least, as she could exact a very large subsidy for acting as an auxiliary.—But in these conjectures he had entirely mistaken the character of the lady.

Bred in a country where a very free system of gallantry prevails,[2] Signora Sporza certainly did not view it in the light that a virtuous woman ought. In her youth, she had been a coquette, and she retained something of that appearance at an age when coquetry is less tolerable: which gave a handle to her enemies to insinuate that she had carried matters beyond the point at which simple coquetry is supposed to stop; this, however, they were never able to ascertain;—and as those who were most industrious to spread the insinuation were, with better grounds, thought to be in that predicament themselves, their malice had the less effect. Her constant good-humour, humane disposition, and easy manners, rendered her highly agreeable to society in general; and she had lived on the best terms with her husband, undisturbed with jealousy, notwithstanding his being an Italian.

Her talent for raillery she managed with such address, as to render it entertaining in general, without being offensive in particular. Mere, dull, downright scandal, which had no object but the gratification of malice, she detested, and considered the circulation of every story to the disadvantage of others, as inexcusable even although founded in truth. When a connection of a particular kind subsisted between two people, of different sexes, nobody was more quick than Signora Sporza in perceiving it; yet she was never heard to give the least hint of her knowledge or suspicion of such an intrigue. If the parties met openly at her assemblies, she received them with her usual politeness; if either of them made her acquainted with their intimacy, she would not suffer them to visit her afterwards. She never would be the confident of a love intrigue; because accessaries, she said, were as guilty as the principals, with far less temptation; besides, she added, as the loving couple generally quarrel afterwards, and sometimes go the length of hating each other, part of this hatred may extend to those who encouraged their connection.

Another of this lady's maxims was, that nothing should ever be told concerning one friend of another, particularly to a husband of his wife, or to a wife of her husband, which would give them pain to know. If what is told is false, all the world agrees, that the talebearer has done a very ill thing; and if it happens to be true, in Signora Sporza's opinion, a much worse; for a malicious falsehood, said she, ceases to do harm when the truth comes to be known, but the mischief attending a malicious truth is more durable. Jealousy, whether well or ill founded, she considered as the greatest plague of society; a jealous husband or wife she thought the most odious of all odious animals, and as carefully to be excluded from good company as mad people or cut-throats. She had no scruple in declaring that, in her opinion, the man was devoid of principle who intrigued with any gentlewoman, however willing she might be, before such gentlewoman was provided with a husband, or at least within a very short time of being so: and she thought *that* man was very little better who did not take due precautions to prevent his intercourse with a woman of reputation from becoming public, even although the lady was married.

As Signora Sporza had no favourable opinion of Zeluco from her first acquaintance with him, and even strongly suspected the nature of his views on Laura; it will seem extraordinary that she did not communicate these suspicions to Laura, or to Madame de Seidlits, for both of whom her esteem and affection hourly increased;—the truth is, it was this very affection that prevented her. She expected to make Zeluco's attachment to Laura, and his influence with the minister, of service to her friends in other schemes which she meditated for their benefit; but she saw plainly from the avowed principles and undeviating conduct of both the mother and daughter, that on the slightest idea of his views on Laura, they would renounce all connection with Zeluco, and spurn at every advantage that could attend it. Having a very high opinion, therefore, of Laura's prudence, on which she relied much, and believing in her aversion to the man, on which she relied more, she permitted him quietly to proceed in his scheme, convinced however that he would be successful only in promoting her's.

There certainly was little delicacy in Signora Sporza's way of thinking on this, and some other subjects; and as she was of a friendly benevolent disposition, and possessed some excellent qualities, it is to be regretted that they were intermingled with any of baser alloy.

Our only reason for describing men and women as animals of heterogeneous composition, made up of bad as well as good materials, is, that we have hitherto always found them so; but we shall be happy to delineate uniform and perfect characters as soon as we have the good fortune to meet their prototypes in nature. There is room to fear, however, that they are as difficult to find as they would be agreeable and easy to describe; and that the race of those perfect beings incapable of weakness, and invulnerable to vice, who are ever armed at all points, and cased in virtues as the knights of chivalry were in mail, has intirely failed, as well as that of those tremendous giants, void of every virtue, and replete with every vice, who lived in the same ages;—till these opposite extremes, men intirely good or completely wicked appear again, we must be contented with that mediocrity of character which prevails, and draw mankind as we find them, the best subject to weaknesses, the worst imbued with some good quality.

In a character, such as that of the person whose story we have the unpleasant task of recording, there are, perhaps, fewer good qualities than in any other, because the basis of Zeluco's character was cruelty, at least a total disregard to the feelings of his fellow-creatures, when any interest or gratification of his own was in question.

This disposition of the mind, we conceive, admits of fewer good qualities, and is connected with a greater number of bad than any other of which human nature is susceptible.—Montaigne, indeed, has said, *"Nature a (ce crains-je), elle-meme attaché à l'homme quelque instinct à l'inhumanité."*[3] But it is to be hoped, that the instinct he mentions belongs only to devils, and that a *disinterested* pleasure in the sufferings of others exists not even in the most wicked of human breasts. It is sufficiently deplorable, that any of mankind are capable of pursuing what they consider as their own interest, and sometimes interest of a very frivolous nature, at the expence of extreme misery to their fellow creatures. The proofs, however, of this degree of cruelty need not be drawn from the stories of giants, and records of chivalry; they are frequently found in more authentic history, and may be adduced from the conduct of too many of the heroes and great men of antiquity; not to mention the great men of our own days, whose sentiments and conduct, however different from those of the former in every other respect, have a wonderful resemblance to their predecessors, in this article of insensibility and disregard of the misery of others.

CHAPTER XXX.

A perfidious Attempt.

As Zeluco now found more frequent opportunities than ever of being in company with Laura, he continued his assiduities with increased zeal, and strove by every means of insinuation with which he was acquainted to gain her good opinion; but with all the pains he took and the art he used, her behaviour to him never exceeded the bounds of common politeness, and sometimes a kind of politeness which savoured a little of dislike.

Although few men had less tenderness than Zeluco for the self-love of others, none could feel more exquisitely when their own was wounded; he perceived Laura's indifference with indignation, and would have endured it with still more impatience, had he not found a balsam to alleviate the smart in the very root from whence it sprung. His vanity, while it made him feel the indifference of Laura, persuaded him that she was deficient in penetration, and did not relish the graces with which he thought himself adorned, as women of taste usually did. *"L'amour propre,"* as Rochefoucault finely observes, *"empêche bien que celui qui nous flatte soit jamais celui qui nous flatte le plus."*[1] It might be thought that this mean opinion of Laura's taste would tend to diminish the force of his attachment to her; but we must remember that Zeluco's love was entirely sensual; he thought Laura's face the most beautiful, and her person the most piquant, he had ever seen. The qualities of her mind he regarded not.

The attentive and complaisant manner in which Madame de Seidlits always behaved to him, convinced him that he enjoyed *her* good opinion; he perceived also, that she had a taste for show and magnificence, and was a little out of countenance sometimes on account of the want of those superfluities which custom has rendered almost necessaries in a certain rank of life. On this weakness he founded an opinion, that, with proper management, she might be gradually brought to wink at the connection he wished to form with her daughter; a piece of complaisance, however shocking, which he had already met with in more than one instance.

He resolved therefore to begin his horrid design by fixing an obligation of an important nature on her, unknown both to her daughter and Signora Sporza: he waited on her one forenoon, when he knew the two other ladies were abroad; and preluding what he had to propose with many apologies, he said, "That the high esteem he had for, and the sincere concern he took in her interest, had prompted him to make some inquiry into her circumstances; and that he was much grieved to find they were so ill proportioned to her merit. As your husband," continued he, "belonged to another service, I find it will be difficult to have this remedied by the bounty of this court; but you will oblige me infinitely (especially if you will agree to keep it a secret from every other person without exception), by permitting me to be your banker for an annual sum, till such time at least as your own affairs are better arranged." So saying, he presented her with a note of very considerable value.

The blood mounted into Madame de Seidlits's face at this proposal, and she immediately replied, with an air of surprise and displeasure, That she was sorry he had taken the trouble of making an inquiry of such a nature; that he had received an erroneous account of her affairs, which were not in a situation to justify her in accepting assistance of that kind from any person; but more particularly from one with whom she had no natural connection. She added, That she should always have a proper sense of the obligation which, unexpected and unsolicited on her part, he had already conferred on her; but she was determined to be exceedingly cautious of permitting a load to be increased which she had already felt too heavy for her to bear without great uneasiness. Having said this she withdrew, throwing such a look at Zeluco as his conscious heart interpreted into a suspicion of his base design. He remained some time fixed to the spot, and then returned to his own house in much disturbance of mind.

He was now convinced that he had made a false estimate of the character of Madame de Seidlits; that he had betrayed his scheme on her daughter, and dreaded that he should be deprived of the pleasure of visiting her any more, without which he felt he could enjoy little comfort or repose.

After much reflection, and after forming and rejecting various plans to remove the effects of this rash step, and reinstate himself in the good opinion of Madame de Seidlits, he at length sent her the following letter:

"I AM much afraid, my dear Madam, that I have offended your delicacy by my proposal this morning, which I am now convinced was made in too abrupt a manner, owing to my having received some vexatious news of a domestic nature, which will oblige me to embark for Messina within a few days; having little expectation of returning to Naples, I grasped too eagerly at the happiness of serving a person I so highly esteem, and whom there is reason to fear I shall never see again. I hope you will forgive my precipitate zeal; for however just your reasons may be for rejecting the satisfaction aimed at, I hope you will never have any for denying some share of your regard to him who is, with the highest esteem, and the warmest prayers for your happiness,

"Madam,

"Your most obedient,

"And most humble servant,

"ZELUCO."

Although Madame de Seidlits's pride had been alarmed by Zeluco's proposal, she had no suspicion that it was dictated by any base motive; and therefore she was not without uneasiness even before receiving this letter, lest she had behaved with too much loftiness to a well-meaning and friendly man. She became entirely of this opinion the moment she perused the letter; her candid mind was filled with remorse for her own behaviour, and sorrow for his threatened departure.

She directly sent him a letter, apologizing for her behaviour, and entreated him not to leave Naples without seeing her once more.

CHAPTER XXXI.

—Tamen ad mores natura recurrit
Damnatos, fixa et mutari nescia.—

Juv. Sat. xiii. 239.[1]

WHEN Signora Sporza and Laura returned from their airing, Madame de Seidlits informed them, that Zeluco had paid her a visit, and that he intended to leave Naples. She mentioned this in such a manner that they naturally thought the sole design of his visit had been to acquaint her with his sudden departure; this she did to prevent any inquiry concerning the real motive of his visit, which, in compliance with Zeluco's request, she intended to conceal.

Signora Sporza was greatly surprised at Zeluco's sudden resolution; it appeared unaccountable to her, who was convinced his affections centered at Naples, and did not believe that any business would appear of sufficient importance in the eyes of a man of his character and fortune, to draw him from the place where his affections were fixed.

Laura was uneasy because she saw her mother so; for independent of that circumstance, she would have been pleased with the departure of a man whose company was disagreeable to her.

The reader needs not be informed that Zeluco had no intention of leaving Naples, and that the story of vexatious news, which obliged him to embark for Sicily, was an invention, calculated to remove all suspicion of his real plan from the mind of Madame de Seidlits, and to convince her, that his proposal could be dictated by pure benevolence alone; for if, previous to making it, he had already formed the resolution of quitting Italy, with no view of returning for several years, and little chance of ever seeing her or her daughter again, the offer must have been well intended, whether she thought it became her to accept it or not.

But it was necessary that he should seem in earnest before he sent the letter to Madame de Seidlits; therefore he announced his intention to the domestics of his own family, ordered several things to be prepared and packed up, called in his debts, ordered inquiry to be made about a proper vessel for transporting him and his suite. In short, he acted his part so well, that none of his acquaintance, except Signora Sporza, had any doubts of his intention.

When Zeluco received Madame de Seidlits's answer to his letter, he began to resume his old opinions; his mind, habituated to hypocrisy and deceit, could not enter into the natural movements of an honest heart, apprehensive of having acted ungenerously, and throbbing with eagerness to make reparation; he imagined her answer displayed an inclination to accept of his offer, and thought her stately behaviour had been assumed on purpose to enhance the value of her future acquiescence, or perhaps was a temporary triumph, with which the good lady chose to indulge her vanity; but having been driven to immediate decision by the unexpected news of his departure, she was now ready to capitulate on reasonable terms.

He did not continue long in this way of thinking; for when he waited on her the following day, and Madame de Seidlits having repeated her apology for the coolness of her behaviour at their last interview, he began to hint, though in a distant way, at a renewal of his former proposition; but was immediately stopt short, by her rejecting it with equal firmness, though with less anger than at first. She added, in the most obliging manner, That she had taken the liberty of requesting to see him; because she could not bear the thoughts of his leaving Naples after such a cold interview as their last, without expressing that sense of gratitude which she should ever retain for his goodness to her on a late occasion, and without wishing him a good voyage.

There was so much virtuous dignity and unaffected candour and benevolence in the whole of her discourse and deportment, as overawed his insidious tongue, and checked every presumptuous hope that began to spring up in his breast.

At his taking leave, Madame de Seidlits, with some degree of solemnity and fervour, said, "Heaven direct you, Sir, wherever you go, and bless you with all the prosperity and success which your disinterested conduct and benevolent character deserve." The conscience of Zeluco smote him at this petition, and he felt a pang sharp as the stiletto of the Portuguese.

Disappointed, humbled, and self-condemned, in broken accents, and with a faultering tongue, he was withdrawing, without having the assurance once to pronounce the name of Laura, when Signora Sporza and that young lady entered the room; even then he was unable to recover himself so far as to address them in his usual manner; after bowing to each, without uttering a word, he hurried out of the room.

His agitation spoke more powerfully in his favour with Madame de Seidlits, than he could himself have done had he been ever so cool and recollected; that confusion which proceeded from disappointment, perfidy, and conscious guilt, she imputed to the sensibility of a benevolent heart, on being separated from friends, without the hope of seeing them again for a long time.

Laura, without being so fully convinced of its justice, acquiesced in the construction of her mother.

Signora Sporza could not account in a satisfactory manner for the behaviour of Zeluco, but she was too much convinced of the selfishness of his disposition, to believe that he could be much affected with any thing unconnected with his own personal interest or pleasure.

He was under the necessity of continuing the preparations for his departure for some days; but on the arrival of the first vessel from Sicily, he pretended that he had received letters, informing him that the business which required his presence was happily and unexpectedly terminated; so that his voyage was no longer necessary.—This news he allowed to reach the ladies in the common course of circulation, fearing that their delicacy might be hurt by his sending a formal message to acquaint them with it; as that would imply his thinking his motions of more importance to them, than they might incline to have believed; but on his waiting on them a few days after, he was highly pleased when Madame de Seidlits chid him for omitting to send her a piece of intelligence which gave her much pleasure. He looked at Laura, in hopes of her shewing marks of agreeing with her mother; but as she felt differently, she seemed as if she had not heard what her mother had said. Signora Sporza, looking slily at Zeluco, said, "I am less surprised than my friend, having all along had a prepossession that something would occur to prevent this voyage."

CHAPTER XXXII.

The Importance of a Man to himself.

ZELUCO was now on a better footing than ever with Madame de Seidlits, visited her more frequently, and became more and more enamoured of her daughter. The natural gracefulness of her manner, the lively good sense of her conversation, and the winning sweetness of her temper, would have attracted the admiration of every man of sentiment, although these qualities had been connected with a face and person of the common kind. Even in the eyes of Zeluco, sunk as he was in sensuality and debased by vice, the filial affection, the graceful modesty, and benevolent heart of this amiable young woman gave additional poignancy to those external beauties which hitherto he had esteemed as all that is valuable in woman.

From the observations which Zeluco had made on the conduct of mankind, confirmed by what passed within his own breast, his opinion was, that virtue was mere varnish and pretext, and whatever apparent disinterestedness, generosity, or self-denial, there were in the conduct of any person, that if the whole could be chymically analyzed and reduced to their original elements, self-interest would be found at the bottom of the crucible;[1] he was, besides, of a suspicious temper, and convinced that for the most of their actions, mankind have secret reasons very different from the ostensible. If, therefore, the motive announced was of a generous or disinterested nature, he never believed it to be the real one, but turned his eyes in search of a motive where self-interest predominated.

In the present case, not being able to conjecture any advantage that could accrue to Laura, from behaving with so much reserve to him (as to disliking him, he thought that impossible), nor any benefit which Madame de Seidlits could derive from rejecting his proposal, especially as he had annexed no condition to it; he laboured to discover what could impel two women who were not devoid of common sense to act in such an irrational manner. And after much deliberate reflexion, he at length imputed the whole of their conduct to a scheme concerted between the mother and daughter, with the aid of Signora Sporza, to take advantage of his passion for Laura, and, by assumed dignity in the one and reserve in the other, to allure him into a marriage.

Replete with this notion, he determined to be more sparing in his attentions to Laura, to pay his court with ostentatious assiduity to a young lady of family and considerable beauty then at Naples; and by alarming Madame de Seidlits and Laura with jealousy, and the fear of losing him for ever, induce them both to more complaisance.

He acted the part he intended so well, that within a short time it was generally believed at Naples, that a treaty of marriage was on foot between Zeluco and the young lady in question; and he took particular care that Signora Sporza, and her two friends, should have more reason than others to be convinced of the truth of this report.

In requital for the pains he gave himself in his new assumed character, he had the vexation to perceive, that those of all his acquaintance who took the least interest in his behaviour, and in the news he had circulated, were precisely the persons he wished to affect the most; that Madame de Seidlits and Signora Sporza heard and believed it with the most perfect indifference, and if there was any alteration observable in the behaviour of Laura, it was that she seemed a little gayer than formerly.

Finding that a stratagem, which he imagined would have greatly disconcerted the supposed scheme of the ladies, and produced something favourable to his own views, had intirely failed, he now thought proper to relax in his assiduities to the young lady in question, and renew them to her whom, for some time, he seemed to have abandoned.

He was the more eager to return to his former society at Signora Sporza's, as he understood that Mr. N——, the English gentleman formerly mentioned, spent a great deal of his time with her, and in the company of Madame de Seidlits and Laura. He could hardly indeed allow himself to imagine that any woman who had eyes, could prefer this Englishman to himself; yet, recollecting that the tastes of women are wonderfully capricious, he felt some sensations of jealousy on hearing of the visits of Mr. N——. Having prepared a plausible story to account for his late absence, and what he thought a mighty well-turned apology, he again waited on Madame de Seidlits. He had no opportunity, however, of pronouncing his apology, for as no notice had been taken by Laura, or her relations, of his retreat, the same inattention was paid to his return. He was received as if he had passed the preceding evening with them; Signora Sporza saying, just as he was about to make his apology,—This is lucky enough, as N—— cannot be with us; we were in want of somebody to form our party.—Pray, Signor, draw a card.

Baffled in all his plans of seduction, his usual amusements becoming insipid, and his former pleasures nauseous; feeling himself incapable of any enjoyment out of the company of Laura, the obdurate and haughty spirit of Zeluco was obliged to relinquish every idea of obtaining the object of his wishes by, what he called, conquest, and to think of proposing articles of union.

This last recourse was the more mortifying to him, as it was a favourite maxim of his, that no man in his senses would ever think of entering into the state of matrimony, but by the door of wealth, or with the view of using it as the ladder of ambition; yet impelled by desires which he could not gratify on other terms, he now found himself obliged to sue for admission into that state without the attractions of either wealth or ambition.

After a long internal struggle, he at last waited on the mother of Laura, and without much ceremony or circumlocution, for he had not the least doubt of success, he acquainted her with his honourable intentions respecting her daughter. Few things could have been more agreeable to Madame de Seidlits than such a proposal.

During the first violence of her grief and dejection of spirits on her husband's death, she felt the diminution of her fortune as an inconsiderable evil after so great a misfortune; but now that the sharpness of her sorrow was somewhat blunted by time, she began to be more sensible of the inconveniences and mortifications attendant on narrow circumstances.

Her husband, like most Germans, was fond of show, and had encouraged his wife in a more expensive style of life than he could well afford. She herself, in other respects of a very amiable character, was not without vanity; she was desirous that her house, furniture, and equipage, should not only be genteel but splendid. It is not surprising, therefore, that the minute œconomy which was absolutely necessary in her present circumstances should be highly disagreeable to her, even on her own account, but still more so on account of her fondness for Laura, whom she eagerly wished to see possessed of all the elegancies of life, and for whose smallest pleasure she was ever ready to sacrifice any gratification of her own; indeed, all her own gratifications, even those of her vanity, were more sensibly enjoyed by her in the person of her daughter than in her own.

As Madame de Seidlits foresaw that Laura's marriage with Zeluco would probably be accompanied with many conveniences to herself, would put her beloved daughter into that state of affluence and splendor which so well became her, and as Zeluco was a man of whom she had a good opinion, she heartily rejoiced at the proposal which he made. Having therefore in polite terms thanked him for his good opinion of her daughter, she said she would inform her of his proposals, and then leave the matter to her own decision.

"That is all I wish, Madam," said Zeluco.

"For," continued Madame de Seidlits, "Laura's dutiful behaviour gives her a claim to the utmost indulgence, and her excellent understanding renders it improper for me *strongly* to influence, far less to control her on such an occasion."

"Control!" repeated Zeluco; "have you reason to think your daughter's affections are already engaged?"

"I know they are not," said Madame de Seidlits; "had that been the case, I should have begun by telling you so."

"Then, Madam," said Zeluco, "it is to be hoped there will be no need of control."

Madame de Seidlits was not so sure of Laura's agreeing to Zeluco's proposal as he seemed to be, and therefore had spoken in doubtful terms, which he thought unnecessary, and a little ridiculous.

Having obtained leave to make his proposals to Laura herself, he withdrew, fully convinced that they would be most acceptable; but somewhat abashed, that to arrive at the wished-for goal, he was under the necessity of taking the detested road to matrimony.

CHAPTER XXXIII.

Maternal Affection.—Filial Duty.

That very evening Madame de Seidlits took occasion to mention Zeluco to Laura, in terms agreeable to the good opinion she had formed of him, and the gratitude which she felt for the good office he had done her; and then added, "she was convinced he would make a good husband."

"Perhaps he might," said Laura, "to a woman who loved him."

"A man of generosity and worth must command the esteem of a virtuous woman," answered Madame de Seidlits; "and that, my dear, is often a stronger pledge of happiness in the married state, than the fantastical notions some women form of love."

Alarmed at the significant manner with which Madame de Seidlits pronounced this;—Laura, looking earnestly at her mother, cried, "Heavens! what does this mean?—has Signor Zeluco—sure he cannot think—"

"Yes, Laura," said Madame de Seidlits, "he thinks of you, and you only;—and this day he offered to make you mistress of his hand and fortune."

The blood immediately forsook Laura's face; she became as pale as snow, and seemed ready to faint.

"My dearest child," exclaimed Madame de Seidlits; "what is the matter?"

"Oh! mother," said Laura, in a feeble voice, "will you give me to a man I cannot love?—will you order your Laura—?"

"How can you talk so, child," said the mother; "when did I order you?"

"Alas!" said Laura, "is not every indication of your wishes obeyed as an order by me?"

"For which reason," replied Madame de Seidlits, "I have no wishes but those which you can with pleasure obey."

"It has been the happiness of my life," said Laura, "to obey,—to anticipate your wishes, when it was in my power; but can you wish me married to a man whom I cannot love? or would you make such a requital to the person who has obliged you, as to give him a wife without fortune, and without the least affection, without even—"

"For Heaven's sake, my dear, do not talk in that manner," interrupted Madame de Seidlits; "you well know, I can desire nothing but what is for your good; but I beg you may hear me calmly, your decision on this matter is of great importance: you must be sensible of the sad reverse of fortune which has befallen you by the death of your father; his rising prospects in the army, his generous spirit, and above all his love for us both, have accustomed you to a style of life very different from what our present circumstances can support. In the meanwhile, Signor Zeluco, a man of a friendly and benevolent character, and of a vast fortune, offers you his hand, and is ready to rescue you from all the inconveniencies of poverty, and to place you in a state of affluence which you never before experienced. But you say, you do not love him.—Well, if that continues to be the case, there is no more to be said; I shall never desire you to give your hand to a man whom you cannot love;—but I fear, my dear, you are misled by false and romantic notions on that head."

"Is there any thing unreasonable or romantic," said Laura, "in refusing my hand to a man who in no degree interests my heart. But you have alluded to the inconveniencies of our present confined circumstances,—as affecting *me* in a more *particular* manner. I know not," continued Laura, "if I understood my mother right?"

"The narrowness of our circumstances are a source of unhappiness to me *on your account only*," replied Madame de Seidlits.

"From this moment then, my dear Madam, let that source be dried up," said Laura, "for our present circumstances, confined as they are, give me no uneasiness; and be assured, that if you can bear them cheerfully, all the inconveniencies attending them are bliss to me, in comparison with affluence as the wife of Zeluco."

"Well, my dearest girl, I have done; you have said enough, and more than enough;—you shall never again hear him mentioned as a lover by me."

"My dear mother," cried Laura, with tears of affection, "how can I requite you for this goodness?"

"By following the dictates of your own virtuous heart," said Madame de Seidlits; "be you happy, my dear child, and I am contented."

"I *am* happy!" exclaimed Laura, throwing her arms round her mother's neck; "how can I be but happy while I am blessed with such a parent?"

Madame de Seidlits then informed her daughter, that Zeluco had desired to have an audience of her by himself, in which he would make his proposals; which she had agreed to.

Laura begged with earnestness, that her mother would take on herself the office of acquainting Zeluco with her determined sentiments. But Madame de Seidlits urged her promise, and that Zeluco might consider himself as disrespectfully used, adding, with a smile, "you must allow me, my dear, to carry *one* point in this negociation." Laura acquiesced, and next morning mustered up all her resolution for a scene which she thought on with a good deal of uneasiness.

CHAPTER XXXIV.

Si on croit aimer sa maitresse pour l'amour d'elle on est bien trompé.

ROCHEFOUCAULT.[1]

ZELUCO called at Madame de Seidlits's the day following; after he had waited a few minutes alone, Laura entered the room pale and in evident emotion, without looking him in the face, pointed to a chair, and desired him to be seated, placing herself at the same time at a respectful distance.

"No doubt," said he, "your mother has informed you, Madam, of the sentiments with which your beauty and merit have inspired me, and with the purport of this visit."

"She has, Sir," said Laura, "and I am sensible of the honour your good opinion does me; the obligation you conferred on my mother demands, and has my warmest gratitude;—but—"

Zeluco, construing Laura's confusion in his own favour, stepped across the room, seized her shrinking hand, and exclaimed, "Talk not of gratitude for trifles, my whole fortune is now at your disposal; and you will, I hope, name an early day that the rites of the church may unite us for ever."

The security implied in this abrupt address offended the delicacy and roused the spirits of Laura; she disengaged her hand, and throwing an indignant look at Zeluco, said, "Carry your fortune, Sir, to some woman more desirous and more deserving of it; I have claim to share it with you on neither account."

Zeluco, surprised and picqued at her manner, answered, "I am sorry you seem offended, Madam; I hope there is nothing in the proposal I have made to hurt your pride."

"Without giving grounds for an accusation of pride," replied Laura, "I may be surprised at being pressed to fix a day for a purpose I never agreed to, and never shall."

"I understood, Madam, that your mother had been so obliging as to explain my sentiments and plead my cause; having her approbation, I flattered myself I should have yours, and that you would be willing to abridge unnecessary delay."

"My mother, Sir, has a warm and grateful heart, and is penetrated with a sense of your services on a late occasion; I hope I also have becoming sentiments on that head, of which the best proof I can give, is by assuring you at once, that it is not in my power to repay the partiality you express for me in the manner you desire. I hope, therefore, you will here terminate a pursuit which must be vain, and is so little worth your while."

"I was informed, Madam," said Zeluco, "that your heart was disengaged."

"You were informed rightly," said Laura.

"What then are your *objections* to me?" said he.

"Since the reasons which determine me," said Laura, "seem valid to those to whom I think myself accountable, I must be excused from an explanation to any other person."

The possibility of his honourable proposals being rejected, had never once entered into the contemplation of Zeluco; on the contrary, he was convinced that all her former reserve was assumed for no other purpose but to allure him to this point; on finding them refused in so decided a manner, his heart swelled with anger, which he could with difficulty suppress.

Laura, perceiving the struggle, added, "I do not mean to offend you, Sir; but I think it my duty, on such an occasion, to assure you, that my determination is unalterable. I sincerely wish you happiness with a more deserving woman."

"You are infinitely obliging, Madam," said he, his eyes flashing with rage.

"I must beg to be excused from attending you any longer," said she, retiring with some degree of precipitation.

She was no sooner gone, than Zeluco struck his clenched fist twice, with frantic violence, on his forehead, and rushed out of the house, before Madame de Seidlits, who meant to have waited on him, had time to reach the room.

The grateful heart of this well-disposed lady was hurt when she understood that Zeluco had left her house in so much displeasure; and even after hearing her daughter's account of the scene which had passed between them, she thought that Laura ought to have softened her refusal, and borne more calmly those signs of vexation and disappointment which Zeluco had displayed; "Which, after all, my dear," added Madame de Seidlits, "are proofs of his love."

"They might have been mistaken for marks of hatred," said Laura, "and could not have been more disagreeable to me had I known them to be really such."

When Zeluco returned to his own house, he poured out a thousand execrations against the sex in general, and the pride and folly of Laura in particular; abused his servants, and displayed many of those ridiculous extravagances, which wounded vanity and disappointment prompt men of peevish and passionate tempers to exhibit. But after having sworn, raged, stamped, bounced and blasphemed for two hours together, he recollected at last, what was very obvious from the first, that these extravagances would not bring him nearer his object; the fermentation excited by this unexpected disappointment settled in a gloomy reserve, during which he avoided society, and passed great part of his time in meditating some scheme for getting Laura into his power, that he might at once satisfy his desires and his revenge.

He once thought of causing her to be seized, forced aboard a vessel, and of passing over with her to Tunis. And he had some conversation with a bold enterprising fellow, who commanded a trading vessel, then at Naples, was well acquainted with the Barbary coast, and had lived a considerable time at Tunis; this man, Zeluco had first become acquainted with at Palermo, and had taken great pleasure in listening to his adventures. He sent for him on the present occasion, and stating a case from which the seaman could not guess at the scheme he meditated, he sounded him with respect to the practicability of some such plan.

But while his mind was agitated with this villanous project, he occasionally visited Madame de Seidlits, who, by the complacency of her behaviour to him, endeavoured, as much as lay in her power, to compensate for that of Laura, which she could not help thinking had been too harsh to a person who had conducted himself in so obliging a manner to them both. And she made no scruple of declaring to him, that she would have been better pleased that Laura had listened more favourably to his suit; which possibly might be the case at some future period. She advised him, however, not to urge her farther at present; adding, That she would acquaint him, as soon as she perceived any change in the sentiments of Laura in his favour.

This discourse of Madame de Seidlits tended to turn the mind of Zeluco from the mad and vindictive projects with which it was occupied, the difficulties and danger of which also became more apparent to himself as he cooled.

But still feeling himself in an aukward and mortified situation, and unable to suppress the over-boilings of wrath and indignation at the sight of Laura, he determined on making another tour through Italy, and perhaps through France, in the hopes that a variety of objects would dissipate his vexation from the constant contemplation of one. When he arrived at Rome, he endeavoured to extinguish a passion which gave him unremitting pain, by plunging into that current of dissipation and debauchery from which he had of late abstained. This expedient had no better effect than his rage, execrations, and blasphemy had formerly produced. Invited to every splendid assembly and magnificent entertainment, indulging every gratification of sense, he *seemed* to be passing his days in joy, and his nights in pleasure; but was in reality the victim of chagrin and of disgust. His passion appeared to gain fresh force from the efforts made to subdue it; and the lovely form of the virtuous Laura, ever present in his mind, obscured even in his vitiated imagination all the allurements of those meretricious charms by which he endeavoured to efface it.

Unable to pursue his original plan, or to support a longer absence from Laura, after pouring out a fresh torrent of execrations against her, he sent an apology to the Cardinal B——, with whom he was engaged to dine, ordered post-horses, and returned to Naples with the rapidity of a courier.

Madame de Seidlits received him with her usual politeness, but gave no hint of any change of sentiment on the part of Laura. He had the additional mortification, in a short time, to find, that though the mother seldom allowed herself to be denied when he called, yet it frequently happened that Laura did not appear during the whole of his visit.

While Zeluco's aim was seduction, all that he had expected from Signora Sporza was connivance; when he was afterwards driven to the resolution of making proposals of marriage, he considered her mediation as unnecessary, being fully convinced that his terms would be accepted as soon as made. Disappointed in both his plans, and excessively galled at Laura's not appearing when he visited her mother, he again had recourse to Signora Sporza, spoke highly of his admiration of her young friend, and ended a very pathetic harangue, by swearing, That his passion was, and had ever been, of the purest and most honourable nature.

"Of what other could it be, Signor?" said she. "Could any body suspect you wicked enough to attempt an affair of gallantry with a woman of birth, who is unmarried?"

He agreed that nothing could be more horrid than such an attempt; but that he had offered her his hand and fortune in the most respectful manner, which, to his great surprise and vexation, she had rejected.

"It is natural," replied Signora Sporza, "that you should be vexed on such an occasion; but there are so many instances of women refusing men who offer to marry them, that I see no reason for your being greatly surprised." It was with difficulty that Zeluco could conceal the anger which glowed in his breast at this observation of Signora Sporza; after a short pause, however, he said, There was reason to fear that Laura had conceived a prejudice against him; and entreated of Signora Sporza, with whom he knew that Laura was quite confidential, to advise him what was the best method of removing this prejudice, and rendering her more favourable to his wishes.

"I know of no qualities," replied Signora Sporza, "by which a man has a greater chance of making a favourable impression on the mind of Laura, than by sincerity, good temper, and benevolence; and were I to offer an advice, it would be, that you should rely on these, and these only."

Although Signora Sporza pronounced this with a serious countenance, the irony did not escape the observation of Zeluco: without seeming to take notice of it, he laid it up in his memory, and thanked her for her good counsel; adding, That he was sorry to perceive that Laura seldom appeared when he visited Madame de Seidlits; that probably this happened from her suspecting that he would renew his suit: he begged that Signora Sporza would assure her, that he intended not to tease her with solicitations; but that he earnestly wished for the happiness of being received by Madame de Seidlits on the general footing of a friend; which he could not think was the case, when any of her family thought themselves obliged to be absent when he visited her.

Signora Sporza was so pleased with the apparent reasonableness and humility of this request, that the rancour and indignation which lurked in the breast of him who made it, entirely eluded her notice. She promised to acquaint her friends with what he had said; and the following day sent Zeluco an invitation to meet them both at her house.

Madame de Seidlits joined with Signora Sporza in representing to Laura, that there was no necessity for her behaving with peculiar reserve to Zeluco after the declaration he had made; and she agreed to behave as they required, without arguing the point; although she would have been infinitely better pleased to have kept herself secluded from the company of Zeluco.

Zeluco now had frequent opportunities of being in company with the object of his wishes. He passed whole evenings with the mother and daughter, attentively studied the characters of both, and endeavoured to adapt his behaviour, and every sentiment he uttered, to what he thought would please them most; and notwithstanding the restraint to which this obliged him to submit, he had, on the whole, a sensation in their company more agreeable than in any other society however jovial or voluptuous. And had not his own character been intrinsically vicious, the continuation of the self-command he was thus obliged to assume, and the efforts he made to please, might, perhaps, have effected a favourable change in his own disposition. For nothing is more powerful in alluring the heart of man to virtue, than the society of amiable, accomplished, and virtuous women.

CHAPTER XXXV.

——Novas artes, nova pectore versat
Concilia.——— VIRG.[1]

IT was already remarked, that a portion of vanity formed part of the character of Madame de Seidlits, and sometimes obscured the lustre of her best qualities; she was apt too frequently in conversation to introduce the names of persons of very high rank, with whom her husband had been intimate in Germany, and who had occasionally visited her when she resided in that country. She paid a minute attention to the ornaments of her person, and sometimes adopted a style of dress which suited her better at an earlier period of her life. Having been distinguished for beauty in her youth, of which there were some remains, she seemed more pleased with the share which she still retained, than sensible that far the larger portion was fled. This error in calculation many women fall into who have not the good qualities of Madame de Seidlits to compensate it; for her general deportment was genteel and elegant, her temper cheerful and complacent, her disposition benevolent and generous.

In Laura Zeluco observed a depth of reflection and solidity of understanding, which he thought incompatible with her sex, and is very uncommon at her age. This was joined to an elegant simplicity of manner, and a total want of affectation, equally uncommon; ever ready to remark, and fond of displaying, the accomplishments of others, she seemed insensible of those with which she herself was so eminently adorned.

No daughter ever had a stronger sense than Laura of what she owed to her mother; the affectionate care and solicitude with which Madame de Seidlits had watched over her infancy, and the unceasing attention she bestowed on her through life, were, in the mind of this young lady, obligations never to be repaid; and independent of all sense of obligation or filial duty, she had a high esteem for her mother's personal qualities. Neither gratitude nor esteem, however, prevented her seeing the weaknesses above enumerated; her clearness of sight was to her, in this particular, a source of uneasiness: and if she suspected any other person of being equally clear-sighted, she could not help feeling a temporary dislike to that person. As often as any of the little failings above enumerated began to make their appearance, she endeavoured, with all the address in her power, to turn away the attention of the company, and with theirs, she would have been glad had it been in her power to have turned away her own.

But it was her happiness to reflect upon, and her delight to display, every graceful and good quality that belonged to her mother. Easy even to indifference about the common forms of respect when they regarded herself, she had a jealous sensibility of the smallest neglect or want of attention to her mother.

Zeluco remarked this peculiarity in the character of Laura; he saw that the compliments he sometimes ventured to pay to herself were always heard with indifference, and sometimes with disgust, while every just and well-founded compliment paid to her mother seemed to give pleasure to the daughter; declining, therefore, the beaten road of insinuation, he tried to gain access to the heart of the one by the praises he bestowed on the other.

It behoved him, however, to be on his guard, in what manner, and on what occasion, he risked his compliments; it was necessary they should seem at once just and *à-propos*. He once mistook his aim so far as to compliment Madame de Seidlits for a quality she certainly did *not* possess, and was instantly warned of his error by such a glance of indignation from the expressive eye of Laura, as prevented his ever repeating it.

But as often as, on proper occasions, he remarked with justice and delicacy on the good and amiable qualities that *really* belonged to Madame de Seidlits, which he frequently did with equal penetration and address, it was evident that Laura listened with looks of more complacency than she ever displayed when he spoke on any other subject. He acquired by study and use such a masterly manner of dwelling on this favourite theme, that Laura's aversion began to diminish; and she could not help feeling sentiments of approbation and good-will to the person who furnished her with so sweet a source of enjoyment.

This alteration in the sentiments of Laura was observed with more pleasure by her mother than by Signora Sporza, whose esteem for Laura and her dislike of Zeluco had increased with her acquaintance with both. Her dislike of the latter, however, did not proceed entirely from her own penetration; she had received such an account of him from a female correspondent at Palermo, as confirmed and greatly augmented her original bad opinion, and made her averse to the idea of his ever becoming the husband of her young friend, notwithstanding the temptation in point of fortune for such an alliance. But being convinced that her mentioning her sentiments on this subject to the mother or daughter, would prevent their ever again having any connexion with Zeluco, she therefore was silent; at the same time determined, if it should be necessary, to speak in sufficient time.

But although Signora Sporza concealed from Madame de Seidlits and her daughter the opinion she had of Zeluco, her real sentiments were detected by the jealous and penetrating eyes of the man himself.

There is perhaps no sentiment which it is so difficult to conceal from the person who is the object of it, as violent hatred: a moderate adept in the art of dissimulation may impose on those for whom he feels no esteem, or whom he even holds in contempt; and, if he has an interest in it, may persuade them that he has a high respect or even veneration for them: and this, in some measure, accounts for so many people of the highest rank being ignorant of the true rate at which they are estimated. For the indications of contempt are easily restrained, and those of admiration as easily assumed; but it requires the powers of a finished hypocrite to hide hatred or aversion. Such strong feelings it is difficult to control, and prevent their discovering themselves by some involuntary appearance in the countenance or manner. It is not surprising, therefore, that Zeluco became fully convinced that Signora Sporza had a very unfavourable opinion of him, and was averse to his ever succeeding with Laura. The rancour which gathered in his breast on this discovery, was of the most deadly kind; but he endeavoured to hide it till he should find a proper occasion of giving it vent; and being, notwithstanding her sex, a better dissembler than Signora Sporza, he for a long time succeeded.

CHAPTER XXXVI.

Full oft by holy feet our ground was trod,
Of clerks good plenty here you mote espy.
A little, round, fat, oily man of God,
Was one I chiefly mark'd among the fry:
He had a roguish twinkle in his eye,
And shone all glittering with ungodly dew,
If a tight damsel chaunc'd to trippen by;
Which when observ'd, he shrunk into his mew,
And straight would recollect his piety anew.

THOMSON.[1]

ALTHOUGH Zeluco perceived with pleasure the change which had taken place in Laura's behaviour to him, he did not chuse to rely entirely on his own address; but as he now believed he had no aid to expect from Signora Sporza, he resolved to seek other allies, and even attempted to draw them from the church itself, a quarter in which one would think he had little interest.

Father Mulo was an ecclesiastic, more remarkable for the rigidity of his manners and opinions, than the depth of his intellects.—Father Pedro was a monk of a different order, indulgent in his disposition, agreeable in conversation, naturally shrewd, and what piety he possessed was far from being of a morose kind. He had adopted the ecclesiastical profession from necessity not inclination, and he endeavoured to assume an air of gravity and self-denial, which was equally discordant with the turn of his mind, the rotundity of his person, and to his rosy complexion, all of which announced him *Epicuri de grege porcus*.[2] The warmth of Father Pedro's constitution had formerly drawn him into some scrapes from which it required all his address to disengage himself, and rendered him exceedingly cautious ever after. He had behaved with peculiar circumspection ever since he had been at Naples; and being a man of more understanding than most of his brethren, he was chosen by Signora Sporza as her father confessor, and through her recommendation he now acted in the same capacity to her two friends, in preference to Father Mulo, who was their relation. In a short time, Father Pedro, whose manners were gentle and insinuating, gained the entire confidence of Madame de Seidlits, and was rather well thought of by her daughter. Father Mulo was by no means pleased with the choice his relations had made, yet as they behaved to him in all other respects with much deference and attention, no open breach took place between the Father and any of them on this account.

Zeluco having informed himself of the character of those two monks, and knowing their connection with Madame de Seidlits, he thought it might be of importance to gain them to his interest.

He began with Father Pedro, whose favour he endeavoured to acquire by all the address and powers of insinuation he was master of, setting out by chusing him for his ghostly Father, and to the gentle penance which he enjoined for the venial faults which Zeluco thought it expedient to confess; he frequently imposed upon himself a mulct in money, which he delivered into the hands of the Father, to be applied to whatever pious use he thought proper.

This behaviour on the part of Zeluco gave great satisfaction to Father Pedro, who not only received his visits with pleasure at his convent, but more frequently waited upon him at Zeluco's house.

After a pretty free repast, during which the Father displayed much good humour and jovialness, Zeluco seizing what he thought a lucky moment, informed him of his passion for Laura.

This ghostly Father assuredly had never imagined, that the sudden veneration which Zeluco professed for him, proceeded either from an admiration of his character or countenance; on the contrary, he had all along suspected its real source. He was not a man of very great delicacy of sentiment, and certainly was not troubled with prejudices of a superstitious nature; yet there were occasions on which he thought it expedient to affect as much terror for the horns of Satan as his brother Mulo was really impressed with. Zeluco had no sooner mentioned his passion for Laura, than the Monk started as if a culverin[3] had unexpectedly exploded at his ear, displaying as much astonishment and horror in his countenance, as if the devil had appeared before him in full uniform, with his cloven feet, longest tail, and largest pair of horns.

"What is the matter with you, my good Father?" said Zeluco; "do you perceive any thing unnatural or extraordinary in my desiring to be united in holy wedlock with a virtuous and beautiful young lady?"

The Father, although he had long perceived Zeluco's fondness for Laura, had never heard of his proposing marriage to her, nor had he any idea that such was his intention. When Zeluco mentioned his love, the Father took it for granted that he was about to request his aid on a different system; but finding that he really intended marriage, the Monk began to imagine that he had played off his pantomime a little inadvertently, and was at a loss how to give a plausible account of his own affected surprise; he endeavoured to colour it, however, as well as he could, by saying, That as his business with Zeluco was of a spiritual nature, he could not help being very much surprised at the mention of a thing so different from what he was accustomed to have any concern in.

"I do humbly hope, my worthy Father," said Zeluco, "that you will think you have a natural concern in this, as I can assure you my happiness not only in this world, but very possibly in the next, depends on my being able to prevail on this young lady to accept of my hand; for my heart is so fixed upon her, that I do not know what desperate measures I may be drove to if she continues obstinately to refuse me."

The Monk seemed to soften by degrees; Zeluco giving him a full account of the proposals he had made, the settlements he had offered, Laura's unaccountable obstinacy; and concluded by informing the Monk, that he had laid apart a sum of money which, in case of success in his honourable proposals, he would request the Father to accept, and appropriate to whatever pious or useful purpose he thought most expedient; but on this express condition, that it should remain an everlasting secret to all the rest of the world; "because," added he, "an ostentatious display of such donations destroys, in my opinion, any little merit there may be in making them."

The Father agreed to this last condition with some seeming difficulty, praised Zeluco's modesty and charitable disposition; and finally assured him of all the assistance in his power. "In the first place," said he, "I will use my influence out of friendship to you: secondly, From the regard I have for Madame de Seidlits and the young lady herself, who so perversely opposes her own happiness; and lastly, and above all, I will use my interest in your favour for the sake of religion and the poor, as both must be benefited by the success of your honourable views."

This Ecclesiastic, partly from probity and partly from prudence, would have rejected a bribe to assist in any project which he thought wicked or unlawful, but he had no scruple in allowing himself to be well rewarded for doing what he approved, and would, of himself, have been happy to promote without any bribe at all.

Indeed he had no notion that Madame de Seidlits, or her daughter, had a serious intention of standing out against a match which he thought so advantageous for both. He imputed their refusal to affectation, caprice, or a desire of indulging a few feminine airs; and he had a meaner opinion of Zeluco's understanding, on account of his being in this manner the dupe of a little female vanity.

And so impatient was he, that the *poor* should reap the fruits of Zeluco's promised liberality, that the first time he found Madame de Seidlits alone, he expressed much surprise that she had never told him of Zeluco's addresses to her daughter.

Madame de Seidlits replied, That after Laura had given her negative, she thought it best not to mention a subject which might be disagreeable to Signor Zeluco, and was so foreign to those in which the Father was usually employed.

"It is true," replied Pedro, "I am principally interested in your spiritual concerns, but by no means indifferent to the temporal welfare of your family."

Madame de Seidlits then informed him of all the particulars.

"I have such an opinion of Signora Laura's filial duty and affection," said Pedro, "that I am convinced, if you were to press this matter earnestly upon her, she would consent."

"It is not impossible but she might," said Madame de Seidlits, "for which reason I shall be particularly careful not to press her."

Father Pedro expressed astonishment at her taking so little concern in an affair of such importance to her daughter's happiness.

"It is because it is of so much importance to her happiness that I leave it to her own judgment," said Madame de Seidlits; "Laura is endowed with prudence and good sense, and she is certainly the best judge of her own feelings; if Zeluco ever becomes more agreeable to her, importunity would be superfluous; and if he does not, it would be cruel: besides, I have given her my word never to urge her on the subject, and I will assuredly adhere to my engagement."

CHAPTER XXXVII.

For he a rope of sand could twist,
As tough as learned Sorbonist,
And weave fine cobwebs, fit for scull
That's empty when the moon is full;
Such as take lodgings in a head
That's to be let unfurnished. BUTLER.[1]

THE Father was prevented from reply, by Laura's entering the room with Father Mulo. Before any account is given of the conversation which this venerable man introduced, it is necessary to throw a retrospective glance on incidents which occurred long before; from this an idea may be formed of the characters of Colonel Seidlits, and others, connected with our purpose.

Without recapitulating the circumstances by which the Colonel and his lady became first acquainted, it is sufficient to observe, that their marriage took place before the Father knew any thing of the matter; but he expressed infinite concern, and probably felt some, on hearing that his relation was the wife of a heretic. When she went with her husband to Germany, the zealous Father continued from time to time to remind her in his letters, of the dangers she incurred in a land of heresy, and furnished her with the best arguments he had at his disposal, to enable her to adhere to the religion in which she was bred, stimulating her at the same time to attempt the conversion of her husband, by which she would acquire immortal glory, effect her husband's salvation, and secure to herself the comfort of his company both in this life and that which is to come.

The Father being infinitely delighted with both the style and arguments of those letters, he could not deny himself the gratification of shewing copies of them to several of his acquaintance, and as the intention of shewing them could not be mistaken, his acquaintance in general were good-natured enough to praise them to the Monk's contentment; one old maiden aunt of Madame de Seidlits's, however, whose zeal for religion and hatred to heretics increased with her years, seemed to approve of the correspondence less than any other person to whose inspection he had submitted it. When Father Mulo hinted this to her, she told him, that she was so provoked at the odious heretic who had seduced her niece, that it was not in her power to wish in earnest for his conversion, for she could not bear even to hear his name mentioned, and she was certain she should faint at the sight of him whenever she met him, were it even in Heaven.

But the Father had too much ardour for making converts, to follow the suggestions of this virgin; he therefore continued to transmit such morsels of eloquence as, in his opinion, could not fail to operate the conversion of Colonel Seidlits.

But the reverend Father's zeal being far more conspicuous than his arguments were convincing, Madame de Seidlits never thought proper to communicate them to her husband; while he, on his part, left his lady, without molestation, in the full enjoyment of her religious opinions, and at perfect liberty to worship God in the manner which her conscience approved. This he had promised when he married her, and he would have thought it inconsistent with honour to have tried to bring her over to his own persuasion, even although he had been certain of succeeding. The Colonel has been blamed for this by many zealous Protestants; we do not mean to approve or censure his conduct in this particular, but only mention the fact, leaving it to better judges to decide whether he was blame-worthy or not.

Madame de Seidlits herself, who was pleased with all her husband's behaviour to her, was peculiarly delighted with what she called his delicacy in this point; and when Father Mulo insisted peremptorily, in one of his letters, on knowing whether she had ever made any attempt to convert her husband, or had shewn him the forcible reasoning contained in his letters to her; she was obliged to acknowledge that she had done neither, and gave for her reason, that her husband having left her at liberty on the subject of religion, she thought it would be a bad requital in her to tease him.

Father Mulo, in answer, endeavoured to demonstrate the weakness of that argument. It is not necessary to transcribe the whole of the Father's letter, the following paragraph will, in all probability, be thought sufficient:

"It was natural enough in you, my dear Madam, to apprehend that your own arguments would be too feeble to convince your husband; but it is surprising that you do not perceive, that those I provided you with are of a very different nature; indeed, they are such as seldom fail to persuade even the weakest minds. From this you may judge what impression they would make on a person of such good sense as you describe your husband to be.

"You say, that it would be improper in you to tease *him*, because he never attempts to disturb *you*, nor allows any other person to trouble you on the subject of religion: but you do not distinguish, my dear Madam, the great difference between the two cases. For your husband, indeed, to make any attempt, or to allow any to be made by others, for the purpose of seducing you from your religion to his, would not only be improper, but also highly criminal, and for this very sufficient reason, *because it is criminal to draw any person whatever from truth to falsehood*. But for you to labour, without ceasing, to prevail on your deluded husband, to abjure his own faith and adopt yours, is in the highest degree meritorious; *because it is highly meritorious to lead any person whatever, and far more a beloved husband, from falsehood to truth, or from darkness to light*.

"After having cleared up this point, I have only just to hint, that instead of reasoning upon what I inform you it is your duty to do; your safest course, my dearest cousin, will, for the future, be to perform it implicitly, for reasoning is by no means what you shine in: and although you are generally allowed to be endowed with very good common sense, and sufficient understanding to conduct common affairs; take my word for it, your immortal soul is of too much consequence to be entrusted in your own hands."

This remonstrance had not the effect which, in Father Mulo's opinion, such forcible reasoning and such rational requests ought to have produced. What contributed, perhaps, to render Madame de Seidlits the more unwilling to touch on such subjects, was an incident of which she was informed about the very time when the Monk was urging her so earnestly.

CHAPTER XXXVIII.

No sooner could a hint appear,
But up he started to picqueer,
And made the stoutest yield to mercy,
When he engaged in controversy,
Not by the force of carnal reason,
But indefatigable teazing. BUTLER.[1]

A YOUNG Protestant clergyman, a distant relation of Colonel de Seidlits, came about this time to Berlin. He had applied himself with ardour to the study of controversy. He was distinguished by his wonderful faculty of creating disputes where they were least expected, and by his invincible courage in maintaining them when begun: he often asserted, and with truth, that he had never yielded an argument in his life. He was greatly admired for the flow of his pulpit eloquence, and the force of his reasoning, by all who were previously of his own opinion. The longer this happy Ecclesiastic lived, he seemed to be the more confirmed in the favourable impression which, from his boyish years, he entertained of his own talents, and in his contempt for those of others; and became at length so powerful in self-conceit, that he would, without hesitation, have engaged a whole conclave of his adversaries, being convinced not only that he could overturn all their arguments, but that the prejudices of education, the considerations of interest, and the allurements of ambition, must all yield to the irresistible strength of his demonstration.

This gentleman was sometimes invited to dinner by Colonel Seidlits, and was made welcome by his lady as often as she saw company in the evening.

In return for those civilities, he thought it incumbent on him to point out to her the absurdities of the Popish religion, as preparatory to her conversion to Calvinism. With this view he was apt to introduce questions of a controversial nature, and at one time threw out a sneer at the doctrine of transubstantiation[2] in the presence of Madame de Seidlits.

This was repeated by one of the company to Colonel Seidlits, who, the next time he saw the clergyman alone, said to him mildly, "I am not certain, my good Sir, whether I ever informed you that my wife is of the Roman Catholic church."

"You never informed me," replied the other; "but it is long since I knew that Madame de Seidlits had that misfortune."

"You may, if you please, leave her misfortunes to those who are more naturally concerned in them," said the Colonel; "but since you knew of what I was in hopes you had been ignorant, I own I am surprised that you could speak of one of the articles of her faith in the manner you did, in her presence."

"I recollect what you allude to," said the clergyman; "but really the article in question is so absurd and incomprehensible, that it is impossible to mention it otherwise than in terms of derision."

"Pray," replied the Colonel, "do you believe in all the doctrines to be found in the public creeds and formularies of our own church."

"That I do," replied the Divine; "and would die at the stake, were it necessary, avowing them."

"Then I hope you have a better reason for thinking transubstantiation absurd, than merely its being incomprehensible?"

"There is no article in any of the Protestant creeds *so* incomprehensible as that you mention," replied the Divine.

"I did not know there were degrees in incomprehensibility," said the Colonel; "if there is any proposition which I am quite unable to comprehend, it will be difficult to state another which I can comprehend less."

"I will undertake to make you comprehend distinctly every article of the creeds you allude to," said the Divine, with an undaunted air.

"Rather than impose such a task upon you," said the Colonel, "allow me to continue to believe them without fully comprehending them."

"Well, Colonel, you will do as you please, but surely it would afford you great satisfaction if your lady could be prevailed on to embrace the same religion that you profess."

"No; I cannot say it would," replied the Colonel, coldly.

"Good God! that seems very unaccountable; will you be so good as to tell me your reason," said the other.

"Because the thing cannot happen, Sir, without either my changing my religion, and I intend no such thing, or by my endeavouring to persuade my wife to change her's, which I have solemnly promised never to do: besides, I am certain that Madame de Seidlits is an amiable woman, and a most excellent wife, with the religion she professes; and there is no knowing what alteration a change of sentiments might make."

"What alteration, but a favourable one, can accrue from renouncing one of the worst religions in the world for the best?"

"As to which is the worst, and which the best," said Seidlits, "the world is much divided."

"The Protestant religion is gaining ground every day," said the Clergyman; "and there is reason to hope, that in a short time there will be more Protestants in the world than Papists."

"That to be sure is very comfortable news," said the Colonel; "but it can have no weight in the present argument; because, ever since the beginning of the world, there has been greater numbers devoted to false religions than to the true; and even now, if the question were to be decided by a plurality of voices, the religion of Mahomet might perhaps carry the palm both from the Protestant and Roman Catholic."

"But you yourself are a Protestant;—*you at least* prefer the Protestant form of worship to all others," said the Clergyman.

"I certainly prefer no other form of worship to the Protestant," replied the Colonel.

"Then I would be glad to know," said the Clergyman, with a triumphant air, "*wherefore* you prefer no other?—the same arguments which convinced you might convince your lady?"

"No," said the Colonel, "that they could not."

"Why so?" said the Clergyman. "By what powerful arguments were you persuaded to adhere to the Protestant religion?"

"By this powerful argument," replied the Colonel, "that I was born in Berlin, and bred at Koningsberg."[3]

"That answer smells of infidelity, Colonel, and implies that you consider religion merely as an affair of geography, and of little or no importance in the world," said the Clergyman.

"It implies more than I intended then," replied Seidlits, "for although I do think that nine hundred and ninety-nine in a thousand of mankind are determined in the religion they profess by the place of their birth and education; I do not infer from thence, that religion is of no importance: on the contrary, I am convinced that those who cherish religion, perform the relative duties of life in the most conscientious manner."

"So you put all religions on the same footing?" said the Clergyman.

"By no means," answered Seidlits; "I know indeed of no religion which does not inculcate morality; but as I have not had any opportunity of observing the influence of other religions on men's conduct, I speak of the Christian religion only;—which, if I am not mistaken, contributes greatly to render mankind better and happier even in this life."

"You speak of the reformed religion, I presume," said the Clergyman; "for as to the absurd tenets of the Roman Catholic creed, it is impossible for you, or any man of sense, to respect them."

"I speak not of the creeds which, since the Christian æra, have been composed by the fathers of either church," replied the Colonel; "I have not leisure, perhaps not understanding, sufficient to weigh or compare them with due precision. My observation regards only the precepts given, and the example set, by the Author of Christianity himself, and in which both churches are agreed. The good effect which a due impression of those divine precepts has upon the mind seems, I confess, very evident to me, whether the individuals on which it operates are Roman Catholics or Protestants."

"That you, by accident, have met with Roman Catholics who were reckoned good moral men, I shall not dispute," said the Minister; "but that any part of their goodness proceeded from their religion, is what I can never admit."

"Why not?" said the Colonel; "the moral precepts of both religions are the same."

"The spirit of those who profess them are very different, however," resumed the Minister. "When did the Protestants display the same spirit of persecution that the Papists have so often done?"

"Let us remember," replied Seidlits, "that the church of Rome was established in power when the first reformers began to attack its doctrines; that an attack on its doctrines endangered the power and riches of its clergy. That it is natural for mankind, when they have long been in possession of power and wealth, to be exceedingly unwilling to relinquish them; and the clergy do not form an exception to this general rule: they, as well as others, are apt to be extremely angry with those who attempt to dispossess them; besides, let us recollect, that all established governments think they have a right to use severities against revolting subjects, whatever good grounds those subjects have had for revolting,—and——"

"But remember," interrupted the Clergyman, "the perfidy and cruelty displayed by the Roman Catholics in the massacre of St. Bartholomy—think of the shocking reign of the gloomy bigotted Philip, and the enormities of his unrelenting general the Duke of Alva."[4]

"I do think of them with horror," said the Colonel, "and I have no mind to palliate such dreadful instances of human wickedness and delusion. I only meant to hint, that those ought not to have credit for not displaying the same spirit who were not in possession of the same power. I am willing to believe, however, that with equal power they would not have committed equal excesses. Though I am sorry to say, that instances might be mentioned, which create a suspicion that more power would have perverted the spirit of some of the most distinguished reformers, and might possibly have the same effect on their successors. It is therefore fortunate for the clergy of Holland, Switzerland, some parts of Germany, and other countries in Europe, that there is little danger of their degenerating from that cause."

"I doubt much, whether that is a fortunate circumstance," replied the Clergyman; "for although riches, power, and pomp have a mischievous effect when prostituted to the unworthy, yet they are suitable to the character we bear of the ambassadors from Heaven, and might give more weight to our admonitions."

"Power and wealth are the great corrupters of the human heart," said Seidlits, "and might spread their baneful influence even to the *ambassadors* themselves; in which event, in lieu of that spirit of toleration, benevolence, and humility, which distinguishes them at present; a great accession of power and riches might gradually inspire them with pride and ambition, and render them at last little better than so many cardinals and popes."

"Never, never," cried the Clergyman; "the spirit of Protestantism is too averse to any such alteration."

"The spirit of human nature, however, has a mighty tendency that way," said Seidlits.

"Learning and deep reflexion correct the depraved tendencies of our nature," resumed the Ecclesiastic, "and leave the mind equally free from the degrading absurdities of superstition, and the impious sophistry of scepticism."

"That is a state of mind devoutly to be wished," said Seidlits.

"Is it not?" cried the Parson with exultation; "you yourself allow that superstition is degrading to the mind of man," continued he.

"I do," replied the Colonel; "and the more readily, as I never said it was otherwise."

"Well, I will now prove to you, that scepticism is as uncomfortable as the other is degrading: I hope you have no pressing business at present," continued the Parson, "because, to put the subject in a clear light, it will be necessary to divide it into three heads, and then subdivide each of these into four principal branches.

"To begin then with the first and most important of those three heads.

"Any degree of doubt or uncertainty, particularly on matters of high importance, has been considered in all ages as irksome, and——"

"I ask pardon for interrupting you," said the Colonel; "it is only to know whether you mean to prove, that to a well-disposed mind a state of certainty is more agreeable than any degree of doubt on religious subjects?"

"That is precisely what I am going to demonstrate," resumed the Parson.

"I will save you the trouble," said Seidlits, "for there is nothing of which I am more firmly convinced."

"Is it not astonishing then," said the other, "that so many should be so foolish as to persevere in a state of uncomfortable doubt?"

"Very astonishing indeed," said the Colonel; "especially as it is in every body's power to believe whatever will afford them most comfort."

"I perceive," said the Parson, "you have perused my treatise upon the faculty of believing."

The Colonel nodded.

"I there clearly prove, that the Roman Catholics have too much faith, and some sects of the Protestants too little; and then carefully point out the golden medium which mankind ought to adhere to."

"It is very fortunate for mankind," said the Colonel, "that *you* know it."

"It is so," resumed the Parson; "for of this happy medium it may be said, more emphatically than of any thing else, *nescire malum est*."[5]

"If I am not mistaken," said Seidlits, "an answer to your work was published by a certain French Abbé, who, according to the custom of his countrymen, seemed very fond of jesting."

"That was a most abominable, and a most provoking performance," cried the Parson with great vehemence; "but jests are no arguments, Colonel."

"No; nor arguments are no jests," said Seidlits; "yet this provoking Abbé endeavoured to make a jest of all your arguments."

"There will be no jesting in Hell, however," said the Parson, with a vengeful aspect.

"True," said the Colonel; "when you have once got him there, the laugh will be on your side——"

"But pray, Colonel," resumed the Minister, "do you imagine that your lady has ever read my book?"

"I should rather think not," said the Colonel.

"What a pity!" exclaimed the other; "it would go a great way to cure her of many prejudices."

"The remedy would be rather violent," said the Colonel.

"Perhaps it might seem a little so at first," rejoined the Clergyman; "but were I to converse with her on those subjects, I should begin in gentle terms."

"That would be very proper," said the Colonel.

"The sooner I begin then the better," said the Parson; "after I have talked with her for a few hours, she will be able to decide between the two religions on rational principles."

"I have already decided, on what I think rational principles," said the Colonel, "not to disturb her."

"You have decided very erroneously," resumed this persevering Ecclesiastic.

"Let me intreat you, my good Sir," interrupted the Colonel, "not to interfere in my domestic concerns, but to mind your own business."

"I beg leave to inform you, Colonel Seidlits," said the Clergyman, with a dignified air, "that I consider the propagation of gospel truths, and the unmasking of imposture, particularly those of the church of Rome, as *my* business; and I will embrace every opportunity of doing both, in spite of the united opposition of men and devils."

The Colonel having looked very earnestly for some time at this violent Reformer, at length said, "I beg your excuse, Sir, for having engrossed so much of your valuable time; it is a mistake I shall never again fall into." So saying, he pulled off his hat, made a low bow, and walked away. The moment he entered his own house, he gave orders that his relation should be no more admitted.

CHAPTER XXXIX.

Multa putans, sortemque animo miseratus iniquam.

VIRG. Æn. l. vi.[1]

THE attention which Colonel Seidlits displayed in preventing his lady from being disquieted in her religious opinions, and the delicacy of his behaviour on every occasion, was felt by her with affectionate gratitude. She was, however, by no means so easy in the contemplation of her husband's being a protestant, as he was in that of her remaining a Roman catholic; and although the arguments of Father Mulo did not prevail on her to attempt his conversion, yet few things could have afforded her greater satisfaction than to have seen her husband adopt from conviction, what she considered as the only true religion. But with what a face could she speak to him on a subject which he never mentioned to her, and which he permitted no person whatever to disturb her about? Any attempt on her part to alter his sentiments, implied that she considered herself as wiser than he; whereas she only considered herself as more fortunate, in having been educated in a better religion.

These and similar considerations, which occupied the mind of this worthy lady, were sometimes on the point of being sacrificed to the anguish she felt as often as the idea of her husband's continuing in heresy, and all the dreadful consequences occurred to her terrified imagination; for the natural clearness of her understanding and the serenity of her disposition, were clouded and disturbed by the terrific aspect and unrelenting severity of some of the doctrines in which she had been instructed.

This anxiety of mind on her husband's account always increased in proportion to the hazards he was exposed to in the exercise of his profession, and became particularly severe in the course of a tedious illness, into which he fell in consequence of a blow by the butt-end of a musket, which he received on his breast at the battle of Hochkirchen.[2] This contusion produced a spitting of blood, and was supposed to lay the foundation of that illness of which he afterwards died.

Soon after the battle, the Colonel was carried to a place of safety. And Madame de Seidlits, having obtained a pass from Marshal Daun, hastened to the village in which her husband was; where she attended him during his long illness with equal patience and tenderness. At one time he was, by the mistake of the physician, thought in immediate danger. The anxiety which had so long lurked within the breast of Madame de Seidlits now became too violent for her to conceal; the very acute sorrow which she endured from the thought of losing a husband she highly esteemed and dearly loved, was absorbed in the keener anguish arising from the awful idea of the danger which threatened his immortal soul; and this impressed her with the more dread that it seemed to give him none.

Her terrors on this subject were augmented by a letter which she received from her indefatigable relation Father Mulo; who, having heard of the Colonel's illness, most charitably intreated her to exert herself now or never; as there was no possibility of salvation for her husband, unless he relinquished heresy, embraced the catholic faith, confessed his sins, and obtained absolution. One argument, he thought, proved the good policy of this measure beyond the power of reply; it was this:—"The protestants themselves," said this ingenious Priest, "admit, that well-meaning and virtuous persons may be saved, notwithstanding their dying in the Roman catholic persuasion; whereas we assert, that no heretic, however virtuous in other respects he may be, can enter into the kingdom of heaven: it is apparent, therefore, that your husband runs no risk in following your advice, but the greatest by neglecting it."

The agitation and confusion of Madame de Seidlits's mind prevented her from seeing this kind of reasoning in the same light which her good sense would have presented it in a calmer moment.

One day, therefore, when her apprehensions on the Colonel's account were at the height, after much circumlocution, with infinite delicacy, but in the most pathetic terms, she communicated her fears to him, and concluded by urging him to forsake his own religion, and embrace that of the church of Rome.

Having heard her with the utmost attention and some degree of surprise, the Colonel said, "I fear, my dear, you are too much alarmed on my account; but I assure you I have passed an uncommonly good night, and I feel myself better than I was yesterday." "I am most exceedingly glad to hear it," said Madame de Seidlits; "but let this be no reason for preventing a measure of infinite importance, which cannot be taken too soon, but may be delayed till it is too late."

"My dearest Theresa," said the Colonel, taking hold of her hand,

"I view your present solicitude and importunity in the true light; I consider them as fresh proofs of that noble friendship and affection which has been the happiness of my life, and of which I ever had a grateful conviction; but I must assure you, that although I have never urged you, nor permitted any other person to urge you, on the same subject on which you now press me, it is not because I have less concern for your soul than you have for mine; nor is it from a want of partiality for the religion which I myself profess."—"From what motive then has your forbearance proceeded," said Madame de Seidlits. "From a conviction," replied he, "that you are as certain of salvation in your religion as I can be in mine." "You must believe, then," said Madame de Seidlits with quickness, "that both religions are equally good." "No, my love, that does not follow; for although I think there is much good in both, still I think my own is the preferable; yet," continued he gaily, "as you possess so much more of yours than I do of mine, I imagine the superiority in quantity will make up for the deficiency in quality, and render you as secure as you can wish."

"My dear Colonel," replied Madame de Seidlits, "is this a subject, or is this a proper occasion for jesting?"

"I beg pardon, my dear," said the Colonel, "I will be very serious: in one great and essential point we have the happiness to be of one opinion; both religions agree, that it is our duty to live a life of integrity, and do all the good we can to our fellow-creatures."

"For which reason," interrupted Madame de Seidlits, "I am so anxious to do the greatest good possible to him who is infinitely the dearest to me of all my fellow-creatures."

"None of them can be more grateful," replied the Colonel, "than I am for those good intentions; and you cannot doubt of my being willing to render you the same service; yet if you were to continue to press this upon me, and I the same upon you, the unavoidable effect of our eagerness to make each other eternally happy, would be the making each other eternally miserable; for what can be worse in this world or the next, than everlasting disputes between man and wife? Let us therefore avoid all disputable points," continued he, "and endeavour to promote our own happiness, and of our neighbours, by every means in our power. The most probable reason I can conceive for the unequal distribution of the comforts of life, is to afford mankind opportunities for the exercises of benevolence, gratitude, and other virtues, which I am inclined to believe is the most likely way of acquiring the favour of the Deity. We certainly have it frequently in our power to add to the happiness or misery of our fellow-creatures, to God Almighty we can neither do good nor harm; and therefore I cannot help thinking, that the conduct of our lives is of infinitely more importance, than our religious opinions, or the forms of our worship.—It has been already settled between us," continued he, "that you shall educate our daughters in your way of thinking, as our sons shall be educated in mine;[3] our mutual endeavour will be, to render them virtuous women and honest men, which implies benevolence and liberality of sentiment; if we succeed, I have no doubt, notwithstanding our having taken different roads, but we shall all meet in heaven."

"God Almighty, in his infinite mercy, grant it may be so," cried Madame de Seidlits, in a transport of affection; "for I am certain heaven will be no heaven to me without those I so dearly love." Then recollecting herself a little, she took occasion from what her husband had just said, to urge the last argument of her confessor:—"Since you have no doubt," said she, "of our meeting in heaven, although I retain my religion, and since those of our church declare there is no admission for those who persist in heresy, why will you not, my dearest husband, take the safer course, and embrace the catholic faith?"

Here the Colonel, smiling through the tears which his lady's endearments had previously forced into his eyes, replied, "I confess, my beloved Theresa, that this last argument is so unworthy of your excellent understanding, that I am convinced you have had it suggested by some one of far inferior sense and candour to yourself. Consider that, in my conscience,—for whether I am right or wrong is out of the question;—but in my conscience I think the protestant religion preferable to that which you profess; yet you advise me, as the safest course I can take, to embrace yours; that is to say, to commit a piece of gross hypocrisy, and with a view to what? to impose on men? No; there might be sense in that; for men are imposed upon daily by hypocrites: but this piece of hypocrisy to which you advise me, is with a view to impose upon God, and to get smuggled into heaven as a Roman catholic, while in my heart and conscience I remain a Protestant."

Madame de Seidlits seemed embarrassed; after a short silence she said, "I fear my anxiety makes me absurd; forgive me, my dear," continued she, "for teasing you in this foolish manner."

"I shall think myself for ever obliged by the affectionate and generous anxiety of my Theresa," said Seidlits.

"How could I allow myself to think for a moment that such integrity, such manly generosity of mind, as you have always displayed," said she, taking her husband by the hand, "and such strict adherence to the dictates of conscience, can be rejected? These also were the virtues of the man whose memory you so much revere, your noble friend and patron the Marshal."

"Ah! my Theresa," cried Seidlits, "can the long course of honour and integrity pursued by the gallant Keith[4] be forgotten and rejected of Heaven, because he was born in a protestant country, or perhaps entertained erroneous speculative opinions? I well knew the uprightness of his mind, have seen many instances of his humanity and benevolence even to his enemies, and have myself received proofs of his generous friendship; it will be my latest boast to have been a witness to those noble exertions in which he finished a life of honour in the field of Hochkirchen, where the gallant Prince Francis of Brunswic,[5] a family so fertile in heroes, also fell. I thank Heaven I had the honour of assisting the Marshal's intrepid endeavours in rallying and inspiriting our disordered troops, in following him again and again to the charge; by which means the elated enemy was checked, our troops protected, the great monarch he served, and who honoured him with his friendship, enabled to retreat in such order as to pitch his camp within a few miles of the field from which he retired. This great officer himself refusing, although dangerously wounded, to quit the field, continued his exertions, till he received a second wound, which proved instantly mortal. And shall a parcel of ignorant monks, a gang of useless drones, deal damnation around on all who have not a ready faith in their legends and their—? But I ask your pardon, my dear," said Seidlits, checking himself; "I did not mean to say any thing disobliging; but I heartily wish you would observe the dictates of your own understanding more, and listen to the suggestions of others less; the virtuous conduct which you have hitherto pursued is your best security for happiness here and hereafter; permit me to endeavour to secure mine in the manner most agreeable to my conscience, and of course the most likely to be successful."

"Forgive me, my dearest friend," said Madame de Seidlits, "for this once, and I shall assure you, all the monks on earth shall never prevail on me to give you a single hint of this nature again. I am not a little ashamed of what I was foolishly induced to say;—Heaven be praised that you seem so much better than you were last night."

CHAPTER XL.

Shall man be left abandon'd in the dust,
When Fate relenting, lets the flow'r revive?
Shall Nature's voice, to man alone unjust,
Bid him, tho' doom'd to perish, hope to live?
Is it for this fair Virtue oft must strive
With disappointment, penury, and pain?
No; Heav'n's immortal spring shall yet revive;
And man's majestic beauty bloom again.

BEATTIE.[1]

THIS was the first and last dispute on religion that ever passed between Colonel Seidlits and his lady, although both continued attached to *that* in which they had been bred; yet, from this time, Madame de Seidlits seemed to adopt, in many particulars, the liberal sentiments of her husband. They lived together in the happiest union for several years after the general peace.

Laura, their only child, was educated, according to the agreement between them, in her mother's religion.

It was already remarked, that the Colonel never fully recovered his health after the contusion in his breast; on the slightest cold, and sometimes without any known cause, he was liable to be seized with fits of oppressive and difficult breathing; a severe attack of this nature obliged him, by the king's express order, to quit the field in the middle of that short war between Prussia and the emperor respecting the succession of Bavaria.[2] Having returned by slow journies to Berlin, he soon after had the happiness to hear of his son's distinguishing himself by relieving the Baron Carlostein from the Austrian Hussars. And at the conclusion of the peace, he retired to his small villa, with his wife and daughter, where he had the pleasure of entertaining the two friends, as has been mentioned. Carlostein he never saw more; but Captain Seidlits spent all the time he could be spared from his regiment in his father's family, with whom he lived in the greatest harmony.

But Colonel Seidlits's health gradually declined; this however was more apparent to others, than to those constantly with him; and

Madame de Seidlits was for a long time deceived by the cheerful air her husband always assumed in her presence; for his mind remained in full vigour notwithstanding his bodily weakness. Having perceived, however, for some days, that he shewed uncommon solicitude in arranging and settling his affairs, she took notice of that circumstance to him with an air of apprehension.

"Is it not a sufficient reason," said he, "my dear friend, that I know I must die some time or other, and that I do not know how soon?"

"But why disturb your mind with business at present?" said she, "you are certainly in no immediate danger."

"You are not then of the opinion of the Duc de la Rochefoucault," replied the Colonel, "who says, *Il n'y a que la mort qui soit certaine, et cependant nous agissons comme si c'étoit la seule chose incertaine.*"[3]

"That is applicable to me as well as to you, my dear," said Madame de Seidlits.

"It is so," replied the Colonel; "and if I had become apprehensive of your dying as often as you prepared yourself for death, I should have been in continual apprehension ever since I knew you." The Colonel said this with such an easy air, that Madame de Seidlits became less alarmed.

But although the Colonel had none of the oppressive asthmatic attacks as formerly, he felt his strength melting fast away; he permitted none of his family, however, to attend him through the night; an old soldier alone, who had been long in his service, lay in his bed-chamber.

A few days after this conversation with his lady, having had a very disturbed night, he perceived the near approach of death. He caused himself to be raised in his bed in the morning, a little before the hour at which his family usually entered the room; they were unconscious of his illness through the night; his lady, with Laura and Captain Seidlits, sat around his bed;—when the Colonel, smiling, said in a faint voice to his son, "It is a long while, Seidlits, since I assured my wife, that notwithstanding the difference of our sentiments on certain subjects, this company should all meet in heaven."

"I hope you will keep your word, Sir," said the young man; "but not for a long time."

"It is my hope," replied the Colonel, "that it will be long before the rest of the company follow; but I feel that I must set out soon."

"Ah, father!" cried Laura, with a voice of sorrow. Captain Seidlits looked with anguish at his mother-in-law.[4]

"Why do you talk so, my dear?" said Madame de Seidlits; "you seem a little faint this morning; but you have often recovered from more oppressive symptoms."

"Never, never! my beloved friend," said he; "but you would not wish me to struggle any longer; the hope of perfect recovery has been long over, and the struggle is ending."

"Alas!" cried she, starting from her seat greatly alarmed, "send for a physician."

"If you love me," said he, "let there be no intrusion."

She sunk on the bed, grasping his hand; "Let my latest breath," continued he, "declare my unaltered affection. I regret that I have been able to make so small a provision; but what can a soldier provide? I have served an heroic monarch with fidelity; he knows it. Your conduct, my Seidlits," looking at his son, "has thrown comfort and gladness on the heart of your father, and made my declining years the happiest of my life. I know you will behave with duty to your mother, and affection to your sister. Farewel, my beloved Theresa;—farewel, my sweet Laura;—farewel, my Seidlits:—I resign you to *his* protection, into whose merciful hands I resign my own soul.—God Almighty bless you;—once more, farewel; —but I hope—I trust not for ever.—My eyes grow dim!—a dark mist overhangs them!—I see you not, my Theresa!—My children!—my organs fail!—yet my soul departs intire.——Father of mercy, receive my soul!"—His voice failed, and after a few sobs, this gallant soldier expired.

Madame de Seidlits remained in speechless affliction, holding the cold hand of her husband for a considerable time after he had breathed his last. Laura, kneeling by her mother, wept without uttering a syllable; and Captain Seidlits, unable to comfort either, stood motionless with grief, till a servant entering the chamber, Seidlits supported Laura and her mother to their apartment, and then retired to his own.

CHAPTER XLI.

La gravité est un mystere du corps, inventé pour cacher les défauts de l'esprit.
ROCHEFOUCAULT.[1]

COLONEL SEIDLITS left his family in very moderate circumstances. The king appointed a pension to his widow, and soon after promoted his son, who had only the rank of Lieutenant, to the command of a troop of dragoons. This young man behaved with great generosity to his mother-in-law; and continued for some time after his father's death to live with her and his sister; but, on his being obliged to attend his regiment, Madame de Seidlits took the resolution of returning to her native country, which she put in execution notwithstanding the strongest solicitations on the part of Captain Seidlits, whose friendship and affection for them both made him exceedingly desirous of their remaining in Germany.

When we were led into this long digression, we left Madame de Seidlits in conversation with Father Pedro, which was interrupted by the coming of Laura and Father Mulo. The latter always harboured fears that Madame Seidlits's long residence in a country of heretics had diminished in her mind that salutary horror in which he thought they should be held by every sincere catholic. To counteract this, and to revive her faith in those points which he considered as most essential, he sent her, since her arrival at Naples, a large folio of divinity, earnestly entreating her to peruse it attentively along with her daughter, telling her at the same time, that she might rely on having the second volume as soon as they had read the first.

"Have you perused that admirable work, my dear daughter?" said Father Mulo, seeing the book lie on the table.

"I have begun it," replied Madame de Seidlits; "it is a book of too serious a nature to be read over superficially."

"It is indeed a work of great weight, and requires the utmost attention," said Father Mulo.

"It were fortunate," said Laura, "if the authors of books which require so much attention could write them so as to command it."

"The business of an author is to write books," said Father Mulo, with becoming gravity; "it is the duty of the reader to command his attention when he peruses them."

"You are indeed too hard upon authors, my good young lady," said Father Pedro, "to expect that they should not only write their books, but also be obliged to command the attention of their readers. My learned brother has, with more regard to distributive justice, divided the toil between the author and the reader."

"In my humble opinion," replied Laura, smiling, "he allots too large a proportion of the task to the courteous reader. It is not so easy a matter to command one's attention on perusing certain books as you seem to think. I own I never found mine more disobedient than in the perusal of that very admirable work which the reverend Father recommends."

"Your taste, I am afraid," said Father Mulo, addressing himself to Laura with much solemnity, "is in some measure corrupted by books of prophane history, or of amusement, whose merit consists in their eloquence, or perhaps in their wit."

"And you may judge, my dear daughter," added Father Pedro, "how little value ought to be put on that kind of merit, by its being often to be met with in the writings of infidels and heretics."

"I should be better pleased," resumed Laura, "to meet it elsewhere; but I hope, Father, you do not think that where there is wit there must also be infidelity."

"Why really daughter," said Father Mulo, answering with more gravity of manner than depth of reflection, "where there is much of the first, there is often reason to suspect some of the last."

"I cannot be of that opinion," said Madame de Seidlits; "for I have generally found true wit in better company; and although we sometimes find infidelity accompanied by wit, how much oftener are we shocked with pert ostentatious infidelity without any wit at all?"

"I am convinced my mother is in the right," cried Laura; "and I hope you will allow, Father, that there is not a necessary connection between them."

Father Mulo, perceiving at length that he had spoken a little inconsiderately, was obliged to own, though with evident reluctance, that he hoped there was not.

"I am *certain* there is not," added Laura; "and I am obliged to my mother for having made me remark instances, both in conversation and in reading, where not only the strength of the arguments, but also the purest wit, was on the side of virtue and piety."

"I can assure you, young lady, from my own experience," said

Father Mulo, with an air of great sagacity, and wishing to retract his first assertion, "that it is almost always the case;—true wit and eloquence are generally on the side of orthodoxy."

"How comes it then that this author," said Laura, pointing to the large volume, "has not seasoned his work with a little wit or eloquence, since there is nothing sinful in them; and they would have made it more universally read, and of course more useful?"

"How comes it?" repeated Father Mulo, who was not famous for quick replies on emergencies of this kind,—"how comes it, did you say?"

"Why it comes by the diabolical malice of Satan," cried Father Pedro, stepping in to the relief of his brother; "it is all owing to the spite of our great spiritual enemy, who is ever ready to enliven the works of the wicked; and has, it would seem, perplexed the sense and darkened the reasoning of this excellent author, so as to render it a little laborious for the young lady to read his work with the attention it requires."

"The greater the effort, the more meritorious will it be in the young lady to perform that duty as she ought," resumed Father Mulo.

"True, brother," said Pedro; "and thus the malice of Satan is defeated, and like the words of Balaam the son of Beor,[2] what was intended as a curse is converted into a blessing."

Father Pedro had a sovereign contempt for his venerable brother; and as he wished to retain his influence with Madame de Seidlits without participation, he was too ready to display him in a ridiculous light before her, as in the present instance.

But perceiving that he should have no further opportunity that day of prosecuting the object of his visit, he withdrew, leaving Father Mulo to dine with his two relations, which he did accordingly, and in such a manner as gave them no suspicion of his having already made a very ample repast at the house of a pious old lady, whose time of dining was two hours earlier than that of Madame de Seidlits; for it must be allowed in justice to Father Mulo, that although he reasoned but feebly, and thought with difficulty, he digested with uncommon force and freedom.

CHAPTER XLII.

————— With tract oblique
At first, as one who sought access, but fear'd
To interrupt, side-long he works his way.
As when a ship by skilful steersman wrought
Nigh rivers mouth or Foreland, where the wind
Veers oft, as oft so steers, and shifts her sails;
So varied he.——

MILTON.[1]

FATHER Pedro having found Madame de Seidlits less tractable than he expected, resolved, on the next occasion, to sound Laura herself, and try to dispose her to the purpose he had in view. Accordingly, a few days after, on being left alone with her, he turned the conversation on the subject of charity; mentioned some individuals who distinguished themselves by the exercise of this virtue, and dwelt particularly on Zeluco, whom he represented as one of the most charitable persons he had ever known; adding, That those were happy who were blessed with benevolent and charitable inclinations, but much more were they to be envied, who were also blessed with the means of putting such inclinations into action.

Laura agreeing with him in this sentiment, he said, "Would not you be happy, my daughter, to be in this enviable situation?"

"I flatter myself," replied she, "that if I ever had a great desire to be rich, it proceeded from a disposition to relieve the distressed. But it has been remarked, Father," added she, "that those who have nothing to give are wonderfully generous; and I myself have known some who, when they had not the power, expressed the strongest inclination of being liberal; yet when they afterwards came to have the power, seemed entirely to lose the inclination. Those observations give me diffidence in myself; I am not certain what alteration riches might make in my own disposition."

"I have no diffidence in you," said the Father.

"Of this, at least, I am certain," said Laura, "that if I could know beforehand, that wealth would have the same effect on me that it seems to have had on some of my acquaintance, I should refuse it were it offered to me."

"Depend upon it, my dear daughter," said Father Pedro, "those you allude to never had charitable and benevolent dispositions; they have only affected to have them, when they well knew that nothing was expected, nor would be received from them. Their real dispositions appeared afterwards when they became rich. But in you, my dear child, exists the reality, not the semblance, of benevolence; and riches could only enable you to extend your generosity, not render it more sincere."

Laura thanked him for his good opinion.

"I should have still a better opinion of you," said Father Pedro, "if I had not been informed that you refused this very enviable power."

"I have no idea of what you mean," said Laura.

"Tell me, in the first place, my dear daughter, whether you really refused your hand to Signor Zeluco?"

"I did," said she, without hesitation.

"And what good reason could you have, my dear child, for rejecting so generous a man?"

"You will allow, Father, that a woman may have good reasons for refusing a man for her husband, although she does not think proper to reveal them to her Father Confessor."

"You ought to have very good reasons indeed, daughter, for declining such a fortunate and happy match."

"But my particular sentiments and feelings might render it a very unhappy match."

"How could it be unhappy for you," said the Father, "who would reap every advantage by the alliance."

"If my husband could reap none," said she, "that circumstance alone would make it an uncomfortable alliance to me."

"Do not mistake me, my dear child; your husband would certainly acquire a beautiful, accomplished, and I hope a pious wife; but the gifts of fortune are all on his side. There are many beautiful and accomplished young ladies in Italy who would be happy to be united to Signor Zeluco: but what probability is there of your having the offer of a husband of superior fortune to his?"

"Not the least," said Laura; "but, my good Father, I thought the question between us related to happiness, not merely to fortune."

"It does so," answered Father Pedro; "and what do you think of the happiness of having it in your power, as well as in your inclination, to do good to others; to feed the hungry, clothe the naked, protect the orphan, and make the widow's heart sing for joy."

"According to your own account, Father," said Laura, "all this is done by Signor Zeluco's fortune already; to embarrass such a generous and charitable man with the additional expences which a wife occasions," she added with a smile, "would be diverting into different channels that bounty which, at present, flows entirely upon the naked, the orphan, and widow."

"There is no occasion for turning it into another channel," said the Father, a little peevishly; "but I perceive you are in a jesting mood."

"You shall not be angry, Father," said Laura; "if you are offended, I must be to blame."

"Nay," replied he, "I am not offended, child; your vivacity cannot offend me; I wish, however, it may not lead you into error."

"If it ever should, Father," said Laura, "I beg you will not, by way of expiation, enjoin me to give my hand to Zeluco, for that is a penance I shall never submit to."

Laura pronounced these last words with such strength of emphasis, as, joined to what her mother had said, greatly damped the sanguine hopes of Pedro with regard to the success of his mission.

CHAPTER XLIII.

> S'il y a un amour pur et exempt du mélange de nos autres passions, c'est celui qui est caché au fond du cœur et que nous ignorons nous-memes.
> ROCHEFOUCAULT.[1]

In the mean time, Signora Sporza became so very fond of her two relations, that she preferred their company to those numerous assemblies in which she had been accustomed to pass her evenings. Having perceived that Laura had no great relish for them, she formed a small select party at her own house, which met two or three times a week, and to which the Honourable Mr. N——, and a few others, were constantly invited.

This gentleman had long been on a footing of friendly intimacy with Signora Sporza, and now found an additional power of attraction to her parties in the lively and judicious conversation of Laura. Few men's company was more universally acceptable than Mr. N——'s; but what rendered him peculiarly agreeable to Madame de Seidlits and her daughter, was his acquaintance with the Baron Carlostein and Captain Seidlits. He became known to the first during his residence at Potsdam; and the Baron, on his expressing an inclination to see the camp at Magdeburg,[2] gave him a letter of introduction to his friend Captain Seidlits, who was there with his regiment; and Mr. N—— always spoke of those two gentlemen in high terms of commendation.

Laura was seldom or never in company with Mr. N——, without making fresh inquiry concerning her brother. It was not in Mr. N——'s power to talk much of him, without his friend Carlostein's being included in the circumstances of the narrative; and every anecdote relating to those gentlemen seemed highly interesting to Madame de Seidlits, and still more so to Laura.

"Pray, Sir," said she to Mr. N——, one evening when the rest of the company were engaged at cards, "Is my brother as fond of horses as ever?"

"He is remarkably fond of his horses," replied Mr. N——; "and no officer in the army is esteemed a better rider."

"He is very graceful on horseback," said Laura.

"He is very much so," replied Mr. N——.

"I do not think the scar on his face at all disfigures him," said Laura.

"He had no scar on his face, madam, when I saw him," replied Mr. N——.

"No scar," said Laura, with surprise.

"No, madam;—not Captain Seidlits: his friend the Baron, indeed, has a very honourable scar covered with a piece of black plaster, which does not disfigure him in the least."

"I thought you had mentioned him," said Laura, blushing very deeply.

A considerable degree of intimacy was gradually formed between Mr. N—— and this young lady. It was hardly possible for them not to have a mutual esteem for each other. Laura had received the most favourable impression of Mr. N—— from Signora Sporza, who had spoke of him as a man of sense, integrity, and benevolence; and her own observation of his conversation and behaviour, confirmed her in the justice of her friend's representation. He, on the other hand, while he agreed with the general opinion of the graces of Laura's face and person, was still more struck with her other accomplishments, with the genuine modesty and unaffected dignity of manner which accompanied her beauty: she was equally free from coquetry and disguise; her sentiments of those around her might be easily guessed by her behaviour.

To those of whom she had but an indifferent opinion, she observed such a degree of cautious and polite reserve as rendered it very difficult for them to be on a footing of any degree of freedom or ease with her, however strongly they were desirous of being so. But to those of whom she thought well, and particularly to Mr. N——, she behaved with a natural frankness, expressive of confidence and goodwill.

Yet although this engaging frankness of manner was extended to her male friends as well as her female, it was always attended with such expressive purity and dignity as precluded licentious hopes or wishes; for innate modesty pervaded the easy openness of her manners, appeared in all her words, actions, and gestures, and presided even in her dress. As often as the mode seemed to lean to the opposite side, Laura had the art of making her's retain the fashionable air, while she corrected the circumstance which she disapproved.

Mr. N—— had the same degree of esteem and approbation of Laura, which she made no difficulty of declaring for him; and there was no engagement which he would have preferred to passing an evening at Signora Sporza's, when he knew that Laura was to be of the party.

CHAPTER XLIV.

Characteristic Sketches.

Mr. N—— had for his servant out of livery,[1] one Buchanan, a Scotchman, to whom his master's growing attachment to Laura gave the greatest concern; and his concern augmented in proportion to the beauties and accomplishments which he himself could not help observing in that young lady, and the good qualities he heard ascribed to her; for he had too good an opinion of his master's taste and penetration to think him capable of a lasting attachment to one who was not remarkably accomplished. But Laura had one failing which, in this man's opinion, neither beauty, nor fortune, nor understanding, nor an assemblage of every good quality of mind or person could compensate—she was a Roman Catholic.

That his master should be captivated, and possibly drawn into a marriage with a woman of that religion, Buchanan considered as one of the greatest misfortunes that could happen to him, and he knew it would be viewed in the same light by Lady Elizabeth, Mr. N——'s aunt, by whom he had been placed with her nephew. The strong attachment this man had for his master, and his extraordinary zeal for his welfare, prompted him to intermeddle in matters which did not properly belong to him, and to offer his advice much oftener than it was wished or expected.

One day when Mr. N—— dined at home, and expected nobody but Mr. Steele, who lived with him, the latter invited Mr. Squander, and he brought along with him a certain Mr. Bronze,[2] one of those gossiping companions, who know every body, are of every body's opinion, and are always ready to laugh at every body's joke; who nestle themselves into the intimacy of men of fortune and rank, allow themselves to be laughed at, are invited on that account, or to fill a vacant chair at the table; and sometimes merely to afford the landlord the comfort of having at least one person in the company of inferior understanding to himself, whose chief employment is to fetch and carry tittle-tattle, become at length as it were one of the family, and are alternately caressed and abused like any other spaniel in it. This person had, many years ago, come to Italy with a party of young English, who, as they posted through the country, dropped him sick at Ferrara; and having resided ever since in Italy, he was thought to have some taste in pictures, antique intaglios,[3] cameos, statues, &c. and had picked up a considerable fortune by selling them to his countrymen who came to Rome or Naples.

Mr. Squander would not, for his own private satisfaction, have given a horseshoe for all the antiquities in Rome, and had no more taste in painting than his pointer; yet, thinking that he must carry home a small assortment of each, were it only to prove that he had been in Italy, Mr. Bronze had been recommended to him as a great connoisseur, who would either furnish him with what he wanted, or assist him in purchasing it.

Buchanan waited at the side-board.—They talked of an assembly, at which Messrs. N——, Squander, and Steele, had been the preceding evening. The former spoke with warmth of the beauty of Laura. The antiquarian, who had also seen her, said, Her face had a great resemblance to a certain admired Madona of Guido's.—Mr. Squander observed, That he thought she was very like a picture which he had seen at Bologna, but whether it was painted by Guido or by Rheni, he could not recollect.[4]—Mr. N—— said, smiling, That it was probably done by both, as they often painted conjunctly;—"but, however that may be," continued he, "the young lady I mentioned has one of the finest countenances that I ever saw either in nature or on canvass." Buchanan, who was sorry to hear his master praise her with such warmth, shook his head.

"You have seen many handsomer in Scotland," said Squander, addressing himself to Buchanan.

"I will not presume to make any comparisons, Mr. Squander," replied Buchanan; "for, on the present occasion, I doubt they would be thought odious."

Mr. N—— had often desired Squander to leave off the indecent custom which he had, of addressing the servants, but without effect. So taking no notice of what passed between him and Buchanan, he proceeded to praise Laura's accomplishments, particularly her voice, and her execution on the piano forte.

"*Your* countrywomen," said Squander, renewing his attack on Buchanan, "prefer the Scotch fiddle."—The Antiquarian laughed very heartily, and all the footmen tittered at this jest, which Squander himself called a bon mot.[5]—"A bon mot!" repeated Steele.—"Yes, by G—d," said Squander, "and as good a one as ever George Bon Mot uttered in his life. What think you, Buchanan?"

"It certainly bears this mark of a good joke, Mr. Squander," said Buchanan, "that it has been often repeated; yet there are people who would rather be the object than the rehearser of it."

"You are a wit, Mr. Buchanan," said Bronze, tipping the wink to Squander, "and you will certainly make your fortune by it."

"If I should fail that way, Mr. Bronze, I may try what is to be done by the haberdashing[6] of intaglios and cameos, and other hardware," said Buchanan.

"A great many more of *your* countrymen, indeed, have made their fortune as pedlars than as wits," resumed Squander.

The Antiquarian burst into a loud fit of laughter at this sally, clapping his hands, and crying, Excellent, bravo!

Buchanan, observing that Mr. N—— was displeased at what was going on, made no reply, till Squander pushed him, by saying, "What have you to say to that, Buchanan?"

"All I have to say, Mr. Squander, is, that I have known some of my countrymen, as well as yours, who were beholden to their fortune for all the applause their wit received."

Although Mr. N—— could with difficulty refrain from smiling at this remark, assuming a serious air, he told Buchanan, There was no need of his further attendance; and when he withdrew, Mr. N—— started another subject, which prevented the Antiquarian and Mr. Squander from abusing Buchanan, for which he saw them prepared.

Mr. N——, however, spoke not in his usual affable manner to Buchanan the whole evening, and when he went out, addressing one of the footmen instead of Buchanan, as was his custom, he said, he was going to Madame de Seidlits.

Buchanan, imagining that his master was highly displeased with him, imputed it to his having shaken his head at the praises of Laura; and was now more convinced than ever, that Mr. N—— was desperately in love with her, and in immediate danger of proposing marriage to her.

Under this apprehension he resolved to use every means, even at the risk of greatly offending his master, to prevent a measure which he thought diametrically opposite to his interest and happiness. Knowing that a certain Baronet, who was uncle to Mr. N—— by the mother, and whose presumptive heir Mr. N—— was, had lately arrived at Rome, and was soon expected at Naples; Buchanan imagined the most likely means he could use to accomplish his purpose, was to inform the Baronet; he therefore determined to write to him all his fears relative to his master. Buchanan had been educated at an university, and had learning sufficient to render him a pedant; to have an opportunity of displaying his learning therefore, in all probability, was an additional motive for his writing the following letter to the Baronet:

"Honoured Sir,

"Hearing of your arrival at Rome, I think it my indispensable duty to inform you, that my master, and your nephew, the Honourable Mr. N——, has been seized with a violent passion for a young lady denominated Laura Seidlits, who lately arrived at this city from Germany. The young woman is of a comely countenance—*Vultus nimium lubricus aspici*,[7] and, as far as I have hitherto been able to learn, of a very tolerable reputation. Yet, notwithstanding the fairness of her character and countenance, she is at bottom a black Papist.—*Hinc illæ lachrymæ!*[8]—This is the cause of my affliction; for were she as beautiful as Helen of Greece, Cleopatra of Egypt, or even as Mary Queen of

Scots, she being, like the foresaid Mary, of the Popish persuasion, would be a most unsuitable spouse for my master. Yet there is hardly a day goes over his head that he is not in this young woman's company, and the Lord above only knows how far a headstrong youth, instigated by passion, may push matters, more especially as he generally meets her at one Signora Sporza's, a very pawky* gentlewoman, who understands what's what as well as any woman in Naples, and being the relation of the foresaid Laura, will leave no stone unturned to get her linked to Mr. N——.

"I once had hopes, that as the young woman attends mass regularly every day—for those poor deluded creatures shew more zeal for their own superstition than some Protestants do for true religion—I had once hopes, I say, that she might object to marrying a Protestant. But I am informed, that as the song is, *Her mother did so before her*,[9] which has greatly diminished my hopes of refusal on her part; for it is natural to conclude that the mother has given the daughter a tincture of her own disposition, and you know, Sir, that

> *Quo semel est imbuta recens, servabit odorem,*
> *Testa diu.*[10]

"I am sure I need add no more to convince you of the misery that such a match as this would occasion to all Mr. N——'s relations, particularly to his honoured aunt, who holds Antichrist and all his adherents in the greatest detestation. You must likewise be sensible, that a Popish wife, however fair her aspect, must give but a dark prospect to a Protestant husband, inasmuch as her religion instructs her that she is not obliged to keep faith with heretics.—*Heu, quoties fidem mutatosque Deos flebit!*[11]

"These reflections are so manifest, that you will wonder they do not occur to Mr. N——; but you must remember, that he is blinded by the mist of passion, and in that state people cannot perceive the force of reason;—*Quid enim ratione timemus aut cupimus.*[12]—Yet if you could find a plausible pretext for desiring Mr. N—— to meet you at Rome, instead of allowing him to wait for you here at Naples, I am convinced he would obey your summons; and when he is removed from the opportunities of seeing this young woman, he may possibly be beyond the influence of her attraction, and above the wiles of her

* Sly. [Moore's note.]

co-adjutors; and you may then prevail upon him to listen to the voice of reason, abandon this land of superstition and delusion, where we have sojourned too long, and return directly to Britain; whereas it would be as easy to whistle the *lavrocks out of the lift*,* as to make him agree to this proposition while he remains within eye-shot of this same Laura Seidlits.

I am, with all due respect,
Honoured Sir,
Your most obedient servant,
GEORGE BUCHANAN."

The gentleman to whom this letter was addressed had already received a hint from a friend of his at Naples to the same purpose; he therefore determined to follow Buchanan's advice, and actually wrote to his nephew, that it was not in his power to proceed to Naples as he had intended, and expressing a strong desire of seeing him and Mr. Steele at Rome.

However fond Mr. N—— was of Laura's company, he could not think of allowing his uncle, for whom, independent of other considerations, he had a very great respect, to return to England without waiting on him; he therefore took his leave of Signora Sporza and her two friends a few days after receiving this letter, and he and Mr. Steele set out for Rome, accompanied by Buchanan and two footmen.

Signora Sporza told him at parting, That she was herself engaged to a lady of her acquaintance, who had business of importance at Rome, to make that jaunt with her, so that she expected very soon to have the pleasure of meeting him in that city.

Squander, and two or three other young Englishmen, finding their time pass a little heavily without Mr. N—— and Steele, followed them on the third day after they set out.

* The larks from the sky. [Moore's note.]

CHAPTER XLV.

L'hypocrisie est un hommage que le vice rend à la vertue.
ROCHEFOUCAULT.[1]

ZELUCO plainly perceived at their next meeting the ill success of the Father's negociation, in spite of the palliations with which it was communicated. As his hopes had been greatly raised, his disappointment was great in proportion; his enraged spirit, unaccustomed to restraint, on this occasion was deaf to the dictates of caution, and rejected the mask of hypocrisy; he raved like a madman, poured curses on both mother and daughter, particularly the latter, on whom he vowed vengeance for what he termed her insolence, and for all the trouble and vexation she had given him.

Father Pedro crossed himself, and began to repeat his Pater Noster.

"Come, come, Father," said Zeluco, "do not let you and I keep up the farce with each other any longer. I know you have too much sense to lay any stress on these mummeries; and I am not such a fool as to think that a woman is to be won by crossings or prayers."

"You have as good a chance that way, however," replied the Father, "as by swearing and raging like a fury."

"I will have her one way or another!" exclaimed Zeluco.

"And what way do you intend to take next?" said Pedro.

"I'll have her by force.—I'll have her seized, and carried aboard a vessel.—I'll fly with her to Algiers! to the West Indies!—any where!" exclaimed he with a loud voice, and stamping with his foot; "for she shall be mine;—by all the Gods, she shall!"

"Of all the Gods?" said Father Pedro, calmly: "the God of Hell was the only one who was driven to the miserable shift of committing a rape to get himself a wife;[2] do you intend to imitate *him*, Signor?"

"I do not care who I imitate," roared Zeluco, "were it the devil."

"In the present case, however, you will not even have the satisfaction of imitating him throughout; for although you may hurry *yourself* to hell, you have little chance of carrying the lady along with you. I would advise you, therefore, to adopt some less desperate expedient."

"What expedient?" cried Zeluco. "I can think of none; I can hardly think at all.—But if thou canst assist me in obtaining this woman, thou wilt eternally oblige me, Priest; and thou shalt have money enough to build a church."

Although Zeluco in his rage thus threw himself open, and put himself in some degree in the Father's power, the latter was resolved not to follow his example, and put himself in Zeluco's. He plainly perceived, indeed, that Zeluco did not imagine that he had acted from motives of piety; but whatever suspicions he might entertain, Pedro considered that there was some difference between being suspected of a villany, and actually avowing it; he therefore assured Zeluco, that he would have no farther connexion with him in this business, and that he would inform against him if he made any criminal attempt on Laura. He acknowledged, he said, that as he had thought his marriage with that young lady would be happy for both, and agreeable to the worthy lady her mother, besides conducing to other good purposes, he should have been extremely happy to have promoted it; but after the furious and unwarrantable projects he had just heard of, he desired to have no more to do with it, directly or indirectly.

This calm remonstrance brought Zeluco to his senses; he now perceived that the person he had to deal with, and whose assistance he still thought might be of use, was of too wary a character to act without a cover, to which he might retreat on occasion.

After a little recollection he replied, in conciliating terms, "Surely, Father, you cannot imagine that what has escaped me in a moment of passion is my serious intention; my own reflections would very soon have convinced me of the folly and wickedness of an attempt which your prudence has in an instant put in a just light. I think myself most happy in such a friend on whose wisdom I may rely, and whose counsels I shall ever be ready to follow. My love and respect for the virtuous young lady is such, that I will use every lawful means in my power to obtain her hand. I know the well-placed confidence which she has in you, and most earnestly beg that you will use your influence with her in my favour. In the mean time, my dear Father, I am sensible of the trouble which I give you; the only way in which you permit me to shew my gratitude, is by enabling you to extend your benevolence to the deserving and the necessitous. I beg, therefore, you will accept of this, which you will apply to whatever pious purpose you think proper:"—So saying, he put a purse of sequins into the Father's hands, assuring him of double the sum, independent of what he had already promised, on the successful conclusion of the business.

"Now, my son," replied the Monk, "you talk rationally; and reason always suggests a mode of action opposite to what is prompted by rage. You have already gained the good opinion of the young lady's mother; please to recollect how you gained it; not by violence, but by gentleness, by rendering her an essential service: and although the young woman herself seems indisposed towards you, yet who knows what a sense of gratitude might do?—it might have the same effect on the daughter that it has had on the mother. The last obligation you laid on the family was of a pecuniary nature, which is more apt to make an impression on an old heart than on a young; but there are obligations which make deeper impressions on young hearts than on old."

"What obligations are those? I am ready to do whatever you direct."

"Opportunities of this kind may occur," said the Father, "and then your own good sense will direct you how to profit by them. In your rage you proposed methods the most likely to make her detest you, and love those who should have the good fortune to free her from you; you spoke not like yourself, but like a *robber*, like a *ravisher*. A man who attempted what you threatened would draw upon himself her just hatred, whereas he who did the reverse, who had the good fortune to save her from such an attempt, might probably gain her love."

Having said this in a very significant manner, Father Pedro took his leave. In spite of Zeluco's endeavours to prevail on him to be more explicit, after remaining for some time in profound meditation, "He who has the good fortune," said he, repeating to himself the words which Pedro had pronounced with emphasis; "he who has the good fortune to save her from such an attempt might probably gain her heart.—Who can make such an attempt?—How can I deliver her from dangers to which she is not exposed?"

He conjectured however, that the Father meant to convey a hint to him respecting some emergency which he knew would occur, although he was resolved not to be farther explicit; and determined to observe his words and actions attentively, in the hopes of discovering his meaning more clearly.

Two days after, he was able more fully to comprehend the Father's idea; when he informed Zeluco that he had just left Madame de Seidlits and her daughter; that Laura having often expressed a curiosity to visit Mount Vesuvius,[3] her mother, who had formerly opposed it, had now agreed to it, on his offering to accompany her and Signora Sporza; that accordingly he and these two ladies were to dine next day at Portici,[4] visit the mountain in the evening, and return to Naples the same night.—"If you are eager to be of the party," added he, "I will endeavour to obtain the ladies' consent."

Zeluco, engrossed by reflection, did not give an immediate answer.

"But I know," continued the Father, "you have been there already; and possibly do not chuse to return again."

"Pray, my good Father," said Zeluco, rousing from his reverie, "at what hour do you propose returning to town?"

"It is impossible to say exactly," replied Father Pedro; "I dare say it will be late enough, for I find Signora Laura wishes to see the explosions to the greatest advantage; but I perceive we cannot have you. I shall not, however, inform the ladies that I made you the proposal, or that you so much as know of the expedition, lest they should accuse you of want of gallantry. Adieu. I can stay no longer at present."

"What servants do you take with you?" resumed Zeluco.

"I really do not know," said the Father; "but I must be excused, I cannot stay any longer now;—one of my penitents waits for me.—Servants!—let me see—there will be no need of many servants. I presume we shall have only Jachimo. The muleteers will be with us till we regain the carriage; and then we shall have only the coachman and Jachimo to attend us to town." Saying this, the cautious Monk hurried away, leaving Zeluco satisfied respecting the meaning of his former hints.

CHAPTER XLVI.

——Revenge, at first thought sweet,
Bitter ere long, back on itself recoils.

MILTON.[1]

ZELUCO now determined to plan an attack on the ladies as they returned from the mountain, to drive off the assailants, and assume the merit with Laura of having saved her from robbery and assassination.

Having communicated his design to his valet-de-chambre, the

confidant and accomplice of many of his villanies; the scheme seemed practicable and safe in all respects, except in the necessity which appeared of employing many agents. The valet however undertook the business with the assistance of only one person, and spoke with a confidence of success seldom acquired otherwise than by experience in similar scenes.

Being now convinced of Signora Sporza's dislike to him, and having a violent suspicion that it was through her means that Laura was so ill disposed towards him, Zeluco expressed some anxiety with regard to Signora Sporza, lest she might suspect the source of the attempt.—The valet assured him, that *she* should be particularly attended to, for he would order his companion to fire his pistol so close to her ear, that, though charged only with powder, it would confound her sufficiently to prevent her from making observations, and terrify the rest of the company into non-resistance.

This suggested a horrid piece of wickedness to the vengeful mind of Zeluco, which however he did not communicate to the valet; but next day, when he understood that every thing was arranged, he desired to see the pistol with which the man was to arm his companion:—"You are certain it is charged with powder only," said he. "I am very certain," replied the valet; "for I charged it myself." "Let the fellow fire then directly at her head; this will frighten her into silence," said Zeluco, "and render every thing easy."—He then gave him very particular directions in what manner they were to behave to Laura; and, sending the valet to fetch something from a distant part of the house, he slipt two bullets into the pistol: the hatred and thirst of revenge, which burned in his breast against Signora Sporza, overcoming his caution, and prompting him to a measure which might have produced a discovery of the whole plan.

Before these two emissaries set out, Zeluco again repeated to the valet not to allow his companion to touch Laura, but to pull Signora Sporza entirely out of the carriage, and then fire the pistol in her face, which would be the signal for Zeluco himself to make his appearance.

In the evening Zeluco waited on Madame de Seidlits, where he found Father Mulo; he affected great surprise when she told him that her daughter, Signora Sporza, and Father Pedro had set out that same morning on an expedition to Mount Vesuvius; and that they were not as yet returned.

When the night advanced without their appearing, Madame de Seidlits became uneasy; the noise of every carriage gave her hopes that it was theirs; and every disappointment when the carriage passed increased her uneasiness.

When Madame de Seidlits first began to express her apprehension, Zeluco withdrew on pretence of an engagement; and Father Mulo remained, as he said himself, to comfort Madame de Seidlits, in case any misfortune should really have happened to Laura and the rest of the party.

Madame de Seidlits had heard, in general, of people being sometimes hurt by the fall of the substances exploded from the mountain: her alarmed imagination prompted her to make particular inquiries on this subject; and Father Mulo's retentive memory supplied her with every instance of that kind which had happened for many years back; but he added, at the close of every example, that such a misfortune having happened to the people he mentioned, could not be considered as a positive proof that the same had befallen any of the company for whom she was so much interested; and if the like had happened to *some of them*, still it was possible that Laura was not the unfortunate person: "For which reason," added he, "my dear Madam, you ought to keep yourself in perfect tranquillity, and hope for the best; because vexing yourself will be of no manner of use, but is rather a tempting of Providence, and may draw down upon your head the very misfortune you dread, or some other as bad." By such reasoning Father Mulo endeavoured, with uninterrupted perseverance, to quiet her fears.

What effect this method of conveying comfort might have produced on the mind of Madame de Seidlits can never be known, for her imagination was too much alarmed to permit her to attend to his discourse: besides, although it may seem a bold word, no ecclesiastic ever possessed the faculty of speaking without being listened to in greater perfection than the reverend Father Mulo.

On leaving Madame de Seidlits, Zeluco mounted his horse, and rode directly towards the place which he had fixed on for the attack. Having perceived his emissaries in waiting, he turned his horse without seeming to take notice of them, and rode slowly backwards and forwards till he saw the carriage coming briskly along. The valet and his companion, with masks on their faces, riding furiously up to the carriage, ordered the driver to stop on pain of having his brains blown out; the driver instantly obeyed, and Jachimo fell from his horse on his knees, supplicating for mercy in the name of the Father, Son, and Holy Ghost; to whom, after he had recovered his recollection a little, he added St. Januarius.[2]—Father Pedro also prayed with much seeming fervency, invoking the aid of St. Dominic,[3] and a whole host of other saints.

After the valet had taken the ladies' purses, which were instantly presented to him, the other fellow dragged Signora Sporza out of the chaise; she exclaimed that every thing had been delivered to them, and attempted to get into the carriage again; but the fellow, standing between her and it, presented his pistol, which flashed without going off. Zeluco seeing the flash, and hearing the screams of Laura, galloped towards the carriage, hallooing,[4] and threatening the assailants with immediate death if they did not desist; but the fellow, whose pistol had snapped, fearing that he should not be thought to have performed his part properly, if he did not actually fire it, cocked it once more, and fired it off in such a hurried manner, that both the bullets passed the head of Signora Sporza, and one of them lodged in Zeluco's shoulder.

This staggered him a little; but the attackers flying, he came up to the carriage in time to prevent Laura from rolling out of it; she had retained her presence of mind while she considered the assailants simply as robbers; and after delivering their money, seeing Signora Sporza pulled violently out of the carriage, she called to Father Pedro to assist her; but on hearing the pistol fired, which she imagined had killed her friend, she fainted in the chaise. Signora Sporza also was greatly alarmed; but seeing the aggressors fly, she rose from her knees, on which she had sunk when the pistol was fired, and assisted Zeluco and Father Pedro in their endeavours to recover Laura, who, as soon as she recognised Signora Sporza and the Father, and understood that the danger was over, exclaimed, "What blessed angel has delivered us from the ruffians?" Father Pedro immediately answered, "We all owe our deliverance to Signor Zeluco." "Signor Zeluco!" cried Laura, with painful surprise. "Yes, my daughter," added he; "and here he is to receive our grateful acknowledgments."—"We are all highly indebted to you, Signor," said she: "How providential was your coming!" added Father Pedro.—"Considering the hour of the night," said Signora Sporza, "his coming seems miraculously so."

Zeluco then informed them how he was induced to meet them; that as he drew near the carriage, hearing the shrieks of Signora Laura, he had rode up to the ruffians, one of whom, he said, he could have taken, had he not been more anxious to relieve them than to seize him.

The driver and Jachimo having now recovered from their terror, the carriage was prepared, and the company moved towards the town. Jachimo told the driver as they went, that he had made an observation which he would communicate to him as a friend, because it might be of use on future occasions of the same nature; it was this: that while he continued to implore the first three Persons to whom he had addressed his prayers, no interposition had been made in his favour; but that as soon as he began to implore the protection of St. Januarius, Signor Zeluco had appeared for the rescue of the company. "*Certo,*" said the coachman, "St. Januarius takes the greatest care of all his votaries on Mount Vesuvius and the neighbouring district, *ad ogni uccello suo nido è bello;*"[5] but out of sight of the mountain, he assured Jachimo that St. Januarius was as regardless of prayers as his neighbours, and not more to be depended upon than those he complained of.

When the company arrived at the house of Madame de Seidlits, Father Mulo was giving her a circumstantial account of a robbery with assassination, which happened many years before on the road between Portici and Naples; and, as he with wonderful accuracy remarked, looking at his watch, much about the hour in which he was then speaking; he also detailed the providential manner in which the murderer was discovered, and how he was broken on the wheel,[6] to the edification, as Father Mulo expressed himself, of all the beholders, and the great comfort of the murdered person's widow.

The powerful faculty hinted above, which the Father possessed, and which shone with peculiar lustre in narrative, prevented these anecdotes from affecting Madame de Seidlits so much as they would otherwise have done. The sight of the company which now entered her house relieved her, however, from a set of very disagreeable reflexions.

Father Pedro, in the presence of the ladies, gave her the history of their adventure, in which the generous intrepidity of Signor Zeluco made a conspicuous figure; and the watchful care of Providence in sending him to their deliverance was mentioned in the most pious terms.

Madame de Seidlits then poured out the grateful effusions of her heart in thanks to Zeluco, who modestly acknowledged that, on seeing her alarmed at the ladies not returning, and being himself exceedingly uneasy, he had on leaving her immediately mounted his horse, and galloped towards Portici, which he should ever consider as the most fortunate incident of his life, with whatever consequence the accident which had happened to himself should be attended.

"Accident!" cried Madame de Seidlits; "What accident?"—and then perceiving blood on his clothes,—"Alas! Signor," said she, "you are wounded! send directly for a surgeon!"

Father Pedro, who, notwithstanding the blood, had reasons of his own for thinking that he was not at all, or in no dangerous degree hurt, said it would be best that Zeluco were removed to his own house, where the wound would be examined more conveniently, and proposed to accompany him immediately.

Madame de Seidlits, wringing her hands in the utmost grief, begged that all possible care might be taken of him; for she should never again know comfort if any accident should accrue to so worthy a man, particularly, added she, looking to Laura, on such an occasion.

Her daughter, with more composure, but with visible emotion, begged of Father Pedro not to leave Zeluco till his wound was dressed, which she hoped would not be found dangerous.

Father Mulo desired Zeluco to be of good cheer, for Heaven *seldom* permitted villany of this kind to pass unpunished; but that in case this wound should prove mortal, he might *rely upon it*, that the planners of such a daring attack would be brought to open shame; for, sooner or later, murders were always discovered.

Signora Sporza observed to Zeluco, who by this time was not the least alarmed in the company, that the wound could not be dangerous, as he had been able to sit on horseback while they were coming to town.

Zeluco was then put into a carriage, and slowly transported to his own house, accompanied by Father Pedro, who did not chuse to make any particular inquiry, nor to express the surprise he really felt at there being a wound at all; for, as the carriage went slowly, he was afraid of being overheard by the servant that walked by its side. The wounded man himself was silent, except that once he muttered, "Damn the aukward blockhead!" and afterwards, "What a cursed blunder!"

As soon as he was placed in his own bedchamber, "Is the surgeon come?" said he to Father Pedro.

"Do you really wish for a surgeon?" said the Father.

"Certainly; don't you see how I bleed?"

"I see blood; but I had hopes it was not from your veins?"

"It is a cursed business; pray send for a surgeon," cried Zeluco impatiently.—This was done accordingly.

The valet and his accomplice had returned before Zeluco had even reached the town. The former, on hearing that a surgeon was sent for, and seeing blood on his master's arm, was astonished, and cried, "How is it possible, Sir, that you can be wounded? For——"

"Peace, babbler," said Zeluco.

"Can any thing be more natural," said Father Pedro with a sarcastical smile, "than for pistols to make wounds, especially when fired by two such bloody-minded ruffians. But I must now leave you, Signor; you may depend on my prayers for your recovery, and that you may soon reap the fruits of your generous valour." He then withdrew, convinced that the wound was fictitious, and invented as a natural incident in the farce, which would be better acted by the master, the servant, and the surgeon, without his taking any part.

CHAPTER XLVII.

A Medical Consultation.

As Father Pedro went out, a Physician and Surgeon[1] entered the room together. It was found that the bullet had entered the arm, near the shoulder, and without having injured the bone or joint, was felt beneath the skin on the opposite side.

It was extracted without difficulty after an incision. The Doctor and Surgeon then retired to another room to consult. The latter was a Frenchman of some humour, a considerable share of shrewdness, and much of a coxcomb.

"This wound is nothing," said the Doctor.

"We must try to make *something* of it, however," replied the Surgeon.

"It will heal of itself directly," resumed the Doctor.

"It must therefore not be left to itself," said the Surgeon.

"What farther do you intend," said the Physician; "little more seems necessary, except applying some fresh lint every day."

"*Lascia far' a Sant' Antonio,*"[2] replied the Surgeon, "I will take care that his Excellency shall not be exposed to danger on the high road for at least a month to come."

"Unless it be to prescribe some cooling physic, and such a low regimen as will prevent his suffering from want of exercise, I can do nothing," said the Physician.

"That is doing a great deal," said the Surgeon; "it keeps the patient in low spirits, and renders him obedient."

"But after all, how do you intend to treat the wound itself?" said the Physician.

"I intend to treat it *secundum artem*,"[3] replied the Surgeon.

"*Benè, benè respondisti*,"[4] said the Physician; "and so much for the wound.—Now, pray what say you to the news?" continued the Physician; "they talk of a Russian fleet in the Mediterranean."[5]

"Whether that will take place or not," said the Surgeon, "depends entirely on the king's pleasure."

"How so?" said the Physician; "How can his majesty prevent it?"

"By threatening to sink them if they presumed to enter the streights," replied the Surgeon. "The Toulon fleet will be sufficient."

"Toulon fleet!" cried the Physician; "why, what king do you mean?"

"Why, the king of France to be sure," replied the Surgeon; "What other king *can* I mean?"

"*Vi prego di scusarmi*, Signor,"[6] cried the Physician; "but in speaking of the king *in* Naples, I thought the king *of* Naples might perhaps be meant."

"*A fe di Dio*, Signor," replied the Surgeon; "*non m'è venuto mai in pensiero*;[7] but I believe," added he, looking at his watch, "our consultation has lasted a decent time enough."

The Physician being of the same opinion, they returned to the patient's bedchamber. The Physicians ordered a low diet, and cooling ptisans[8] in great abundance.

"What do you think of the wound?" said Zeluco to the Surgeon.

"It would be rash to speak decisively at the very first dressing, Signor," said the Surgeon.

"But what is your general notion?" resumed Zeluco.

"Why, Signor, if my friend here will answer for keeping down the fever, I will do my best to save your Excellency's arm."

"Save my arm," exclaimed Zeluco! "I would rather be damned than lose my arm, Sir."

"That may be, Signor," said the Surgeon, "but people are not always allowed their choice on such occasions."

"Zounds, Sir!" exclaimed Zeluco; "do you think there is any danger of my losing my arm?"

"I am determined to save it, if possible," said the Surgeon, "and it will afford me great pleasure to succeed."

Here the Physician interfering, begged of Zeluco to be composed, for nothing retarded the cure of wounds more than impatience; he hoped, by the great skill of his friend, every thing would terminate to his satisfaction, provided he would be resigned, and follow the directions that from time to time would be given him.

With much internal chagrin, Zeluco was obliged to assume the appearance of serenity, and he promised to obey the injunctions of those two learned gentlemen.

CHAPTER XLVIII.

The French Surgeon.

THE following day the Physician and Surgeon did not think it expedient to take the dressings from the wound, but renewed their injunctions that Zeluco should be kept exceedingly quiet, take his medicines punctually, and strictly adhere to the coolest regimen. As the wound now was more painful than at first, the patient became apprehensive of losing his arm, and complied with the directions given, though not without breaking out frequently into violent execrations on the unlucky chance by which he was reduced to the necessity of suffering such penance.

Madame de Seidlits had sent a message, desiring that the Surgeon might call at her house when he left his patient.

He went accordingly, and found Father Mulo with her.

"I am extremely happy, Madam," said the Surgeon, "to have this opportunity of paying you my devoirs; it is an honour I have long wished for. I perceive, by the brilliancy of your looks, that you are in charming health."

"Pray, Sir," said Madame de Seidlits, with impatience; "How do you find—?"

"I ask you ten thousand pardons, Madam, for interrupting you," said the Surgeon; "but I beg to know, before you proceed, how the amiable and accomplished young lady your daughter does?"

"My daughter is very well, Sir," answered Madame de Seidlits; "now will you be so obliging——"

"You may command whatever is in my power, Madam," said the Surgeon, bowing very low.

"Then pray tell me, Sir, how you left your patient?"

"I have a great many patients, Madam; but I presume your ladyship inquires, at present, for Signor Zeluco."

"I do, Sir, and earnestly beg to know how you left him?"

"Much better than I found him, Madam—I have cut a bullet out of him."

"Poor gentleman!" cried Madame de Seidlits.

"He is not the poorer for that, Madam," said the Surgeon; "he is a great gainer by what has been taken from him."

"I hope he is in no manner of danger?" said Father Mulo, who was still with her.

"Alas! Father," said the Surgeon; "how often are our hopes fallacious:—a heretic hopes to go to Heaven, which is impossible; Is it not Father?"

"That certainly *is* impossible," said Mulo.

"I knew," continued the Surgeon, "that you would be fully convinced of that great and comfortable truth."

"But you do not think this poor gentleman in danger?" said Madame de Seidlits.

"A person of your ladyship's excellent understanding must know," replied the Surgeon, "that gun-shot wounds are often attended with danger."

"This is only a pistol-shot wound," said Father Mulo.

"Very judiciously observed, Father," said the Surgeon; "*that* certainly makes a difference; it happens unluckily, however, that even pistol-shot wounds prove sometimes mortal."

"The bullet, I understand, passed through his arm *only*," said Father Mulo.

"Had it passed through his heart *also*, it would have been more dangerous to be sure, Father," said the Surgeon.

"You have extracted the ball—I think you said so, Sir?" resumed Madame de Seidlits.

"I have, Madam, and quite in the manner recommended by Mons.

Lewis at Paris; it is by much the safest. I never made a sweeter incision in my life."

"It must have been very painful," said Madame de Seidlits, shrinking like one who suffers.

"Painful!—not in the least, Madam!" replied the Surgeon; "I performed it with the greatest ease."

"I imagine," said Father Mulo, "the lady meant, that the operation must have been painful to the *patient*."

"To the *patient*; Oho!" cried the Surgeon; "your Ladyship spoke of the *patient*,—did you?"

"I did indeed, Sir, I fear he suffered a great deal," said Madame de Seidlits.

"Why, yes; a good deal perhaps, though I should think not a vast deal neither.—I have seen many suffer more;—in short, there is no knowing," said the Surgeon, carelessly; then added with earnestness, "but of this I do assure you, Madam, that Monsieur Lewis's method is by much the best. I had the honour of being a favourite eleve[1] of his—and in some instances, have improved on his ideas."

"I dare say, Sir," said Madame de Seidlits, willing that he should withdraw, "you will do all that can be done for this gentleman. I shall be glad to know how he is after the next dressing. I have heard your skill much commended."

"You are extremely polite and obliging, Madam," said the Surgeon, bowing; "your ladyship, no doubt, has passed some time at Paris?"

"I never did, Sir.—I shall expect to hear from you to-morrow."

"I am surprised at that," said the Surgeon; "I could have sworn that you had lived a considerable time at Paris?"

"Pray, Sir," resumed Father Mulo, "will you be kind enough, before you go, to say whether or not you think this gentleman's wound will be long in healing; for I have not yet been able to gather from your discourse what your opinion is."

"The art of surgery, my good Father," replied the Surgeon, "consists in healing wounds *well* and *radically*, not soon and superficially; the last is the art of charlatans."

"I honour the art of surgery, Sir," said Madame de Seidlits; "it is one of the most useful that mankind possess, and particularly so to the bravest class of mankind."

"Your politeness can only be equalled by your excellent understanding, Madam," said the Surgeon. "The art of surgery is not only the most useful, and most honourable, but also the most ancient of all the arts; it can boast higher antiquity than the art of medicine itself."

"Perhaps it may be so," said Madame de Seidlits.

"I will have the honour of proving it to your ladyship," said the Surgeon; then coughing and adjusting himself like one going to make a formal harangue, he began—"The earliest race of mankind—"

"I am fully convinced it is as you assert," said Madame de Seidlits, interrupting him, "but I must really beg your forgiveness for being obliged to leave you at present. You will be so good as to let me know how your patient does after the next dressing?—Your humble servant, Sir.—Adieu, Father."

When Madame de Seidlits was withdrawn: "Is it possible," cried the Surgeon, "that this lady was never at Paris?"

"She never was, I assure you," replied Father Mulo.

"That seems very extraordinary," said the Surgeon.

"I had a notion," resumed the Father, "that there was a considerable number of people in the world who never were at Paris."

"Your reverence's notions are all wonderfully well founded," said the Surgeon; "but my surprise at present proceeds from my not being able to conjecture where or how Madame de Seidlits could acquire so much politeness and liberality of sentiment."

"She was educated in a convent," said the father.

"That clears up the matter at once," said the Surgeon; "for so were you, Father, and yet perhaps you never were at Paris any more than the lady."

"Never in my whole life," answered Father Mulo.

"Nor at Moscow neither," added the Surgeon.

"No, never," answered the Father; "though I have *heard* a good deal about *Muscovy*, particularly of late."

"O, you have?" said the Surgeon.

"I have, indeed," answered Father Mulo; "some people tell me it is larger than Naples. What is your opinion?"

"About what?" said the Surgeon; "I fear I do not quite understand what your reverence means."

"I only asked which you believed to be the largest city, Naples or Muscovy?"

"Why, I should think Naples the most populous," answered the Surgeon, "though Muscovy stands upon rather more ground."

"I had some suspicion of that kind myself," said Father Mulo.

CHAPTER XLIX.

An Anodyne Sermon.

Impediat verbis lassas onerantibus aures. HOR.[1]

WHEN Madame de Seidlits left Father Mulo and the Surgeon, it was partly to get free of the loquacity of the latter; and also because Laura, who did not chuse to appear herself, waited with impatience to know the Surgeon's opinion of Zeluco. That young lady had passed a very disturbed night, owing, in some measure, to the fright, but more to the uneasiness she felt on account of Zeluco's wound, or perhaps rather on account of the occasion on which he had received it; for it is more than probable that Laura would have felt less concern had he received the same wound in any other cause. Of all mankind the person she wished least to be obliged to was Zeluco.

Madame de Seidlits having perceived her daughter's anxiety, although she had herself been agitated by the alarming manner in which the Surgeon had spoken, affected a degree of composure which she had not, and spoke to Laura as if there were no doubt of his recovery; she afterwards desired Signora Sporza and Father Mulo, to talk the same language to her. The former did so naturally; for there appeared something mysterious and suspicious to her in the whole adventure, and she never once believed him in any danger.

Father Pedro visited Zeluco daily, but never thought proper to ask any particular explanation of the accident by which he was wounded; nor did the latter ever talk to him but on the general supposition that the attack had been made by real robbers. Yet they so far talked without disguise to each other, that the Father informed Zeluco of Laura's distress on his account, the mother's precaution in softening the accounts of his illness to her daughter, advising Zeluco, as the best means of keeping alive the interest which that young lady took in him, that he should not be in too great a hurry to announce his perfect recovery; and declaring, at the same time, that he had better hopes than ever of his success.

Several days after the adventure, Father Pedro found the three ladies together, and endeavouring to suit the account he gave of

Zeluco with the sentiments he wished to inspire; he said, "That, for his part, he did not know what to think of Signor Zeluco's state of health; that sometimes the Surgeon imagined the wound disposed to heal, that soon after he declared that it had a worse appearance, and threatened the most dangerous consequences. But what gave him the greatest uneasiness was, that the Physician, a man of great skill and penetration, had told him, that he suspected some secret anxiety of mind preyed upon his patient, producing a slow fever, which gradually undermined his strength, and destroyed the effect of the medicines; and he was much afraid would render a wound, which might otherwise have been cured, the apparent cause of his dissolution." Madame de Seidlits threw a look at Laura, as the Father pronounced these words, and the young lady herself betrayed symptoms of great emotion.—"Avaunt, thou prophet of evil!" cried Signora Sporza, with an air of raillery, "see you not that this audience cannot bear a sermon from the Lamentations of Jeremiah.[2] Nor is there need for such gloomy forebodings, I will be answerable for it, that our heroic Knight Errant's wound will heal in due time, in spite of the secret sorrow which preys on his tender heart."

Signora Sporza continued to slight every idea of danger, and endeavoured to keep up the spirits of her friends, which seemed ready to sink under the artful insinuations of Father Pedro.

Signora Sporza, in consequence of the engagement above mentioned, set out for Rome with her companion a few days after this conversation, having taken an affectionate leave of her two friends, both of whom were a little hurt at the want of concern she displayed on account of the illness of Zeluco, who, they imagined, merited more regard from her than she was willing to allow.

When she departed, Father Pedro circulated, without restraint, such reports as he thought would answer his purpose. One day Madame de Seidlits was told, that Zeluco was a little better, the next a great deal worse; at one time it was given out, that the Surgeon feared it might be necessary to amputate his arm, as the best means of saving his life. And the Father was always at hand to lament, that his generous intrepidity should be attended with such consequences.

One day he filled Madame de Seidlits's mind with the greatest apprehensions for Zeluco's life; asserting that the agony of his wound was excruciating; that he had not slept for the three last nights, and that the fever threatened his brain.—"What a benevolent and liberal friend," exclaimed the Father, "are the poor about to lose!" And so he left both the mother and daughter in very great concern.

He had hinted to Zeluco himself, that he intended to give this impression, that he might act accordingly, and give suitable answers to all inquiries made about his health. The Father's view was to imprint, in the first place, a strong degree of compassion in the breast of Laura, in the hope that this would render her more favourable towards Zeluco; and he purposed returning that same evening to the ladies with exaggerated accounts of Zeluco's tortures, which, by totally depriving him of sleep, augmented the fever; and when he should perceive Laura's compassion strongly interested, he intended again to urge his suit in the hopes of obtaining some favourable declaration from Laura, in the event of Zeluco's recovery.

This shrewd plan, however, was a little deranged. Father Mulo called on Madame de Seidlits two hours after Pedro had left her. When he had sat a little while, she begged he would be so obliging as to pay a visit to Signor Zeluco, endeavour to see him, and return afterwards to her; for his case, as she was informed, altered every hour, and she did not know whose account to depend upon. Laura joined in this request, that she might be relieved from the Reverend Father's conversation, which she had always felt uncommonly oppressive.

Father Mulo's connection with Madame de Seidlits's family was known to all Zeluco's servants; therefore, although they had received orders to admit nobody to his chamber except the medical people and Father Pedro, yet they imagined that Father Mulo was meant to be comprehended in the exception. He was accordingly introduced.

But as Zeluco expected no such visit, he was not exactly in the situation he would have chosen, had he known of the Father's coming. The wine and sweet-meats which were on the table had been placed there on Father Pedro's account, who was always pleased to find a collation of that kind ready arranged when he called. Father Mulo expressed great satisfaction at seeing him look so much better than he expected, adding, That it would afford consolation to his friends, particularly to Madame de Seidlits, when he should inform them how well he looked.

"Alas! Father," said Zeluco, "nothing is more deceitful than looks. I am in continual pain. I have not slept at all for these three nights. The physician thinks I might be better if I could get some sleep; but nothing he orders has the effect, the agony of my arm is so violent. Oh!—"

"You had best take a glass of wine; allow me to help you," said the Father.

"I dare not taste wine," replied Zeluco; "but I beg you will help yourself to some; and pray, my good Father, try at the same time, if you can, to taste those biscuits; you seem fatigued with walking in this sultry weather. There is a napkin to dry you with; you are in a very violent perspiration. Pray take another glass of wine—I will endeavour to suppress my complaints while you refresh yourself. The *lachryma Christi*[3] is excellent; do taste it."

Father Mulo acknowledged that he was indeed very much fatigued, having visited many penitents that morning, and walked a great deal. After he had eat and drank very plentifully, thinking himself bound to repay Zeluco for his agreeable repast, he prepared to do it in the most ample manner in the only coin he ever carried about with him, a consolatory exhortation. He turned, therefore, from the buffet, and addressed himself to Zeluco in these words: "The accident which has befallen you, my dear son, in all human probability, is the most fortunate that could have happened; you have had time during your confinement to reflect on your past life, and to repent of your manifold iniquities. As for the pain, it is temporary and trivial in comparison of the pangs which sinners endure in purgatory. Of what account are the frivolous enjoyments of sense? of what avail are all sublunary—?" &c. &c. &c.

In this strain and with an uniform monotonous voice, mightily resembling the drone of a bee, the Father continued his harangue with wonderful perseverance and shut his eyes, as was his custom when he prayed and admonished. It is difficult to say how long he might have continued, had he not been surprised into a full stop, in the midst of a sentence full of unction, by the snoring of Zeluco; who, unwilling to interrupt the Relation of Laura, and unable to attend to what he said, had been long lulled into sleep by the lethargic hum of his voice.

Father Mulo opening his eyes, perceived the situation of Zeluco; as it was no ways uncommon to the Father to find many of his audience in the same condition at the end of his sermons, he betrayed no marks of surprise on the present occasion; but after having with wonderful composure finished what remained of his bottle, and eat a few more biscuits, he walked softly out of the room, told the servant that his master had most providentially fallen into repose, and desired that he should on no account be disturbed till he awaked of himself.

Father Mulo, not chusing to be troubled with inquiries into particulars, sent a general message to Madame de Seidlits, importing that Signor Zeluco was a great deal better. This afforded much pleasure to both the mother and daughter; and the same evening, when Father Pedro called on purpose to strengthen the impression he had already made, they congratulated him on the comfortable accounts they had received of Zeluco. As Father Pedro had not seen nor heard of him since he had been last with the ladies, he was a good deal surprised at the intelligence; he could see no motive Zeluco could have for deviating from the plan that had been settled between them, and therefore declared his disbelief of the account which ladies had received. "Have you seen Signor Zeluco since you were here?" said Madame de Seidlits. Father Pedro owned that he had not.—"Then our accounts are later than yours, and may be depended on; they come from Father Mulo, who was with Signor Zeluco, and sent me the message after he left him."

"There is some mistake," said Pedro angrily; "he cannot possibly be better."

"One would imagine, however," said Laura, "that there is nothing to put you out of humour in the intelligence we have received, and which it is certainly possible *may* be true."

"The reason that I have to fear that it is not," resumed Father Pedro, recollecting himself, "makes me averse to your adopting an opinion which will give double uneasiness when found to be false."

"Whether it is false or true may be soon ascertained," said Madam de Seidlits, who immediately sent a footman to inquire. The messenger returned in a few minutes, and informed them, that Signor Zeluco had been asleep for several hours; and that he slept so calmly, there was every reason to hope he would be greatly better when he awoke.

"Heaven be praised!" exclaimed the Father; "some powerful soporific must have been administered to produce such a lasting effect."

Zeluco was at length awoke by Father Pedro himself, who was greatly irritated at what had happened, and burned with impatience to vent his ill-humour.

"You seized a very seasonable moment truly for slumbering," said he, after a long altercation.

"I seized it not," replied Zeluco; "I am hoarse with telling you, that, in spite of all I could do, it seized me."

"After I had melted them with the accounts of your sufferings, assuring them you had not slept for nights, when I returned with the strongest hopes of improving on this favourable disposition of Laura's mind," continued Pedro, "it was too provoking to find them informed that you were in perfect ease, sound asleep, and the effect of all my labour annihilated."

"If the whole world had been to be annihilated, I could not help it," cried Zeluco; "your brother Mulo has power to lull Prometheus asleep, in spite of all the efforts of his vulture.[4] I'll tell you, Father," added Zeluco with vehemence, as if he intended a stronger illustration, "*your* own eloquence is scarcely more powerful to rouse and animate, than *his* drowsy monodies are to benumb the senses."

This last stroke softened the wrath, and smoothed the brow of Father Pedro. "Well, well, my friend," said he with a smile, "repining at what is past can do no good; all may yet be repaired; that this long and unexpected repose has been of service to your health must not be denied to the ladies, but remember that you are to recover very slowly, and that you may possibly relapse."

After a consultation of some length, they separated as good friends as ever.

END OF THE FIRST VOLUME.

ZELUCO.

CHAPTER L.

Il est aussi facile de se tromper soi-même sans s'en appercevoir, qu'il est difficile de tromper les autres sans qu'ils s'en apperçoivent.

ROCHEFOUCAULT.[1]

About this time, Madame de Seidlits received accounts of the failure of a house at Frankfort, in which her husband had placed most part of the money he had left for the use of his widow and daughter. In the same house also was the residue of the money produced by the sale of her furniture and other effects, when she left Germany; part of which had served to defray the expence of her journey, the rest she had ordered to be remitted to her banker at Naples, and expected every day to hear that this was done, when the sad news of the failure arrived.

This news was accompanied, as is usual on such occasions, with the comfortable assertion that it was only a temporary stoppage of payment; for that the house would pay all they owed in time. However that might be, Madame de Seidlits felt very great immediate inconveniency from the accident; she had already contracted debts at Naples, for the discharge of which her sole reliance was upon this money: she concealed this misfortune from Laura, to save her the shock of such calamitous news, and in hopes that she might in a few posts have the first statement confirmed, that there would finally be no loss by the bankruptcy. In this distressing situation she lamented the absence of Signora Sporza, who was the only person to whom she could freely speak on such a subject; and she once thought of writing to her for a small supply of money for her immediate occasions; but fearing that this might not be convenient, or perhaps not agreeable, and having naturally a great reluctance to lie under a pecuniary obligation, she determined rather to part with her jewels, even those which she had received from her husband, and on that account valued far above their intrinsic worth; she accordingly applied to a jeweller, and sold them for a sum sufficient for the discharge of her most urgent debts.

Father Pedro having seen the jeweller, with whom he was acquainted, coming out of Madame de Seidlits's house, entered into conversation with him, and endeavoured, from a prying disposition not uncommon to monks, to sift from him what his business with her was; for he well knew that Madame de Seidlits was not in circumstances to purchase jewels. The jeweller, in consequence of her injunctions, evaded his questions, which more and more excited the curiosity of Father Pedro, who did not rest till he learned from one of the jeweller's workmen, what his master's business with Madame de Seidlits was.

This gave the Father an idea of the distress of her circumstances far beyond what he had hitherto entertained, and inspired him at the same time with fresh hopes of success in the scheme he was so sanguinely engaged in. He immediately communicated the intelligence to Zeluco, adding, That he imagined it would be no longer necessary for him to exaggerate the uneasiness of his wound, but rather to admit the idea which the ladies had already received of its being better; although his general health was still delicate, this plan would allow him the benefit of enjoying the fresh air, the pleasure sometimes of seeing and paying his court to Laura, while the perplexed state in which the mother's circumstances seemed to be, with the admonitions which the father undertook on every proper occasion to give both to the mother and daughter, might at length dispose them to listen to his proposal.

Zeluco waited on Madame de Seidlits and Laura the following day; they both manifested sincere satisfaction at seeing him. Madame de Seidlits cautioned him, with all the solicitude of friendship, to be very careful of himself till his health should be fully restored; and Laura, impressed with a sense of obligation, and softened by the danger in which he had been, behaved with more cordiality than she had ever shewn to him before. He continued to visit them very frequently, and was always received in the same manner.

Father Pedro congratulated him on the very friendly reception which he met with, from which he augured an agreeable answer when he should next speak to Madame de Seidlits on the subject of Zeluco's suit, which he hinted he intended to do very soon; but the same circumstances which had imparted this confidence to the mind of the Father, revived Zeluco's original hopes of obtaining Laura without marriage. He imagined that the proud spirit of both mother and daughter, humbled by misfortune and terrified by the horrors of impending poverty, would in a short time acquiesce in the settlements he determined to make, unclogged with the ceremony he detested.

He wished not, therefore, that the Father, by a precipitate renewal of the proposal of marriage, should render it more difficult for him to succeed upon his own terms, as he expected, though perhaps at a more distant period.

The wound in his arm was now on the point of healing; but the fears he had undergone, the medicines he had taken, the regimen he had followed, had weakened him considerably, giving him also an appearance of sickness, which corresponded with the accounts that had been spread of his danger, and enabled him to support a delay in the gratification of his desires with a degree of patience which he could not have displayed had he been in perfect health.

He begged of Father Pedro, therefore, not to urge his former suit at present, expressing an apprehension of disgusting the ladies by too much importunity; then talked of his sorrow at the thoughts of the distress they were in, wished that the Father would prevail on Madame de Seidlits to accept of a sum of money, with which he directly presented him, on the pretence of its coming from a person who suspected her situation, but was unknown to Father Pedro and to herself, and was determined to conceal the transaction from all the world.

Although Zeluco behaved on this occasion with a good deal of address, spoke with great gentleness and in plausible terms, Father Pedro's penetration pervaded his hypocrisy, and he at once saw his motive and drift.

Father Pedro, it must be confessed, was not a monk of that rigid self-denial and sublime piety that will intitle him, an hundred years after his death, to canonization.

Had Laura been inclined to meet Zeluco on his own terms, very possibly he would have winked at the connexion, or given her absolution on easy terms; but his mind revolted at the thought of being accessary to betraying her: besides, the virtues of Madame de Seidlits and her daughter commanded his entire esteem; whereas the money he had from time to time received from Zeluco had not produced a single sentiment in his favour. He wished well to both the former, and would have cheerfully served them in any thing not attended with great inconveniency to himself; but he would not have abstained from a pinch of snuff when his nose required it, to have saved the other from the gallows.—For these reasons Father Pedro refused the money; saying, He was sufficiently acquainted with Madame de Seidlits, to know that such an offer would offend her; that as for his own part he had been induced to interfere in this business, with the sole view of rendering him the most essential service that, in his opinion, one man could do to another, by assisting him in his avowed inclination of marrying one of the most accomplished, beautiful, and virtuous women in Europe: "But," continued he, "Signor, if you have altered your mind, my interference of course must end here."

To this Zeluco replied, That he was sensible of what he owed to the Father; that he would ever take the warmest interest in both the ladies; but wished not to have his former proposal pressed on them at that particular time.

CHAPTER LI.

Les passions les plus violentes nous laissent quelquefois du relâche; mais la vanité nous agite toujours. ROCHEFOUCAULT.[1]

ZELUCO, who was of a most suspicious temper, now imagined that Father Pedro acted in concert with Madame de Seidlits, and that the desperate state of her affairs had produced an alteration in the sentiments of her daughter, of which they had informed him that he might push a renewal of the proposal of marriage without delay.—He thought also that the Monk's zeal had made him overshoot his commission, by imprudently mentioning the circumstance of the sale of the jewels; for he was convinced, that one reason for their wishing to have the ceremony speedily concluded, was to prevent *this* and other proofs of their poverty from appearing. As he now believed therefore, that it was in his power to obtain Laura in marriage whenever he pleased, that very conviction acting on his capricious and vicious disposition, disinclined him from it, and determined him to renew his original scheme of seduction, which he flattered himself the distresses of poverty, joined to the credit of his late exploit, would greatly facilitate.

Laura, though unacquainted with the disagreeable accounts which her mother had received from Germany, or with the exact state of the circumstances in which she had been left by her father, knew in general that they were narrow, and therefore would have been pleased with a more severe system of œconomy than was agreeable to her mother. A knowledge of this was one reason why Madame de Seidlits had always represented their situation in the most favourable light to her daughter.

This young lady, notwithstanding the admiration she never failed to excite, was by no means fond of appearing often in public. What are called public amusements, she had but a very moderate relish for, and stood in no need of them as a resource for passing her time.

She had such a taste for reading, as afforded a very pleasing source of entertainment and improvement to her mind, without inclining her to despise or neglect other occupations becoming her age and sex. Her natural good sense, taste and accomplishments, while they rendered her independent of company, made her more entertaining in it; without being over-reserved, nothing could be more modest than her deportment; and very few women possessed the talent of conversing in a more easy and agreeable manner. Her mind being undisturbed by passion, serene through innocence, naturally cheerful, and easily amused, she could have lived happy in a very limited society, and in the delightful occupation of promoting her mother's happiness, and that of all around her.

Madame de Seidlits was somewhat of a different character; although Laura was the warmest object of her affection, yet she stood in need of amusements, and had a taste for a greater share of elegant superfluities than her revenue could supply. Had she conformed herself exactly to her daughter's taste, they could have lived free from debt upon the pension and interest of the money left by her husband; but as she often followed her own, they must have been embarrassed in a short time, even although their banker's failure had not happened.

The particular article of expence which gave Laura most uneasiness, was what regarded her dress. Her own taste in dress was elegantly simple, and, in her, was so becoming, that all who beheld her were of opinion that additional ornament would tend to diminish the lustre of her beauty; yet when in compliance with her mother's taste she adopted ornaments to the height of the mode, the same beauty shone conspicuous through all the variations, and in spite of the extravagances of fashion.

While Madame de Seidlits endeavoured to assume the appearance of serenity and cheerfulness before Laura, she could not resist a real depression of spirits. She saw the necessity of retrenching the limited plan of expence she had with difficulty hitherto observed, and was uncertain whether any system of œconomy would relieve her from a species of distress which her spirit could ill support, and which she felt with keener anguish on Laura's account—who in reality could have supported the misfortune which was so carefully concealed from her, infinitely better than her mother.

Meanwhile, Zeluco visited Madame de Seidlits with most assiduous punctuality, and was always received with a cordial welcome. He saw the dejection of Madame de Seidlits, and the anxiety of Laura, with secret satisfaction and apparent concern; he imputed both to the distress of their circumstances, and was in daily expectation that Madame de Seidlits would apply to him for relief, which he imagined would entitle him to still greater familiarity in the family, involve her in repeated obligations to himself, and finally terminate in the success of his base designs upon the honor of Laura.

Zeluco's passion was of the grossest nature; he called it love, but with more propriety, even at its height, it might have been denominated hatred; it was entirely selfish, unconnected with sentiment, or the happiness of its object; even in the midst of desire, he felt resentment against Laura, for the neglect and indifference which she had evinced towards him.

He took every opportunity, when he found Madame de Seidlits alone, of insinuating a desire of obliging her, and lamented, with mildness and much respect, that she was so reserved, and seemed unwilling even in the smallest instance to give him the pleasure of being of service to her.

He sometimes, on Madame de Seidlits being called out, was left for a few minutes with Laura; to her he expressed the most tender concern for her mother's health, "which he dreaded was not so good as usual; was afraid of some concealed anguish, either in her body or mind, and with the most insinuating solicitude begged to know whether Laura suspected what it was; not that he presumed to make too particular an inquiry, only in general, whether she did not suspect that her mother had some secret affliction, and whether it was bodily or mental."

Laura's answer on all such occasions was, "that she hoped he was mistaken in imagining that any thing particular disturbed her mother; but even if it was so, she would be cautious of prying into what her parent judged proper to conceal."

In the mean while, Madame de Seidlits flattered herself that Laura began to view Zeluco with more favourable eyes than formerly, and entertained hopes that she would at length consent to his proposals: she was determined however to leave her to herself, and adhere to the promise she had given, never to solicit her on the subject. But she found means, without apparent design, of leaving them frequently, for a considerable space of time, together, in the expectation that he would gradually strengthen Laura's disposition in his favour, and seize some happy occasion of renewing his suit, for the success of which she was more anxious than ever.

The idea that Laura, whom she justly thought formed for adding lustre to the highest and most brilliant rank of life, should undergo the mortifications of poverty, was what she could bear with less firmness, than the thought, horrid as it was, of mortifications of the same nature occurring to herself. Here Madame de Seidlits fell into a very general error, and what parents are peculiarly liable to, in the establishing of their children in marriage. Her daughter's happiness, not her own, was what she had chiefly in view; but in estimating this, her own ideas of happiness, not her daughter's, were what she chiefly considered.

Laura had remarked some appearance of dejection in her mother's spirits, before it was hinted to her by Zeluco; but had not made any inquiry about the cause, partly because she hoped it proceeded from no cause of importance, and partly for the reason she had given to Zeluco.

She had remarked that her mother had less dejection in Zeluco's company than when he was not present; on this account she herself was pleased with his visits; she thought herself under great obligations to him, and in consequence of these sentiments, the whole of her conduct was so much altered, that he became persuaded not only that her former prejudices were overcome, but that she had conceived a great partiality for him. He was much less surprised at this, than he had been formerly at her having viewed him with indifference; which his vanity never permitted him to think was natural, but rather the artificial offspring of Signora Sporza's malice. But she being now at a distance, he fondly believed that his personal accomplishments began to operate the same effect on the heart of Laura, which, in his opinion, they usually did on the hearts of women of sensibility and discernment.

Madame de Seidlits had for some time expected letters from a friend at Berlin, who had engaged to write to her the real state of her banker's affairs, and how much he would be able to pay his creditors, as soon as the trustees appointed for that business should make their report. Several posts had already arrived since the time when she expected this account, without her having received any letter on a subject which interested her so much. She was sitting one day with Laura, when the servant returned from the post-office, and told her there were no foreign letters for her. She could not help discovering marks of disappointment and vexation.—"I am sure, my dear mother," said Laura, "will let me know, as soon as it is fit I should know, what it is which gives her uneasiness."—"Being disappointed when I am in expectation of letters from my distant friends, always vexes me, my dear," said Madame de Seidlits; "I cannot help it."

"I hope you will have agreeable accounts soon," said Laura.

"I hope I shall, my dear," replied Madame de Seidlits, with a sigh, and directly fell into a fit of musing, which brought tears into the eyes of Laura, who turned to the window, that they might not be observed by her mother.

Zeluco was introduced.—The face of Madame de Seidlits brightened, and she received him with cheerfulness and every mark of regard. The heart of Laura, who perceived the immediate effect his presence had on her mother, throbbed with warmer gratitude and good-will towards him, than even when he delivered her from the supposed robbers.

A female acquaintance of Madame de Seidlits at this instant called on her.

"You are low-spirited of late," said she to Madame de Seidlits, "and keep the house too much. I am come to carry you into the fresh air for a couple of hours."

"I beg you will go," said Laura eagerly to her mother; "you really have been too much confined."

"I will with pleasure, my dear," said Madame de Seidlits.—"You will entertain Signor Zeluco, while he chuses to stay."

CHAPTER LII.

Reserve with frankness, art with truth ally'd,
Courage with softness, modesty with pride. POPE.[1]

WHEN Madame de Seidlits and her friend had driven away, Laura asked Zeluco whether he chose to hear an air on the harpsichord; he answered, he should prefer it to any concert, provided she would accompany it with her voice.

She played and sung a lively air; this did not exactly suit Zeluco, who wished to make serious and very pathetic love to her; he could not avoid, however, praising the tune, and the execution.

"Since that air is to your taste, Signor," said Laura, who was highly pleased with him on account of the good effect his visit produced on her mother, "I will play another in the same style."

"You play like an angel—and are an angel," cried Zeluco.

"Do angels deal in music of this sort?" said Laura, running over the keys with infinite rapidity, and singing a very gay air.

Zeluco being persuaded, that he had been left by the mother to give him an opportunity of renewing his proposal to the daughter, and that she herself had, for some time, expected this with impatience; he construed her gaiety into a desire of captivating him, and meditated how to address her in terms expressive of love, without conveying any idea of matrimony. He dreaded any hint of that kind, and imputed her frank and obliging behaviour to a disposition in Laura, of which he determined to take the advantage.

Having finished the air, and perceiving that Zeluco was grave and pensive; she said, with a sweetness of voice and manner which would have turned a less determined villain from his purpose, "You do not seem to relish this so much, Signor."

"I relish," cried he, "every thing you do, and every thing you say; and beg to be heard on a subject of infinite importance to my happiness."

"You have a right, Signor, to expect to be heard by me on any subject which you yourself have not agreed to avoid," said Laura with a solemn and serious air, which the impassioned manner in which he had spoken, obliged her to assume.

Although Zeluco was a little surprised at the sudden alteration which had taken place in the features of Laura, he resumed his rapturous tone: "How can I avoid expressing my admiration of beauty so angelic?" cried he, throwing himself on his knee, and attempting to seize her hand.

"Whatever you have to say, Signor," said Laura, withdrawing her hand, and speaking with firmness and dignity, "you will certainly speak more at your own ease, and to my satisfaction, by keeping your seat."

"Hear me, Madam," said Zeluco, embarrassed and overawed.

"I will hear nothing," replied she, "while you continue in that posture;—it is too ridiculous."

Zeluco rose.—"Now, Sir," said she, "what have you to say?"

"I am much concerned, Madam," resumed he, hesitating, and entirely driven from his purpose; "I am sorry, I say, that I have offended you;—but I really flattered myself, that after the marks of regard which I had the good fortune to—but those are trifles.—My esteem and regard are unbounded,—and the honour I proposed,—that is, the happiness of calling you mine—My fortune, my life, I consider as nothing—that is, I mean, when put in competition."—In this incoherent manner he went on without knowing what he said.

There is a dignity and elevation in virtue which overawes the most daring profligate. No man of sense, however free in his morals, ever attempted a woman, till he imagined that she had some inclination he should. Let him use what delicate terms he pleases, to what purpose can he be supposed to express his own wishes, if he does not suspect that she has the same wishes with himself? This is the true point of view in which women ought to consider addresses of this nature—In what other point of view can they be considered? A woman is solicited to grant what dishonours herself. Well, her solicitor, if he is not a fool, will not, in conscience, expect that she will stoop to this without a motive, or merely to please him; what then does he expect? Why, that she will consent to please herself.

The coolness and modest dignity of Laura's manner gave at once such a check to Zeluco, that she did not discover his aim. She saw only his embarrassment, which she imputed to his being conscious of having broken the engagement which he had entered into, not to renew his proposal of marriage; for, although she had been surprised, and displeased with the manner in which he had addressed her, yet she never once suspected his real scheme.

Willing, therefore, to relieve his confusion, and to be quite certain of what he meant; she, with a milder aspect, addressed him in these words: "Signor Zeluco, I wish to know whether I am to construe what you say into a renewal of your former proposal."—Although conscious that she mistook his intention, he answered her question by a bow.—"Then," resumed she, "I must repeat what I formerly declared on that occasion; I am truly sensible of the honour which your opinion does me. I should be happy to have any proper opportunity of shewing the sense of obligation which I have for the generous services which you rendered me. You are entitled to my lasting gratitude—more is not in my power to bestow;—and gratitude alone would, in a wife, be a poor return for the generous love you profess. After this avowal, and declaring with the same breath," continued she, "that the proposals you made, in point of liberality, exceed my utmost wish; it is evident, that my reason for declining them is of a nature not to be overcome, and ought therefore to be an obstacle of as great weight with you as it is with me. Indeed, if I had not been persuaded that it had at length appeared so in your eyes, I should have taken care to avoid any occasion for an explanation, equally disagreeable for you to hear, and me to repeat."

Having said this, she withdrew to another room, and left Zeluco so much surprised and confounded, that he remained fixed to the spot for some minutes before he recovered presence of mind sufficient to return to his own house.

He was now convinced, that all his conjectures were erroneous, and that, notwithstanding domestic distresses, so far from having any design upon him, Laura was determined never to accept of him as a husband. He had not pondered long on this, till, in proportion as his fears of losing her augmented, his desire to marry her increased, and before the ensuing morning he would have purchased at the highest price that very situation which, the day before, he dreaded being drawn into, and had determined to use all his address to avoid.

He plainly perceived, that her reason for refusing him proceeded from dislike; but although this conviction rankled in his breast with the severest anguish, he could not refuse his admiration of the delicacy and propriety of her sentiments, the candour and dignity with which they were expressed; while the beauty and elegance of her face and person never had appeared more attractive.

CHAPTER LIII.

Nunc animum pietas, maternaque nomina frangunt. Ovid.[1]

He now regretted the language he had held to Father Pedro, and resolved to renew his confederacy with him on the basis on which it had formerly stood, resolving at the same time, that in one shape or other she should be *his*, whatever danger or guilt might attend the accomplishment of his desires.

Ever since their last conversation, Father Pedro had kept a watchful eye upon Zeluco, being suspicious that he meditated some design upon Laura which he durst not avow. These suspicions he intended to communicate to Madame de Seidlits, but he was prevented by Zeluco's intreating him to renew the matrimonial treaty. He endeavoured to give some plausible reason for his former behaviour, and Pedro was too well pleased with his present disposition to criticise with much severity his late conduct. But he was sincerely sorry that Laura seemed so determined to reject a measure which, in his eyes, appeared absolutely necessary in the present state of her mother's circumstances.

He again spoke to Madame de Seidlits on the subject of Zeluco's addresses to Laura, enumerating the advantages that would result to herself, as well as to her daughter, from this alliance.

Madame de Seidlits thanked him for the interest he seemed to take in her family, adding, "That perhaps she saw the advantages of such an alliance in the same light that *he* did, and had stronger reasons than he was acquainted with, for wishing that Laura were of the same way of thinking. But having the most complete conviction of the good sense, virtuous inclinations, and dutiful disposition of her daughter, to whom her approbation of Zeluco was perfectly known; she was resolved to adhere to her engagement, not to press her farther on that subject. There never was one human creature, Father," continued she, "who had a stronger desire to oblige another, than Laura has to oblige me; she knows that few things could give me so much pleasure as her consenting to marry him; yet she continues to reject him. What can this proceed from but a rooted dislike? whether this be well or ill founded, it would equally render her miserable to be united to a person she so dislikes; and it would be the height of cruelty in me to exert maternal influence in such a cause."

Father Pedro said, "He feared that Laura sacrificed her happiness to an ill-grounded prejudice."

"She shall, at least, not sacrifice it to my importunity," replied Madame de Seidlits.

The efforts which Madame de Seidlits was obliged to make, to conceal the bad state of her affairs from Laura, to appear cheerful while in reality she was sad, and to adhere to her promise and resolution of giving no hint to her daughter in favour of Zeluco, hurt her health; she lost her appetite, grew thin, and uncommonly pale: when any body took notice of this, by an affected cheerfulness, and by assertions which her whole appearance contradicted, she rendered her illness more visible and more affecting.

"Alas! Madam," said Laura, "why will you conceal the cause of your illness?"

"I am not ill," replied she, with a sickly smile.

"Let this be decided," said Laura, "by a physician."

"Indeed, my dear, a physician could be of no service to me."

"I am certain you are not well—you are always sorrowful."

"Can physicians cure sorrow?"

"You have then some secret sorrow," cried Laura, catching at her mother's last expression, as if it had been an avowal.—"Tell me—O tell me the cause of your affliction;—confide in me,—trust your Laura."

"I do confide in you, my beloved girl;—I could trust my soul with you;—but you alarm yourself without a cause.—I am happy, my love, in your affection and goodness."

Laura could not refrain from tears at these expressions of her mother; but finding that she declined to acknowledge the cause of her uneasiness, she pressed her no farther: perceiving, however, that her mother's dejection of spirits continued, and that she became more and more emaciated, the young lady was at last so greatly alarmed, that she communicated her fears to Father Pedro, intreating his counsel.

Hitherto he had abstained from the subject, in expectation that Laura would adopt this very measure.

"I have been as uneasy as you can be, my dear daughter, at the visible alteration in your mother's spirits and health; and observing that she avoided giving any reason for it, I could not help endeavouring, by every means I could think of, to discover whether she had received any news to disturb her, or what the cause of such dejection could be, that every possible method might be tried for its removal."

"And have you discovered the cause?" cried Laura, impatiently.

Father Pedro had heard of the failure of the banker; he began by informing her of what he had learned on that head.

Laura was in some degree relieved by this account; her imagination had figured something worse: she dreaded that some disease of an incurable nature afflicted her mother, which, out of tenderness to her daughter, she concealed.

"The distress which this man's misfortune brings will be temporary," said she; "he will surely pay some proportion, if not the whole, of his debts. My mother feels the present inconveniency more on my account than her own. I will shew her how light it sits on my mind, and how cheerfully I can conform to any circumstances.—The king's pension remains—the house here, and the farm, remain.—A little time will make my mother forget this loss; she will recover her health, and I shall again be happy."

The Father then mentioned the circumstance of selling the jewels.

This affected Laura at first, because it was a proof of her mother's immediate distress; but soon after, she said, "I am glad of it, it will put her at her ease for some time at least,—perhaps till the banker is able to pay part of what he owes. I am much happier, Father, than I was before I knew the whole source of my dear mother's low spirits."

"I wish," said the Father, "this were the whole."

"O! merciful Heaven!" cried Laura; "What! is there more?"

"Shall I speak," said Pedro, "my real sentiments?"

"Yes, certainly," cried Laura, trembling.

"Without any cover or disguise?" added he.

"I did not think you had ever used any," said Laura.

"When we are obliged to blame those we love," resumed he, "it is natural to do it in the mildest manner."

"If I have failed in my duty to my mother, use the severest," said Laura.

The Monk then reminded her, That her mother had always entertained a favourable opinion of Signor Zeluco, which had been confirmed and augmented by time and more intimate acquaintance; that she had heard his proposal of marriage with great satisfaction, for few things are more agreeable to a prudent and affectionate mother, than to see her daughter united in marriage with a man deserving her esteem; that on finding her daughter's ideas different from her's on this subject, she had sacrificed her own, and with a generosity which few parents possess, had never again given her a hint on the subject; but it was even then pretty evident the sacrifice had cost her a good deal: that Zeluco's gallant behaviour since that time, and the very important service he had rendered her, had renewed and sharpened her mother's original wishes, that so deserving a man were as agreeable to her daughter as to herself, and probably had inspired her with fresh hopes that his conduct would produce that effect on such a generous and grateful heart as Laura's: that being disappointed in these flattering expectations at a moment when her own private affairs were so much deranged, had, he feared, corroded the breast of Madame de Seidlits, and was the true cause of all her inquietude; for she was endued with that noble and exalted affection which inclined her to be ready to communicate to her daughter the largest portion of all her comforts, and endeavour to keep to herself the whole of what was painful in their common lot, as appeared conspicuous in her concealing from Laura the bankruptcy which so cruelly affected their circumstances, and allowing the whole vexation of that unexpected misfortune to prey upon her own spirits, and undermine her health.

Here the Father paused, to give Laura an opportunity of speaking; but perceiving that she kept her eyes fixed on the ground, and seemed unable to make any reply, he added, "That, upon the whole, it was very difficult for him to offer any advice, or point out a remedy; because, he acknowledged that Laura's taste, even her prejudices, ought to have weight in the choice of a husband, and that it would be hard to blame her for indulging them. He would not venture to assert, that religion required her to sacrifice them, as Providence certainly might, if it thought proper, find other means of preserving the health of her mother; and might, in its own good time, free that worthy woman from her present difficulties, and prevent her future life from being imbittered with penury, which her elegant taste and liberal disposition could so ill endure."

"Father," said Laura, whose eyes were now overflowing, "I am unable at present to converse with you,—leave me to myself,—I will, if I can, talk with you more fully to-morrow morning."—They parted.

CHAPTER LIV.

Fallit te incautam pietas tua.— VIRG.[1]

LAURA continued reflecting on every thing that the Monk had said, and insinuated—Zeluco's disinterested passion—his kindness to her mother—the obligation he had laid on herself—her mother's wishes, at first so plainly signified, and afterwards with such delicacy suppressed—her maternal tenderness through all her life, particularly displayed by her endeavour to conceal the affair of the jewels and the bankruptcy;—and, finally, the declining state of her mother's health, which filled her with the most alarming apprehensions.

In consequence of revolving those considerations in her mind, her dislike to Zeluco began to appear in her own eyes an unreasonable prejudice, which gratitude and filial affection, with united voice, called upon her to overcome.

The next day Laura informed her mother that she was willing to bestow her hand on Signor Zeluco. Joy was very strongly mixed with the surprise which appeared in Madame de Seidlits's countenance. Yet she addressed Laura in these terms: "I desire, my dear, that no sacrifice may be made to any supposed wish of mine on this occasion; I assured you formerly, and I repeat it now, that I think you have a full right in an affair of this nature to follow your own inclinations."

Laura replied, That this alteration of sentiment had taken place in consequence of her serious reflexions on Signor Zeluco's conduct to them both.

Madame de Seidlits then embracing her daughter, expressed her satisfaction in the most affectionate terms; and communicated the glad tiding to Father Pedro, who was then entering, and immediately joined in Madame de Seidlits's congratulations.

Laura, however, said, That as she had, in a very serious and formal manner, refused Zeluco when he last made his court to her, it was very possible he might since that time have altered his sentiments as well as herself.

"That I can answer for is not the case," said Father Pedro.

"There is no need of any one's answering for it," said Madame de Seidlits; "the truth will appear of itself. If Signor Zeluco does not shew as much ardour as ever to obtain my daughter's hand, he never shall obtain it with my consent."

Laura, smiling, thanked her mother for being so punctilious where she was concerned; and said, She would explain herself in a letter to Signor Zeluco, which she hoped the Father would deliver to him.

Madame de Seidlits objected to her writing. The Father, she said, might, if he pleased, acquaint Signor Zeluco that her daughter was more favourably disposed towards him than formerly, and then leave him to take his course.

Laura said, If her mother would trust to her expressing herself with propriety on a subject of so much delicacy, she would prefer writing, as there was one point that required explanation.

"I have perfect confidence in your prudence, my dear," said Madame de Seidlits; "write what you think proper." She then left Laura and Father Pedro together.

Laura directly wrote what follows:

"Signor Zeluco,

"In the conversation I lately had with you, I candidly told you my sentiments; with the same sincerity I now inform you they are altered; and that I am ready to accept of your proposal. It will not surprise me if such apparent levity should induce you to renounce the too favourable opinion which you had of me; should that be the case, you certainly can have no scruple in declaring it.

"It is proper that I should further inform you, that since I last saw you, I have learnt that, by the failure of a house at Berlin, great part of the money left by my father for the use of my mother, and which would have eventually come to me, is, in all probability, irrecoverably lost.

"Laura Seidlits."

Having sealed this letter, she gave it to Father Pedro, who carried it directly to Zeluco, whom he found alone in his garden, ruminating a half-digested plan of a very atrocious nature, the object of which was the possession of Laura.

The Monk announced by his countenance that he brought agreeable news, and delivered to him Laura's letter; which, in spite of the cold terms in which it was conceived, as it pointed a more speedy and safe road to the gratification of his desires, filled him with pleasure, and entirely dissipated the dark and desperate purposes over which his mind was brooding.

He told Father Pedro that he would himself be the bearer of the answer to the letter; and immediately waited on Madame de Seidlits and Laura with all the expressions of joy usual on similar occasions.

From this moment there was a visible change for the better in the spirits and health of Madame de Seidlits; she was now convinced that her daughter had overcome her groundless dislike of Zeluco, was secured in a comfortable and genteel situation for life; of course nine-tenths of her anxiety were removed. Laura was rejoiced at the favourable alteration in her mother, reflected with satisfaction on the efforts she herself had made for the sake of a parent whom she tenderly loved, and flattered herself that an union agreed to on her part from such a pious motive, would be more fortunate than could naturally have been expected, considering the extreme indifference, to call it by no stronger a name, which she felt for her intended husband.

Zeluco soon became urgent with Madame de Seidlits that an early day might be fixed on for the marriage ceremony; saying, that he would in the mean time order the settlements to be made according to the terms formerly proposed.

She expressed a desire that the ceremony might be postponed at least till the return of Signora Sporza from Rome; one reason of Zeluco's impatience was, that it might be over before her return; dreading a delay, or perhaps a total prevention from that quarter; but, without giving any hint of such fears, he earnestly insisted on the ceremony's taking place immediately after the settlements were ready; urging that Signora Sporza would be most agreeably surprised to find that all was over at her return; and that it would give him double pleasure to salute her on their first meeting, not as a person intended to be, but who actually was, his relation. Madame de Seidlits agreed to leave it to Laura's decision, promising, at Zeluco's request, not to write to Signora Sporza till the point should be determined.

He knew that Laura wished the ceremony should be private; he directed Father Pedro to hint to her that this would be impossible after Signora Sporza's return, whose decided taste for parade and ostentation they all knew.

Laura was more easily brought to agree to an early day than was expected; having already given her consent, despising all affected delays, and wishing to have every thing conducted with as much privacy as the nature of the case would admit, she decided for the earliest day that had been mentioned. Besides the motives already mentioned, there was another which influenced this unfortunate young lady more than all the rest; she felt her original reluctance to any connexion with Zeluco threatening to return; and she wished the ceremony over, that it might be no longer in her own power to shrink from what she now thought both her duty and honour required her to perform.

The writings were prepared, and an early day appointed for the private performance of the marriage.

During this interval the heart of Laura, endowed with the most exquisite sensibility, and formed for the purest and most delicate sensations of love, was not agitated with those tender fears and pleasing emotions which fill the virgin's bosom at her approaching union with the beloved object of her wishes; she, unhappy maiden! felt an hourly increasing aversion to the man to whom she was destined to plight her faith, which all the struggles of her reason could not subdue. Her resolution however enabled her, in a great measure, to conceal what her reason could not conquer, and her efforts for this purpose rendered the pangs of her heart the more acute.

The night preceding the day of her marriage she was disturbed with gloomy forebodings, distracted with horrid dreams, and with terrors of a confused nature, which darted like lightning in a black and stormy night across her clouded imagination.

She arose early, endeavoured to banish those dismal apprehensions from her breast, and assumed as much serenity as she possibly could at the approach of her mother, who imputed the marks of disturbance that still remained in the countenance of Laura to no uncommon cause; yet all the endearments of maternal affection which Madame de Seidlits lavished on her daughter, were scarcely able to keep up her spirits: two or three times the trembling heart of Laura was ready to break through all restraint, avow her sad forebodings, and beg that this frightful marriage might be postponed for ever. She was prevented by the satisfaction she perceived it gave her mother, and by the thoughts of the light in which such fickle and childish conduct must put her in the opinion of others.

The marriage ceremony was performed privately, and Zeluco remained that night at the house of Madame de Seidlits.

CHAPTER LV.

All classic learning lose on classic ground. Pope.[1]

A day or two before Laura's marriage took place at Naples, Signora Sporza received a letter from Germany, giving her an account of the severe loss which Madame de Seidlits would sustain by the bankruptcy. This letter directed to her at Naples, had gone in course of post to that city, was there detained for some days by the neglect of her servant, and now conveyed to her the first account she had ever had of an event which gave her very great pain. She well knew the limited boundaries of Madame de Seidlits's finances; that the money which she depended on for paying some pressing debts at Naples was in this banker's hands, and of course that she would be put to immediate and very great distress by this unlucky accident; she became even afraid, lest, terrified by a species of calamity which she had never experienced, Madame de Seidlits should become more urgent than ever with Laura to give her hand to Zeluco, and lest Laura, in compliance with her mother's desire, might at last consent: but what made her more uneasy than all the rest, was her not having it in her power from any fund of her own sufficiently to relieve the distress of her friends.

In this situation she could think of nobody so able, and whom she expected to find so willing, to supply her in what she wanted, as the honourable Mr. N——. She sent a message, desiring that he would come and speak with her as soon as possible. Mr. N—— was not at home. She sent again, begging that he would come to her the moment he arrived.

But her impatience increasing as the time of the departure of the post for Naples drew near, she drove to Mr. N——'s lodging, and calling for Buchanan, told him she had business of importance with his master, and would wait for him till he came home. Buchanan shewed her into a room adjoining to Mr. Steele's dressing-room, and separated from it by a very crazy partition. Steele was there with Mr. Squander and some other young Englishmen. Signora Sporza hearing their voices, thought she distinguished that of Mr. N——. "No," said Buchanan, "it is a party of young gentlemen, who are taking a course of Roman antiquities; they wait at present for the antiquarian who instructs them; but it is my opinion, if the poor man profit no more by *them*, than they do by his lectures, he will soon be in a state of perfect starvation."

A voice was then heard, crying, "Hey, Dutchess, what the devil are you about, you slut?—ay, to her, Pincher; pull away;—tear it from her, boy."

"Who does he talk to?" said Signora Sporza.

"A couple of quadrupeds, Madam," replied Buchanan; "the one is a spaniel, the other a terrier. Those young gentlemen cannot proceed in their studies without them."

Here the door of Mr. Steele's room was opened by a servant, who said the antiquarian had sent to know whether they were inclined to go to the Pantheon that day, or to St. Peter's?[2]

"Damn the Pantheon and St. Peter's both," cried Squander; "tell him we can go to neither at present.—Zounds! cannot the fellow quietly pocket his money without *boring* us any more with his temples, and churches, and pictures, and statues?"

Steele, however, finding them determined against attending the antiquarian, followed the servant, and delivered a more civil message.

While he was absent, Squander, tossing a couple of maps on the floor, cried, "Here, Dutchess, here is *Roma Moderna*;—and there, Pincher—there is *Roma Antiqua* for you, boy—tear away."

When Steele returned, he endeavoured to save Rome from the ravages of those Goths, but Squander told him with a loud laugh, that Dutchess had made a violent rent in St. Peter's, and Pincher had torn the Pantheon to pieces.

Squander then proposed that they should walk to the stable, to examine a mare which he had thoughts of purchasing—Dutchess and Pincher followed them, and Mr. N—— came home soon after.

"I have an unexpected call for money," said Signora Sporza, interrupting his apologies for having made her wait, "I hope you can let me have it."

"I hope I can," said Mr. N——. "How much do you need?"

"Three or four hundred ounces,"[3] replied she.

"I am happy that I can, without inconveniency, spare you four hundred," replied he.

"I do not think it probable that you will be soon repaid," said she.

"I shall not need it," replied Mr. N——.

"You are an angel of a man," cried she, "give me then an order on my banker at Naples for that sum, for I must send it thither by this day's post."

Mr. N—— directly gave her the order.

"O my good friend!" cried she, "I must not tell you how I come to need this money; but, indeed, it would grieve you if you knew who—." Here Signora Sporza's voice was suppressed with grief at the idea of the distress of her two friends, and the tears fell down her cheeks; after a pause, she gave her hand to Mr. N——, who led her to her carriage, without either of them uttering another word.

As soon as Signora Sporza got home, she wrote a most affectionate letter to Madame de Seidlits, complaining of her having concealed the misfortune of the bankruptcy at Berlin, and the distress in which this accident must necessarily have involved her and Laura; and informing her, that she herself had unexpectedly recovered some money for which she had no immediate use, she begged therefore very earnestly, that Madame de Seidlits would accept of five hundred ounces, which she could without any inconveniency let her have directly. Signora Sporza added one hundred ounces, all in her power, to the four hundred advanced by Mr. N——.

Madame de Seidlits was with her daughter when she received this letter, which she immediately shewed to Laura; they were both much affected with this instance of friendship, and agreed that it would have an air of unkindness not immediately to acquaint Signora Sporza with Laura's marriage, by which she would understand that her liberality was unnecessary.

Zeluco not having now the same objection that he had formerly, assented without difficulty to their proposal; and by the next post Signora Sporza received the account of Laura's marriage with equal surprise and concern.

The following day she informed Mr. N——, "That she should always consider herself under as great an obligation to him, as if she had made use of his credit, but that she now found she would have no occasion for it, and desired him to instruct his banker at Naples to that effect."

At the interval of several hours she informed him of Laura's marriage with Zeluco. "Good heavens," exclaimed he, "is it possible!"

"What do you see extraordinary," said she, "in a very accomplished woman of no fortune marrying a very rich man."

"Of no accomplishments," said Mr. N——.

"Even if that be the case, it certainly is nothing extraordinary," said Signora Sporza. "If it is not to be wondered at, I fear it is to be regretted," added Mr. N——.

After this, Signora Sporza seemed desirous to change the subject. She would have had no scruple in acquainting Mr. N—— with any thing which regarded herself alone, but thought she had no right to inform him of the state of Madame de Seidlits's circumstances, and of course impressing him with the idea that this had driven Laura to the marriage. Signora Sporza was also much afraid that Laura, in avoiding one species of distress, had exposed herself to others, which to one of her turn of mind might prove fully as acute; and therefore she did not like to talk on the subject. Mr. N—— seeing her thoughtful and rather reserved, left her, he himself having been somewhat shocked as well as surprised at hearing of Laura's marriage.

Whatever uneasiness that event occasioned to Signora Sporza and Mr. N——, it was heard of with much satisfaction by his valet Buchanan, who lost no time in communicating the news to the Baronet, who also heard of it with pleasure; for although he did not think there was so much danger as Buchanan did, of Mr. N——'s making proposals of marriage to Laura immediately; yet he plainly perceived that he had a very high regard for that lady, and he particularly remarked, that his nephew did not at all relish a proposal which had been made by way of sounding him, that he should accompany his uncle to England without returning to Naples; in short, he thought, that although Mr. N—— might be sensible of the inconveniences of uniting himself to a woman of Laura's religion and country, yet these inconveniences would naturally dwindle in his estimation, in proportion as his admiration of the lady increased. He therefore could not help being pleased with the account of Laura's marriage.

The Baronet observed that Mr. N—— was by no means in his usual spirits after this intelligence, he therefore omitted nothing that he imagined could tend to the amusement of his young friend; and frequently proposed excursions to Tivoli, Frescati, and other places in the neighbourhood of Rome.[4]

Mr. Steele was generally of these parties; but one day, when the Knight and Mr. N—— had agreed to dine at Albano, Mr. Steele was prevailed on to stay and make one at a cricket match with some British gentlemen and their footmen, who were at that time at Rome.

After dinner, the Baronet asked Mr. N——, how he liked the new acquaintance whom his father and aunt had recommended to him, meaning Mr. Steele.

"It is impossible not to like him," replied N——, "for he is one of the best-natured easy tempered fellows alive, and at the same time of the greatest integrity. When he first arrived at Naples, he seemed thoughtful and rather melancholy. This however, being no part of his natural disposition, soon wore away, and now the genuine cheerful and obliging colour of his character is almost always predominant."

"Does he intend to remain long in Italy?" said the Baronet.

"I believe he will remain as long as I do," replied N——, "and no longer, for he does me the honour of being more attached to me than to Italy; and I for my part have the most perfect good-will to him, although he is not precisely the kind of man whom I should have expected my father to recommend to my particular acquaintance; yet I shall ever think myself obliged to him for it. I do not so much as know of what family he is," continued Mr. N——, "nor by what means he got acquainted with ours, for Steele is not spontaneously communicative; and you know, Sir, I am not a great asker of questions."

"I can give you some account of those matters," said the Baronet, "for I have frequently heard your father describe his first interview with this young man's uncle."

But as we know more of Mr. Steele's family than the Baronet did, we shall in the next chapter give the reader a more circumstantial account than was in his power.

CHAPTER LVI.

Anecdotes concerning Mr. Nathaniel Transfer.

Mr. Nathaniel Transfer, uncle to the young man now in question, had made a large fortune in the city of London, where he was born, and where he lived happily till the age of sixty-five. Mr. Transfer's life may surely be called happy, since it afforded him the only enjoyments which he was capable of relishing; he had the pleasure of finding his fortune increasing every year; he had a remarkably good appetite, relished a bottle of old port, and slept very soundly all night, particularly after a bottle of Burton Ale. He might have continued some years longer in the same state of felicity, and perhaps have been conveyed to the other world in a gentle lethargy, without sickness, like a passenger who sleeps the whole way from Dover to Calais, had it not been for the importunities of a set of people who called themselves his friends; these officious persons were continually disturbing his tranquillity with such speeches as the following: "Why should you, Mr. Transfer, continue to live all your life in the city, and follow the drudgery of business like a poor man who has his fortune to make? It is surely time for you to begin and enjoy a little ease and pleasure after so much toil and labour. What benefit will accrue to you from your great fortune, if you are determined never to enjoy it? Good God, Mr. Transfer, do you intend to slave for ever?—You certainly have already more money than you have any use for."

This last assertion was unquestionably true, although the inference those reasoners drew from it was false. The fourth part of his fortune was a great deal more than Transfer had any use for; gathering of pebbles, or accumulating pounds, would have been equally beneficial to him, if he could have taken an equal interest in the one occupation as in the other, and if he could have contemplated the one heap with equal satisfaction with the other. He had not the shadow of a wish to spend more than he did, nor the least desire of benefiting any of the human race by the fruits of his labour. But Mr. Transfer's advisers had forgot the power of habit upon the mind of man. Transfer, like thousands of others, had begun to accumulate money as the means of enjoying pleasure at some future time; and continued the practice so long, that the means became the end—the mere habit of accumulating, and the routine of business, secured him from tedium, and became the greatest enjoyment of which he was susceptible. Not being aware of this himself, poor Transfer at last yielded to his friends' importunity. "Well, I am determined to be a slave no longer; it does not signify talking," says he, "I will begin and *enjoy* without any more loss of time."

He wound up his affairs with all possible expedition, gave up all connexions in business at once, bought an estate in the country, with a very convenient house in good repair upon it, to which he went soon after, determining to rest from his labours, and to take his fill of pleasure. But he quickly found rest the most laborious thing that he had ever experienced, and that to have nothing to do, was the most fatiguing business on earth. In the course of business, his occupations followed each other at stated times, and in regular succession; the hours passed imperceptibly without seeming tedious, or requiring any effort on his part to make them move faster. But now he felt them to move heavily and sluggishly, and while he yawned along his serpentine walks and fringed parterres,[1] he thought the day would never have an end.

His house was at too great a distance from London for his city friends to go down on a Saturday, and return to town on Monday. His neighbours in the country were ignorant of that circle of ideas which had rolled in his brain with little variation for the last forty years of his life; and he was equally unacquainted with the objects of their contemplations: unless it was their mutual love of port wine and Burton ale, they had hardly a sentiment in common with Mr. Transfer, who was left for many a tedious hour, particularly before dinner, to enjoy rural felicity by himself, or with no other company than a few gods and goddesses which he had bought in Piccadilly,[2] and placed in his garden. "They talk," said he to himself, "of the pleasures of the country, but would to God I had never been persuaded to leave the labours of the city for such woful pleasures. O Lombard-street! Lombard-street![3] in evil hour did I forsake thee for verdant walks and flowery landscapes, and that there tiresome piece of made water. What walk is so agreeable as a walk through the streets of London? what landscape more flowery than those in the print-shops? and what water was ever made by man equal to the Thames? If here I venture to walk but a short way beyond my own fields, I may be wet through by a sudden shower, and exposed to the wind of every quarter, before I get under shelter; but in walking through the streets of London, if it rains, a man can shelter himself under the Piazzas;[4] if the wind is in his face while he walks along one street, he may turn into another; if he is hungry, he can be refreshed at the pastry shops; if tired, he can call a hackney coach; and he is sure of meeting with entertaining company every evening at the club."

Such were Mr. Transfer's daily reflexions; and he was often tempted to abandon the country for ever, to return to Lombard-street, and re-assume his old occupations.

It is probable that he would have yielded to the temptation, had it not been for an acquaintance which he accidentally formed with the Earl of ——.

This nobleman, who was very subject to the gout, lived almost constantly in the country. What contributed with his bad health to give him a dislike to the town, was his fixed disapprobation of the public measures at that time carried on, and his indignation at the conduct of his eldest son, who had accepted of a place at court, and voted with administration.

The Earl resided therefore ten months in the year at a very noble mansion in the middle of his estate, and at no great distance from the house which Transfer had lately purchased. After the death of the Countess, his sister Lady Elizabeth, a maiden lady of an excellent character, always presided at his table, with whom Miss Warren, the daughter of a navy officer, who had lost his life in the service, resided as a friend and companion.

The Earl had often heard of a rich citizen who had bought an estate in his neighbourhood, and the whole country resounded with the style in which he had ornamented his garden, and the peculiar charms of a little snug rotunda[5] which he had just finished on the verge of his ground, and which impended the great London road.

As Mr. Transfer sat one day in this gay fabric, smoking his pipe, and enjoying the dust, the Earl passed in his carriage, which, without having observed Mr. Transfer, he ordered to stop, that he might survey the new erection at leisure. The citizen directly popped his head out at the window, and politely invited his Lordship to enter, and he would shew him not only that room, but also the other improvements he had made in his gardens.

My lord accepted the invitation, and was conducted by Mr. Transfer over all this scene of taste. The marks of astonishment which the former displayed at almost every thing he beheld, afforded great satisfaction to Mr. Transfer; the turn of whose conversation, and the singular observations he made, equally delighted his Lordship.

"Pray, Mr. Transfer," said he, pointing to one of the statues which stood at the end of the walk, "what figure is that?"

"That, my Lord," answered Transfer, "that there statue I take to be—let me recollect—yes, I take that to be either Venus or Vulcan, but upon my word I cannot exactly tell which.—Here, you, James,"—calling to the gardener;—"is this Venus or Vulcan?"[6]

"That is Wenus," answered the man; "Wulcan is lame of a leg, and stands upon one foot in the next alley."

"Yes, yes; this is Venus, sure enough," said Transfer, "though I was not quite certain at first."

"Perhaps it is not an easy matter to distinguish them," said the Earl.

"Why, they are both made of the same metal, my Lord," said Transfer.

"She ought to be bone of his bone, and flesh of his flesh," resumed the Earl, "for you know Venus was Vulcan's wife, Mr. Transfer."

"I am bound to believe she was," replied Transfer, "since your Lordship says so."

"You have so many of these gods, Mr. Transfer," said the Earl, "that it is difficult to be master of all their private histories."

"It is so, my Lord," said Transfer, "I was a good while of learning their names,—but I know them all pretty well now.—That there man, in the highland garb, is Mars. And the name of the old fellow with the pitch-fork is Neptune."[7]

"You are now very perfect indeed, Mr. Transfer," said the Earl.

At his departure, my Lord invited Mr. Transfer to dine with him the following day, introduced him to his sister, and was so entertained with his conversation and manners, that he visited him frequently, and often invited him to N—— house, where an apartment was kept for him, to which he was made welcome as often as he found himself tired with his own home, which, to the Earl's great satisfaction, was pretty frequently.

Yet even at N—— house, Mr. Transfer sometimes had occasion to regret Lombard-street, particularly in the forenoons, and when the weather was bad.

One day, immediately after breakfast, when there was no company but Mr. Transfer—"It rains so furiously," said the Earl, "that there is no driving out.—How shall we amuse ourselves, Mr. Transfer?"

"Why, I should think smoking a pipe or two the pleasantest way of passing the time in such raw moist weather," said Transfer.

"Yes; that might do pretty well for you and me," said the Earl; "but as far as I recollect, neither my sister, nor this young lady, ever smoke."

"If that is the case," replied Transfer, "we must think of something else more to their taste, for I scorn not to be agreeable to the ladies."

"Have you got any thing new to read to us, sister?" said the Peer.

"That might do for you and me, brother," said she; "but perhaps Mr. Transfer never reads."

"Forgive me, Madam," said Transfer, "I have no particular aversion to it. I have sometimes read for half an hour at a stretch since I have been settled in the country, and I believe I could hold out longer, if I were not so apt to fall asleep."

Some time after this, Lady Elizabeth expressed her surprise to Mr. Transfer, that, as he was a batchelor, he did not think of having some of his female relations to take care of his family rather than a mercenary housekeeper.

To this Mr. Transfer replied, That he had been put very early to business, and not being accustomed to his relations, he had never cared much for any of them, except his sister, who had lived with him several years in Lombard-street; and as he was then *accustomed to her*, he had a good deal of kindness for her, but that she had made an ungrateful return for all his kindness.

"I am sorry for that," said Lady Elizabeth, "but I hope your sister did nothing very bad."

"Yes, but she did," resumed Transfer; "for she actually married, without my approbation, a young man of the name of Steele, with little fortune, and no experience in business, although she knew that I had a very *warm* man of established credit in my eye for her, provided she would only have had a little patience."

"Provided she had liked the man you had in your eye, and provided he had liked her, you mean, Mr. Transfer," said Lady Elizabeth.

"I beg your Ladyship's forgiveness," said Transfer; "still she would have stood in need of a little patience."

"Could not they have married when they pleased, if they were both willing, and you desirous of the match?" added she.

"I was most desirous of the match," replied Transfer; "but still there was an obstacle."

"What obstacle?" said she.

"The man I had in my eye for my sister had a wife then alive," answered Transfer.

"I confess that *was* an obstacle!" cried Lady Elizabeth.

"But she was dying of a consumption," added Transfer, "and I had reason to believe that he would propose marriage to my sister very soon after his wife's death."

"Did his wife die as he expected?" said Lady Elizabeth.

"Yes; that she did," said Transfer; "but she might as well have lived, for my sister had secretly married the other three weeks before."

"That was unlucky indeed. But what became of your sister and her husband?"

"I never saw my sister from the time of her marriage," said Transfer, "till after her husband became a bankrupt; for he broke within a very few years."

"Poor man!" cried Lady Elizabeth; "but you saw your sister after her misfortune?"

"Yes; I could not help it," said Transfer, "for she burst in upon me, begging that I would engage my credit for re-establishing her husband."

"Which I hope you did," said Lady Elizabeth.

"As I had refused to have any connexion with him, even when he was in some credit, your Ladyship can hardly suppose that I would begin one after he was quite broken," said Transfer.

As Lady Elizabeth was a little shocked at this observation, she made no reply. It was not in her power to say any thing obliging on this occasion, and it was not in her nature to say any thing harsh:—she only was silent. Which the Earl, who was present, observing, "To be sure, Mr. Transfer," said he, "that is not to be supposed."

"But yet," resumed Transfer, "as she was my sister, I told her that if she would give up all connexion with her husband, I was willing to receive her again into my house, and put her child out to nurse at my own expence."

"That was very fair on your part," said the Earl; "well, what reply did your sister make to this?"

"Why, she absolutely refused, my Lord; which is a pretty clear proof," continued Mr. Transfer, "of her loving her husband, though he was a bankrupt, better than her own brother, of whom there was not the least suspicion to his discredit; for which reason I turned her away, refusing positively to do any thing for her husband."

"Well, what became of them?" said the Peer.

"I heard afterwards that they were reduced to great distress.—But what are bankrupts to expect?" continued Transfer; "and as for my sister, she was not to be pitied, because she might have lived perfectly easy both in body and mind in my house in Lombard-street, if she had taken my advice, and abandoned her husband, and sent her child to nurse, or to board in the country."

"Nothing can be more clear," said the Earl, "than that you have acted like yourself, and have done every thing for your sister that could be expected of you.—But after all, what became of her?"

"A relation of her husband's happened to die, and left him a small estate in Yorkshire, of five or six hundred a-year; and as neither he, nor my sister, had any *ambition*, and were afraid of a new bankruptcy if they had settled in town; he retired to his small estate, where he died a few years ago, leaving no other children but the son whom she refused to send out to nurse, and who has now arrived at man's estate."

"Whereas," added the Earl, "if she had followed your advice, and given him out to nurse, she might probably have had him off her hands long ago."

"Why, there is no knowing what might have happened," said Transfer, "for most of those children die before they arrive at the years of discretion, which is very well ordered, as they have nothing to live on."

"Well, but Mr. Transfer," resumed the Peer, "do *you* ever intend to marry?"

"No, my Lord," replied he; "I cannot say I do;—as I never was *accustomed to a wife*, I am not much inclined to matrimony; for through the whole course of my life I have never found any thing agree with me, but what I am accustomed to."

"That is very wisely observed," said the Earl; "but this young man of course will be your heir?"

"Unquestionably," answered Transfer; "the young man never offended me; and as he is my nearest of kin, I should be sorry to do an unjust thing, and leave my fortune to any other body.—No, no; he shall have all at my death, but he must wait till then; besides, it is so far lucky that it saves my making a will, to which I have always had an aversion; for this young man being my lawful heir, there is no need to employ an attorney to leave him his due."

CHAPTER LVII.

Reasons for going into Holy Orders.

Gaudet equis, canibusque. Hor.[1]

The strange apathy which Transfer discovered, and which shocked Lady Elizabeth, seemed to be a source of amusement to her brother;

who, however, was surprised at perceiving that Transfer expressed not the least desire of ever seeing an only sister, and still more that he should have the same indifference towards a nephew whom he considered as his heir, and who he owned had never offended him. The insensibility of Transfer for his sister and nephew seemed to inspire the Earl with an interest in them. He wrote to an acquaintance, who resided in that part of the country in which Mrs. Steele and her son lived, desiring an account of both their characters, and a particular detail regarding their circumstances and manner of life, especially what the views of the son were.

In consequence of this, the Earl was informed, that Mrs. Steele was an agreeable woman, of a cheerful temper and benevolent disposition, without much foresight, and distractedly fond of her son, whom she had never been able to contradict in her life: that he was a young fellow of that genuine and rare good-nature that resists the usual effect of so much indulgence; for, although his mother's study was to gratify, not to correct his humours, this ill-judged partiality had only prevented his improvement, without rendering him capricious, unfeeling, or wicked: that while he remained at school, he had applied himself to nothing; but that ever since he left it, he had applied himself with unremitting diligence to hunting and shooting, in both of which, and in the knowledge of horses and dogs, he had made great proficiency for his age; that he was made welcome wherever he went, and was a great favourite with man, woman, and child, all over the country: and that a noble Lord, of very great influence, who was particularly fond of him, had lately told young Steele, that he would be very happy to have it in his power to be of service to him; adding, "That if he chose to go into the army, he would immediately procure him a cornetcy of dragoons,[2] and would do all in his power to assist his promotion afterwards."

Steele, after expressing his gratitude for so much goodness, declined the proposal, saying, he was quite unfit for the army.

The nobleman was the more surprised at this, as he had a notion that the army was the profession, of all others, for which Mr. Steele was fittest, being genteel in his person, of a bold intrepid disposition, and capable of bearing the greatest bodily fatigue.

"You may, perhaps, have no inclination for the service," said his Lordship.—"But—"

"Nay, my Lord," resumed Mr. Steele, "if there were any likelihood of a war, I should prefer it to any other line of life; because, in the time of war, a soldier is continually occupied, and can have no wish but doing his duty—but then what a sad business must it be in the time of peace?"

"During a successful war," said my Lord, "a soldier will naturally be in high spirits; but I do not perceive why he should be peculiarly sad in the time of peace."

"*I* certainly should, my Lord," said Steele; "your Lordship knows my excessive fondness for shooting, and the chase;—to be obliged to attend my regiment during those seasons would render me quite miserable."

"Why, the same objection," said his Lordship, "may be made to law, physic, and almost every other profession."

"It may so," replied Steele.

"Then you wish to be of no profession," said the Peer.

"Forgive me, my Lord," said the other, "I am sensible that my circumstances are so narrow, that I cannot hope to indulge my taste for my favourite amusements in the style I could wish, without being assisted by the emoluments of some profession."

"What profession then would you choose to be of?" rejoined his Lordship.

"That of a clergyman," replied Mr. Steele.

"A clergyman!" exclaimed the Peer.

"Yes, my Lord," continued Steele; "I confess I have a great desire to enter into holy orders."

"I cannot conceive," said the Peer, "what can be your inducement."

"My fondness for hunting and shooting," answered Steele; "and if, by your Lordship's favour, I could obtain a tolerable living in a hunting county, I should think myself extremely happy. The business of a clergyman, as your Lordship knows, from many examples, is no way incompatible with a passion for those manly amusements, without which I am sure life would seem a very dull affair in my eyes."

"But there are certain duties of a clergyman," said the Peer, "which, in some people's eyes, are not exceedingly entertaining."

"I should think them no great hardships, my Lord," said Steele: "In case of the indisposition of my curate,[3] on particular occasions, I have no manner of objection to reading prayers, or to preaching; and on the whole I do not despair of rendering myself agreeable to the generality of my flock; for, with regard to comforting the sick and relieving the poor, I thank Heaven I am disposed to perform those duties whether I shall ever be a clergyman or not."

"All this is very well," resumed the Peer; "but, my dear Steele, are not there some previous studies necessary before you can be—"

"Certainly;" replied the other, interrupting his Lordship; "and I have of late been preparing myself accordingly. I confess I was too inattentive at school, which renders this task the harder upon me now; yet I hope to surmount all obstacles, and give satisfaction to the bishop. My passion for hunting and shooting instigates me to exertions in study which I never knew before."

"Nay, Heaven forefend," replied the Peer, smiling, "that I should attempt to blunt such laudable instigations. All I have to say is, that when you are once fairly ordained, I beg you will let me know: there is some considerable chance of a living, which is in my gift, being vacant very soon, and you may rely upon it, my dear Steele, that if you continue in your present way of thinking, and are completely dubbed,[4] that I will prefer no man to yourself."

CHAPTER LVIII.

Ille bonis faveatque, et concilietur amicis. HOR.[1]

THIS account of Mrs. Steele and her son did not diminish the inclination the Earl had to serve them, in which he was assisted by Lady Elizabeth. They found no difficulty in prevailing on Mr. Transfer to give Steele an invitation to visit him, with which the young man immediately complied. His appearance, natural complaisance, and everlasting good-humour, rendered him highly agreeable to all the family at N—— House, without excepting Miss Warren, the young lady who lived with Lady Elizabeth. Here it will not be improper to mention by what accident this young lady came to be introduced into the family of the Earl of ——.

Lady Elizabeth happened to pass through the county town at a time when the inhabitants, by ringing of bells, bonfires, and illuminations, were announcing their joy for a victory obtained by a celebrated naval commander. She stopped her carriage at the door of an old female acquaintance, intending merely to leave a message, but understanding that she was a little indisposed, Lady Elizabeth went to see her; as she entered the chamber, a beautiful girl of about thirteen or fourteen years of age, with severe marks of sorrow, went out. After Lady Elizabeth had satisfied herself that her friend's indisposition was but slight, and that she was in a way of recovery, she inquired who that lovely girl was who had just left the room, and why she seemed so much afflicted.

"Alas, poor girl," replied the other, "she has received the account of her father's being killed in the very action for which the citizens are displaying all those marks of joy. Unfortunate girl," continued she, "by her father's death, she is not only deprived of her only surviving parent, but perhaps the very means of subsistence; for there is great reason to fear that her father, who was a very generous as well as a brave man, has left more debts than effects."

"Poor young creature," said Lady Elizabeth, "how much is she to be pitied—how came you acquainted with her?"

"I am a distant relation of her mother's," replied Lady Elizabeth's friend; "on hearing of her father's death, I invited her to my house, that I might sooth her affliction, and prevent her being shocked at seeing her young companions, unmindful of her particular calamity, take part in the general joy."

The humane and benevolent heart of Lady Elizabeth was strongly affected at this recital; she continued for some time in silent contemplation on the hard lot of this unhappy orphan, whose tender bosom was wounded by one of the sharpest arrows in the whole quiver of adversity, at a time when the hearts of all around her were elated with joy.

She desired that the young lady might be introduced to her; she spoke to her the soothing language of sympathy; and was charmed with her appearance, her conversation, and the whole of her behaviour.

Lady Elizabeth afterwards made an application to this young lady's nearest relations, proposing to take on herself the charge of her maintenance and education, to which they agreed with the most ready acquiescence. She carried her to N—— House; the Earl, who had known Miss Warren's father a little, and had a high esteem for his character, was delighted with what his sister proposed, and Miss Warren gained daily upon the affections of both, and was now the confidential friend and inseparable companion of her patroness.

We now return to Mr. Transfer, who became in a short time *accustomed* to his nephew, and at length so fond of him, that he could hardly bear his absence for a few hours.

Not all the interest which Steele had in pleasing Mr. Transfer, however, nor even the more powerful attractions of Miss Warren, could prevail on this young man to remain at his uncle's house, after he received a letter from his mother, written in rather low spirits, and expressing a desire to see him.

He assured his uncle, in spite of his solicitations to the contrary, that he would set out for Yorkshire the very next morning. Transfer complained of this to the Earl, saying, "It was strange perverseness in the young man to prefer his mother's company, who could do nothing for him, to his, who intended to do so much."

"The general run of people would certainly act otherwise," replied the Earl; "but why cannot Mr. Steele have the pleasure both of your company and his mother's? for although she ought not to be put on an equal footing with a man of your *great wealth*, Mr. Transfer, yet the affection the young man shews to his mother is no way unnatural neither."

"I do not assert that it is," said Transfer, "but what would your Lordship have me to do, for I do not love to part with this youth, after having become *accustomed to him*; and perhaps his mother may not allow him to return so soon as I could wish."

"Invite his mother to come with him," replied the Earl, "and then he'll stay as long as you please."

This was an expedient which had never entered into Transfer's mind; but he agreed to it the moment it was proposed. He wrote to his sister to detain her son as short a time as possible, and begged of her to accompany him to his house. Lady Elizabeth wrote also to Mrs. Steele, expressing a desire to be acquainted with her, and urging her to forget old misunderstandings, and accept without delay of her brother's invitation.

Mrs. Steele came accordingly with her son, and was received by her brother with some appearance of kindness, while to her son he displayed as much as was in his nature to discover. The following day she was visited by the family at N—— House; was invited there, and treated in the most obliging manner: she had not resided a couple of months with Mr. Transfer, till he entirely forgot Lombard-street, and felt less desire of forsaking his own mansion for that of the Earl; and at last, being again accustomed to his sister, and she bestowing more attention to amuse him, he became fonder of her company than even of her son's, who, it must be confessed, began to have a greater desire for Miss Warren's company, than for that of either his uncle or mother.

This was a happiness he never enjoyed, however, but in the presence of Lady Elizabeth, to whom his partiality for her young friend was very evident.

The Earl took occasion one day when he found himself alone with Transfer, to mention young Steele's fancy for being a clergyman.

"That is a business," said Transfer, "which there is very little to be made of. I have no notion of purchasing in a lottery where there are so many blanks and so few prizes, my Lord."

"Would you not be happy to see your nephew a Bishop?" said the Earl.

"I should be much happier to see him an independent gentleman," replied Transfer.

"You may enjoy that happiness when you please," said the Earl; "for it is in your power to make him so without injuring yourself, or any person on earth."

This led to a long conversation, in which his Lordship, with less difficulty than he expected, convinced Mr. Transfer, that nothing would do him so much honour, or contribute more to his own happiness, than executing what had been thus accidentally hinted. Mrs. Steele and her son had by their cheerful attention gained the citizen's heart so completely, as almost to alter his nature; he had no enjoyment with which they were not intimately connected; and when the Earl told him, that by giving Steele a genteel independence, he would add the generous ties of gratitude and esteem to those of blood by which the young man was already bound to him, the citizen became impatient till the deed was drawn out, which, to the astonishment of Mrs. Steele and her son, was presented to him as soon as executed.

CHAPTER LIX.

> Neglected, Tray and Pointer lie;
> And covies unmolested fly. PRIOR.[1]

IN the mean while, the shooting season passed away without Mr. Steele shewing any desire of profiting by it; his growing passion for Miss Warren entirely occupied his mind. He long watched, in vain, for a proper opportunity of declaring his sentiments to her, and when the long-expected opportunity occurred, the timidity which always attends sincere and respectful love, prevented him from seizing it. But the affable and obliging character of Lady Elizabeth encouraged him to mention to *her* those sentiments which he had been unable to express to the young Lady herself.

Lady Elizabeth's answer implied that he ought to attempt no engagement of such a nature, without the approbation of his mother and uncle.

He said, he was certain of the former, but deferred speaking to his uncle till he had some reason to hope that his proposals were not disagreeable to Miss Warren.

Lady Elizabeth consented to sound her young friend on the subject, but she first informed her brother.

"I am rejoiced to hear this," said the Earl; "for Transfer and his sister seem both fond of her, and I dare say will be pleased with the proposal; Steele is so very good-humoured a young fellow, that I am convinced he will make the sweet girl happy; and in her he will have one of the best wives in England. But how is she inclined herself?"

"That is what I am not quite certain of," replied Lady Elizabeth; "but Mr. Steele's appearance and disposition must be powerful advocates in his favour."

When Lady Elizabeth mentioned to Miss Warren what passed between her and Mr. Steele, the young lady, with some degree of solemnity and earnestness, begged to know whether her Ladyship or the Earl had any wish, or were at all interested in the answers she should give to Mr. Steele.

"None, my sweet friend," said Lady Elizabeth; "but that it should be dictated by your own genuine uninfluenced inclination."

"The whole of your ever noble and generous behaviour ought to have left me no doubt of such an answer," cried Miss Warren, as she kissed her Ladyship's hand. "I will now, as you desire, tell you my genuine sentiments. It is some time," continued she, "since I perceived Mr. Steele's partiality for me, and thought it not impossible that he might make this proposal. I have therefore had time to weigh the matter fully. Mr. Steele is evidently of a cheerful and obliging disposition; he is agreeable in his person, and I doubt not possesses other good qualities: I know what his uncle has already done for him, and what there is a probability of his still doing; yet all those advantages do not tempt me from the happy asylum I have found at N—— House for these six years past; and although I think myself obliged to Mr. Steele for his good opinion, I would rather remain the friend of Lady Elizabeth N—— than be the wife of Mr. Steele."

"If the one were incompatible with the other, I am the last person in the world that would have proposed it," said Lady Elizabeth.

"I would rather, if left to my own choice," said Miss Warren, "remain the one without being the other."

Lady Elizabeth urged her friend no farther, but in the most soothing terms possible communicated her determination to Mr. Steele, whose whole behaviour was expressive then, and for some time afterwards, of the severity of his disappointment, and the permanency of his esteem for the lady.

The truth was, that Miss Warren, although her heart was disengaged, and although she thought favourably of Steele in some respects, yet being herself a young lady of a very accomplished mind, she perceived Mr. Steele's deficiency in certain parts of knowledge which she thought requisite for securing to a gentleman the esteem of the world.

The effect which her refusal had on Mr. Steele's spirits appeared in spite of his efforts to conceal it; he was teased and distressed by his uncle's inquires into the cause of the alteration in his spirits, and finding no return of taste for his former amusements, he told the Earl that he had a strong inclination to go abroad for a year, and begged of his Lordship to endeavour to make his design palatable to Mr. Transfer.

The Earl, to whom his sister had communicated Miss Warren's determination, approved very highly of Mr. Steele's plan, not only as the most likely measure that could be adopted for dissipating that uneasiness and dejection which obscured the natural gaiety of his disposition, but also for the improvement of his mind, and enlarging the range of his ideas.

He represented therefore to Mr. Transfer, that his nephew's health was evidently on the decline, and that a short excursion to the continent was necessary for its re-establishment. After some struggle, the Earl obtained Mr. Transfer's assent; Steele himself having by the same argument previously prevailed on his mother, not only to abstain from any kind of opposition, but even to be solicitous for his speedy departure.

The Earl's second son, the Honourable Mr. N——, had some

considerable time before this returned to Italy, partly from choice, but in some degree also on account of a complaint in his breast, and was to spend the ensuing winter at Naples. Mr. Steele had occasionally heard the Earl read some parts of his letters, from which, as well as from his general character, he had formed a very high opinion of him, and had a great desire to be of his acquaintance. The Earl therefore gave him a letter to his son, recommending him as a young gentleman in whose welfare he was greatly interested; and Lady Elizabeth wrote to her nephew in the same strain.

When Mr. Steele came to London, he accidentally met with an acquaintance going to Milan; they went together, stopping only one day at Paris, and that merely because the gentleman had some business to transact there, which when he had finished he had the complaisance to tell Steele, that although he himself was perfectly well acquainted with Paris, and had no further business in it, yet rather than lose the pleasure of his company to Milan, he would remain a week or two at Paris, that he might have an opportunity of viewing some of the curiosities of this celebrated capital before he went to Italy.

Steele thanked him, but begged that their journey might not be retarded an instant on his account. "I thought," said his companion, "I heard you say you never had been here before."

"I never was," said Steele.

"Would not you like then to take a view of the town before we go?" said the other.

"Why, faith," replied Steele, "I never had much pleasure in looking at towns; and as for this here, I am heartily tired of it already."

They set out therefore directly for Milan, and the day after their arrival Steele meeting with an English footman, who had already made the tour of Italy, engaged him, and proceeded the following morning to Rome, where he slept one night, and next day he told his servant to order post-horses, that they might continue their journey to Naples.

"Good God," cried the man, "will not your honour stay one single day at Rome?"

"I have some thoughts of it," said Steele, "when I return."

He arrived in good health at Naples, where he soon found Mr. N——, who, independent of the warm recommendations from his father and aunt, was in a short time so pleased with the careless good humour and singularity of Steele's disposition, that he procured him an apartment in the house where he himself lodged; and they had lived together ever since.

The Baronet could not give so particular a detail of Steele's family as has been now given; but he mentioned every circumstance relating to them that was known to himself—after which he and Mr. N—— returned from Albano to Rome, where they found Mr. Steele just returned to his lodgings from the cricket party.

And there we shall leave them, and return to Naples and to Laura.

CHAPTER LX.

> Regretter ce que l'on aime est un bien, en comparaison de vivre avec ce que l'on hait.
> LA BRUYERE.[1]

ZELUCO was not long married before it was pretty generally known, notwithstanding the intention of keeping it for some time secret. The marriage, therefore, was publicly avowed, and Laura appeared in all the brilliancy of dress and equipage, which riches can procure, and the ostentatious taste of her husband exacted. She was universally admired, and the acquaintance of her husband assiduously courted by many who, previous to his marriage, shewed no great inclination to cultivate it.

Possessed of great riches, with the advantage of birth, and having obtained the woman he had long ardently desired, it is natural to imagine that Zeluco now enjoyed happiness, or at least tranquillity; but any tolerable degree of tranquillity is incompatible with perfidy and fraud; besides, this wretched man possessed two qualities which never mingle smoothly in the character of a husband; he was excessively jealous, and excessively vain of his wife's beauty: a wiser man might have been excused for the latter, but the conduct and character of Laura left him without any rational pretext for the former. To drive round the beauteous environs of Naples in the carriage with her mother, to improve her mind by books, and to divert it by music, from certain painful reflections which often intruded themselves, in spite of all her endeavours, were the sole amusements and occupations she was inclined to in the absence of her husband. When he was present, which was by no means the most comfortable part of her time, substituting a sense of duty, all that was in her power, in the place of affection, which she could not command, she adapted her conversation and conduct, as much as she could, to what she thought would please him: but if there are tempers of such an unfortunate frame that even when joined to goodness of disposition it is impossible to please, how then could the efforts of this unhappy young woman prove successful, who had to deal with a peevish temper engrafted on a vicious disposition?

Zeluco's vanity was continually inciting him to carry Laura to places of public resort; yet such was the capricious absurdity of the man, that he was at once desirous of displaying the beauty of his wife, and unable to bear the admiration which it always attracted. And when she was particularly accosted by those gentlemen whom he himself had introduced to her acquaintance, the commonest civility on her part, such as the laws of good manners render indispensable, filled him with chagrin, and seldom failed, for some hours, to throw an additional shade of ill-humour upon the habitual gloom of his temper: so that it was impossible for Laura to gratify his vanity without exciting his jealousy; and it is difficult to determine, even during the period in which his fondness was at the height, whether she afforded *him* more pain or pleasure, while it is certain that his behaviour, from the beginning, filled *her* with vexation and remorse.

An Italian of high rank, from a different part of Italy, happened at this time to come to Naples, where he lived at considerable expence, and in an ostentatious style; he was presented to Laura by Zeluco himself, soon after their marriage: peculiarly pleased with her conversation and behaviour, this nobleman addressed himself more to her than to any other woman, as often as he met her in public. This was remarked by Zeluco, and produced the usual effect on his temper.—Laura, conscious of no impropriety in thought or conduct, imputed her husband's ill-humour on this, as on other similar occasions, to an unfortunate habit of fretting without cause, and took notice of it in no other way than by redoubling her endeavours to please him. Zeluco himself, though he was unable to control the sulkiness of his temper, was, for some time, ashamed to mention to her what occasioned, or rather what increased it, in the present instance. At length, however, he expressed some disapprobation of the attention which this nobleman paid her.

"I will most cheerfully abstain," said Laura, "from going to those places where I have any chance of meeting him."

"How is that possible?" said Zeluco; "he is at every public place."

"I will go to no public place," said Laura.

"That would seem very singular," resumed he.

"The singularity is of small importance," said she, "provided you are satisfied."

"No;" replied he, "it would be improper for you not to go to those assemblies which all people of rank frequent, but you may behave in such a manner when you see him there, as will prevent his speaking to you any more."

"In what manner is that?" said Laura.

"A woman who is displeased with a man's addresses, is never at a loss to find it out," replied he.

"But I have not the least reason to be displeased with the manner in which this gentleman addresses me," said she; "yet, if you *have*, I certainly wish to converse with him no more."

"Every woman who has no desire of pleasing a man," resumed Zeluco, "knows an easy way of breaking up all connection with him, without absenting herself from the places where there is a probability of meeting him."

"Well," replied Laura, endeavouring to smile, "I am a woman quite ignorant of that easy way, yet assuredly I have no particular desire of pleasing the person in question."

"I am not quite sure of that," said he.

"How shall I prove it to you?" resumed Laura.

"By turning abruptly from him," replied Zeluco, "when he next speaks to you."

"Would not that be rude," replied Laura, "to one of his rank, and whom you introduced to me?—but I am sure you say this only in jest.—Come, my way is the best—let me avoid public places—at least till he leaves Naples; it is but three weeks."

"How came you to know so exactly," said Zeluco, with an air of surprise, "when he was to leave Naples?"

"By your informing me," replied Laura.

"My informing you!" said he.

"Yes," replied Laura; "do you not remember that a few days ago you told my mother and me that he was to set out for Rome in less than a month?"

"The news seems to have made a strong impression on you," said Zeluco, peevishly.

"Just enough to make me recollect it now, for the first time since you mentioned it," replied Laura.

"Well, you will behave as you think proper," said Zeluco, in a little better humour; "but you cannot but understand his drift in the great attention he pays you."

"I have seen nothing but politeness in his behaviour to me," she replied; "but the moment he discovers any drift that ought to be disagreeable to you, I shall certainly turn from him in the manner you desire."

Zeluco withdrew, and Laura, with a sigh, exclaimed, "Alas! my mother, had you known this man, the wealth of India could not have brought your consent to his being united to your poor unfortunate daughter."—She then burst into a flood of tears, and having in this manner assuaged the anguish of her heart, she wiped her eyes, summoned all her firmness, and met her mother and husband at dinner with a serene and cheerful countenance.

CHAPTER LXI.

The Prisoners.

Some little time after this, Madame de Seidlits received a very unexpected letter from her son-in-law,[1] dated from Rome, in which he acquainted her, that his friend Baron Carlostein and he were just arrived in that city, and intended soon to pay her a visit at Naples.

Baron Carlostein had long had a great inclination to visit Italy, and had received his sovereign's permission for that purpose; while he was preparing for his journey, it occurred to him, that his friend Seidlits would probably be happy to have an opportunity of seeing his mother and sister, particularly the latter, of whose marriage he had lately heard. The Baron, therefore, asked it as a particular favour of Captain Seidlits to accompany him; and on the Captain's agreeing, the king's leave was obtained for him also; and the two friends set out together. Carlostein soon perceived that his companion had infinitely more impatience to be with Madame de Seidlits and Laura, than admiration of those masterpieces of art which detain the connoisseur and antiquarian in their travels through Italy. That Captain Seidlits therefore might pass as much as possible of the period for which he had leave of absence with his mother and sister, Carlostein had the complaisance to continue his course directly, and with great expedition, to Rome. After a hasty view of what is most remarkable in that city, he proposed to accompany his friend to Naples, remain some time there; and, on his return to Germany, travel all over Italy with that leisure and attention which the curiosities the country presents merit.

Captain Seidlits, in his letter to his mother-in-law, assured her that the banker's failure would not be attended with the bad consequences which was feared at first; and concluded by expressions of the warmest affection for his sister, with compliments to her husband, to whom, he added, he was impatient of being known, and prepared to esteem.

This letter was followed, within a few days, by one from Signora Sporza, informing Madame de Seidlits that Mr. N—— had met with the Baron Carlostein and Captain Seidlits at the Cardinal Bernis'[2] assembly, and had presented those gentlemen to her. She dwelt a good deal on the praises of both, adding, That they were so much approved of by the Roman ladies, that she imagined they would find it difficult to leave Rome so soon as they intended: she concluded by warning Madame de Seidlits and Laura not to be greatly surprised or disappointed if Captain Seidlits did not arrive at Naples so soon as he had appointed.

Baron Carlostein and his friend had been recommended in a distinguished manner to Cardinal de Bernis, who sent them an invitation to dinner some days after the date of Signora Sporza's letter above mentioned. At his very hospitable and magnificent board they met with the Honourable Mr. N——, his uncle, Mr. Steele, and a variety of other strangers; it happened that there was at table one person, at least, from almost every country of Europe; the conversation turned a good deal on national character, and several lively traits were mentioned by way of illustration; but whether it was owing to a notion that the British bear strokes of this kind with less good-humour than the inhabitants of other countries, or whatever was the cause, it so happened, that for a considerable time no mention was made of any peculiar feature belonging to them.

At length the Cardinal, addressing himself to Mr. N——, said, he could not help thinking, that the melancholy generally attributed to the English nation was greatly exaggerated. He mentioned many English gentlemen with whom he had the pleasure of being acquainted, who were as gay as any Frenchmen, without the levity of which his countrymen were so much accused; besides, continued he, politely, "Can any thing be less probable, than that the nation, which perhaps of all others has the best reason to be cheerful, should be the most melancholy."—In return to this, Mr. N—— observed, That what was the most probable, was not always the most true; that, in his opinion, nothing was so much to be envied as that charming quality which seemed inherent in the French nation, of supporting, without murmuring, and even with gaiety, many of those vexatious incidents in life which sink the people of other nations into despondency, or overwhelm them with despair; that it was preposterous to call *that* quality of the mind levity which does what philosophy often attempts in vain. As for the melancholy imputed to his countrymen, he was much afraid, that notwithstanding the particular exceptions which had come under his Eminence's observation, it was but too well founded: and he illustrated his assertion by the following anecdote:

"During a late war between France and Great Britain,"[3] said Mr. N——, "an English vessel of superior force took a French frigate after an obstinate engagement, in which the French officers displayed that intrepidity which is so natural to them. The frigate was brought into a commercial town upon the English coast, and the officers were treated with great hospitality by some of the principal inhabitants: one very rich merchant in particular invited them frequently to his house, where he entertained them in a very magnificent manner.—The first day on which they dined with him, his lady behaved with such peculiar attention to the prisoners, that she seemed to neglect all the other guests at her table. After the company had withdrawn, she spoke highly to her husband of the politeness and easy agreeable manners of the French nation, and added, that it gave her pleasure to perceive that the French gentlemen who had just left them, instead of giving way to vain repining, or allowing their spirits to be depressed by their misfortune, had shewn the utmost cheerfulness and gaiety during the whole repast, all except one gentleman, who seemed much dejected, and almost entirely overcome with the idea of being a prisoner. This she accounted for by supposing that his loss was greater than that of all the rest put together; and she apprehended, from the obstinate silence he had retained, and from the discontent and melancholy so strongly marked in his countenance, that the poor gentleman would not long survive his misfortune.

"I cannot imagine who you mean," said the husband.

The lady described the man so exactly, that it was impossible to mistake him.

"That unfortunate gentleman," said the husband, "is none of the prisoners; he is the captain of the English vessel who took them."

CHAPTER LXII.

Carlostein and Seidlits arrive at Naples.

ALL the allurements of Rome, however, could not overcome Captain Seidlits's impatient desire of seeing his relations at Naples; and the Baron, yielding to his friend's eagerness, agreed to set out sooner than Signora Sporza had given Madame de Seidlits reason to expect.

Mr. N—— would have willingly accompanied them, provided he had been able to prevail on his uncle to go so far as Naples. But that gentleman had received some letters from England, which made him impatient to return directly; and all the fears which were suggested by Buchanan being now dissipated by the marriage of Zeluco to Laura, he rather wished his nephew to remain another season in Italy, as he had been advised for the confirmation of his health.

Mr. N—— accompanied the Baronet on his way home as far as Florence, and there took his leave of him and Mr. Steele, who had received letters from his mother and Mr. Transfer, pressing his immediate return in the most earnest terms. Steele, therefore, to the great satisfaction of the Baronet, resolved to accompany him to England; and on the day they left Florence, Mr. N—— set out on his return to Naples, where Signora Sporza had arrived before him.

Carlostein and Seidlits had reached that city a considerable time before either. On the morning of their arrival, Zeluco had gone to the country with the nobleman whom he had accompanied from Sicily, and was not to return till the day after. Laura determined to pass that interval with her mother.

Madame de Seidlits was delighted with the thoughts of seeing her son-in-law, for whom she had always felt the sincerest esteem and friendship; and Laura had more happiness in the expectation of passing some time with her brother, than in any reflexion which had occupied her mind since her marriage. She likewise experienced a confused sentiment of pleasure and uneasiness, the source of which she did not clearly comprehend, in the idea of meeting Carlostein, who had struck her fancy so strongly in her youth that the impression had never since been entirely effaced.

Immediately after their arrival at Naples, Captain Seidlits waited on his mother-in-law, with whom he found his sister; when the reciprocal congratulations and compliments were ended, Madame de Seidlits, inquiring what was become of his friend, was told, that he had insisted on remaining at the inn by himself for the first day of their meeting at least, that he might be no bar to that domestic kind of conversation so natural among near relations after a long absence. "I cannot bear the appearance of your leaving your friend at an inn the moment you arrive among your relations," said Madame de Seidlits: "we shall have abundance of opportunities for domestic chat; so if you think the Baron can put up with a poor dinner, we had best send for him." Captain Seidlits, who had with reluctance left his friend to dine alone, heard this proposal with pleasure, saying, "If that is the only objection, I shall certainly endeavour to bring him; for I never knew any man have a greater relish for good company, and so much indifference for good fare."

This proposal ofher mother's was not heard with perfect tranquillity by Laura; who foresaw that it would lead to their passing the whole evening together; and from what she had remarked of her husband's temper, she feared that he might not be pleased when he came to know that instead of her having passed the time of his absence with her mother only, a young gentleman besides her brother was of the party; she could not object however without giving a reason to her mother, which she wished to conceal; nor could she, with propriety, withdraw from a company of which her brother, so lately arrived, was one.

Captain Seidlits left them, and returned soon after with his friend.

The Baron Carlostein was at this time on the borders of thirty years of age; he was active and genteel in his person; he had an open manly countenance, which announced candour and good sense; his conversation and conduct confirmed what his features indicated; his general manner was gentle; yet when provoked, which did not slightly happen, his fine blue eyes darted a fire very different from their usual expression.

When Captain Seidlits presented him to his sister as an old acquaintance, he was struck with admiration at the improvement which a few years had made in the graces of her face and person. Her, whom he recollected only as a lively girl, just bursting from childhood, he now beheld a woman in the full bloom of beauty, and formed by Nature's finest symmetry. If he found the appearance of Laura more interesting on account of its alterations, she was the more pleased with his, because it remained the same.

After dinner Madame de Seidlits, renewing an old source of sportive dispute, said to her son-in-law, "I hope your short stay at Rome was sufficient to convert you from your heretical opinions on the article of female beauty; and you will now confess that the fine expressive countenances of the Roman ladies are far more interesting than all the bloom of the Saxon."

Captain Seidlits, however, fought the cause of his countrywomen with an intrepidity worthy of a knight-errant. "I will appeal to Baron Carlostein," said Madame de Seidlits; "his partiality for his country will not blind his judgment nor corrupt his candour—which do you think the finest style of countenance, that of the Italian, or German women?"

"I prefer a mixture of both," replied he, throwing the glance of an instant at Laura.

"*A vous ma sœur*,"[1] said Captain Seidlits, who had accidentally taken up a guitar, the moment before he made this appeal to his sister.

Laura blushed at the import of the Baron's answer, and was embarrassed by her brother's direct application of it; she extricated herself, however, by snatching her guitar out of his hand, saying, "*Volontiers, mon frere*,"[2] and instantly playing one of his favourite airs.

This turned the conversation; and Laura, who was a very great proficient in music, was desired to play several pieces on the harpsichord as well as guitar, which she accompanied with her voice in a manner that would have delighted a far less partial audience.

The evening was spent with entire satisfaction by Madame de Seidlits and the Captain; Laura's enjoyment was blended with great inquietude; Carlostein hardly uttered a sentence, as his friend and he returned to their lodgings, where, pretending to be disposed to sleep, he retired immediately to his bed-chamber, and passed the night meditating on the accomplishments of Laura.

Zeluco at his return received the two strangers with politeness, and many expressions of friendship; their appearance and manners attracted the approbation of all to whom they were presented. He perceived that his connexion with them did himself credit, and therefore was unremitting in his attentions, and entertained them with a profusion of magnificence exceeding what he formerly displayed.

Some such motive of selfishness and vanity is the usual source of *ostentatious* entertainment; friendship and cordial good-will to the guests are satisfied with mere simple preparations for their comfort and conveniency.

As Mr. N—— lived in the greatest intimacy with Carlostein and Seidlits, and was highly respected by them, he was invited to all those splendid feasts which Zeluco's vanity prompted him to give for the entertainment of his brother-in-law and the Baron. Zeluco was also assiduous in contriving parties of pleasure for their amusement; and often accompanied them when they went to visit the environs of this very interesting city. He engaged a certain Abbé of distinguished taste in virtù[3] to attend them as their Ciceroné,[4] and explain the antiquities brought from Herculaneum and Pompeia,[5] and the other curiosities collected in the Museum at Portici. Madame de Seidlits and her daughter were generally of those parties: but Captain Seidlits, as was already hinted, had not so great a relish for virtù as either his friend Carlostein or Mr. N——; nor was he enthusiastically struck with the various natural beauties which adorn the Bay of Naples. Intended from his early youth for the profession of arms, his studies and reflections were pretty much confined to what related to the military art; and he was not solicitous of being thought a connoisseur in any other. Having honestly acknowledged that the Bay of Naples was the most beautiful prospect he had ever seen, he was little disposed to say, and as little to hear, any more about it; and when the Abbé began to descant on ruins, and lava, and antiques, he left others to profit by the lecture, and walked away humming a march or some other favourite air to himself. As little could Seidlits support the Abbé's dissertations on the Roman arms, and their manner of using them; although that learned ecclesiastic explained those matters with an accuracy and minuteness which would have astonished one of Cæsar's best Centurions. All this learning and eloquence were exhausted in vain to shake the early prejudice which Seidlits had conceived in favour of the firelock and bayonet.[6] He became at length completely sick of antiquities, and often cursed those everlasting curiosities, each of which drew a lecture from the Abbé, and were continually crossing their way, whatever road they took in their excursions from Naples.

When Laura was of the party, Seidlits was fond of drawing her from the rest of the company, and conversing with her apart. And she, although not exactly of her brother's way of thinking on the subject of virtù, generally yielded to his solicitation. They talked of their acquaintance in Germany; of domestic affairs; and sometimes their conversation turned upon Carlostein; the virtues of his friend was a subject on which Seidlits dwelt with enthusiasm; he was eager to enumerate instances of his generous nature, and to give proofs of the noble turn of his mind. Laura and Carlostein were the two people on earth for whom Seidlits had the greatest esteem and affection; he was anxious, therefore, that they should esteem each other; and with this view he was apt to dwell on the praises of each to the other. The subject was more agreeable to both than he dreamt of.

CHAPTER LXIII.

The Highlander.

——Cujus
Dextera per ferrum, pietus spectata per ignes.
Ovid.[1]

Captain Seidlits was attended by an elderly man, a native of the North Highlands of Scotland, whose name was Duncan Targe.[2] As there is something singular in this man's story, and in the accidents by which he came into the Captain's service, it is not foreign to our purpose to mention a few of the particulars.

His father, who rented a small portion of land of a nobleman of that country, being upon his death-bed, expressed a desire of seeing his master; the nobleman went directly to the hut of his tenant, and condoled with him on the melancholy state he seemed to be in. "I am greatly indebted to your Lordship," said the dying man, "for the condescension[3] and kindness which you have always shewed to me. I am now dying, my Lord, and would willingly leave to so good a master what I have of the greatest value in this world."

"I am happy to hear, my good friend," said his Lordship, "that you have any thing of value to leave; for I was much afraid that you had lost the whole, or the greatest part, of what you had, when, contrary to my advice, you became surety[4] for your relation at Inverness; but whatever you have, I must insist upon your leaving it all to your little son Duncan here; and whatever his portion is, I am more disposed to add to it, than diminish it."

"Little Duncan is all I have to leave," replied the poor man; "and the greatest uneasiness I have in dying, is the thought of the destitute condition of that poor boy; for my relations at Inverness are all ruined by the same misfortune which has reduced me. I therefore earnestly entreat of your Lordship to accept of this poor orphan, as a pledge of my regard, and the only legacy I have to bestow."

"I do accept of him with all my heart and soul," cried his Lordship; "and if he proves as honest a man as his father, nothing but death shall part him and me."

"Praise be to the Almighty," cried the dying man, with uplifted eyes and arms. "Thanks to the gracious God of heaven and earth for all his goodness to me and mine!—Oh! my good Lord," continued he, addressing the Nobleman, "you have made me a happy man."—Here the sudden gush of joy overwhelmed the feeble heart of this poor man; he fell back on his heath pillow, and expired.

The Nobleman led the boy home to his castle, and after placing him some years at school, took him to attend his own person. He was in this situation when the rebellion broke out in the year 1745;[5] in which his master unfortunately taking a part, young Targe, being then a stripling of fifteen or sixteen years of age, accompanied him, and continued inseparably attached to his Lordship after the battle of Culloden, during a considerable time in which they skulked among the most remote parts of the Highlands.

On this trying occasion, Targe, being a youth of a hardy Highland constitution and spirit, had the satisfaction of repaying his master for all his former kindness by his unshaken fidelity and grateful attachment. In one or two instances he actually saved him from starving among the mountains, by bringing him, at the risk of his own life, provisions from those places where his Lordship could not appear without a certainty of being discovered. At length they both escaped to the continent, where this unfortunate Nobleman died; after which, Targe was taken into the service of Marshal Keith, by whom he was recommended to Colonel Seidlits, and now attended his son.

Buchanan and Targe generally attended their masters in their excursions around Naples. Mr. N—— had remarked an intimacy between them ever since Captain Seidlits and he met at Rome. On perceiving them walking apart from the other servants in close conversation together, "I'll lay a bett," said Mr. N—— to Captain Seidlits, "that your servant is from Scotland."

"He certainly is originally from that country," replied Seidlits; "but I cannot conceive how you came to discover this so readily."

"Nay, I should not have discovered it," said Mr. N——; "but I was convinced by my servant's sudden and great intimacy with him that *he* had."

Some time after this, Zeluco and his Lady, Madame de Seidlits, Carlostein, Mr. N——, and Captain Seidlits, went to pass the day and dine at Portici; neither Buchanan nor Targe had been ordered to attend their masters on that occasion. As the company were returning to town, Captain Seidlits took notice of this accident to Mr. N——; and they amused themselves with various observations on the source of the great friendship which was so suddenly formed between their two domestics. While they were conversing, Mr. N—— saw one of his footmen coming at full gallop towards them from Naples.

"What is the matter, Dick?" cried Mr. N——.

"Lord! Sir," the man replied, "Captain Seidlits's servant, Duncan Targe, has cut poor Mr. Buchanan almost to pieces."

"Impossible!" cried N——; "what! his own countryman?"

"Yes, please your Honour; they had a quarrel about the Queen; and so they fought in the garden with broad swords."

"About the Queen!—Nonsense!" cried Mr. N——; "what Queen?"

"The Queen of Scotland, please your Honour," said the servant.

"The fellow's certainly mad," said N——. "There is no Queen of Scotland, fool."

"I don't know whether there is or not," replied the servant; "but I am sure that Mr. Buchanan called her a w——; upon which Mr. Targe called him a liar: so they challenged each other; and so Mr. Buchanan is desperately wounded; and so I was ordered to come and acquaint your Honour."

Being able to get no better explanation from this messenger, Mr. N—— and Captain Seidlits rode on before the rest of the company; and after proper investigation, were informed of all the particulars of this curious adventure.

CHAPTER LXIV.

Dear is that shed to which his soul conforms,
And dear that hill which lifts him to the storms,
And as a child, whom scaring sounds molest,
Clings close and closer to the mother's breast;
So the loud torrent, and the whirlwind's roar,
But bind him to his native mountains more.

GOLDSMITH.[1]

WHEN the party was arranged for dining at Portici, and Buchanan understood that neither he nor his friend Targe were ordered to attend, the former invited his countryman to dine upon hotch potch, and minched collops,[2] two Scottish dishes, which he had previously instructed the cook at the inn how to dress. The invitation was joyfully accepted by Targe. After dinner, as neither was an enemy to the bottle, they pushed it pretty briskly between them, and the conversation became more and more animated every moment; while they talked of absent friends, the days of former years, the warlike renown of Scotland, the great men it had produced, and the romantic beauties of the country, they were in perfect unison; and when Targe, who had a tolerable voice, sung the songs of Lochaber, Gilderoy, the Last Time I came o'er the Muir, and the Flowers of the Forest,[3] the sympathetic tears flowed mutually from their eyes; but with all the prejudices which those two Caledonians had in common, there were some articles in which they differed diametrically.

Targe's birth and education have been already mentioned, and his political attachments accounted for; but Buchanan was born and educated among the Whigs of the west of Scotland, the descendants of the ancient Covenanters, who suffered so much oppression and religious persecution by the absurd policy of the ministers of Charles the Second, and his brother James, which is still remembered with horror in that part of the country.[4]

His father was a farmer, who was at an expence which he could ill afford, by supporting him at a neighbouring university[5] for several years; for the poor man's great ambition was to breed him to the church, or, as he himself expressed it, to *see his son George shake his head in a pulpit*. But while the youth was prosecuting his studies, the father's hopes were blasted, and Buchanan's plan of life entirely altered, by the natural consequence of an illicit connexion he had with a young woman.

This transgression being viewed in a more atrocious light in that part of Scotland than in the metropolis of England, and poor Buchanan being threatened at once with the public reprehension of the church and the private indignation of his own relations, fled to London, and was kindly received by some of his countrymen; in whose breasts compassion for the delinquent had greater influence than horror for his crime.

Several attempts for placing him in a more independent way having failed, and Buchanan being impatient of remaining a burthen on his friends, he accepted of an offer of going into the service of the Earl of——, where he remained several years, and was afterwards, at the recommendation of Lady Elizabeth, placed with her nephew on his going abroad.

As Buchanan's political sentiments were so different from those of Targe, it would have been fortunate if the two friends had kept clear of any discourse on such subjects; but while Buchanan was endeavouring to prove that the city of Naples was inferior in beauty to that of Glasgow, the view from the Castle of Edinburgh far more sublime than that from the Castle of Saint Elmo, and the palace of Casserta, though larger, in much worse taste than Holyrood House;[6] Targe interrupted him, and remarked with a sigh, that "it was a thousand pities that the just proprietor of that palace, the lineal descendant of so many kings, should be obliged to live like a private person in Italy."[7]

"It would be a much greater pity," Buchanan remarked, "to see popery and arbitrary power established in Great Britain and Ireland."

"I do not believe there was any danger of either," replied Targe.

"*Your* creed on that subject is not gospel, Mr. Targe," said Buchanan; "in my opinion it was prudent in the nation therefore to secure those important points, by the limitations made at the Revolution."[8]

"Those limitations," answered Targe, "might have been applied to king James and his descendants;[9] and the same restraints which have kept one race of kings within the limits of law, would have kept another."

"There is an essential difference between the two cases," replied Buchanan; "a man will be very happy to accept of a good estate to which he has no immediate claim, upon conditions which the possessor of the estate and his posterity would think it a hardship to have forced on them, particularly if they believed the estate had been transmitted to them through a long line of ancestors. And it is natural to suppose, that the latter would be more apt to break conditions which they considered as unjust, than the former to destroy the sole foundation of his right; it is therefore wise, Mr. Targe, in the British nation to adhere to the family it has placed on the throne, as long as they adhere to the conditions on which they were there placed; and I have not heard that any of them ever shewed a disposition to infringe them."

"Whatever reason the nation had to complain of the father, his descendants were innocent," replied Targe; "and if they had a particle of equity or gratitude in their character, they never would have attempted to break through those conditions on which they were replaced on the throne of their ancestors."

"Why, truly, Mr. Targe, if ever you heard of any kings who were withheld by mere considerations of gratitude or equity from extending their power, or encroaching on the rights of their subjects, when they thought they could do it with safety, you have the advantage of me; and I am apt to believe, that if ever such there were, the edition is now pretty much exhausted, and not likely to be renewed."

"You seem to have a very bad opinion of kings," said Targe.

"I cannot say I was ever intimate with either kings or princes," replied Buchanan, "so that I can say nothing about them from personal acquaintance; but from what I have heard of them by word of mouth, and read of them in history, I must confess my opinion of them in general is not very favourable."

"I hope you do not think them naturally worse than other men," added Targe.

"No, Mr. Targe, I certainly do not; but they are so accustomed from their youth to be flattered and dawted,* to have every thing done for them, and to make so few exertions of their own; often surrounded by those who have an interest in leading them astray, and sometimes by such a worthless set, that if they are not at the beginning naturally better than other men, they run a great risk of becoming artificially worse. But be they good, bad, or indifferent, I am clear for the subjects keeping such a portion of power in their own hands, as will render it very dangerous for the monarch to make any attempt against their

* Indulged. [Moore's note.]

rights; and I am clear in another point, Mr. Targe, that when a king is such a gawk* as to fly with his young one into an enemy's land, it would be the height of folly ever to let either the one or the other back to the nest."

"Well, I cannot help thinking it extremely unjust," replied Targe, "to deprive an innocent person of his right, and to make him suffer so severely for the faults of others, if faults there were."

"Unjust!" cried Buchanan; "Does not Heaven visit the iniquity of fathers upon their children?"[10]

"Heaven has a right to do what it pleases," said Targe; "but, please God, I never would take it on *me* to do such a thing, had I the power to-morrow."

"But the thing is done already," said Buchanan, "and cannot be undone, without more fighting about it than the cause is worth."

"Many a brave man, not only in Scotland but also in England and Ireland, have shed their blood in the cause of the house of Stewart," said Targe.

"I wish those who are disposed to shed their blood in such a cause much good of it," said Buchanan, shrugging his shoulders; "as for my own part, I shall be as ready as my neighbours to fight for my religion or my country, but as for shedding one drop of my blood for the difference between one king and another, when the good of the country is no way concerned, I beg to be excused."

"Do you not think fighting for your king is fighting for your country?" said Targe.

"Very often it is just the reverse," replied Buchanan; "fighting for a bad king, I consider as fighting against my country."

"Yet you must acknowledge," resumed Targe, "that kings reign by the appointment of God; and therefore it seems to be a very daring thing in man to attempt to dethrone them."

"The pestilence is by the appointment of God," retorted Buchanan; "yet we use every means in our power to drive it out of the land."

Targe seeming a little disconcerted and displeased at this observation, Buchanan filled a bumper, and gave for his toast, "The Land of Cakes."[11]

This immediately dispersed the cloud which began to gather on the other's brow.

---

* Gawk, a Saxon word still used in Scotland, signifies a cuckow, a silly fellow. [Moore's note.]

Targe drank the toast with enthusiasm, saying, "May the Almighty pour his blessings on every hill and valley in it!—that is the worst wish, Mr. Buchanan, that I shall ever wish to that land."

"It would delight your heart to behold the flourishing condition it is now in," replied Buchanan; "it was fast improving when I left it; and I have been credibly informed since that, it is now a *perfect garden.*"[12]

"I am very happy to hear it," said Targe.

"Indeed," added Buchanan, "it has been in a state of rapid improvement ever since the Union."[13]

"Damn the Union," cried Targe; "it would have improved much faster without it."

"I am not quite clear on that point, Mr. Targe," said Buchanan.

"Depend upon it," replied Targe, "the Union was the worst treaty that Scotland ever made."

"I shall admit," said Buchanan, "that she might have made a better—but bad as it is, our country reaps some advantage from it."

"All the advantages are on the side of England."

"What do you think, Mr. Targe," said Buchanan, "of the increase of trade since the Union, and the riches which have flowed into the Lowlands of Scotland from that quarter?"

"Think," cried Targe; "why, I think they have done a great deal of mischief to the Lowlands of Scotland."

"How so, my good friend?" said Buchanan.

"By spreading luxury among the inhabitants, the never-failing forerunner of effeminacy of manners. Why, I was assured," continued Targe, "by serjeant Lewis Macniel, a Highland gentleman in the Prussian service, that the Lowlanders in some parts of Scotland are now very little better than so many English."

"O fye!" cried Buchanan, "things are not come to that pass as yet, Mr. Targe; your friend the serjeant assuredly exaggerates."

"I hope he does," replied Targe; "but you must acknowledge," continued he, "that by the Union Scotland has lost her existence as an independent state; her name is swallowed up in that of England: Only read the English news-papers; they mention England as if it were the name of the whole island. They talk of the English army—the English fleet—the English every thing; they never mention Scotland, except when one of our countrymen happens to get an office under government; we are then told with some stale gibe, that the person is a Scotchman; or, which happens still more rarely, when any of them are condemned to die at Tyburn, particular care is taken to inform the public, that the criminal is originally from Scotland: but if fifty Englishmen get places or are hanged in one year, no remarks are made."

"No," said Buchanan; "in that case it is passed over as a thing of course."

The conversation then taking another turn, Targe, who was a great genealogist, descanted on the antiquity of certain gentlemen's families in the Highlands, which he asserted were far more honourable than most of the noble families either in Scotland or England. "Is it not shameful," added he, "that a parcel of mushroom Lords, mere sprouts from the dunghills of law or commerce, the grandsons of grocers and attornies, should take the pas[14] of gentlemen of the oldest families in Europe?"

"Why, as for that matter," replied Buchanan, "provided the grandsons of grocers or attornies are deserving citizens, I do not perceive why they should be excluded from the king's favour more than other men."

"But some of them never drew a sword in defence of either their king or country," rejoined Targe.

"Assuredly," said Buchanan, "men may deserve honour and pre-eminence by other means than by drawing their swords. I could name a man who was no soldier, and yet did more honour to his country than all the soldiers or lords or lairds of the age in which he lived."

"Who was he?" said Targe.

"The man whose name I have the honour to bear," replied the other; "the Great George Buchanan."[15]

"Who? Buchanan the historian!" cried Targe.

"Ay, the very same," replied Buchanan in a loud voice, being now a little heated with wine, and elevated with vanity, on account of his name. "Why, Sir," continued he, "George Buchanan was not only the most learned man, but also the best poet of his time."

"Perhaps he might," said Targe coldly.

"Perhaps!" repeated Buchanan; "there is no dubitation in the case. Do you remember his description of his own country and countrymen?"

"I cannot say I do," replied Targe.

"Then I will give you a sample of his versification," said Buchanan, who immediately repeated, with an enthusiastic emphasis, the following lines from Buchanan's Epithalamium on the marriage of Francis the Dauphin with Mary Queen of Scots.

> Illa pharetratis est propria gloria Scotis,
> Cingere venatu saltus, superare natando
> Flumina, ferre famem, contemnere frigora et æstus,
> Nec fossa & muris patriam, sed marte tueri,
> Et spreta incolumem vita defendere famam;
> Polliciti servare fidem, sanctumque vereri
> Numen amicitiæ, mores, non munus amare
> Artibus his, totum fremerunt cum bella per orbem,
> Nullaque non leges tellus mutaret avitas
> Externo subjecta jugo, gens una vetustis
> Sedibus antiqua sub libertate resedit.
> Substitit hic Gothi furor, hic gravis impetus hæsit
> Saxonis, hic Cimber superato Saxone, et acri
> Perdomito Neuster Cimbro.——[16]

"I cannot recollect any more."

"You have recollected too much for me," said Targe; "for although I was several years at an academy in the Highlands, yet I must confess I am no great Latin scholar."

"But the Great Buchanan," said the other, "was the best Latin scholar in Europe; he wrote that language as well as Livy or Horace."

"I shall not dispute it," said Targe.

"And was over and above a man of the first-rate genius," continued Buchanan with exultation.

"Well, well, all that may be," replied Targe, a little peevishly, "but let me tell you one thing, Mr. Buchanan, if he could have swopt* one-half of his genius for a little more honesty, he would have made an advantageous exchange, although he had thrown all his Latin into the bargain."

"In what did he ever shew any want of honesty?" said Buchanan.

"In calumniating and endeavouring to blacken the reputation of his rightful sovereign, Mary Queen of Scots," replied Targe, "the most beautiful and accomplished princess that ever sat on a throne."

"I have nothing to say either against her beauty or her accomplishments," resumed Buchanan; "but surely, Mr. Targe, you must acknowledge that she was a —— ?"

"Have a care what you say, Sir!" interrupted Targe. "I'll permit

* To swop is an old English word still used in Scotland, signifying to exchange. [Moore's note.]

no man that ever wore breeches to speak disrespectfully of that unfortunate queen."

"No man that ever wore either breeches or a filibeg,"* replied Buchanan, "shall prevent me from speaking the truth when I see occasion."

"Speak as much truth as you please, Sir," rejoined Targe; "but I declare that no man shall calumniate the memory of that beautiful and unfortunate princess in my presence, while I can wield a claymore."†

"If you should wield fifty claymores, you cannot deny that she was a Papist," said Buchanan.

"Well, Sir," cried Targe, "what then? She was like other people, of the religion in which she was bred."

"I do not know where *you* may have been bred, Mr. Targe," said Buchanan; "for aught I know, you may be an adherent to the worship of the scarlet whore yourself. I should be glad to have that point cleared up before we proceed farther."

"I cannot say that I understand your drift, Sir," replied Targe; "but I am an adherent neither of a scarlet whore, nor of whores of any other colour."

"If that is the case," said Buchanan, "you ought not to interest yourself in the reputation of Mary Queen of Scots."

"I fear you are too nearly related to the false slanderer whose name you bear," said Targe.

"I glory in the name; and should think myself greatly obliged to any man who could prove my relation to the Great George Buchanan," cried the other.

"He was nothing but a disloyal calumniator," cried Targe, "who attempted to support falsehoods by forgeries; which, I thank heaven, are now fully detected."

"You are thankful for a very small mercy," resumed Buchanan; "but since you provoke me to it, I will tell you in plain English, that your bonny Queen Mary was the strumpet of Bothwell, and the murderer of her husband."[17]

No sooner had he uttered the last sentence, than Targe flew at him like a tiger; and they were separated with difficulty, by Mr. N——'s groom, who was in the adjoining chamber, and had heard the altercation.

---

* A part of the highland dress which serves instead of breeches. [Moore's note.]

† The highland broad sword. [Moore's note.]

"I insist on your giving me satisfaction, or retracting what you have said against the beautiful queen of Scotland," cried Targe.

"As for retracting what I have said," replied Buchanan, "that is no habit of mine; but with regard to giving you satisfaction, I am ready for that, to the best of my ability; for let me tell you, Sir, though I am not a Highlandman, I am a Scotchman as well as yourself, and not entirely ignorant of the use of the claymore; so name your hour, and I will meet you to-morrow morning."

"Why not directly?" cried Targe, "there is nobody in the garden to interrupt us."

"I should have chosen to have settled some things first; but, since you are in such a hurry, I will not balk you. I will step home for my sword, and be with you directly," said Buchanan.

CHAPTER LXV.

—Et dulcis moriens reminiscitur Argos.[1]

THE Groom interposed, and endeavoured to reconcile the two enraged Scots, but without success. Buchanan soon arrived with his sword, and they retired to a private spot in the garden. The Groom next tried to persuade them to decide their difference by *fair boxing.* This was rejected by both the champions, as a mode of fighting unbecoming gentlemen. The Groom asserted that the best *gentlemen* in England sometimes fought in that manner; and gave as an instance a boxing match, of which he himself had been a witness, between Lord G.'s *Gentleman* and a *gentleman*-farmer at York races, about the price of a mare.[2]

"But our quarrel," said Targe, "is about the reputation of a Queen."

"That, for certain," replied the Groom, "makes a difference."

Buchanan unsheathed his sword.

"Are you ready, Sir?" cried Targe.

"That I am.—Come on, Sir," said Buchanan; "and the Lord be with the righteous."

"Amen!" cried Targe; and the conflict began.

Both the combatants understood the weapon they fought with; and each parried his adversary's blows with such dexterity, that no blood was shed for some time; at length Targe making a feint at

Buchanan's head, gave him suddenly a severe wound in the thigh.

"I hope you are now sensible of your error," said Targe, dropping his point.

"I am of the same opinion I was," cried Buchanan; "so keep your guard." So saying, he advanced more briskly than ever upon Targe; who, after warding off several strokes, wounded his antagonist a second time. Buchanan, however, shewed no disposition to relinquish the combat; but this second wound being in the forehead, and the blood flowing with profusion into his eyes, he could no longer see distinctly, but was obliged to flourish his sword at random, without being able to perceive the movements of his adversary, who, closing with him, became master of his sword, and with the same effort threw him to the ground; and standing over him, he said, "This may convince you, Mr. Buchanan, that your's is not the righteous cause; you are in my power, but I will act as the Queen whose character I defend would order, were she alive. I hope you will live to repent of the injustice you have done to that amiable and unfortunate Princess." He then assisted Buchanan to rise. Buchanan made no immediate answer; but when he saw Targe assisting the Groom to stop the blood which flowed from his wounds, he said, "I must acknowledge, Mr. Targe, that you behave like a gentleman."

After the bleeding was in some degree diminished by the dry lint, which the Groom, who was an excellent farrier,[3] applied to the wounds, they assisted him to his chamber; and then the Groom rode away to inform Mr. N—— of what had happened; but the wound becoming more painful, Targe proposed sending for a surgeon. Buchanan then said, That the surgeon's mate, belonging to one of the ships of the British squadron then in the Bay, was, he believed, on shore; and as he was a Scotsman, he would like to employ him rather than a foreigner. Having mentioned where he lodged, one of Mr. N——'s footmen went immediately for him. He returned soon after, saying, That the surgeon's mate was not at his lodging, nor expected for some hours; "But I will go and bring the French surgeon," continued the Footman.

"I thank you, Mr. Thomas," said Buchanan; "but I will have patience till my own countryman returns."

"He may not return for a long time," said Thomas. "You had best let me run for the French surgeon, who they say has a great deal of skill."

"I am much obliged to you, Mr. Thomas," added Buchanan; "but neither Frenchman nor Spanishman shall dress my wounds when a Scottishman is to be found, for love or money."

"They are to be found for the one or the other, as I am credibly informed, in most parts of the world," said Thomas.

"As *my* countrymen," replied Buchanan, "are distinguished for letting slip no means of improvement, it would be very strange if many of them did not use that of travelling, Mr. Thomas."

"It would be very strange, indeed! I own it," said the Footman.

"But are you certain of this young man's skill in his business when he does come?" said Targe.

"I confess I have had no opportunity to know any thing of his skill," answered Buchanan; "but I know for certain that he is sprung from very respectable people. His father is a Minister of the Gospel; and it is not likely that his father's son will be deficient in the profession to which he was bred."

"It would be still less likely had the son been bred to preaching," said Targe.

"That is true," replied Buchanan; "but I have no doubt of the young man's skill; he seems to be a very *douce** lad; it will be an encouragement to him to see that I prefer him to another, and also a comfort to me to be attended by my countryman."

"Countryman or not countryman," said Thomas, "he will expect to be paid for his trouble as well as another."

"Assuredly," said Buchanan; "but it was always a maxim with me, and shall be to my dying day, that we should give our own fish-guts to our own sea-mews."[4]

"Since you are so fond of your own sea-mews," said Thomas, "I am surprised you were so eager to destroy Mr. Targe there."

"That proceeded from a difference in politics, Mr. Thomas," replied Buchanan, "in which the best of friends are apt to have a misunderstanding; but though I am a Whig and he is a Tory, I hope we are both honest men; and as he behaved generously when my life was in his power, I have no scruple in saying, that I am sorry for having spoken disrespectfully of any person, dead or alive, for whom he has an esteem."

"Mary Queen of Scots acquired the esteem of her very enemies,"

* Douce, a Scottish expression, meaning gentle and well-disposed. [Moore's note.]

resumed Targe; "the elegance and engaging sweetness of her manners were irresistible to every heart that was not steeled by prejudice or jealousy."

"She is now in the hands of a Judge," said Buchanan, "who can neither be seduced by fair appearances, nor imposed on by forgeries and fraud."

"She is so, Mr. Buchanan," replied Targe; "and her rival and accusers are in the hands of the same Judge."

"We had best leave them all to his justice and mercy, then, and say no more on the subject," added Buchanan; "for if Queen Mary's conduct on earth was what you believe it was, she will receive her reward in heaven, where her actions and sufferings are recorded."

"One thing more I will say," rejoined Targe; "and that is only to ask of you, Whether it is probable that a woman, whose conscience was loaded with the crimes imputed to her, could have closed the varied scene of her life, and have met death, with such serene and dignified courage as Mary did?"[5]

"I always admired that last awful scene," replied Buchanan, who was melted by the recollection of Mary's behaviour on the scaffold; "and I will freely acknowledge, that the most innocent person that ever lived, or the greatest hero recorded in history, could not face death with greater composure than the Queen of Scotland; she supported the dignity of a Queen, while she displayed the meekness of a Christian."

"I am exceedingly sorry, my dear friend, for the misunderstanding that happened between us," said Targe affectionately, and holding forth his hand in token of reconciliation; "and I am now willing to believe, that your friend Mr. George Buchanan was a very great poet, and understood Latin as well as any man alive."

Here the two friends shook hands with the utmost cordiality; but Targe, observing that Buchanan's face seemed a little pale, and that the wound in his thigh bled profusely through the dressings, begged that he would allow some other surgeon to be brought; and Mr. N——'s footman swore, if he did not he would certainly bleed to death.

Buchanan having rebuked Thomas for swearing, added, "You know, or at least ought to know, Thomas, that let him bleed as he pleases, no man can die till his time is come; but even if I were to die of this wound, I should be sorry that the last act of my life was that of preferring a foreigner, not only to a countryman, but to one born in the same parish with myself, which this young man was. As for Mr. Targe here, I take you to witness, that I declare him innocent, happen what may." As he pronounced these words, the young surgeon, who had been so long expected, entered the chamber, and having examined Buchanan's wounds, and made proper applications, he strongly enjoined his patient to keep quietly in his room for some time, without attempting to walk, otherwise the wound in his thigh would be very tedious in healing; and there might even be some risk of a fever. And the patient agreeing to follow his injunctions, the surgeon promised him a speedy cure.

Mr. N—— and Captain Seidlits heard with satisfaction the prognostic of the surgeon; and were equally astonished and entertained when they were informed of the cause and circumstances of this quarrel.

CHAPTER LXVI.

——Placet impares
Animos sub juga ahenea
Mittere HOR.[1]

THAT course of dissipation in which Laura was involved for a considerable time after the arrival of her brother and Carlostein, was by no means agreeable to the natural turn of her mind, yet it certainly was of service to her in her present situation. An unremitting succession of balls, assemblies, operas, and other public entertainments, however they may be oppressive to those who enjoy domestic happiness, are relaxations from domestic misery.

The dispositions of Zeluco and of Laura scarcely touched in a single point; it was impossible therefore that there could be any cordial adhesion or agreement between them: he was vain and ostentatious, she modest; he was dissembling, she open; he was malicious, she candid: some of his pleasures were of so gross a nature that the mere mention of them was shocking to her; the gentle affections of the heart, the emotions of filial affection, the glow of friendship, the effusions of gratitude, and meltings of compassion, which alternately delighted and afflicted, but always occupied the feeling soul of Laura, were sentiments of which Zeluco had hardly any idea.

Neither did the most sublime beauties of nature, the most exquisite imitations of art, or the works of genius of any kind, to all of which she was feelingly alive, afford any enjoyment to the mind of Zeluco; although from vanity and affectation he pretended to admire some of them, and had made himself master of the common cant of *virtù*. Zeluco, in short, had no taste in common with Laura; so that this ill-assorted pair could not carry on a conversation interesting to both on any one subject. It is true, Laura had *never* liked him; all that Father Pedro had reported in his favour, joined to the good opinion of her mother, were not sufficient to overcome the bad impression she had early received of Zeluco; but till she actually became his wife, she could form no adequate notion of a character whose depravity developed to her abhorring heart more and more every hour.

As soon as Laura's beauty had become familiar, and of course began to pall on the jaded senses of Zeluco, she lost, in his eyes, the only attraction she had ever possessed; for he was incapable of deriving satisfaction from any of her numerous accomplishments, and the purity of her mind equally abominated his conversation and his tastes. He sought in venal beauty, and in variety, the pleasure which he no longer had in the chaste charms of Laura: the consequence of this pursuit was tedious intervals of *ennui*, and its never-failing companion, ill-humour; for what he intended to mitigate was found to irritate the evil that oppressed him. Wretched himself, he could not support the sight of the happiness of others, and particularly nothing provoked him so much as the idea of his wife's being in a state of composure, while he felt himself tormented with malignant passions; and he often endeavoured to exhaust the virulence which corroded his own breast upon the unhappy Laura, who, before her marriage, had never known but from description what envy or ill-humour were.

Hard, however, and painful to support as his ill-humours were, it appeared not so disgusting to Laura as the fits of fondness for her with which he was occasionally seized; and such was the unsupportable caprice of the man, that his fondness was sometimes displayed immediately after having insulted her with the most unprovoked ill-usage. On those occasions he was an object of horror to her, and had what she suffered been known, this beautiful woman, who shone at every public place of entertainment in all the brilliancy of diamonds and of equipage, would have been an object of universal compassion.

In the mean time, the opportunities which Carlostein daily had of seeing and conversing with Laura, convinced him that the beauty and elegance of her face and person were equalled by her good sense and other mental accomplishments. She, on her part, thought him the most engaging of men, and felt a warmer approbation of him than of any other man whose good qualities had ever before attracted her esteem. She was conscious of a real friendship for Mr. N——, and had the highest opinion of the worth of his character; but the sentiments which she now experienced for Carlostein were of a still more interesting nature. When Mr. N—— visited her, she was pleased the moment she saw him enter the room; but if he did not come when expected, the disappointment did not so far affect the natural cheerfulness of her temper, as to prevent her from enjoying other company. But if the same happened with respect to Carlostein, if any accident prevented his coming when there was reason to expect him, her real cheerfulness fled, and nothing but an affected substitute remained with her for the rest of the evening.

Alarmed at this, and sensible of the impropriety of an attachment which was gradually gaining upon her: "Ah! let me banish this man from my thoughts," said she often to herself; "let me remember that I am the wife of another."—This immediately brought the image of that other before her mind's eye, in all the deformity of vice; and the contrast was so striking, and so much in favour of him whom she thought it a duty to forget, that he was pressed nearer to her heart by the very efforts she made to remove him; and the more she struggled, the deeper was the hook from which she wished to disengage herself fixed in her vitals.

After remaining several months at Naples, and seldom passing a day without being in company with Laura, Carlostein had not ventured to give a hint of his passion, but had endeavoured to conceal it from her, and the rest of the world, as much as he could: while she, on her part, behaved with such circumspection, that neither her mother, brother, Signora Sporza, nor any other acquaintance, had an idea of her having any particular attachment to Carlostein. Even Zeluco, though cursed with a jealous temper, ever on the watch, and convinced that he never had possessed the affections of his wife, harboured no particular suspicion of Carlostein.

How well so ever Laura and Carlostein succeeded in concealing their sentiments from the rest of the world, they failed with regard to each other. Laura had too much penetration not to perceive that she occupied the attention of Carlostein in an uncommon degree; and she sometimes remarked this on occasions when a less acute or less interested observer would have been apt to think that she engaged his attention less than any other person in company. While his behaviour to her, in the eyes of others, appeared uniform and unvaried, because it was always respectful; *she* perceived a variety of shades in his conduct in her presence, which depended, in some degree, on the company present, yet always harmonised with the humour she seemed to be in.

The sex in general are very penetrating on this subject, and it rarely happens that a man is sincerely in love with a woman, without his passion's being known to her before he is fully convinced of it himself. Notwithstanding that Carlostein therefore had never said a syllable on the subject of love to Laura, nor had presumed to indicate any such sentiment by his looks, or in any particular deviated from that delicacy of behaviour due to a woman of virtue; she was as fully convinced of his attachment to her, perhaps more, than if he had made a solemn and earnest declaration of it.

It is more than probable, that Carlostein had some idea also that he was not an object of indifference to her; for although there are accounts of ladies who, while they are passionately fond of their lovers, make them believe, for years together, that they could not endure them, it must be acknowledged that these examples are oftener found in romances than in life, and when found in real life they afford a stronger proof of the lady's pride and the lover's passion, than of the good sense of either. For our behaviour, in all respects, from things of the greatest importance to trifles, is, in spite of ourselves, different to those who engage our affections, from what it is to every other person; and the very effort to behave in the same manner to the beloved object as to others, discovers to an acute observer what is meant to be concealed; for although love is often simulated by those who have it not, it is more difficult to conceal it where it really exists: Carlostein, therefore, ought not to be accused of vanity or presumption, in flattering himself with no common share of the good opinion of Laura.

But he was not more fully convinced of her partiality for himself, than of her dislike to her husband; which Laura endeavoured with equal care and as little success to hide. Such, however, was his veneration for the character of Laura, that he presumed as little from the certainty of the latter as from his conviction of the former; indeed, he could hardly allow himself to wish for a success which he could not enjoy but at the expence of the future peace of mind of the person he loved; and if he ever permitted himself to suppose that the woman he so greatly admired might have a moment of weakness, such was his notion of her disposition and principles, that he was convinced it would be followed by everlasting remorse on her part, and of course by misery on his; for he could not hope that all her partiality for him, or all the sophistry he could use, would persuade a woman of real virtue and dignity to live in a manner inconsistent with both.

If, in consequence of these reflexions, Carlostein had withdrawn himself entirely from a connection of such a dangerous tendency, he would no doubt have acted a more prudent part;—but having no delight equal to that of conversing with Laura, no wish on leaving her company but that of meeting her again, the effort was above his power;—all he could do was to endeavour to hide a passion which he was unable to subdue.

CHAPTER LXVII.

Il n'y a point de déguisement qui puisse long-temps cacher l'amour où il est, ni le feindre où il n'est pas. ROCHEFOUCAULT.[1]

It is not improbable that the sentiments which Carlostein and Laura mutually entertained for each other would have been discovered by Zeluco, had not his suspicions been fixed on another object; for, notwithstanding the candid behaviour of his wife, when he spoke to her concerning the Nobleman, as was mentioned above, the sparks of jealousy which glowed in Zeluco's breast had never been entirely extinguished, but were rekindled more fiercely than ever on the return of that Nobleman from Rome.

As Laura now appeared at all public places, he had frequent opportunities of accosting her; and although she received his compliments with an air of great reserve, yet he omitted no occasion of addressing her.

One evening in particular, at a very numerous assembly, Laura being in company with Signora Sporza, her husband, her brother, and Carlostein; this Nobleman no sooner saw her than he made up to Zeluco's party, and as usual directed his whole assiduity to Laura. Zeluco observed this with *stifled* rage, and *apparent* good-humour; Laura alone discerned the hurricane in his heart through all the sunshine of his countenance.—She rose to withdraw—the Nobleman offered his hand—she seeming not to observe his motion, turned to her husband, who desired Carlostein to hand her to her carriage. She immediately presented her hand to him, and the Nobleman seized it.—"I believe, Signor," said Carlostein, "the lady intended me the honour."—At that instant Laura withdrawing her hand from the other to prevent farther dispute, took hold of Zeluco's arm, begging him to accompany her to her carriage, which he did, and drove home.

When the assembly broke up, as the Nobleman pressed across the Corridor in some hurry towards his carriage, his legs were for a moment crossed by the sword of Carlostein, who instantly loosened it from his belt, making an apology; the other, without paying any regard to this, pushed forward, saying, in an imperious tone, "Make way, Sir."—"Make you way, Sir," cried Carlostein, provoked at his insolence, and pushing him to one side. The Nobleman drew and made a pass at Carlostein, whose sword being in his hand, he put aside the thrust, and returning it, hit his antagonist smartly near the eye with the point of the undrawn sword, and with a jerk threw the Nobleman's sword quite out of his hand.

Carlostein then walked calmly to his own carriage, where he found Signora Sporza and Captain Seidlits, who, instead of going directly to Zeluco's, where they were to sup, proposed driving a little to enjoy the refreshing breeze from the bay, to which Carlostein assented, without saying a word of what had just happened.

Meanwhile one of Zeluco's servants having heard an imperfect account of the squabble, hastily entered the room where Madame de Seidlits, Laura, and Zeluco were, telling them, "That the Nobleman and Carlostein had fought, that one of them was desperately wounded, and the other killed on the spot."

"Which of them is killed?" said Zeluco.

"I cannot tell," said the servant; "all I know for certain is, that one of them is dead."

"Go and learn which, blockhead," cried Zeluco.

As the servant went out, Carlostein entered with Signora Sporza and Captain Seidlits; but Laura's spirits underwent such painful agitation from the servant's intelligence, that, after struggling for some time to hide her emotion, she suddenly fainted, and fell from her chair. Being carried to bed, she continued greatly disordered, and even after her mother had acquainted her with the true state of the case, which she did as soon as she was herself informed of it, Laura was not able to stir abroad for near a week.

Laura having fainted just as Carlostein appeared, Zeluco's jealous temper, ever ready to put the worst construction on the most innocent occurrence, imputed her being so violently affected to her suspecting from the servant's account that the Nobleman was the person killed, and her being confirmed in that suspicion when she saw Carlostein enter the room in good health.

This very idea was a sufficient reason to render Zeluco fonder than ever of Carlostein's company; he invited him very frequently to his house, because he thought that his presence was highly disagreeable to his wife; and this idea seemed the more probable, as Laura, being conscious of the real cause of her fainting, was evidently more constrained and embarrassed in his company than she had formerly been, all which Zeluco imputed to her aversion to that gentleman on account of his quarrel with the Nobleman.

He was confined to his room for several weeks with an inflammation which came on his eye, and some of his friends were imprudent enough to vapour a little about his determination of calling Carlostein to an account as soon as he was fully recovered. Carlostein, who was of a cool temper, took no notice of these, being resolved to regulate his conduct by the behaviour of the Nobleman himself, and not by that of his officious friends; but Captain Seidlits, who was of a more fiery disposition, did not behave with the same moderation.

In a company where the Captain was, the conversation turned on the quarrel; a friend of the Nobleman's gave a representation of it more favourable for him than was consistent with truth: "I am convinced," said Seidlits, "you have not received that account of the matter from the Nobleman himself, for he knows that it happened very differently."—"Do you not allow," said the other, "that the Baron's sword was in the scabbard?"—"I do," replied Seidlits.—"It was highly insulting then," said the other, "to make use of it in that state; why did he not draw it?"[2]—"It was a present from the king, his master," replied Seidlits; "my friend has a high value for that sword, and does not like to draw it on *slight* occasions." Here, contrary to the expectation of some of the company, the conversation dropped; but it was afterwards repeated to Laura.

The next time she saw her brother, she blamed him for making so haughty an answer; adding, that it might have bad consequences.—"I am sorry to have done what you disapprove of, my dear sister," said Seidlits; "but as for the consequences, I regard them not, and I am sure Carlostein regards them as little as I do."

Signora Sporza, who with Mr. N—— was the only other person present, observed to Seidlits, "That he might, if he pleased, despise the open resentment of a fair enemy, but he would do well to remember, that in the country where they were, there was a mode of avenging injuries, which his friend Carlostein ought to be on his guard against, otherwise than by relying on courage alone."[3] She hinted at the same time, that there was a greater risk of a vengeance of the latter kind from the Nobleman and his relations, than of that which Captain Seidlits seemed so much to despise.

Laura left the room abruptly when this remark was made, but not before Signora Sporza observed her change colour, and appear greatly agitated. This was the first time that Signora Sporza had any suspicion of Laura's partiality for Carlostein; Mr. N—— had conceived some notion of it a few days before, from an incident not worth mentioning, and which would have escaped the observation perhaps of any other person. He found a pretext for withdrawing soon after Laura left the room; and, upon her return, Signora Sporza was confirmed in her suspicions, for in spite of the pains which Laura had taken to wash away the traces of tears, it was plain she had been crying.

CHAPTER LXVIII.

> Nam tibi cum facie mores natura pudicos,
> Et raras dotes ingeniumque dedit.
>
> Ovid.[1]

The words which had fallen from Signora Sporza, concerning the resentment of the Nobleman who had been hurt by Carlostein, and the mode of revenge he might adopt, made a lasting impression on Laura. She thought Carlostein in the greatest danger of being secretly murdered, if he were not openly called to the field; she considered herself as the original cause of the hazard to which he was exposed, and which she feared was increased by the imprudence of her brother: her imagination dwelt on the horrors that might ensue.

Zeluco one evening said to her, that he had an inclination to go the following day to Puzzoli, and to cross the bay between that town and

Baia; and as she had expressed a desire to see the Ponte di Caligula, the baths of Nero, the tomb of Agrippina, and the other ruins of that seat of ancient luxury,[2] he would take her with him. Laura assented. But going to bed with her thoughts brooding over the same train of reflexions which had infested her mind for some days past, she dreamt of bravos and assassination the whole night. She sometimes thought she beheld Carlostein stretched on the ground, pale and bloodless;—at other times the blood seemed to flow from a recent wound in his side; and as often as she stooped to lend him assistance, she imagined that her husband prevented her by terrifying looks and insulting language. Those visions disordered her so much, that she resolved next morning to decline the proposed jaunt to Puzzoli.

Some time after she arose, Zeluco sent her word, that Captain Seidlits and he waited for her at breakfast. The Captain had accidentally called earlier than usual, and as soon as his sister entered the room, he told her that he and Carlostein intended to accompany Zeluco and her to Baia. Laura endeavoured to excuse herself. "What is the matter now," said Zeluco; "you had no objection last night?" She still wished to decline going; but Zeluco suspecting her only reason was because Carlostein was of the party, determined that she *should* go. He and Laura went in the carriage accordingly, Seidlits and Carlostein accompanying them on horseback. After wandering some time along this beautiful coast, Zeluco told Seidlits, he would lead him to see something peculiarly curious; but, as it was at some distance and difficult of access, he begged of Carlostein to remain with Laura till their return.

Seidlits agreed to the proposal, because he thought it would be agreeable to his sister to be entertained during this interval by his friend: Zeluco made it, because he thought it would be in the highest degree disagreeable to her; Laura heard it with surprise, and Carlostein with pleasure.

When Zeluco and the Captain left them, they walked slowly on without considering where they went, and without exchanging a word, till they arrived at a shady seat, from which the various beauties around might be seen to advantage;—here Carlostein expressed a fear that she was fatigued with walking. She immediately sat down, and he placed himself at her side.

Carlostein and Laura, thus unexpectedly seated together, seemed entirely absorbed in reflexion, and as regardless of the sublime and luxurious scene before their eyes, as if they had been blind; their mutual constraint was so great, that neither was capable of expressing a distinct idea. Carlostein made several efforts to begin a conversation, which proceeded no farther than one uninteresting question and answer; Laura had been so terrified with the dreams of the preceding night, that she could think or speak of nothing but what *they* suggested. The careless and blunt temper of her brother disquieted her very much; and she greatly dreaded some mischief from that quarter.

"I fear, Sir," said she, making a great effort to break the silence, and forcing a smile, as if the fear she expressed had not been serious; "I fear you have an imprudent friend in my brother."

"Madam!" cried Carlostein, with surprise.

Laura repeated what she had said.

"I consider your brother," replied Carlostein, "as the most valuable friend that ever man had. I owe my life to him."

"Nay," resumed she, "I have no design to make a breach between you; but my brother has sometimes a thoughtless and provoking way of speaking, which may lead to very bad consequences, and of which it is the duty of a friend to warn him."

"I do not conceive," said Carlostein, "to what you allude."

"Nothing," resumed she, "rankles more in the heart than contemptuous expressions."

"Unquestionably," answered he.

"Nor," added she, "is there any kind of injury more apt to provoke men to revenge."

"I am convinced of it," said Carlostein, unable to guess to what she alluded.

"Then surely," continued Laura, with hesitation, "it was imprudent in my brother to speak, as I hear he did on a late occasion."

"I am convinced you labour under some mistake, Madam," said Carlostein. "Captain Seidlits, although as fearless as any man alive, is not apt to give wanton provocation."

"I was told," said Laura, "that conversing lately on the unfortunate scuffle in which you were involved, he used terms which might drive your antagonist to measures he otherwise would not think of."

"The accident which happened in consequence of that foolish affair," said Carlostein; "he who gave the first provocation brought it on himself; Captain Seidlits knows that nobody else was to blame, and I dare say he will assert this as often as the affair is talked of."

"But why irritate him with contemptuous expressions? perhaps he might become sensible he is in the wrong. What my brother says may be carried to him, and excite him to measures which otherwise he would not think of adopting."

"What measure he may chuse to adopt, it is his business to weigh with attention," said Carlostein; "but certainly is not worth Captain Seidlits' consideration."

"Friendship," said Laura, "might make him consider that contemptuous language; may stimulate to a mode of revenge which no degree of courage can obviate, and no skill can ward off." She spoke these words with agitation, and the tear trembled in her eye: then, recollecting the import of what she was saying, her face was instantly suffused with blushes; yet mustering up all the woman within her, and endeavouring to conceal the true source of her concern, she added; "he does not think on the remorse and misery *he himself would feel*, should his imprudence be attended with any fatal consequence to——." Here perceiving that her voice faultered, her embarrassment increased; she hesitated, and was incapable of uttering a distinct word.

It was hardly possible for Carlostein not to see the real motive of her concern and embarrassment; whatever satisfaction he might have in the discovery, he had too much delicacy to seem to perceive either.—"Your brother's friendship," said he, "has ever been a source of happiness to me; I should reckon myself unfortunate indeed, if it should ever become a cause of uneasiness to him, and will use every precaution to prevent such an effect, of which, however, I think there is no danger."

Laura gently bowed her head, by way of thanking him; for although somewhat recovered from her perplexity by Carlostein's reply, she was still afraid to trust her voice with words. She then rose, and after they had walked a little way without speaking, Carlostein began to point out some of the most striking beauties of the landscape in their view; and she assented to his remarks in a manner that evinced how very little they occupied her thoughts. At length, seeing Captain Seidlits and Zeluco approaching, they moved in silence to meet them.

The latter observing the reserved manner in which Laura and Carlostein advanced, concluded that their *tête-à-tête* had been as disagreeable as he intended it should; and the melancholy air which Laura retained, in spite of all her efforts to seem cheerful, he imputed to displeasure for having been left with Carlostein.

Replete with this notion, Zeluco let slip no occasion, while they remained at the inn where they dined, of saying things which he thought would vex and disconcert his wife, without being perceived by Carlostein or Seidlits.

"Has any one heard how his eye is to-day?" said he, naming the person with whom Carlostein had the quarrel.

"I heard," said Seidlits, "that it still continues swelled and inflamed."

"I am told he runs some risk of losing it altogether," said Zeluco, looking maliciously at Laura.

"I hope not," said Laura, naturally, and without observing the manner in which he had spoken.

"Would it give you a *great deal* of pain, Madam?" rejoined he.

"I should certainly be concerned that such a misfortune happened to any body," replied she, "particularly on such an occasion."

"You will never be forgiven by the ladies, Signor," said Zeluco, addressing Carlostein, "for spoiling this fine spark's ogling."

The venom of jealousy in Zeluco's breast was put into a ferment by Laura's answers, natural and mild as they were. When the company were preparing to return, "Be so obliging, Signor," said he, to Carlostein, "as to take my seat in the carriage, and let me have your horse; I should like to *ride* to town."

This obliging husband made the proposal with no other view than that of distressing his wife.—Laura's heart beat tumultuously when she heard it; the agitation which she had felt during the conversation she had just had with Carlostein, on which she already had made some reflexions, added to the glow of joy she was conscious of, on hearing her husband's proposal, determined this virtuous woman to evade it;—turning from Carlostein therefore to Captain Seidlits, "I have something particular to communicate to you, brother," said she, holding forth her hand; "I beg you will favour me with your company in the carriage."

"With pleasure," cried Seidlits, taking his sister's hand. "Your wife and I have had a quarrel," added he to Zeluco, "and I see she wishes for an opportunity to make it up." So saying, he went with her into the carriage, leaving Carlostein disappointed, and Zeluco ready to burst with anger.

Whatever self-approbation Laura felt from this victory of her reason over her inclination, yet, when she observed the desponding look of Carlostein, as the carriage passed him, her heart whispered, that if Zeluco should renew his proposal, she ought not to provoke him by a second refusal. She was not put to the temptation. The carriage moved on, and her brother was obliged to ask her oftener than once, what she had to communicate to him, before he was able to raise her from the reverie in which her thoughts were absorbed, when the carriage proceeded to town.

Zeluco having invited the two gentlemen to sup at his house, where they met with Madame de Seidlits and Signora Sporza, he could not give vent to the anger which he had so absurdly conceived against his wife, but assumed the appearance of good-humour and extraordinary affection for her. Laura was too much accustomed to him to be his dupe on this occasion. She saw clearly into the real state of his thoughts, and being quite convinced of his rancour, she, who herself was all candour, was so shocked at his affected kindness, that in spite of her unwillingness to give her mother uneasiness, she could not remain with the company, but was obliged to leave them abruptly, on the pretext of ill health.

Madame de Seidlits had intended to remain that night with her daughter, but being at that time in a delicate state of health herself, she was prevailed on to return to her own house, upon Signora Sporza's offering to stay all night with Laura. This was infinitely agreeable to the latter, who wished to be secured from the company of her husband.

CHAPTER LXIX.

No more can faith or candour move;
But each ingenuous deed of love,
  Which reason would applaud,
Now, smiling o'er his dark distress,
Fancy malignant strives to dress
  Like injury and fraud. AKENSIDE.[1]

ZELUCO retained all his hatred to Signora Sporza, though he thought it expedient to let it lie dormant for the present, and to behave to her with the attention due to a relation of his wife's family. She saw through his dissimulation, and repaid his hatred with a fixed aversion; but this she carefully concealed from Madame de Seidlits, because she knew that it would give her uneasiness. Signora Sporza's affection for

Laura was increased by her perceiving that she was unhappy in her marriage; and perhaps by being convinced that she entertained the same sentiments of Zeluco with herself. She did not take the same pains therefore to conceal her sentiments from Laura that she did from Madame de Seidlits. Laura, however, would understand none of her hints, and discouraged all conversation on that subject.

Signora Sporza saw the true motive of her young friend's reserve; and notwithstanding that it would have been agreeable to herself to have talked freely of Zeluco's behaviour and character, yet she could not help approving of Laura's prudence in declining all conversation on such a delicate subject. She beheld with more concern that Laura was sinking into dejection of spirits; and although she strongly suspected her partiality for Carlostein, as well as his passion for her, so far from considering this as an aggravation of Laura's misfortune, she thought an attachment of this kind might prove a salutary antidote against the gloomy despondency, or even despair, with which her young friend was threatened.

With regard to Signora Sporza it has been already hinted, that whatever her manner of *acting* had been, she was rather a free *thinker* on subjects of this nature; for although she had a high idea of Laura's virtuous principles, she could not but be sensible of the danger of such attachments. It would appear however, that she thought any danger worth risking that could make a diversion from the dismal state of mind into which Laura was falling, from a continued contemplation of her miserable connexion with a morose and jealous husband.

Zeluco was the greatest of all self-tormentors; his envious and gloomy mind was eternally suggesting fresh causes of disquiet to itself. The two ideas which plagued him at present were, first that Laura disliked him, and also that she was fond of another. There was no cure for the first, but his becoming an honest man, which was not in his nature; and the cure of the other was nearly as difficult; for to remove suspicions from the breast of a man given to jealousy, and prevent their returning, would be changing his nature. This passion has a tendency not only to sour the temper, but to obscure the understanding, else how should

—Trifles, light as air,
Be to the jealous confirmation strong
As proofs of Holy Writ.—[2]

Laura's having shewn a disposition to remain at home on hearing that Carlostein was of the party to Baia; her having preferred her brother's company to his when they returned; her having left the company abruptly at supper; and her dejection of spirits from the time that the Nobleman was confined by the hurt in his eye, Zeluco imputed to the interest which she took in this Nobleman, and to her dislike to Carlostein on that account.

Zeluco was one of those amiable creatures who being seldom at peace with themselves cannot bear that their neighbours should enjoy tranquillity. Laura used the pretence of ill-health for a considerable time after her being obliged to retire from the company at supper, merely that she might be allowed to keep her apartment, enjoy the society of her mother and Signora Sporza, and be spared from that of her husband.

When she seemed a little better, her brother was added to the number of her visitors; and even after she went abroad, she visited nowhere but at her mother's or Signora Sporza's. Zeluco explained her reserve, low spirits, and love of retirement, in the same manner that he had done her previous behaviour; and his sullenness augmented daily. Laura was endeavouring one day to divert her melancholy with her harpsichord, Zeluco heard the sound while he sat in his own apartment, and it redoubled his ill-humour. He suddenly entered the room where she was playing, and threw himself on a chair opposite to her with every mark of displeasure.

She had observed that taking any notice of him, particularly by speaking to him, on such occasions, never failed to draw from him some brutal answer; she therefore said nothing, but played an air of such soothing melody as might have subdued the rancour of a dæmon.

"You are mightily fond of Italian music, Madam," said he, after some minutes of silence.

"I am, indeed," replied she, stopping for a moment, endeavouring to smile upon him, and then resuming the instrument.

"You prefer whatever is Italian, I have observed," rejoined he, with a malignant look.

"I cannot entirely say that," answered she, quitting the harpsichord; "but their music is generally preferred to that of any other nation."

"Yet you are half a German," resumed he.

"More than half," said Laura. "I was born and educated in my father's country."

"It is a wonder then that you have not some partiality for your countrymen."

"I esteem them highly," said Laura; "all the world acknowledge them to be a brave and worthy people."

"But you think the Italians more *amiable*?" added he, prolonging the last word.

Laura made no answer, but applied again to the harpsichord, wishing to put an end to a dialogue which she found highly disagreeable, although she did not comprehend the motive or tendency of it.

Zeluco started up, and walked with a hurried step across the room, and then turning suddenly to Laura, "You dislike the Baron Carlostein, Madam, do you not?" resumed he.

"Dislike him, Sir?" said she, alarmed and blushing.

"Yes, Madam, you hate him."

"I should be glad," said she, "to have no reason to hate any body."

"And what reason have you for hating him, Madam?"

"I have not said that it is *him* I hate," replied she with some degree of indignation.

"Oh! you have not *said* it," rejoined he, mistaking the implication of her words; "you have only *shewn* it by your behaviour."

"I do not comprehend your meaning," said she.

"Why would you not admit him into the carriage on your return to Baia?"

"I wished to converse with my brother," said she.

"Perhaps you would have preferred another to either," added he, looking maliciously in her face.

"I do not know that I should," said Laura.

"But I know it, Madam; I know who interests you more than all the world, and on whose account the Baron Carlostein is the object of your displeasure."

Laura could not hear this name without emotion. She again coloured, repeating with a faultering voice, "*My displeasure!*"

"Yes, Madam, *your* displeasure," cried Zeluco, with a raised voice; "you cannot hide it, you redden with resentment at the bare mention of his name; but I would have you to know, that he is a man whom I esteem; and I wish the blow he dealt to that fine essenced mignon[3] had beat his brains out."

As he pronounced this with violent emphasis and action, he struck his cane through a mirror, and rushed out of the room, leaving Laura filled with contempt and indignation at his ridiculous and frantic behaviour.

Zeluco, like many other peevish and fiery tempered people, was apt to display his ill-humour at the expence of his furniture; but Laura had never seen him so violently agitated on any former occasion.

She was not sorry, however, that his suspicions, since suspicions of some person or other he must have, were directed to a man quite indifferent to her.

A footman entering the room as Zeluco went out, she mentioned the mirror having been accidentally broken, and ordered another directly in its place to prevent farther remarks on the subject; and she determined to pass that evening with Signora Sporza.

CHAPTER LXX.

The Indiscretion of a Friend.

Hitherto Laura had been successful in her endeavours to hide from the servants the ill-footing on which her husband and she were; but Zeluco had spoken during the foregoing dialogue in such a loud tone, that a maid of Laura's, who was in one of the adjoining chambers, heard a great part of it.

This maid felt herself quite overloaded with so much important intelligence, and seeing nobody at home to whom she could conveniently consign it, she hastened to Signora Sporza, whom she knew to be the friend of her mistress, and immediately informed her of all she had heard; and wherever there might have been a gap in the narrative from her not having heard distinctly, she took care to fill it up from her own imagination: so that the whole appeared an uninterrupted scene of brutal abuse on the part of Zeluco, and of patience and resignation on that of Laura.

When she had finished, *"Voilà un homme,"* said Signora Sporza, speaking in French, that the maid might not understand her; *"voilà un homme fait exprès pour être cocu."*[1] She then cautioned the maid very earnestly not to mention what she had heard to Madame de Seidlits, or to any other person, as it might be of very bad consequence to her mistress.

The maid feeling herself greatly relieved by what she had already told, and being averse to do any thing which would injure Laura, thought she might safely promise not to mention it; which she accordingly did, with a sincere intention to keep her word.

As the maid withdrew Baron Carlostein was introduced, and soon after Signora Sporza had a proof in herself of what most people experience; how much easier it is to give good advice than to follow it: for she was so full of indignation at what she had heard, that she could not contain herself more than the maid, but told the whole to the Baron, who was much more affected than surprised at the information; for, from the idea he had formed of the character of Zeluco, and what he had observed of his behaviour, particularly on the day of the jaunt to Baia, he was convinced that Zeluco and Laura lived unhappily together, and conjectured, that scenes similar to that which Signora Sporza had recounted to him, sometimes passed between them.

In her narration, Signora Sporza discovered great indignation against Zeluco; in listening to it, Carlostein seemed to think only on the unhappiness of Laura: while she abused the former, he compassionated the latter. After having exhausted her rage, however, pity became predominant in *her* breast also, and she was actually shedding tears when Laura herself entered the room. As Laura seemed surprised at finding her friend in this state, and began to inquire into the cause of her affliction, Carlostein thought it became him to retire, and leave them at freedom.

Laura then expressed the most tender anxiety for her friend, and begged to know what distressed her.

"Alas! my sweet friend," said Signora Sporza, "why should I disturb you with my sorrows?"

"That I may do all in my power to alleviate them," said Laura, "that you may shew you have too much confidence in me to hide the cause of your grief from me."

"Have *you* shewn that confidence in me?" replied she.

"Yes," replied Laura, "in every thing that concerned myself alone, or could be remedied. Tell me, therefore, what grieves you, and prove that you think me your friend."

"I think you an angel," said Signora Sporza, passionately; "and I love you with all my soul; but he who is the cause of my present affliction is a monster whom I detest as sincerely as I love you." She then threw out expressions which plainly indicated that she was acquainted with the scene above-mentioned, and knew that she was very ill treated by her husband.

"Good Heaven!" cried Laura; "was this the subject of your conversation with the Baron Carlostein, when I entered?"

Signora Sporza owned that they had been conversing on this subject. Laura then begged of her to send to him directly, and intreat him not to give the most distant hint of what she had told him to Captain Seidlits. "You do not know," continued she, "the violence of my brother's temper, and were he to hear any thing of this nature, the consequence would be dreadful indeed."

Signora Sporza directly wrote a letter to Carlostein in the terms which Laura required; and he immediately returned for answer, that he was aware of the consequences that might follow the mentioning any of the circumstances she had communicated to him, and assuring her he never should.

This quieted Laura's anxiety on this head, and as she could no longer entirely avoid conversing with Signora Sporza on the subject of her husband's ill treatment, she endeavoured to soften it, saying, That the particulars had been exaggerated, and that some vexatious news had put him into ill-humour at that time, and made him behave in a manner different from his usual conduct.

CHAPTER LXXI.

Mr. N—— hears from the Baronet.

In the mean time the honourable Mr. N——'s intimacy with Carlostein and Seidlits continued, and gradually grew into friendship, especially with the former, for the character and tastes of Mr. N—— were more analogous to those of Carlostein than of Seidlits; yet he had also a very great degree of esteem for the latter. It is remarkable, that the friendship between Mr. N—— and Carlostein was not interrupted by their being fond of the same woman: both esteemed her highly, neither had a wish inconsistent with her honour; and although Mr. N—— perceived that Laura had a stronger attachment to Carlostein than to any other person, he had also that degree of candour which so few possess, of being able to acquiesce in a preference against himself.

Mr. N—— had heard no accounts of his uncle the Baronet, or Mr. Steele, since he parted with them at Florence; and he had begun to be uneasy about them, when he received a letter from the former, dated Paris, the import of which was to inform him, that they should be detained in that place longer than they intended, by a hurt which Mr. Steele had received in consequence of a fall from his horse, in attempting to leap over a gate in a field a few miles from Paris; that a French gentleman, who saw the accident, had brought him to town in his carriage, much bruised; but he was already better, and would soon be quite well.

The Baronet next mentioned, that one *Carr*, a Scotchman, who pretended[1] to be an acquaintance of Buchanan, had called on him, saying, "He had lately come in a trading vessel from Naples to Marseilles; that on his landing he had met with a young sailor, who, some years since, had gone to the East Indies as midshipman in an English frigate, which had been lost on the coast of Malabar,[2] but he, with a few others of the crew, were saved; that after various distresses he had been taken into one of the vessels of the country, and again shipwrecked in the Persian gulph; had remained several years in Persia, afterwards had found means to get to Alexandria, and from thence in a trading vessel to Marseilles, where this Carr had met him, and they had travelled together on foot to Paris; but on account of his sharing his purse with this poor sailor, who then lay sick at their lodgings, Carr pretended that his own finances were exhausted; on which account he applied to him for a small supply of money to enable them both to proceed to London. The Baronet concludes his letter in this manner: "You may believe, my dear N——, that I was willing to relieve a man who had behaved so generously; but I wished, in the first place, to ascertain the truth of this Scotchman's story, which I own I thought a little romantic. I gave him, therefore, only a guinea in the mean time, and desired him to return next morning with some proof that he was of Buchanan's acquaintance; and I sent Mr. Steele's servant, Tom Dawson, with him to his lodging, with another guinea to the English sailor: Tom returned within a couple of hours, and informed me he had seen the sailor, who was a young man of three or four and twenty, of the name of Warren; that Carr had shewn him a letter which he said was from Buchanan to a countryman of theirs at Edinburgh; that having broken open the seal of this letter, Carr desired Dawson to carry it to me as the only testimony he could give of the truth of his story.

"After perusing it I own I have no doubts of the truth of what Carr told me, and shall certainly supply those two poor fellows with money sufficient to carry them home. Buchanan's epistle is so characteristic that I had it transcribed, and now send you the copy. As you are no very enthusiastic virtuoso,[3] it may possibly entertain you as much as any manuscript lately dug out of Herculaneum.

"There is another composition which I should be very well pleased to get a sight of, and that is by no less a personage than Steele's servant, Dawson. He told his master the other day, he wished to go to Versailles, and being asked what business he had there; he said, "He had received a letter from Ben Jackson, your father's groom, desiring him to be sure to send him a description all about France and Paris; and he therefore wished to add a word or two about Versailles, being the king's country-house." Steele who, you know, would suffer great inconveniency himself, rather than deprive any person depending upon him of such a gratification, immediately assented; and he tells me, that Dawson has been scribbling ever since his return. An account of Paris, and of the French nation, from such a hand, must of course be entertaining. I am sorry, therefore, I cannot send it you with the inclosed.

Adieu, my dear Edward,—Believe me ever sincerely

Yours,

* * * * *."

CHAPTER LXXII.

Buchanan's Letter.

To Mr. Archibald Campbell, Tobacconist, at the Sign of the Highlander, Cannongate, Edinburgh.

DEAR ARCHY, Naples.

"I Received your kind epistle, with the agreeable news that all our friends in the west country are well. I would have acknowledged the favour long ago, but could not find a private hand to carry my letter; for I do not choose to put my friends to the expence of postage, and therefore I make it a rule never to write by the post to any but strangers.[1]

"Your fears of my having forgot you are very ill founded, for although it has been my lot to sojourn many years among strangers, yet, thanks be unto God, I never learned to prefer foreigners to my own countrymen: on the contrary I do feel, that I like my old friends the better in proportion as I increase my new acquaintance. So you see there is little danger of my forgetting *them*, and far less my blood relations; for surely blood is thicker than water.

"As for my master the honourable Mr. N——, he is an exception; for he has been my benefactor, and it is impossible for me to be more attached to the nearest relations I have than to him: he is a kind-hearted and noble-minded gentleman indeed; and although he is most generous on proper occasions, he avoids the idle expence of many of his countrymen, whose extravagance, when they are on their tours, as they call them, renders them the prey and laughing-stock of all the countries through which they pass. And if you were only to see the sums which those thoughtless young lads, who have ten times more money than wit to guide it, throw away on useless *nigg-nyes*,* while thousands around them are pinched for the necessaries of life, it would make the very hair of your head, my dear Archy, stand up like the locks of Medusa.

"Before we left England, which, as I wrote to you at the time, Mr. N—— was advised to do on account of his health; I endeavoured to persuade him to go and drink goats whey among the healthful hills of the Highlands, where there are neither coughs, colds, nor shortness of breath, and where he could have lived like a king at a moderate expence; but he was prevailed on to try Italy, which has, to be sure, succeeded pretty well; but I am still in hopes that he will some time or other make a visit to Scotland, for he always speaks with respect of our country, which the ignorant and worthless of the English never do.

"You desire my opinion of Italy and its inhabitants, which I shall now give you without prejudice or partiality. The Italians are a most ingenious people. I have been even tempted to think that there is something favourable to ingenuity in the very air or soil, or something else belonging to this happily situated peninsula of Italy, for it became in the first place the seat of the empire of the world by the valour and address of its inhabitants; when I say the world, I mean all but the

* Nigg-nyes, or bawbles. [Moore's note.]

northern part of Great Britain, which the Romans were so far from subduing that they were obliged to build walls and ramparts across the island; first, between the Firths of Forth and Clyde, and next, from Carlisle to Newcastle,[2] to defend themselves from our ancestors the Caledonians.

"But when the Roman empire was overturned by the Goths, Rome became the seat of a new kind of empire, and that is the empire of the Popes. In short, the inhabitants of Italy first subdued mankind by open force; and secondly, by imposition and pawkry.* And after several ages of Gothic darkness, where does the light of knowledge first dawn again? Where do the arts first appear, and where are they carried to the greatest perfection? Why in this same Italy. This looks, I say, as if there were something peculiarly favourable to ingenuity in this country. But whatever may be in that notion, with all the disadvantages to which they are exposed from a miserably bad government, the present race of Italians certainly are a civilized, discreet, sober people, not so frank as the French, nor yet so reserved as the English; but with more shrewdness of understanding perhaps than either.

"In the formation of statues and graven images they are supposed to surpass all the nations in Europe; for in our own country, you know, this occupation was never much encouraged, because, in the opinion of several serious Christians of the Presbyterian persuasion, it flies in the teeth of the second commandment.

"The Italians are fond of music to an astonishing, and even to an unwarrantable degree; the number of eunuchs which they employ at a great expence, is a pretty plain proof that they spare nothing to have their ears tickled; they even oblige them to sing in the very churches; yet surely they might find houses enough to keep concerts in without profaning the house of God.—What would you think, Archibald, of hearing a dozen of fiddlers playing in the High Church of Edinburgh before and after sermon on the Lord's-day? I am sure it would shock you, as it did me, to a very great degree.

"Some people endeavour to defend this, saying, that it assists devotion, and a great deal of idle *clish-maclaiver*† of the same kind; for my part I have no good opinion of that sort of devotion which a parcel of fiddlers can assist. And people may argue as they please,

* Pawkry, cunning. [Moore's note.]

† Idle tittle-tattle. [Moore's note.]

but assuredly fiddles are better contrived to promote dancing than either meditation or prayer. At the same time it must be confessed, that Italian music, when performed in a proper place and on proper occasions, is very delightful to hear; though the best of it never thrilled through my heart so pleasingly as the sweet melody of some of our own tunes.

"As to the vulgar notion, that the Scottish music was invented by David Rizzio, the Italian secretary to Queen Mary,[3] it is contrary to history, to tradition, and to common sense; for nothing requires a greater degree of popularity, or would be a stronger proof of a man's being esteemed and universally admired in a country, than his forming the national taste in music; but David Rizzio, poor creature, was universally hated during the short time he lived in Scotland; and if any tunes had been known to be of his invention, that circumstance alone would have been sufficient to prevent their ever being sung or played in that country.

"You inquire also concerning the city of Naples compared with other places:—I will only say in a few words, that it is a large and populous town, pleasingly situated in the view of a spacious bay, little inferior in beauty to Loch Lomond itself.[4] The houses are built of free stone, several stories high, so that it has a more lofty appearance than London, but not quite so sublime as Edinburgh.[5]

"But it is not in the appearance of the fields, or of the cities, nor in the customs or genius of the inhabitants, that the country where you reside has the great advantage over this land of darkness, but in the important article of religion; which here consists almost entirely of external show and gewgawry,[6] of bowings, courtesies, and various gesticulations, of fantastical dresses, processions, and other idle ceremonials, which are in no way connected with true piety, and altogether opposite to the simplicity of the gospel, which you, my dear friend, enjoy the inestimable privilege of hearing preached in its native purity and truth.—As for your high dignified clergy, their lordships, and their eminencies, and his holiness himself, I have heard some of them perform, and if I may judge of the rest by those I have heard, they are mere pigmies upon pedestals, compared with the preachers you have an opportunity of hearing every Lord's-day.

"Having now briefly touched upon most of the points you mention in your last letter, I must recommend the bearer to your friendly offices; his name is Andrew Carr, of the Carrs of the South, his father being a shoemaker in Selkirk;[7] he came to this country in the service of an English gentleman, whom he was obliged to quit through the malice of the valet de chambre, who taking advantage of the young man's being overtaken with liquor on the last St. Andrew's day,[8] turned him off, on the pretext of his being an habitual drunkard.

"He remained however at Naples, in expectation of being taken into the service of some other English gentleman, and being young, thoughtless, and of a canty* turn of mind, he lived for some time very idly. When any of the English servants were allowed a day of pleasuring, as they call it, Andrew was sure to be of the party; and, at this rate, all the money he received from his late master would soon have been *cast at the cocks*:†—but in the midst of this, he received a letter from his mother, at Selkirk, informing him of his father's death, by which she and his sister were reduced to great poverty and distress. This news made a most laudable alteration in the conduct of Carr; he shunned all those parties of which he had formerly been so fond. And when our Dick pressed him very much, saying, "You used to be as fond of mirth and good wine as your neighbours;" Andrew shook his head, and replied, "Gif I drink wine, Richard, my mother and sister must drink water;" and the very next day he called on me with forty dollars, which he desired me to pay to Mr. N——'s Banker, for an order on a house at Edinburgh, to remit the value to his mother. Mr. N—— was so much pleased when he heard of this, that he doubled the remittance to Carr's mother, and also furnished him with money sufficient to defray the expence of his journey through France to Edinburgh, where, by my advice, he intends to establish himself as a dancing-master, being one of the best dancers of an English hornpipe, a Scottish jigg, or a strathspey, that I ever saw. It is a thousand pities that he continued so long at the shoe-making trade, because the constant stooping has given a roundness to his back and shoulders which hurts his air a little in dancing of a minuet; but he is to remain three weeks or a month at Paris to improve himself, which will remove that impediment.

"I desire, that you will put my namesake, little Geordy, to Mr. Carr's school, and I beg that you will assist him by your recommendation.

"I send by Mr. Carr two tortoise-shell snuff-boxes, one for you, and the other for Mr. Mackintosh; they are in the Neapolitan taste,

* Cheerful. [Moore's note.]

† Thrown away. [Moore's note.]

only instead of their usual ornaments, I caused the maker to inlay the first with a golden thistle, with the inscription, *Nemo me impune lacessit;*[9] and the other, with a cat rampant, which is the crest of the Mackintoshes, and the motto, *Touch not the cat bot* a glove.* I hope you will accept of them as small tokens of my friendship to you both. I send also a blue velvet bonnet as a new year's gift to little Geordy. I must now end this long letter, begging to be respectfully remembered to the laird of Clairvoky and his lady, to Mr. Hector Monro, and his cousin Æneas, to black Colin Campbell, and blind Saunders, and to all enquiring friends on the water of Enrick;[10] and so my dear Archy,

I remain, your affectionate cousin,

GEORGE BUCHANAN."

CHAPTER LXXIII.

Dawson's Letter.

ALTHOUGH the Baronet could not with propriety get a sight of the letter which Dawson had been so long and so carefully composing for the benefit of his friend Ben Jackson, we have had the good fortune to procure a copy, faithfully taken from the original; which is here inserted as a companion to the foregoing.

A Monseer,

Monseer BENJAMIN JACKSON, che le Count de————,

————Shire.

Engliterr.[1]

DEAR BEN,

HAVING received yours per course, this serves to let you know, that I am well and hearty, and so is Sir ——; but as for Mr. Steele, he had a fall from his horse in taking a very easy leap, which hurt him a little, but he is growing better thank God, for he is as good a soul and as generous to servants as any alive:——it was all the horse's fault, *that* I must say in justice to Mr. Steele, who put more trust in this lazy toad than he deserved; being deceived by the owner, who pretended he was a very good leaper. Now to say the truth, I have not seen many tolerable horses fit for hunting in all this town; and as for the women,

* Without. [Moore's note.]

about which your sister Bess makes inquiry, they are all for the most part painted, at least their faces: then for the rest, they hardly ever nick their tails, I mean of the horses, for England is the only country for horses and women. I do not believe that all Paris can produce the like of Eclipse, and your sister Bess.

Since you and your sister Bess desire it, I shall now write to you a little about the description of this here town and country. In my own private opinion, Paris is but a tiresome town to live in, for there is none of the common necessaries of life, as porter or good ale; and as for their beef, they boil it to rags. Wine to be sure is cheaper here, but not so strong and genuine as in London.

I have been at the French King's palace, which they call Versailles in their language; it is out of town, the same as Kew or Windsor is with our king. I went first and foremost to see the stables, which to be sure is very grand, and there they have some very good looking horses, especially English hunters: it grieved me to see so many of our own best subjects in the service of our lawful enemy, which to be sure the French King is.

We little think how many of our fellow-creatures are seduced from England to distant countries, and exposed to the worst of usage, from both the French and Spaniards; for none of them know how an English horse ought to be treated.

When I was at Versailles, I saw the Dowfiness,[2] which is all the same as the Prince of Wales's wife with us; she is one of the prettiest women I have seen in France, being very fair and blooming, and more like an English woman than a French, and not unlike your sister Bess, only her dress was different.

She rides like the ladies in England, with both her legs on the same side of the horse, whereas I have seen many women since I came abroad ride on horseback like men, which I think a bad contrivance, and I am surprised their husbands permit it. But I am told the women here do whatever they please, for all over France "the gray mare is the better horse."[3] Yet what contradicts this, and which I cannot account for, is what I heard my Lord D——'s butler tell yesterday; which is this, that by a law which he mentioned, but I have forgot its name, though it sounded something like a leek.[4]—By that there law, he said, that no woman can be king in France; that is, he did not mean by way of a bull,[5] for he is of English parentage, born at Kilkenny, but he meant, that no woman can ever be queen in France, as our women in

England are. As for instance, suppose the king has no sons, but only a daughter, then when the king dies, this here daughter, according to that there law, cannot be made queen, but the next near relation, provided he is a man, is made king, and not the last king's daughter, which to be sure is very unjust. But you will say, can there be no queen in France then? Yes, whoever the king marries is queen; and as long as her husband lives she may govern him, and rule the nation as much as she pleases; but when he dies, she is not permitted to rule any longer, except the next king pleases.

Now this shews, and you may tell your sister Bess so, that in spite of all the coaxing and courting which the French use to the women, yet they are false-hearted towards them at the bottom, and do not respect them so much as to the main point, as we English does; and yet one of those d——d Parlivoos[6] will go farther with some women in a day, than an Englishman in a month—all owing to their impudence; for a common man has as much impudence in France as a man-midwife[7] has in England. By the bye, Ben, I wonder you allow Tournelle, my Lord's French servant, to be so much with your sister Bess; he pretends to teach her the French cortillong,[8] but who knows what sort of cortillongs he may try to teach her; in my own opinion, old John Lancashere could teach her dancing as well, and this would be more decent for the reputation of her vertue: but you need not shew this part of my letter to Bess, but make your own use of it.

I have seen the French horse-guards which they call Jangdarms;[9] the men are smart-looking young fellows enough, but the horses are poor washy things in comparison of our dragoons.

The Swiss guards are stout men, clothed in scarlet, the same as our soldiers; but they have moustaches on their lips like the rat-catcher in St. Giles's.

The French foot guards are dressed in blue, and all the marching regiments in white, which has a very foolish appearance for soldiers; and as for blue regimentals, it is only fit for the blue horse or the artillery.

I believe the French army would have no great chance with our troops in a fair battle upon plain ground. It is lucky for the Mounseers, that there is no road by land between Dover and Calais; but as it is, I wonder the king does not send some regiments by sea to take Paris, which could make no great resistance; for there is no walls round the town, and there would be a good deal of plunder.

But after all, I like Paris better than Naples, though it is so near Mount Vesuvius, which all strangers go to see, the same as they do St. Paul's, the Monument, and lions in the Tower of London:[10] it is to be sure continually smoking and throwing out fiery ashes and other combustibles, such as none of our English mountains does. I went one night to the top of it with Mr. N——'s valet Buchanan, and one Duncan Targe, another Scotchman; I thought I should have been choked with the smoke and sulphurous smell. But as for Buchanan and Targe, it gave them no disturbance; the reason of which I take to be, that the Scotch are accustomed from their infancy to brimstone and bad smells in their own country. I do not say this by way of disparagement to them two, who are not bad kind of men—only a little proud; but of the Scotch in general, who in my opinion ought to be restrained by act of parliament to their own country, otherwise I do believe, in my own conscience, sooner or later, they will eat up Old England.

I have sent unto you, by the bearer, a pappy mashee[11] tobacco box, and a dozen pair of gloves, for your sister Bess, who will also deliver to you this letter, which I have taken three days in writing, to oblige you and Bess; and I durst not write by the post, for if the French found this letter, they would take me up for a spy, and shut me up in the Bastile during my life; and in England I am told all foreign letters are opened by the ministry, in which case this might bring you into trouble, because of the box and gloves, which being counterband against the act of parliament, the king would be enraged if he knew of such a thing, which stands to reason, all smuggled goods being so much money out of his pocket.—All from dear Ben, with my kind love to your sister Bess.

Your Servant to command,

THOMAS DAWSON.

CHAPTER LXXIV.

A Letter from the Baronet to the Honourable Mr. N——.

A FEW posts after the arrival of this packet, Mr. N—— received the following letter from his uncle:

MY DEAR EDWARD, Paris.

I will now give you a little more of Carr the Scot, and the English seaman.—In consequence of Dawson's having mentioned to his master, that the latter seemed sickly, and was but very indifferently accommodated in lodgings, Steele had the humanity to do what I ought to have done, but which I confess I neglected. He sent a physician to visit him, who having given it as his opinion, that the young Englishman required nothing but rest and proper diet to re-establish his health, Mr. Steele then sent for the landlord of the house where Carr and he were quartered, desiring that he would immediately give them a more convenient apartment, and let the young man have that particular diet which the doctor recommended; for all which he indemnified the man by an immediate advance of money, and sent a message to the sailor, that he wished to see him as soon as he could easily walk to the hotel, which was at no great distance from their inn.

Carr and Warren came together two days after receiving this message; the latter is a well-looking man, of about twenty-three or twenty-four years of age; he appeared emaciated, but is naturally of a stout constitution, and mends daily. He was desired to sit down, and he gave a short account of his disasters and long residence in Persia, in a modest and sensible manner.

But I leave you to imagine our surprise and pleasure, when in the course of the conversation we discovered that this sailor is brother to Lady Elizabeth's young friend Miss Warren; the same who went in a frigate as a midshipman to the East Indies the year before her father's death, and was supposed to have been lost in the passage, as neither the vessel nor any of the crew were afterwards heard of. You must remember Lady Elizabeth's relating those circumstances to you and to me at N—— House, one day after Miss Warren left the room, which she did on your mentioning an East India ship's having struck on a bank in going out of the Channel; and your aunt at the same time begged of you to be guarded in your discourse in that young lady's company, as every hint relative to naval engagements or shipwrecks was apt to rouse within her mind the painful recollection of her own family misfortunes. I will not attempt to describe young Warren's joy, on my informing him that I was acquainted with his sister, and that she was well and happily situated; nor how suddenly that joy was checked, when he inquired about his father. I answered, "I had heard nothing of him very lately;" but the youth had observed, that Steele made a sudden involuntary movement at the question, and he saw me look sorrowful when I made the answer. "Alas," cried he, wringing his hands, "my father is dead—I shall never see him more." We were silent, which rendered his suspicions certainty. The young man then burst into tears; after allowing them to flow for some time in silence, I told him that his father had died in battle, exerting himself gallantly in the cause of his country. The satisfaction which this communicated was visible through his tears; he made me repeat all the circumstances I knew, again and again. I shall never forget the emotion and ardour which appeared in the youth's countenance while he listened.—"My father," cried he with exultation, "was a brave officer."—"That he was," said I. "I had the honour of knowing him; his behaviour during the action in which he fell was praised, and his death regretted by the whole fleet." The young man continued to shed tears.

Steele is a worthy fellow—I like him more and more; he took hold of Warren's hand, and was going to say something consolatory to him, but his voice failing he also burst into tears, and he only could utter the words *damn it*, while he hastily rubbed his eyes, in a kind of indignation at finding himself crying. I said every thing that I imagined could sooth young Warren;—we ordered an apartment for him at our hotel;—poor Carr was exceedingly happy; he said he had always suspected that Mr. Warren was of genteel parentage, and even attempted to make an apology for some parts of his own behaviour which he thought had been too familiar. You may easily conceive how this was received by one of Warren's sensibility; he shook him by the hand, called him his benefactor, and said he would never forget what he owed to him. Carr however declared he knew what belonged to a gentleman and the son of an officer, and only desired leave to continue to attend him in the quality of a servant till his arrival in England; and notwithstanding all Warren could urge, he would remain with him on no other conditions.

I have prevailed on this young man to accept of my credit for what is immediately necessary for his decent equipment. All his misfortunes have not damped his fondness for his profession. He has no views nor hopes independent of it; and his most ardent wish after seeing his sister, is to return to his duty, in the hopes of promotion as an officer. Steele is wonderfully attached to him, and Warren seems to have the warmest esteem or most grateful affection for Steele; who is now so well that we think of leaving this in a few days, and my next letter, I hope, will be dated from N—— House. God bless you, my dear Edward!

CHAPTER LXXV.

A second Letter from the Baronet to the Honourable Mr. N——.

Two or three weeks after this, Mr. N—— received another letter from his uncle, of which what follows is an extract:

"Our reception at N—— House was most joyful; Steele's mother and his uncle Transfer were both there when we arrived. The former flew with impatience into her son's arms before he had finished his compliments to your father and Lady Elizabeth. Transfer assured Steele as he shook him by the hand, that he was not so happy even at the peace, although he had then gained six thousand pounds by the rise of stock. While the mother, uncle, and nephew were entertaining each other, I presented young Warren to his sister. The tenderness of this scene exceeds my power of description; your father was moved even to tears, while Lady Elizabeth beheld it with a smile of serene satisfaction. I do not know how to account for this, for who is more alive to the feelings of humanity than her Ladyship? Perhaps she had anticipated the meeting in her imagination; so that when it actually took place, nothing happened but what she had foreseen; whereas your father was taken by surprise, or perhaps Lady Elizabeth's attention to support her young friend during this pathetic interview prevented her from being so much affected herself as she would otherwise have been.

"Young Warren behaved with great propriety, for his behaviour was natural. His first expressions were those of the most affectionate tenderness for his sister; his next, of gratitude to Lady Elizabeth and your father, for the parental kindness they had shewn to his orphan sister; the mention of which brought the recollection of their own father into the minds of both. The fine countenance of Miss Warren, bathed in tears, fell upon her brother's shoulder, while he, greatly agitated, was scarcely able to sustain her and himself.

"In this attitude they continued for some time in the midst of a group too much affected to give them any interruption.

"Miss Warren seeming to recover herself, and attempting to apologize to the company, Lady Elizabeth took her by the hand, and said, 'I beg you will come with me, my dear, I have something to say to you.' Then supporting Miss Warren with one hand, and drawing her brother after her with the other, she conducted both into another room. 'You must have many things to communicate in which you will be under restraint from the presence of even your best friends.' So saying, she left them together, and returned to the company.

"Mrs. Steele was inclined to have a tête-à-tête with her son; but Transfer, who observed her drawing him apart, opposed it, unless he were admitted of the party; he swore he loved his nephew as well as his sister could love her son, and he had no notion of allowing him to be seduced from him on the very day of his arrival.

"After Warren and his sister had been together about an hour, he called in Carr, whom the young Lady was most desirous of seeing. She seems almost in love with this fellow ever since her brother informed her of Carr's behaviour to him; and respects him so much for the goodness of his heart, that she cannot bear to hear him turned into ridicule on any account.

"I read Buchanan's letter the other day to your father and Lady Elizabeth. We laughed a little at an expression in it concerning Carr's air in dancing a minuet. Miss Warren did not quite relish the jest. I do in my conscience believe that had a man, with the face and person of the Belvidere Apollo,[1] neglected her brother in his distress, no future attention to herself could have made this young Lady respect him so much as she does this poor fellow.

"The enthusiastic affection of Miss Warren for her brother bodes well for our friend Steele, who is her passionate admirer as much as ever; and if I am not greatly mistaken, the Lady views him already in a different light from what she did before he went abroad. I am so much convinced of this, that I have ventured to give Steele some encouraging hints to that purpose. Your father also wishes him to renew his addresses, and I am certain that Steele's heart prompts him to the same; his natural diffidence, however, joined to the abhorrence he has for importuning any body, have hitherto restrained him; he derives little encouragement from Miss Warren's affable behaviour to him, which he entirely imputes to complaisance for her brother, whose friendship for Steele increases daily. But in my opinion, independent of all consideration of her brother, the damsel herself now views honest Steele with other eyes than she did formerly. Indeed both your father and Lady Elizabeth declare that he is improved in many respects by his travels. Possibly you may lay claim to part of the honour of this, for I believe you were his only *ami du voyage*.[2] Adieu, my dear Edward. I rejoice in the accounts of your continued good health, and hope you will stay no longer abroad than the time requisite for confirming it, so as that you may never again need to quit Old England on that account."

CHAPTER LXXVI.

Prudent Conduct of Laura.

It is now full time to return to Laura, from whom the reader may perhaps think we have been absent too long. When we left her, she had prevailed on Signora Sporza to write to Carlostein, and had seen his answer, wherein he gave assurances not to give the least hint to his friend Captain Seidlits of the ill-footing on which Zeluco and his sister were. After the discovery made by the maid to Signora Sporza, it was no longer in Laura's power to adhere to the plan she had formed, by avoiding conversations with Signora Sporza on a topic which she introduced as often as they were together by themselves. And in the course of those conversations Signora Sporza made no scruple of giving it as her opinion, that Laura ought not to submit to the caprices and ill-humour of a man she did not love, and whom it was impossible she ever should; one, whose love for her was already exhausted, and which, if it should ever return, must, now that his true character had developed itself, prove a curse, not a blessing, to his wife: the best measure which Laura could adopt therefore, was to inform her mother and brother of the true state of the case, and to separate, on the best terms they could procure, from her husband for ever.

Nothing was more earnestly desired by Laura than a separation upon any terms from Zeluco; but as this could not be done without informing her mother of the misery of her situation, she could not bear to give a parent, for whom she felt the most tender affection, the remorse of thinking that *she* had been the most active cause of her child's misery. She was also afraid of her brother, whom she knew to be of a temper to call her husband to a severe account for his conduct towards her, the consequences of which in every point of view appeared to her dreadful; a third consideration, it is probable, had some weight with her—she had reason to believe she was with child.

Laura, therefore, insisted firmly with Signora Sporza to be allowed to judge for herself in this particular, and convinced her that she should be highly offended if Signora Sporza gave the least hint of the terms on which she was with her husband to her brother, or any other person. What had already happened, however, made Carlostein an exception; and Signora Sporza indemnified herself for the restraint she was obliged to use to others by speaking her sentiments very freely to him, even in the presence of Laura, on this subject, which now engrossed her thoughts.

Notwithstanding the precautions which Laura took to keep her mother from the knowledge of what would give her too much uneasiness, if that lady had not been a little dazzled by the glitter of magnificence which appeared in the equipages and domestic establishment of Zeluco, and flattered by his specious behaviour to herself, she would have discovered that her daughter was unhappy. With regard to Captain Seidlits, he thought his sister so very amiable in all respects, that it never entered into his mind that the man who possessed her, and who could have no motive but love for his original attachment to her, did not think himself happy in the acquisition; and although it sometimes occurred to him, from the pensive and melancholy air of his sister, that she might not be so very fond of her husband as could be wished, he considered that as a misfortune which she had in common with many women, and for which there was no remedy; and he turned his thoughts from it as from an idea which if indulged could only plague himself, without being of service to his sister.

It has been already remarked, that the many fine qualities and accomplishments which Laura possessed, and which would have fixed the esteem and affection of a man of worth and sentiment, had little attraction for the jaded senses and corrupt taste of Zeluco, who sought in venal beauty and in variety a relief from *ennui*, and its never-failing companion ill-humour; but all those palliations, instead of diminishing were found to augment the incurable disease under which this wretched man laboured; who, when he became unsupportable to himself, often endeavoured to exhaust the virulence which corroded his own breast upon her, who, before she knew him, had never known what *ennui* or ill-humour was.

Distressing, however, as his ill-temper was, it did not seem so dreadful in the eyes of his wife, as the returns of fondness with which he was occasionally seized; and sometimes, from unaccountable caprice, those fits of fondness would come immediately after he had been insulting her with the most unprovoked ill usage.[1] An attachment, therefore, which Zeluco formed about this time, and was considered as a source of great affliction to his wife, proved in reality one of the most comfortable incidents to her that had occurred since her marriage.

CHAPTER LXXVII.

Nerina.

——genus huic materna superbum
Nobilitas dabat, incertum de patre ferebat.
VIRG.[1]

Two ladies had lately arrived at Naples; one of them an elderly woman, the other about three or four and twenty, and of uncommon beauty. The account given of them by the banker on whom they had a credit, and which was supported by letters to individuals at Naples, was, that the youngest had a moderate fortune in her own possession, on which she lived in a genteel and independent manner, and had come to pass a few months at Naples, that she might enjoy the benefit of a purer air than that of Rome; that the elder lady was aunt to the younger, and the widow of an officer; that she was in reduced circumstances, and dependent on her niece.

Such was the account given of those two ladies, whose real history was as follows:

The young one, whose name was Nerina, was the offspring of a secret amour between an unmarried woman of family in Genoa, and a musician. The affair had been hushed up; the lady being delivered at the house of a female relation in the country, the infant given to the wife of a peasant to suckle, and the father retiring to Venice, where he lived on the profits of his profession and on the money which he received from the child's mother. His demands became more exorbitant than it was in her power to satisfy; he wrote menacing letters, but no threats could procure from her or her relations what satisfied the rapacity of the musician; on which he formed a scheme to carry away the child from the peasant's cottage, and convey her to his own house at Venice. He succeeded in his project by the connivance of the maid who had the care of the child. Having this pledge in his hands, he imagined that the mother or her relations would be more solicitous to furnish him with money: it happened otherwise; the unhappy mother retired to a convent, where in a short time she was seized with a fever, of which she died. After this her relations set the musician at defiance, and gave themselves no further trouble about him or the child. The musician was a man of the most profligate principles and manners; he lived with a woman of the same character, who was a singer at the Opera. With this couple Nerina was educated; she had a pretty good voice, and promised to be remarkably handsome. They expected that in a short time the circumstances of the family would be greatly augmented by a proper use of both; but Nerina was not of a disposition to share the profits arising from her personal accomplishments with any person whatever; at the age of fifteen therefore she abandoned her father's house, and the territories of the Republic, in company with a Venetian Nobleman. She was acquainted with the circumstances of her own birth; and although in her disposition she had more affinity with her father than with her unfortunate mother, yet in conversation she seemed to consider herself as descended from her mother alone, and never mentioned her father, more than if she had not known of his existence. She lived with the Venetian, till his flow of money, which was considerable at the beginning of their connexion, began to ebb; she then left him for a young Englishman, with whom she embarked in a high tide of fortune, and at last quitted him for the same reason that she had quitted the Venetian. She afterwards established herself at Rome, and wishing to acquire a decent character, she took an elderly woman into her service, who she pretended was a relation of her mother's, and lived for some time with as much affected modesty as a great deal of natural impudence would permit.

It is said that people are apt through life to set too great a value on those things which they have found it difficult to procure in their youth, and too little on those to which they have been accustomed. Nerina had been bred in a family in which there was a great scarcity of money, and a profusion of what is sometimes, however improperly, called love. Whether it was owing to this, or from whatever cause it proceeded, certain it is, that Nerina, in all her dealings, shewed the utmost attention to the former, and made very little or no account of the other.

While Nerina lived in this *decent* style at Rome, she was protected by a certain Cardinal, who sometimes saw her in secret, and by whose friendship she flattered herself that she should be enabled to pass the rest of her life without having need of other protectors; but before she could get matters arranged to her satisfaction, an accident happened to the Cardinal, which, according to his own calculation should not have happened for several years, and which Nerina did not wish for till the arrangements above-mentioned had taken place. The Cardinal died the day after he had passed an evening with Nerina, during which he had been more profuse than ever of his expressions of *friendship*.

Nerina was so violently affected by this premature accident, that, in her rage, she could not abstain from many abusive expressions against his Eminence, for having so long delayed what she thought it was his duty to have performed; but her passion subsiding by degrees, she at length mustered up all her philosophy, which directed her, without farther loss of time, to have recourse to several protectors to indemnify her for her loss of one of the Cardinal's importance.

Among those was a young man of a noble family of Milan, who became desperately in love with her, and for whom she affected a reciprocal flame, but with this difference, that the young man's continued to burn with undiminished fervour after the fuel which fed Nerina's was quite exhausted. As soon as she perceived that his money was gone, and understood that he had but distant hopes of a fresh supply, a chilling alteration seemed to take place in the bosom of Nerina; and the youth, instead of smiles and caresses, was received with formality and cold politeness.

The imprudent youth, unable to bear this kind of behaviour from a person who commanded all his affection, proposed marriage as the only recompence he could make to her, now that his finances were exhausted.

This offer made an immediate impression on the mind, and some alteration in the behaviour of Nerina; but after weighing every circumstance, and balancing the advantages and disadvantages of closing with the proposal, she concluded that it would be attended with more trouble than she was willing to bestow, and more risk than she chose to run. She therefore fell on means, without appearing to have given the information, of acquainting her lover's relations that he had got into bad company at Rome, and that if he were not removed immediately, he was in danger of taking an irretrievable step of the most fatal consequence to his honour and happiness. She amused the youth himself with evasive answers, till one of his relations arrived at Rome, with peremptory orders from his father, for his immediate return to Milan; which the young man with infinite reluctance at length obeyed, after mutual oaths of eternal love, and many tears on his part as well as that of Nerina, whose agent received a liberal recompence for the intelligence.

The young man being thus disposed of, and Nerina having a desire to see Naples, she did not think those acquaintance whom she had occasionally seen, unknown to her Milanese lover, and to each other, of importance enough to induce her to baulk her fancy.

She went accordingly, and established herself with her pretended aunt, in the manner that has been mentioned.

CHAPTER LXXVIII.

Il y a dans la jalousie plus d'amour propre que d'amour.

ROCHEFOUCAULT.[1]

ZELUCO accidentally meeting with Nerina, was sufficiently touched with her face and figure, to wish to cultivate her acquaintance. He found no unsurmountable obstacle to this, but Nerina, knowing him to be a man of great fortune, thought it worth her while to use all her powers of attraction, which, particularly to a man of Zeluco's character, were very strong, till by degrees she cherished what was only a transient desire into a violent passion.

He wished however to conceal his connexion with Nerina from his wife and her relations; and although he visited her very frequently, it was always in secret, so that their intimacy might have remained much longer unknown, had all the world taken as little pains to discover it as Laura and her relations. But Laura received two letters in one day, both from unknown and *sincere friends*, giving her a faithful account of her husband's intimacy with Nerina; and explaining how she might detect it. One of those friends was a woman with whom Zeluco had intrigued, and who took this step to be revenged of him for his infidelity; the other was a lady who suspected that her husband was fond of Laura, and hated her on that account, although well convinced that he would not succeed. It would have been mortifying to those two benevolent creatures, had they known how very little their intelligence affected Laura. She was in the act of throwing their letters into the fire when her husband entered the room: "You seem very eager to burn those letters," said he. "Their contents are of a nature too indifferent for me to be eager about them," replied she.—"Pray, who are they from, if it be not a secret?" added he.—"It *is* a secret?" said she.—"Indeed!" said he, snatching one of the letters that was not consumed, from the fire, "may *I* be admitted as a confident?"—"You had better not read it," said Laura coolly, and without attempting to take it from him.—"Why so?" said he. "Because," replied she, "the contents will be as little satisfactory to you as the method of obtaining them is honourable."

"So you are afraid of my reading it," said he. "I have no fears on the subject," replied Laura, walking towards the door.

"Stay, Madam," cried Zeluco, who knew the hand, and having observed the name of Nerina in the letter, suspected the contents; "I have no intention to read this scroll, only your affecting not to know from whom it came, surprised me."—"It is no affectation, I have not the least notion," said Laura.—"What then, they were both anonymous?"—"They were," added she.—"Some jest, I suppose," said he, throwing the letter again into the fire, "or perhaps some piece of malice."—"Very possibly," said she, and left the room.

While Zeluco had held the half-consumed letter in his hand, he recognized the writing of the Lady with whom he himself had intrigued. Knowing the jealousy of her disposition, and perceiving Nerina's name in the middle of the letter, he immediately suspected its contents; and *albeit, unused to the blushing mood,*[2] he underwent something approaching to it, on perceiving that he had betrayed unjust suspicions of his wife, at the very instant that she received information of his own infidelity.

For some time after this incident, Zeluco behaved with more attention to Laura, and affected a greater share of good humour than was natural to him, while she shewed no symptom of being in any degree affected by the intelligence conveyed in the anonymous letters; nor did she ever after by any allusion or hint revive the recollection of them.

In the mean while Mr. N—— prevailed on Captain Seidlits to make a tour with him into the two Calabrias,[3] and other parts of the kingdom of Naples. Carlostein having declined to accompany them, saying, as he was to remain in Italy after Seidlits, he would postpone it. Zeluco became daily more intoxicated with Nerina; she almost continually occupied his thoughts, and engrossed the greatest part of his time, so that Laura was left at more freedom and in greater tranquillity than she had ever enjoyed since her marriage.

Her husband's vanity with regard to her was considerably abated, so that he no longer insisted, as he had done formerly, on her appearing at every assembly and public place; he was better pleased that she should remain at home at her mother's, or Signora Sporza's, while he was passing his time with Nerina, and of course being missed from assemblies, it might be believed that he was keeping his wife company.

Laura's society at this period therefore was confined to her mother, Signora Sporza, and Carlostein; the latter she saw almost every day, and frequently had opportunities of conversing with him alone at the house of Signora Sporza. This too indulgent friend being exceedingly affected at the settled gloom which she well saw had overspread the mind of Laura, and which she thought the company and conversation of Carlostein alone had the power of dissipating, contrived frequent means of bringing them together; and this she did with such address, that they seemed to happen by accident, and without any previous arrangement on her part. Nothing could be more imprudent than the conduct of Signora Sporza, in leading her young friend into such slippery situations, which she did however from no other inducement than the pleasure she took in seeing Laura pleased and in good spirits; as for Zeluco, she thought he richly deserved the worst that could happen, for, in her opinion, he had already put it out of his wife's power to do him injustice; but there is one consideration, which, had it occurred to Signora Sporza, would have made her act very differently from what she did; and that is, the effect that any essential ill conduct would have had on the mind of Laura herself. Signora Sporza did not reflect that, had this been the case, no alleviation from peculiar circumstances, no provocation on the part of her husband, no certainty of concealment, and no consideration of whatever kind, could have made a woman of Laura's disposition forgive herself, or could have restored her that peace of mind without which happiness cannot exist.

It must be owned that the virtue of few women was ever placed in a more perilous situation than that of Laura, when it is considered that she had a fixed and well-grounded aversion for her husband, constantly kept alive by fresh provocations; for she was by turns teased by his caprices, abused by his unprovoked rage, insulted by his groundless jealousies, and stimulated by his infidelity; while a most amiable and accomplished man, for whom she could not help feeling a great partiality, was desperately in love with her, and with whom she had frequent opportunities of being alone.

She received a second letter from one of her anonymous correspondents, informing her, that her husband and one of his associates, with Nerina, who was also to have a companion, had formed a party to pass a few days at Casserta[4] and other places, and were to set out that very day. Laura was as little affected by this letter as the former; she threw it into the fire, and thought no more of it.

That very day, Zeluco, without the shadow of provocation, but in the mere wantonness of caprice, behaved to her in the most insolent and brutal manner, telling her, "that her *favourite*," meaning the Nobleman who had the squabble with Carlostein, "had abandoned her, and set out for Venice, and he supposed *that* was the cause of her low spirits; on her keeping silence, he told her that her silence proceeded from insolence and pride."

"You are mistaken," said Laura; "I never *was* insolent, and I never had less reason to be proud; I was silent from contempt of an accusation which I cannot think you yourself believe to have any foundation."

"Contempt!" cried Zeluco, fiercely.

"Contempt of a groundless accusation," replied Laura.

"Your contempt is affected, Madam," said Zeluco; "but your melancholy is real."

"My melancholy is indeed real," said Laura, bursting into tears.

After uttering some shocking observations on her being so much affected, and the supposed cause, he said, "I am going to the country for a few days, Madam, and leave you to mourn that your mignon is not at hand to comfort you during my absence."

CHAPTER LXXIX.

The Portrait.

LAURA gave free way to the fulness of her sorrow for a considerable time after her husband left her, but at last, fearing that her mother might call and observe the traces of affliction on her countenance, she went to Signora Sporza's, that she might have time to recover herself, in some degree, before she should meet with Madame de Seidlits.

The servant did not know that the Baron Carlostein was with his mistress, he therefore told Laura that Signora Sporza was alone, and immediately introduced her into the room, where she found them conversing together.

"I have been just telling the Baron, my dear," said Signora Sporza to Laura as she entered, "that I have a letter to write, I beg therefore you will entertain him till I return."

Carlostein perceived the marks of anguish which the last scene with her husband had left on the countenance of Laura; and he conjectured rightly respecting the cause. Without asking a question, or uttering a syllable, his countenance expressed a thousand tender inquietudes on her account. After a considerable silence, he at length said, "Would to Heaven, Madam, it were in my power to alleviate your sorrow, or contribute in any degree to your happiness."

"*My* happiness!" repeated Laura, raising her spread hands, and throwing up her eyes to Heaven.

"Yes, Madam," cried Carlostein with great emotion; "*your* happiness, which is dearer to me than my own, or rather which, more than any personal concern, *is* my own."

"Ah! why," said Laura, "should your fair prospects be obscured by the tempests in which mine——," here she checked herself, and then added, "my thoughts are disturbed, Sir, I am not well.—I know not what I say."

"I have long dreaded," said Carlostein, "that you were not fortunate in all your connections; but you are blessed in some beyond the usual lot; you have the best of mothers, a brother who adores you, and friends who would cheerfully expose themselves to every fatigue and danger to serve you."

"My brother, Sir," said Laura, "first taught me to value his friend; I learned the lesson in my childhood, and it were vain for me to affect not being pleased with the interest you take in me; but a series of unlucky incidents have involved me in a net of misery from which the endeavours of all my friends cannot disentangle me.—Happiness and tranquillity are fled far from me,—I attempt not to recover what is beyond my grasp." Here she burst into a fresh flood of tears, and Carlostein had bathed her hand with his, while in the excess of her despair she was insensible that he had hold of it. He attempted to comfort her by every suggestion that could convey hope or consolation.—"No!" exclaimed she; "death must be my only comforter; there is no hope for so complete a wretch as I am, but in the grave;—and miserable creature that I am," resumed she, after a pause; "I cannot without reluctance even wish for that last refuge of the miserable; how can I have the heart to wish for ease to myself, knowing as I do, that it cannot be obtained but at the expence of my poor mother, who would be left a prey to remorse, horror, and despair."

Carlostein then in the most sympathising manner, and with all the eloquence of passion, declared the highest esteem and attachment to her; that he would consider it as the greatest honour and happiness he could ever enjoy, to attempt whatever could tend to her ease or satisfaction; that he esteemed fortune, and life itself, as valuable only in as much as they should enable him to serve *her*, whose happiness was far dearer to him than life.

"Alas!" cried Laura, "the completion of my misery is the being sensible that you can be of no service to me. I am convinced that your generous friendship would excite you to exertions of difficulty and danger in my favour; but I am in that hopeless state, that my best friends, those united to me by blood, as well as those attached by sentiment, must struggle equally in vain to free me from the horrid rock of misery to which I am fixed by chains which no earthly hand can break."

"Accursed chains!" cried Carlostein, "they were forged in hell, and ought not to bind an angel!"

"They will ever bind me," said Laura.

"O loveliest and dearest of women!" cried Carlostein, with enthusiasm; "why did I not know you sooner; often did I hear the praises of the accomplished Laura Seidlits—whom I had only seen in childhood; but could I imagine there was such perfection, such elegance, such soul-subduing loveliness, united in woman."

Declarations of this nature, uttered with all the energy of truth and passion, by a graceful and amiable man, for whom she had the warmest friendship, at a time when she was full of indignation at the brutal behaviour of a hated husband, could not fail to make a lively impression on the heart of Laura, endued with exquisite sensibility, and formed for friendship and love.

"Why did not your brother and I," exclaimed Carlostein, "follow you to Italy sooner?—Why did we loiter at Berlin and Vienna while the fiends were weaving this web of wretchedness?—O! would to heaven we had hurried directly to Naples!"

"Would you had!" said Laura, in a languid voice.

"Bless you—bless you, my angel, for that wish!" cried Carlostein, encircling her waist with his arms.

In this situation Laura seemed for a short time to have lost the power of recollection; but raising her eyes, they met the portrait of her father, which hung on the opposite wall of the room.—She gave a sudden scream, and struggled to get free.

"What is the matter, my angel?" said Carlostein.

"Ah! loose me;—unhand me, Sir," cried she with a voice of terror, and sprung from his yielding arms.

"What terrifies you?" said he.

"Look there!" cried she, pointing to the portrait.

"I see a picture," said Carlostein.

"I see an angry father," said Laura, with a trembling voice.

Carlostein then endeavoured to sooth and calm her spirits by the most endearing expressions; but as often as he approached her, she moved from him, and entreated him to be gone.

"If I have offended you," cried he, "most earnestly do I beg your forgiveness."

"I cannot forgive myself," replied Laura.

"In what are you to blame, angel of purity?" exclaimed he.

"Leave me; O leave me!" repeated she; "it is not meet for us to be thus together.—Pray withdraw."

"When shall I see you again?" said Carlostein, in a plaintive voice.

"You shall hear from me soon," answered she; "but at present, if you have any esteem for me, leave me."

Carlostein retired, and Laura, turning to the portrait of her father, continued for a considerable time contemplating it with earnestness, and then exclaimed, "Blessed effigy of one to whom honour was dearer than life, how much am I beholden to you!"

When Signora Sporza returned, she seemed surprised at the absence of Carlostein. Laura said, he was obliged to go, and immediately turned the discourse to other subjects.

The two following days Carlostein found no opportunity of seeing Laura; being uneasy at the idea of having offended her, he told Signora Sporza, that he was afraid her friend had misunderstood some part of his conduct which he wished to explain, and begged she would deliver a letter for that purpose, as he was unwilling to send it by a servant.

Signora Sporza complied with his request, and the next day presented him with the following answer from Laura.

"To the Baron Carlostein.

"The uneasiness you express at the idea of my being displeased with you, may now be at an end.—I never thought you capable of any formed plan inconsistent with my honour. But I am sensible that the pleasure I took in your conversation, and in the thoughts of your friendship, has led me into improprieties and dangers which a prudent and virtuous woman should avoid.

"The ties by which I am bound to my husband are sacred, however miserable they render me. Although his behaviour deprives him of my esteem, it cannot justify my ill conduct.

"Having said this, you cannot, with reason, blame the resolution I have taken, never again to meet you alone. I am persuaded, my cousin Sporza would not have permitted such meetings if she had not a higher opinion of me than I deserve.

"It will be vain for you to endeavour to prove the innocence or safety of our meeting as formerly; the only effect of such an attempt would be to diminish the good opinion I entertain of you.

"Adieu, and may Heaven bless you! Every proof of regard and confidence, consistent with duty, you may always expect from the wretched

Laura."

CHAPTER LXXX.

——Miseri quibus
Intentata nites. HOR.[1]

HOWEVER vexed Carlostein was at the thoughts of being deprived of the pleasure of seeing Laura as formerly, he was too well convinced of the propriety of her conduct, and too much afraid of losing her good opinion, to make any immediate attempt to prevail on her to alter it.

He immediately signified, in a letter which Signora Sporza delivered to her, his gratitude for the friendship with which she honoured him; adding, that although he perceived not any danger in the meetings which she had determined to discontinue, yet he acquiesced in her decision, and would conform himself in that, and in every thing else, to her pleasure.

He saw her occasionally, however, at her own house, where he was frequently invited by Zeluco; and as, after the scene at Signora Sporza's, Laura's behaviour to Carlostein was a little more constrained than usual, Zeluco was more and more convinced that his wife struggled in vain to conceal the dislike she had to him.

It is probable that he would have discovered his mistake in this particular, had not his mind been engrossed by his passion for Nerina, for whom he had taken a little villa at some distance from Naples, where his visits, he imagined, would be less observed than while she lived in town.

The symptoms of pregnancy became apparent on Laura, which rendered the retirement she loved more expedient than ever; and as Zeluco was seldom at home, she was for several months almost entirely relieved from his jealousy, ill-humour, and fondness.

In truth, Nerina had as little affection for Zeluco as Laura had; but it was much easier for the one to feign sentiments which she had not, than the other; the first had been reared from her infancy in the school of simulation, in her all the alluring tricks of educated artifice were engrafted on a disposition naturally fraudulent. The other was habituated to truth; had she been inclined to dissemble, she must have failed from want of practice. And if both had been equally mistresses of deceit, still Nerina would have had the easier task in affecting to love Zeluco; she only had to get the better of indifference, whereas Laura had to overcome aversion.

Zeluco had, from the hour of his marriage, observed extreme coldness in Laura; and although, from a very short period after their union, he had never been able so far to overcome the natural sulkiness of his character as to make a fair trial to gain her affection, yet he considered her want of it as a crime; for self-love made him think it impossible that a woman should be cold to him, who was not capriciously prepossessed in favour of another.

Nerina had two objects in view: the one was to persuade Zeluco that Laura was attached to another man; the other, that she herself was desperately fond of him. She had hitherto found no plausible opportunity of insinuating the first, but she endeavoured to convince him of the second by ten thousand little attentions, by flattering fits of jealousy, by occasional resistance, and other allurements, which she well knew how to vary opportunely; she had already drawn very considerable sums of money from him, and had acquired such an ascendancy over him as she hoped to improve into a complete and absolute sway.

If Zeluco happened to dine for two days successively at home, or to mention Laura with any degree of respect, he was sure soon after to find Nerina in apparent languor and ostentatious dejection of spirits: when questioned by him on the cause, she sighed, affected to hide her tears, and begged that he would not inquire into the cause of that for which she had too much reason to fear there was no remedy. On being farther urged, she would sob, shiver, and fall into a convulsive faint; and when she had performed this with admirable nicety of action, she seemed to recover, and after a fresh discharge of tears, lamented the severity of her fate, in being passionately fond of a man who, after the sacrifice she had made, preferred another to her; and, what was still more mortifying, one who hated and despised him.

At other times she insinuated that his wife's relations formed a cabal to manage him entirely; that they had already taken advantage of the easy generosity of his temper, and prevailed on him to settle a large portion of his fortune on her and her children, and had plans of carrying their rapacious views still farther, so that in a short time he would be little more than a factor on his own estate.

CHAPTER LXXXI.

The Displeasure of Captain Seidlits;—the Distress of Laura;—the Prudence of Carlostein;—and good Sense of Mr. N——.

Some time after Seidlits returned from his tour he heard of this connexion with Nerina, and perceived, with an indignation which he could ill suppress, that Zeluco had not the same degree of attention for Laura that he formerly displayed.

Captain Seidlits dropt some expressions to that effect in the presence of his sister. She was alarmed at the consequence of his harbouring such a suspicion, and endeavoured to remove it; but fearing that she had not succeeded, she earnestly begged that he would not ruin her mother's peace by mentioning his suspicion to her.

"It is not to your mother, but to your husband, I mean to talk on the occasion," said he.

Laura then endeavoured to convince him of the impropriety of his interfering undesired between man and wife, adding, That she was sensible of the fraternal interest he took in whatever concerned her, that it was her pride and happiness to have such a friend and protector, and that she would apply to him freely when she needed his interposition.

Laura was so distrustful of her brother's temper, that she renewed her remonstrances frequently on this subject. It happened once or twice that Zeluco entered the room on these very occasions, and she remarked with great pain, that Seidlits could with difficulty conceal his feelings, and that he returned the civilities of the other in a very cold manner.

This increased her fears so much, that, in the presence of Signora Sporza, she acquainted Carlostein with the cause of her uneasiness, and entreated him to watch over his friend, and endeavour to dissuade him from a conduct fraught with the most dismal consequences. Carlostein expressed his satisfaction at the confidence which she placed in him, and promised to do every thing in his power to prevent what she dreaded.

Carlostein soon after happened to meet his friend Seidlits walking by himself, and ruminating on the various instances he had observed of neglect or ill-usage on the part of Zeluco towards Laura.

"You seem thoughtful, my friend," said Carlostein; "something vexes you."

"Something does vex me," said Seidlits.

"You do not intend then, I hope, that it should be a secret to me."

"No certainly.—This Zeluco, I fear, does not use my sister as she deserves."

"I do not know who could," said Carlostein.

"He seems to be of a sulky, ill temper," said Seidlits.

"If that be the case, it is a misfortune to all who are connected with him," replied Carlostein, "but most of all to himself."

"But it ought to be a misfortune to himself only," said Seidlits, "not to her who has the sweetest temper on earth; and I am determined that his ill humour shall not make my sister unhappy.—The same world shall not contain me and the man who behaves ill to Laura Seidlits.—I'll tell him so this very day."

"Have you any particular instance of ill usage to complain of?" said Carlostein.

"Why there is this woman," replied Seidlits, "this Nerina, with whom he passes so much of his time; *that* must be mortifying to my sister, and shews what a brute he is; and besides, his general manner to her is not kind and attentive as it ought to be, and as it shall be, *that* I am determined on."

"My dear Seidlits," said Carlostein, "what answer do you think you would give to any man who should tell you, that he did not approve of your keeping company with a particular woman, and that you ought to behave with more attention and kindness to your wife."

"Well, if any man did speak to me in that manner, I should certainly give him satisfaction one way or other."

"That kind of satisfaction is easily given," said Carlostein; "but your object is to promote your sister's happiness."

"My sole object!" replied Seidlits.

"How would it be promoted should you fall?" said Carlostein.

"Why, that kind of reasoning might be applied with equal justness, if I should demand satisfaction of the man who pulled me by the nose. You might ask what satisfaction I should receive in case I myself should fall. In short," continued Seidlits, "this is not an affair of reasoning, but of feeling; and, by Heavens! this fellow shall not behave improperly to *my* sister."

"Since it is entirely an affair of feeling," replied Carlostein, "some regard should be paid to the feelings of her who is chiefly concerned. Has your sister ever complained of her husband, or given you any hint of his having treated her ill?"

"You know," replied Seidlits, "of what heavenly mildness her disposition is; she will bear much without complaining."

"But as she has never mentioned any thing in the nature of complaint to you," said Carlostein, "it is possible that part of what you suspect is groundless; and if she has reason to complain of some things, it is probable that she considers them of far less moment than what she would suffer by your quarrelling with her husband. On the whole, it is clear that you ought to have a little patience, till it is more evident that your suspicions are well founded, and then I shall be happy to concur with you in taking the most likely measures for your sister's relief."

Although Seidlits remained convinced that his sister had cause to complain of her husband's conduct, yet Carlostein at length obtained his promise that he would not speak on the subject to Zeluco, without first acquainting his friend.

When Carlostein gave an account of this conversation to Laura, notwithstanding his softening some parts of it, she continued exceedingly apprehensive of some fatal scene between her husband and brother. She again mentioned her apprehensions to Carlostein in the presence of Signora Sporza, and knowing that it was part of their plan to visit Sicily before their return to Germany, she expressed her wishes that Carlostein would prevail on her brother to set out with him immediately.

As at this time Laura's spirits were much dejected, and as she found in the company of her brother and Carlostein the only cordial which could raise or support them, nothing but the affection which she had for her brother, and the dread of his being involved in a quarrel with her husband, could have enabled her to resist the arguments which the Baron could not help urging against their leaving Naples till she should recover from her lying-in, and in this he was assisted by Signora Sporza.

Laura's own inclinations were on the same side with the eloquence of Carlostein, yet she had the firmness to persevere in her request that they would depart; she even used the circumstance of her being soon to be confined as a fresh argument: "For since during my confinement I cannot see my friends at any rate," said she, "it is best that you seize that interval for your tour; and by the time you return, I shall be sufficiently well to enjoy your company."

Carlostein therefore gave up the point, and prevailed on Seidlits to adopt the measure which his sister had proposed: "For you must recollect," said he to Captain Seidlits, "the present state of your sister's health; whatever you may *ultimately* resolve on therefore, every altercation between you and Zeluco must be avoided at present, as you would avoid her destruction."

Their journey was agreed on; Mr. N——, who had talked of accompanying them, was prevented; but he supped in company with them and Signora Sporza at Madame de Seidlits's the night preceding their departure. Laura endeavoured to be cheerful, partly to hide her concern for the absence of Carlostein, and partly to convince her brother that she was not so unhappy as he imagined. The effort was superior to her strength of mind; for although she bid adieu to her brother with composure, she trembled and turned pale when Carlostein took leave of her. This was observed by Mr. N——, who stood near him; and it was not the first time that he had remarked Laura's partiality for the Baron—which had no other effect on the generous mind of this gentleman, than increasing the regard he had for Carlostein. His own attachment to Laura had never exceeded the limits of friendship and high esteem; he had from their first acquaintance endeavoured to guard against a passion for a woman of a different country and religion from his own. Had Laura betrayed any symptoms of affection for him, it is more than probable his precautions would have been vain; for, when a man approves greatly of a woman's character and person, nothing is so likely to kindle approbation into love, as his imagining that love already exists within her breast towards him. But Mr. N—— was too free from vanity, and had too much discernment, not to perceive that Laura's regard for him was unmixed with passion; and the same discernment enabled him to perceive that her attachment to Carlostein was pure love.

CHAPTER LXXXII.

> Her tongue bewitch'd as oddly as her eyes,
> Less wit than mimic, more a wit than wise.
>
> POPE.[1]

THE morning on which he left Naples, Captain Seidlits called once more on his sister. She had passed an unquiet night, dejection and sorrow were strongly marked on her countenance. Seidlits was affected in a manner unusual to him; while he embraced her, on taking leave, tears were in the eyes of both. Zeluco unexpectedly entered the room at that instant; Seidlits was fretted, and confused at this intrusion; he was abashed at being seen in tears, which he considered as a weakness unbecoming of a soldier. He saluted Zeluco in an embarrassed and abrupt manner, and hurried to Carlostein, with whom he immediately embarked for Sicily.

Laura continued weeping for a considerable time after her brother left the room, which prevented her remarking that Zeluco was displeased at the scene of which he had been an unexpected witness. His ill humour was indeed so habitual, that it might have made little impression on her although she had.

Carlostein and Seidlits being gone, and Laura far advanced in pregnancy, she never went abroad but for a short airing, or to pass a few hours with her mother, or at Signora Sporza's, where she sometimes met with Mr. N——, for whom she always felt and avowed great esteem.

Zeluco's time was almost entirely dedicated to Nerina, whose caprices increased in proportion to her influence over him, which, although they were generally directed to some interested point, were never carried farther than his temper, the variations of which she attentively watched, could bear.

All her whims and caprices indeed were so completely under her command, and managed with such address, that what has disgusted many lovers with their mistresses, were by her made to operate as stimulants to the passion of Zeluco when it seemed to languish.

She possessed the power of amusing in an extraordinary degree; this she exercised sometimes in a manner that would have shocked a mind more delicate than that of Zeluco, but was admirably adapted to his; he accordingly had frequent recourse to it against the dæmons of *ennui* and remorse, who haunted him alternately.

Nerina never mentioned Laura without the intention of turning her into ridicule, or insinuating something to her disadvantage, with frequent allusions to her altered shape, and the complaints incident to women in her situation.

Madame de Seidlits and Signora Sporza were also the frequent butts of her sarcasms; the first she represented as an antiquated coquet, who, calling every auxiliary of the toilette in support of her faded charms, still attempted fresh conquests. "I am told," said Nerina, "that the ridiculous old Lady stuns the ears of her yawning guests with the enumeration of her German admirers, Landgraves, Margraves, and Barons without number. But, my dear Sir, you ought really to give a hint to the imprudent old gentlewoman not to indulge her vanity at the expence of her teeth; for you may depend upon it, the pronunciation of those horrid names is one cause of their being so very loose."

Signora Sporza she represented as a woman of intrigue, who, finding that two of her poor relations hung a little heavy on her hands, had fobb'd off one of them upon him as a wife, and thus had secured a comfortable maintenance for both.

Her caricaturas were given with such exquisite pantomime and mimickry as might entertain those who were not acquainted with the characters of the persons she intended to ridicule, but must have shocked every person of candour who was.

In establishing the influence which Nerina wished to retain over Zeluco, the force of habit was now joined to the power of amusing. Having accustomed himself to go to her at certain hours, he knew not how to fill up those hours without her, and the desire of visiting her returned periodically. In the midst of apparent levity, and seeming want of design, she observed a predetermined plan in most parts of her conduct to him; and often when he imagined her entirely vacant, or occupied in some very frivolous amusement, she was endeavouring to penetrate into his sentiments respecting certain subjects which she thought he might naturally wish to conceal from her. In consequence of this, it struck her, that notwithstanding Zeluco's passion for Laura was greatly cooled, and in spite of the pains she had taken to make her ridiculous in his eyes, yet he still retained a high esteem for her character. Indications of this, to the infinite mortification of Nerina, broke from him unintentionally sometimes, at the very instant when she was labouring to give him a very different impression. As Nerina was doubtful whether she herself had any hold of Zeluco by this sentiment of esteem, she was determined not to leave it in the possession of the woman whom she considered as her enemy. She secretly informed herself, therefore, of Laura's conduct and manner of passing her time, with a view to discover some ground upon which a fabric of falsehood injurious to the character of Laura might be raised; and after having for some time pursued these researches, by the means of her spies and other agents, without success, she at last formed one of the most horrid projects that ever entered into the head of a profligate woman. This shocking idea suggested itself to her, in consequence of her having observed, that, of late, Zeluco displayed a particular dislike to Captain Seidlits, and of his mentioning to her something of his wife's grief at parting with her brother, and endeavouring to ridicule the pathetic manner in which they had taken leave of each other.

CHAPTER LXXXIII.

Obliqua invidia stimulisque agitabat amaris.

VIRG.[1]

IN due time, however, Laura was safely delivered of a son; and as her husband seldom went near her, even to ask how she did, she had a very quick and complete recovery; in little more than a month after her delivery, she was at church, where Nerina had the mortification of seeing her with undiminished beauty, and in all the grace of elegant simplicity. She could not but observe that Laura attracted the regard and commanded the admiration of all the spectators, while she herself, although ostentatiously dressed, was passed over without attention by the eyes of those who did not know her, and with looks of disdain by those who did. Had Nerina been aware of Laura's coming, she would have avoided such an occasion of comparison, well knowing that the sentiments of the spectators would be against her. This incident, however, redoubled her malice against Laura, particularly as it happened at a time when she was already fretted at Laura's having a son; and the apprehension that he might be the means of turning the heart of Zeluco from herself to his wife.

In prosecution of her plan, Nerina sometimes introduced the mention of Captain Seidlits, remarking with a careless and undesigning air, That he was considered by many people as the handsomest man in Naples.

Zeluco laughed at this, saying, That they were no great judges of male beauty who harboured such an opinion.

"Yet in the opinion of most people," said Nerina, "they are the *best* judges; for you may think what you please, but this is a very general notion among the ladies."

"I did not know before," said Zeluco, "that the proportions of a porter, and the strut of a Prussian serjeant, had been so much to their taste."

"The blunt frankness of his manner is certainly better adapted to a camp than a drawing-room," rejoined Nerina; "yet he undoubtedly is a very great favourite with the Neapolitan ladies; many of whom are thought to have cultivated the acquaintance of your wife, and sung her praises wherever there was a likelihood of their being repeated, for no other reason, than that they might be on a good footing with him; for his great affection for his sister, and her influence with him, are pretty generally known."

These hints, however, had no other immediate effect, than drawing from Zeluco some sarcasms against the person or address of Captain Seidlits.

In the mean time, the infant increased in strength and beauty, and began to distinguish objects; and one day in particular, being dandled by the nurse, he smiled in the face of Zeluco. Hard of heart and unfeeling as he was, the smiles of his child melted him into tenderness.—He caught the infant in his arms, and, yielding to the power of nature, he indulged the affection of a father.

The pleasure of those sensations made so strong an impression, that he could not refrain from praising the beauty of the child in the presence of Nerina.

These praises from him were gall and wormwood to her; they made her for a moment forget her usual caution, and risk discovering her aim by precipitation.

"The child must of course be strong and handsome," said she, "for I hear he is the express image of Captain Seidlits."—"Captain Seidlits!" repeated Zeluco.

"Yes," rejoined she, with a careless air, "nothing can be more natural; the Captain being *half*-brother to the child's mother."

"I never remarked any such resemblance," said Zeluco, after a considerable pause.

"No!" said Nerina; "then perhaps there is nothing in it; and all those who have been struck with the likeness, must be mistaken."

Perceiving that her insinuation had taken effect, with an air of careless levity she turned the discourse to other subjects; Zeluco did not attempt to bring it back to this, but was at intervals thoughtful and musing through the rest of the evening; of this Nerina took no notice, but by gay and licentious songs, by mimickry and a thousand playful tricks, seemed intent on nothing but amusing herself and him.

The poison which this artful woman thus administered continued to ferment in the mind of Zeluco, and occupied his thoughts by day and night. A long familiarity with vice, and every species of profligacy, made that appear probable to him, which to a man of integrity would seem next to impossible.

He now called to his remembrance many circumstances in themselves frivolous, and which had made no impression when they occurred, but which now added strength to the horrid insinuations of Nerina. The mutual regard which had always appeared between Laura and her brother—their sequestered walks at the first arrival of Seidlits—his frequent visits to his sister when alone—her eagerness to have him instead of Carlostein in the carriage with her when they returned from Baia—their mutual tenderness when they last parted, the confusion which Seidlits had betrayed, and his abrupt departure on Zeluco's entering the room—and finally, the resemblance which he imagined had struck so many people between Captain Seidlits and the child. He also recollected, that although his marriage took place five weeks before Seidlits arrived at Naples, yet the child was not born till near ten months after that period.

To those circumstances a ridiculous incident gave a degree of support, which, in the disturbed imagination of Zeluco, amounted to full proof.

He entered the nursery one day when he knew that Laura was not there; after talking a little to the nurse about the child, he had the weakness to say, for the insinuations of Nerina deprived him of cool reflection, he had the weakness to say to the nurse, "Which of your Lady's relations do you think this child resembles most?"

"La, Sir," replied the nurse, "why, his own father, sure."

"Idiot, which of my wife's *relations*, I say?" added Zeluco.

Laura's maid, who was present, wishing to correct the nurse's want of accuracy, interposed, saying, "Your excellency, you know, is my Lady's relation by marriage, though not by blood."

"Who desired you to interfere, mistress?" said Zeluco, angrily; then turning to the nurse, he resumed. "Do you not think he is like his uncle Captain Seidlits?"

"Jesu, Maria!" cried the nurse, "What makes your excellency think so?"

"Speak without evasion, woman," exclaimed Zeluco. "Do you not think him like my wife's brother, Captain Seidlits?"

"O Lord, yes, an't please your excellency," cried the nurse, terrified at his manner; "very like Captain Seidlits."

"You have heard many people remark it," continued he, "have you not?"

"A great many indeed," cried the nurse, who began now to think that as Seidlits was a stately man, Zeluco was flattered by his child being thought like him; besides, she was so flurried by his passionate manner of questioning, that she would have echoed back whatever question he could have asked.

But Laura's maid, who had been silenced at the beginning, could no longer restrain herself; for she had suspected Zeluco of jealousy ever since the adventure of the mirror; and imagined that his present questioning proceeded from the same motive.

"How dare you utter such a horrid falsehood," cried the maid to the nurse, "you base lying hussy, you?"

"It is you who are a lying hussy," retorted the nurse.

"Who did you ever hear say such a thing?" said the maid.

The nurse meant to injure Laura no more than the maid; but was so piqued at the maid's attack, and at her own veracity's being called in question, that she was ready to have supported the lie she had been frightened into, by her solemn oath, rather than have yielded the point to the maid.

"Who did I ever hear say it? I have heard a hundred," said the nurse boldly.

"A hundred! O wretch!" cried the maid, turning up her eyes.

"Ay, a thousand, ten thousand," continued the nurse.

"You never did, you never could," exclaimed the maid, "for the child resembles his own father."

"That does not prevent his being exceedingly like Captain Seidlits," continued the nurse; "and I am convinced, if he lives, that he will be as stately a man to the full."

"Hold your scandalous tongue," vociferated the maid, "you vile, worthless, lying wretch; the child resembles no man but my master."

"He is ten thousand times liker Captain Seidlits," cried the nurse, in a violent rage; "and all the world think so, and say so."

"All the world!" exclaimed the maid, lifting her eyes and arms.

"Yes, all the world," repeated the nurse; "and if you will only call them into the room, they will tell you so to your face."

Zeluco withdrew, frowning and biting his lips. Madame de Seidlits with Laura came into the room soon after, and the altercation ceased.

CHAPTER LXXXIV.

The Danger of vicious Confidences—Indignation of Laura.

In his present state of mind, Zeluco might naturally have questioned his confidential valet on this subject, to know what he had remarked respecting the behaviour of Laura and her brother; but this man was no longer on the same footing with him that he had formerly been.

The valet had long beheld with indignation the influence which Nerina gained with his master, and endeavoured to counteract it by every means in his power; but in besieging the heart and retaining the favour of a person of Zeluco's character, Nerina was a more skilful engineer than the valet; besides, she made use of more powerful artillery than he was possessed of. Nerina therefore, having completely gained the ascendancy, did not chuse that Zeluco should have an old confidential servant about him, who was not devoted to her interest. She took every opportunity of disgusting the master with this man, while by many under hand means she endeavoured to render the man equally tired of the master; pretending all the while that she was the valet's friend.

The fellow was not so easily duped as she imagined; convinced of her enmity, despairing of regaining the favour of Zeluco, and prompted by hatred to both, he waited secretly on Signora Sporza, gave her a circumstantial account of the pretended robbers who had attacked Laura and her on their return from Mount Vesuvius; and assured her that he himself had charged the pistols with powder only, but when it appeared from Zeluco's wound, that one of them had been loaded with ball, he said, he recollected that in a small box in his master's writing-desk, he had seen four pistol bullets the day immediately preceding the expedition; and that on examining the same box at his return, he found only two, from which he concluded that Zeluco had secretly put the other brace into the pistol delivered to the servant, with an intention no doubt of murdering Signora Sporza, for he had given the servant particular directions to fire it in her face. That the wounding of Zeluco, therefore, was entirely accidental, owing to the hurry of the servant, and the balls having missed her.

The valet finished his narrative, by declaring, that his motive for giving her this information, was good-will to Signora Sporza, against whom Zeluco still retained his ancient malice; and a regard for Laura's safety, whose life, he said, was also in danger from a husband so very wicked, and who was entirely under the dominion of a woman, more wicked, if possible, than himself.

After rewarding the man for his intelligence, Signora Sporza enjoined him to mention it to no other person, but to continue to behave to his master as usual, that there might be no suspicion of an understanding between the valet and her; and to remain quite inactive till she had time to consult with her friends what measures should be adopted, of which the valet should receive timely notice; and he might rely on being still more liberally rewarded.

Signora Sporza communicated the whole of this man's narrative to Laura, whom it surprised and shocked exceedingly; for bad as her opinion was of her husband's disposition, she never had thought him capable of this degree of wickedness. She was filled likewise with indignation at the history of the sham attack by which her mother, and she herself had been in some measure imposed upon, while she felt the greatest contempt for the man who was obliged to have recourse to such a pitiful trick, to throw a false lustre on his character.

Signora Sporza gave it as her opinion, that Laura should write to her brother, press his immediate return, throw herself into his protection, and separate for ever from her horrid husband; adding, that his attachment to Nerina, and fear of Captain Seidlits, would induce him to agree to the separation upon proper terms.[1] But Laura, who laid little stress on what Signora Sporza meant by *terms*, felt herself under great difficulty in determining how to proceed; for she thought her brother a very improper negociator with Zeluco: and then, although she had no doubt of her husband's willingness to separate from her, she was afraid he might object to her having the child, from whom she could not without pain be absent, and whom she could not without horror abandon to the immediate care and future example of such a father.

After much reflexion she wrote to her brother, expressing a desire of his speedy return, but not in the most urgent terms; nor did she assign any particular reason, but requested that he would inclose his answer under cover to Signora Sporza. When Laura had finished her letter, she told her friend, that at her brother's return she would explain her views to him in the most cautious manner, and in the presence of his friend the Baron Carlostein.

She determined at the same time, that in case her husband consented to leave the child even for a few years under her care after the separation took place, that she would insist on Carlostein's leaving Naples; and if he refused, she resolved never after to admit his visits, even in the company of her mother or brother. She wished, however, that Carlostein should remain till every thing regarding the separation was settled, because he would be a check to the impetuosity of her brother; and also because she hoped that, through his influence with her husband, he would prevail on him to agree to the article nearest her heart, of leaving the child to her own care and management.

Self-sufficiency was no part of this amiable woman's character, however virtuous her inclinations were; she was conscious of a partiality for Carlostein, which convinced her that her safest course was to forego the pleasure of his company entirely.

In the mean while the heart of Zeluco glowed with rage against Laura and Seidlits, and he revolved in his mind various plans of revenge; but as his wrath was deadly, he wished to adopt such an one as would at once satiate his vengeance and secure his safety.

The last he thought inconsistent with his making Nerina a confidant of his measures; for in spite of his partiality for her, and his believing that she had a great deal for him, he knew that this might not always be the case, and therefore he meditated some plan of revenge which required not her assistance, and which he meant to postpone till the return of Seidlits, being determined to involve both the brother and sister in the same ruin.

As he imagined, however, that he should need an accomplice for some part at least of the scheme, he began to soothe his valet, and behave in a more confidential manner to him, with a view to conciliate matters; but this fellow having been seduced into vice and not originally a villain, was not sufficiently a hypocrite to deceive his master. Zeluco perceived through his affected obsequiousness, that the man was disobliged, and not to be trusted; although he had never been the confident of his master in any thing of so much importance as that which now occupied his thoughts, yet Zeluco was conscious that this man was acquainted with certain parts of his conduct which he would not like to have revealed to the world. On observing therefore the mutinous state of his valet's mind, which he had overlooked before, he determined to keep him in as good humour as he could till Seidlits returned, and then send him on some pretext to Sicily, where he knew how to have him disposed of in a manner more agreeable to his own safety.

CHAPTER LXXXV.

He retir'd unseen,
To brood in secret on his gather'd spleen,
And methodize revenge. DRYDEN.[1]

THE mind of Zeluco being ingrossed with these desperate purposes, he passed much of his time in solitude and meditation.

As he walked early one morning towards the hill of Pausilippo,[2] he observed two men coming out of the grotto: they seemed conversing together when Zeluco first saw them; but as he approached, one fell behind the other, and a little to one side. As he who was most advanced drew near, Zeluco recognised him for an old acquaintance; his name was Bertram, the son of a clergyman of Geneva, who, from a spirit of adventure to which the natives of that city are much addicted, had travelled into Spain, to visit a relation who was secretary to an Ambassador at the court of Madrid, through whose interest this young man got a commission in the Spanish service. Zeluco had been several times in company with him at Madrid and particularly once a short time before Zeluco himself left that city, he had met Bertram at a gaming house, and stript him of all his money: this circumstance served to make each recollect the other. After the usual compliments, "You were very unfortunate the last night we were in company together," said Zeluco.

"It was thought so," answered Bertram.

"I am much afraid that what I won put you to much inconveniency," rejoined Zeluco.

"Such inconveniencies must sometimes be expected by those who play," said Bertram.

"You have quitted the Spanish service, I presume," resumed Zeluco.

"I have," said the other.

"You do not think of leaving Naples soon?"

"It is not in my power to leave it immediately," said Bertram.

"How so?"

"Why," continued Bertram, with a smile; "You find me in the condition in which you left me—without money;—in short, I have overshot my credit, and I now wait for a small remittance to enable me to leave this place."

Zeluco then told him he should be happy to accommodate him in whatever sum he needed; "I am engaged this morning," added he, "but if you will walk a little after it is dusk in the square before the palace, I will soon join you, and conduct you to a place where we may have a cheerful glass together; I am impatient to hear your adventures since we parted."

Bertram promised to meet him at the time and place appointed. They then parted, and each continued his walk; but Zeluco immediately turning, said to Bertram, "You had best not mention my name, nor hint to any person that we are acquainted; the reason of this caution you will know hereafter; but in the mean time, I can only tell you, it will not be in my power to serve you, as I intend, if you do."

Bertram assured him he would not, and they again took leave of each other.

Zeluco remembered, that this Bertram was considered at the time he knew him, as a young fellow of desperate fortune and devoted to gaming, but respected on account of the presence of mind and intrepidity with which he had extricated himself from a very hazardous adventure, in which he was involved before Zeluco arrived at Madrid, and which was much talked of at the time. Zeluco had heard no more of him after he himself left Spain, but imagined he was ruined by play, and had now become an adventurer living by his wits, and ready for any desperate enterprise in which there was a likelihood of bettering his fortune. What added strength to his conjectures was, his having remarked the man who was in conversation with Bertram before Zeluco joined him: this man Zeluco was persuaded he had seen with a chain around his leg, working among the malefactors at Casserta; which very suspicious circumstance, and the fellow's retiring and standing aloof, while Bertram and he conversed, convinced Zeluco that his old acquaintance was just such a person as he was in want of. He had not fully determined in what manner he should employ him, but a variety of disjointed ideas of vengeful import floated in his imagination; and he much wished to attach to his views a man such as he took Bertram to be, needy, daring, and profligate; but he knew that the aid he expected from him was of a nature which made it highly expedient both for his own safety and that of his auxiliary, that their acquaintance with each other should not be known, for which reason he was impatient till they separated, lest they should be observed conversing.

CHAPTER LXXXVI.

———Thou hast been
As one, in suffering all, that suffers nothing;
A man, that fortune's buffets and rewards
Hast ta'en with equal thanks; and blest are those,
Whose wit and judgment are so well commingled
That they are not a pipe for fortune's finger
To sound what stop she please.

SHAKESPEARE.[1]

AT the time appointed, Bertram walked before the palace gate, and was soon joined by Zeluco, wrapped in a Portuguese cloak, who desiring him to follow, conducted him through various winding alleys, to the door of a detached house, which, on ringing a bell, seemed to open of itself, for nobody appeared; but Zeluco, after carefully shutting the door, led Bertram into a room commodiously fitted up, with a cold collation and various kinds of wine on the table.

This apartment Zeluco kept for the purpose of entertaining such friends as it was inexpedient to invite to his own house. Nerina, and others, had frequently met him here:—the servants were previously instructed what they should provide; and the guests were served with whatever they needed, by the means of a turning cupboard, such as is used in convents.

"I hate being incommoded with servants," said Zeluco, "particularly on an occasion of this kind, when I am to enjoy a confidential conversation with an old friend. I have therefore taken care that no domestic shall interrupt us.—Pray help yourself to what you like."

After they had supped and drank a few glasses of wine—"I am much afraid," said Zeluco, "that the four hundred dollars I won from you at Madrid put you to great inconveniency, for I remember I was afterwards informed you were in debt at that time."

"I was indeed," said Bertram.

"Well then, I hope you soon after won double the sum," said Zeluco.

"I have never played since," answered Bertram.

"Never!" cried Zeluco.

"Never;" replied Bertram.

"How did you contrive to pay your debts then?" said Zeluco.

"A brother officer, hearing of my ill luck, paid me an old debt which I had despaired of;—this helped me greatly;—living on half my pay for several months did the rest; at last I had the pleasure of paying all my debts to the last farthing."

"It is next to impossible," said Zeluco, "for an officer in the Spanish service, of the rank you then were, to live on his full pay; I cannot conceive how you contrived to exist on the half."

"More difficult things may be performed by those who are resolved to be just," replied Bertram; "I was under the necessity of living very poorly to be sure; but if I had not, some of my creditors, who were poor trades people, must have starved."

And what if they had, thought Zeluco, and then saying aloud; "So to prevent their starving you half starved yourself?"

"Not quite so, Signor," replied Bertram; "though to be sure my table was not sumptuous."

"This must have been a very cruel course of equity however," said Zeluco.

"I have been repaid by the satisfaction it has afforded me since," replied Bertram.

"I dare swear you often cursed me in your heart," said Zeluco.

"A curse has sometimes escaped my lips," said Bertram; "but I do not remember my having ever cursed any body in my heart."

"I should forgive you if you had.—The loss of four hundred dollars to one in your circumstances was a dreadful misfortune," added Zeluco.

"I hope they were of service to you," said Bertram; "for their loss was one of the luckiest things that ever happened to me. I was obliged to pinch so hard to make it up, that I have thought myself in affluence ever since."

"You are a philosopher," said Zeluco, "and bear misfortunes with great fortitude."

"I have hardly ever had any to bear," said Bertram.

"I am surprised to hear you say so," rejoined Zeluco; "because I was told that the four hundred dollars which I won, was but the conclusion of a very persevering run of ill fortune.—I heard you lost near seven thousand dollars in the space of a month."

"Thereabout," said Bertram.

"And what in the devil's name do you call that?" said Zeluco.—"Surely a man in the situation you then were, who loses such a sum in the course of a month's play, must think himself very unfortunate."

"Not if he previously win it all in the course of a week's play," replied Bertram, "which was precisely my case.—I could never have had the misfortune to lose seven thousand dollars, if I had not first had the good fortune to win them."

"That is not the usual way in which men calculate their own misfortunes," said Zeluco.

"It is the fair way, however," rejoined Bertram; "for the most fortunate man that ever existed will be proved to be unfortunate, if you pick out all the lucky incidents of his life, and leave the unlucky behind; but I had one piece of good fortune which I have not mentioned."

"What was that?" said Zeluco.

"Out of the first thousand dollars, I remitted seven hundred to my father."

"The devil you did," cried Zeluco.

"Yes," said Bertram, "I thank Heaven, I put that out of the power of chance."

"The old boy I hope repaid you three-fold?" said Zeluco.

"Ay, ten-fold," replied Bertram; "for he informed me by the next post, that it had enabled him to clear off some debts that distressed him exceedingly."

"But after your loss with me," said Zeluco, "I am surprised you never again tried your fortune at play."

"It required all my fortitude to abstain from it," said Bertram; "for although deep play is little known among the citizens of Geneva, I was early led into it by a young Englishman with whom I was intimate before I left that city. I continued to play with uncommon success after I went to Madrid. This propensity grew into a passion, and I was thoughtless and unjust enough to risk in play with you the money which I had appropriated for the discharge of what I owed to trades-people and others, for which as I felt a degree of remorse which I never before experienced, I determined to effect the discharge of my debts by the most rigid œconomy; yet I must own I was often strongly tempted to try my fortune once more at play; for it occurred to me that by a few successful throws of the dice I might abridge many lingering months of œconomy; but I reflected on the other hand, that in case I should lose, it would be at the expence of those poor creditors whom, by a strict adherence to my plan of œconomy, it was in my power to pay.—While I was balancing this matter in my mind, I received a letter from my father, which decided the point. I paid the money I had in my hands equally among my creditors, and directly after began my course of œconomy, in which I persevered till I was entirely free from debt; and I have never played, nor been in debt since."

"Your father's letter must have contained very forcible reasoning," said Zeluco, "to produce such an effect."

"It contained a recapitulation of those principles which he had instilled into my mind in my childhood; an adherence to which has been the source of all the comfort I have had in life, and from which I never deviated, in the smallest degree, without remorse."

"I should be glad to see this powerful epistle, or hear what you can recollect of it," said Zeluco.

"I am sorry I have it not about me," said Bertram; "for there is a peculiar energy in my father's style to which my memory cannot do justice. The letter in question was written in consequence of his having heard that I was patronised by a certain man in power, from whom I had reason to expect promotion; from this he took occasion to remind me, that the favour of men was precarious, and often guided by caprice; that they might smile upon me to-day, and neglect me to-morrow, however uniformly zealous I might be to retain their good-will; but he earnestly intreated me to make it my chief study to find favour in the eyes of my Creator, in whom there is no variableness, nor shadow of turning."

"Your father was a clergyman no doubt," said Zeluco, stifling a laugh.

"He was," replied Bertram, "and there never was a worthier."

"But did he give you any hint how you were to become a favourite? I mean," continued Zeluco, "besides the old way by devotion and religious ceremonies."

"My father's devotion lay in his heart," said Bertram, "and was little embarrassed with ceremonies."

"Well then," continued Zeluco, "how were you to carry your point?"

"By the duties of humanity and benevolence to my fellow-creatures, and by the most strict integrity; he recommended particularly that I should listen to the dictates of conscience, which he called the voice of God, and which, even in this life, punishes and rewards in a certain degree, according to our conduct. If ever,"—continued Bertram, giving the words of his father's letter;—"If ever, my son, you should feel a propensity to do an unfair thing, overcome it immediately, for no earthly consideration can make it your interest.—Heaven and earth shall pass away, but this truth shall remain, *Whatsoever a man soweth that he shall reap.*[2] Therefore, my dear Bertram, never, O never, be such a fool as to be a knave."

Bertram repeated this part of the letter with unusual fervour, and Zeluco, who was disposed to turn the whole into ridicule, had certain sensations which spoilt his inclination to mirth. He remained for some time in a kind of reverie; then rousing himself, he looked at Bertram, saying, "Well, Sir, what happened next?"

"I told you," resumed Bertram, "that before I read this admonition, my conscience had been whispering that it was not quite fair in me to risk the money which the poor trades-people stood so much in need of; yet my avarice, or love of play, whichever you please, was endeavouring to silence these whispers with all the sophistry they could muster. But I thank God, my father's letter coming to the aid of conscience, I had the strength to act as I did."

By this time Zeluco plainly perceived that his old acquaintance was a very different kind of man from what he had expected, and would by no means suit his purpose; yet he felt a strong curiosity to know the whole of his history. Zeluco therefore pursuing his inquiries; "Upon the whole, however," resumed he, "you must have passed your time but uncomfortably in the Spanish service?"

"Forgive me," replied Bertram, "after I had paid my debts, my time was spent very cheerfully: my mind was free from self-reproach;

I possessed the friendship of some officers of sense and honour; I enjoyed good health and good spirits, for I so contrived matters that my hours never hung on my hands, but were rather too short for my employments; at night I fell asleep, satisfied with the manner I had passed the day, and rose every morning in spirits to perform my duty, and eager to improve my mind."

In the course of Zeluco's inquiries, Bertram informed him, that after remaining some years in the Spanish service, a brother of his mother's had made him an advantageous proposal, which would have enabled him to live comfortably in his own country, to which he had for some time felt a strong desire of returning; his father, and other relations, having written very pressing letters to that purpose.

"You disposed of your commission, and returned accordingly?" said Zeluco.

"I could not immediately indulge my own desire, nor yield to the intreaties of my friends," replied Bertram; "because there was a rumour of war, which sometime after was verified, so I thought myself bound in honour to remain with the regiment which soon was sent on active service."

"The extraordinary expence to which officers are put during war, would bear hard on you, who had no resource but your pay," said Zeluco.

"Very fortunately I had studied mathematics and fortification at Geneva, and was frequently employed as an engineer, for which I received additional pay; this enabled me," replied Bertram, "to live as well as other officers of my rank, and to remit a small sum of money to a female cousin of mine at Geneva, who had fallen under the displeasure of her other relations."

"This *cousin* was young and handsome, no doubt," said Zeluco.

"On the contrary," said Bertram, "she was an elderly woman, who never had been handsome, but had made a rash marriage, disapproved of by all her relations."

"What then interested you so much in her?" said Zeluco; "her mental accomplishments and virtue no doubt."

"Her accomplishments, poor woman," replied Bertram, "never were conspicuous, and rumour was by no means favourable to her reputation in the other particular: in short, her conduct afforded such just grounds to her nearest relations to abandon her, that I thought myself bound to befriend her, because her other friends were either too angry or too much ashamed of her to afford her any assistance."

"But pray," said Zeluco, "when did you quit the Spanish service?"

"At the peace," replied the other, "when our regiment was ordered home."

"I remember to have heard that one of the captains of your regiment died on the passage; I suppose you were promoted to the company?"

"As I was the oldest lieutenant in the regiment, and had received two wounds in the service, my friends flattered me I should; but it was given to a young officer, nephew to a grandee of Spain."

"That was hard," said Zeluco.

"Not particularly so," said Bertram; "men of family have been allowed advantages in all services; it can hardly be expected that they will serve otherwise; and if this young gentleman had been promoted to a company in any other regiment, it would have been equally hard on the oldest subaltern of that regiment."

"But probably this was a person of little or no merit," said Zeluco.

"Forgive me," replied Bertram; "he is a very spirited young man, and I am convinced from what I know of him, will prove an excellent officer."

"I should have thought it damned hard, however, had I been in your place, that another should carry away the whole reward due to me."

"He did not carry away the whole," said Bertram; "for my behaviour on several occasions was publicly approved of by the general, and praised by the whole army; my worthy father, and all my friends at Geneva, were informed of it, and rejoiced at the intelligence; besides, I have the approbation of my own mind, I am conscious of having been ever faithful to my trust, and of having done my duty as a soldier. I had the happiness of being loved by the soldiers as well as the officers of the regiment; many of the poor fellows were in tears when I left them. You must be sensible that this is a very pleasing reward, and occasions delightful sensations."

CHAPTER LXXXVII.

A sight of horror to the cruel wretch,
Who all day long in sordid pleasure roll'd,
Himself an useless load, has squander'd vile,
Upon his scoundrel train, what might have cheer'd
A drooping family of modest worth.
But to the generous still improving mind,
That gives the hopeless heart to sing for joy,
Diffusing kind beneficence around;
To him the long review of order'd life
Is inward rapture.[1] THOMSON.[1]

As Zeluco had never felt any of the delightful sensations which Bertram alluded to, he became a little impatient at this observation. "Well, well," said he, "all this is mighty fine, but pray, my good Sir, what man was he whom I saw in conversation with you this morning, a little before I joined you?"

"That man," replied Bertram, smiling, "is just liberated from the gallies; he is my only attendant; if my suite be not numerous, Signor, you must allow that it is select."

"Liberated from the gallies!" cried Zeluco, with affected surprise.

"Yes, he was condemned to the gallies or to hard labour for life; it comes to the same thing; his last employment was at the royal works of Casserta with other slaves, some Christian, some Mahometan."

"But how came *you* connected with him?" said Zeluco.

"You shall hear," replied Bertram. "Having quitted the Spanish service, and returned to my sweet native city of Geneva, I lived in the most agreeable manner; and this poor man, a Savoyard by birth, was my footman; he is a good-natured creature, though not very clever, and I sought no other: in the mean time, a worthless fellow, a Piedmontese, came to Geneva, and filling my servant's head with many fine stories concerning Italy, persuaded him to quit my service, and accompany him to that country, whither this Piedmontese was returning from France. They travelled together to Milan, where failing in their endeavours to get into service, and their money being exhausted, they inlisted in an Austrian regiment, but had not been quite a month in this situation, when the Piedmontese was recognised by two Neapolitans, as a person who had been imprisoned above three years before at Naples, on an accusation of robbery with assassination, but had made his escape from prison. An information to this purpose being formerly made, the Piedmontese was taken into custody, and my poor Antonio, who had accompanied him to Milan, and enlisted at the same time, was seized and committed to prison as his accomplice; for the witnesses declared there had been two men engaged in the robbery, although only one had been apprehended at Naples.

"On a requisition by the Neapolitan resident at Milan, they were both sent to Naples, but the Piedmontese had the dexterity to make his escape on the journey, and Antonio alone was brought prisoner to this city. The presumptions against him were greatly strengthened by the circumstance of a seal having been found in his pocket, which it was proved had belonged to the murdered person.

"It was in vain that the wretched Antonio told the manner he had made acquaintance with the Piedmontese—that he had been in service at Geneva at the time the murder was committed;—that he had bought the seal of his companion who had escaped, with many other particulars, all of them true, but none of them credited by his judges: however, as there was no direct proof of his having perpetrated the crime, he was not convicted capitally, but was condemned to a punishment in most peoples eyes more severe, hard labour for life.

"The person who had been robbed and murdered was a man much esteemed on account of his character and manners; by his untimely death, a respectable family were in danger of being reduced from affluence to poverty: this created a general sympathy. The murder was supposed to have been accompanied with circumstances peculiarly cruel; the last excited as much indignation as the former did compassion.

"The more atrocious a crime is, there certainly is the less probability that the individual who happens to be taken up on suspicion of having perpetrated it, is really guilty; for this plain reason, that a much greater proportion of mankind are capable of committing a little crime than a very great one; but it happens frequently, that the just indignation against the crime is rashly and unjustly applied against whoever is first accused; and the very circumstance of uncommon atrocity which ought to render us difficult in the admission of the charge, is sometimes the cause of a precipitate and unjust condemnation. This seems to have been the case in the instance of poor Antonio.

"He has since told me, that he wrote to me immediately after receiving his hard sentence; but whether from the letter's having been neglected by the person to whom he gave it to be put into the post-office, or from whatever other cause, it never came to my hand; but after he had been several months in this situation, I received a letter which gave me the first intelligence of his misfortune; it was written in all the simplicity of truth: to convey an idea of the horrors of his fate required not the aid of eloquence. 'I am condemned,' said he, 'to slavery for my whole life, on account of a murder committed at Naples when I was in your service at Geneva.'"

"The blockhead deserved to suffer," said Zeluco, "for his folly in leaving your service, where he was happier than he deserved."

"The poor fellow," replied Bertram, "made that very observation in his letter; but surely, Sir, his sufferings were too severe for a piece of levity, or that love of variety so natural to us all. I was so shocked with the idea of an innocent man's being unjustly condemned, that my first impulse was to set out immediately for Naples; but on my mentioning this to some of my friends they assured me, that an attestation of the man's having been in my service at the time of the murder, and for a considerable space before and after, would be sufficient to procure his liberty. This was immediately drawn up in due form, and sent to Naples, inclosed in a letter to an eminent lawyer of that city.

"But Antonio's dismal situation haunted me day and night. I could not walk into the fields without thinking on his being chained to endless labour—nor eat a meal without reflecting on the scanty morsel moistened with tears on which the wretched Antonio fed—nor lie down in my bed without dreaming I beheld the unhappy man stretched on the damp pavement of a dungeon. 'Alas!' cried I, 'is it acting up to the Divine precept, *do as you would be done by*, to trust the liberty and life of an innocent man to a letter, which may have miscarried or prove ineffectual. If I go myself, it will be in my power to identify the man, and by a thousand circumstances make his innocence so evident, that I must infallibly procure his immediate liberty.' These and similar reflexions ingrossed my mind entirely. I was by no means satisfied with my own conduct, and you know, Sir," continued Bertram, "that when a man stands condemned at the bar of his own conscience, it is of small importance to his happiness to be thought innocent by all the rest of the world; for my own part I felt myself so unhappy on this occasion, that in compassion to myself, as well as to Antonio, I set out for this city, before I could receive any answer to my letter.

"Most fortunate it was for Antonio and for me, that I did so. The lawyer to whom my letter was addressed was gone to Messina, and my letter disregarded. I found poor Antonio at hard labour at Casserta, among a number of wretches against whom crimes had been *proved* similar to that of which he was *presumed* guilty.

"To paint the poor fellow's joy and gratitude at sight of me," continued Bertram, "is not in my power; but I did not find it so easy a matter to procure his liberty as I expected: I had more difficulty in prevailing on some to whom I addressed myself, only to hear my story, than I thought I should have had in obtaining the whole of my object; and when they had heard it, they seemed to think it of less importance than I ever before believed one human creature's happiness could possibly be to another.

"None of them expressed any doubt of the man's innocence, yet few would give themselves the least trouble to get him relieved: they shrugged up their shoulders, said it was hard on the man, but no business of theirs. I am convinced, Sir, that it would shock you, were I to describe every circumstance of the savage hardness of heart and selfish indifference which were discovered by some. Well, I wish those gentlemen much good of their insensibility. I dare say it may have saved them some unpleasant moments, which I, and I doubt not you, Sir, have felt! But of this I am convinced, that when I succeeded at length in procuring Antonio's liberty, my satisfaction was little inferior to his; and I have no doubt but it will afford me pleasure to my last hour; and so, Sir, I leave you to judge whether or not I have reason to rejoice in having made this jaunt to Naples."

Zeluco's eyes were fixed on the ground during the latter part of Bertram's narrative; and he continued silent and pensive for some time after it was finished. His reflexions seemed not of a pleasing nature, several sighs escaped from him; if he then threw back a glance on his own past life, he would discover no cheering ray reflected from acts of benevolence to brighten the gloomy retrospect, no cordial drop of self-approbation to comfort his drooping spirits.

"I fear my long story has tired you Sir," said Bertram; "here is to your good health," added he, filling his glass.

"I pledge you with all my heart," said Zeluco, endeavouring to shake off reflexion, in which however he did not succeed, till he had almost entirely drowned thought in repeated bumpers.

In the course of their conversation, Zeluco renewed the offer he had made in the morning, of furnishing Bertram with what money he had occasion for, till the letter of credit which he expected should arrive; but Bertram assured him that he was already accommodated. The fact was, that Buchanan having accidentally heard that a servant had been redeemed from slavery by his master, had gone and conversed with the man himself, from whom he heard all the particulars, of which he was so full, that on returning home he entered into the room where Mr. N—— was alone, saying, "O sir, I have something to tell you, which I am sure will do your heart good to hear!"—He then gave him the whole story as he had received it from the Savoyard, concluding with this reflexion: "I really do imagine, Sir, that there is something in the air of mountainous countries exceedingly favourable to kindness of heart.—I have heard several travellers declare that they had met with more hospitality in a short tour in the Highlands of Scotland, than in their journies over all Flanders and the Low Countries, although the last are as full of populous towns as the former is of mountains."

"This Bertram is a citizen of Geneva, whose territories are not mountainous," said Mr. N——, smiling.

"Your honour will be pleased to remember," replied Buchanan, "that Geneva is situated by a fine lake, just as the village of Buchanan is by Loch Lomond; and there are mountains at no great distance from both."

"I had forgot that," said Mr. N——; "but I am so charmed with the behaviour of this man, that I should like to be acquainted with him, although it could be proved against him that he had been born above a hundred miles from any lake or mountain."

Mr. N—— went the very next morning to call on Bertram, and found him as he returned from his first interview with Zeluco, telling him he had done himself the honour of waiting on him expressly to solicit the acquaintance of a man of so much worth. In the course of their conversation, Mr. N—— discovered that he had been well acquainted with Bertram's father when he himself had been at Geneva, and when Bertram was in the Spanish service. Mr. N—— at the same time told Bertram, that he had received many civilities from his relations, and spoke of his father in such terms of regard as brought the tears into the son's eyes; who although he at first had declined Mr. N——'s offer, now told him he would with pleasure make use of his banker for what money he might need, till his own credit should arrive.

Zeluco seemed disappointed on finding that he was anticipated in fixing an obligation on Bertram. He asked, Whether he had mentioned to Mr. N—— any thing of their present meeting.

"I fancy, Sir," said Bertram, a little gravely, "you have forgot that I promised not to mention my being acquainted with you to any body."

Zeluco begged his excuse, saying, he *had* forgot; adding, that it would be no longer necessary to conceal their acquaintance, and invited him to dine with him the following day.

Bertram expressed no desire of knowing Zeluco's reason for his former wish of concealment, or for the secret manner in which they had met. He perceived that Zeluco began to be affected by the wine, and imputed his loss of memory, and his neglecting to explain this, to that circumstance.

CHAPTER LXXXVIII.

> Lentus in meditando ubi prorupuisset, tristibus dictis atrocia facta conjungebat. TACIT.[1]

THE suspicions which rankled in the breast of Zeluco would perhaps have gradually lost their force, and at length died away, had they not been carefully cherished and kept alive by the watchful malice of Nerina. She adapted and linked together every accidental circumstance in such an artful manner, that, to the disturbed fancy of Zeluco, they formed a chain of irrefragable force; the absurd answers of the nurse to his questions, and the passionate interference of Laura's maid, which of themselves had made a strong impression on his mind, received additional strength from the comments of Nerina.[2]

Laura observed an increasing gloom on the countenance of her husband, and was shocked and terrified at the looks he sometimes threw on his child. She mentioned this to Signora Sporza, who, not having observed it herself, persuaded Laura, that what alarmed her proceeded entirely from her viewing the looks and actions of Zeluco through a medium of additional gloom ever since the information given by the valet.

A packet of letters arrived from Captain Seidlits, in which was one addressed to Mr. N——, one to Signora Sporza, and one to Madame de Seidlits, but none to Laura. This omission was a circumstance of new suspicion in the eyes of Zeluco, who was with Madame de

Seidlits when she opened the cover of the letters. He suspected what was really the case, that there was a letter for Laura inclosed in that for Signora Sporza; and had he been without a witness, it is not impossible but he might have had the meanness to have broken open the letter. Madame Seidlits sent it by her own servant to Signora Sporza, and Zeluco remained on the watch to observe whether Signora Sporza did not send or bring a letter to Laura. She thought proper to bring it herself, and Zeluco met her as she was going to Laura's apartment. He accosted her with assumed cheerfulness, said he was going to drive out for a few miles, and being persuaded she would not accept, he invited her to accompany him in the carriage; which she having declined, he bade her adieu, saying, he would return within a few hours; and immediately went out of the house, but returned through the garden to his own apartment, by a door of which he alone had the key, and from thence passed unobserved into a small room adjoining that in which Laura and Signora Sporza were conversing. His design was to discover whether his suspicions regarding the letter were well founded, and to hear what passed between the two friends, when they thought themselves unobserved, and him at a distance.

Zeluco could not distinctly hear every word that passed; but from what he did hear, he understood that a letter had come from Captain Seidlits to Laura;—that the Captain with his friend Carlostein would arrive very soon;—that Laura earnestly wished to be separated from him as soon as possible, provided she should be permitted to take her child with her;—and at last he heard Laura with a raised voice distinctly pronounce these words: "O my dearest brother, had you arrived a few weeks sooner at Naples, I should never have been united to this mean perfidious man!"

Zeluco was so transported with rage on hearing this, that he mechanically drew his stiletto, and was on the point of bursting into the room, and stabbing his wife, when hearing the voice of Signora Sporza, he was again tempted to listen.

Signora Sporza endeavoured to sooth and quiet the mind of Laura by admonitions to patience and fortitude, representing that she would in a very short time have the pleasure of embracing her brother, who would unquestionably fall on means to free her for ever from her odious tyrant; reminding her at the same time, that it was of the utmost importance to manage the temper of the monster, till such time as he should agree to deliver the child to her care.

She then told Laura, that she was obliged to make a few morning visits, but would see her in the evening; and took her leave.

Zeluco remained for some time boiling with indignation in his listening place, which he left at last, and came round to the room in which Laura was. She had just received her child from the nurse when Zeluco entered.—He made a motion with his hand for the nurse to retire, which she directly did, leaving the child in Laura's arms.

Zeluco walked backward and forward for some time with a morose and gloomy countenance, without speaking or seeming to take notice of either.

As this was nothing unusual, Laura paid no attention to it, nor did she remark the dreadful humour he was in, till turning quick upon her, he said, with a fierce look, "Don't you think that child very like his father, Madam?"

"He is much too young," replied she, "for his features to announce any particular likeness."

"I have been told," said he, "that he already displays a most striking resemblance to your brother."

"I am happy to hear it," said Laura, caressing the child.

"Have you the audacity to say so, Madam, and to my face?" exclaimed Zeluco, furiously.

"What is it that you mean, Sir?" cried Laura, rising from her seat; for the child screamed, being alarmed at Zeluco's loud and threatening voice.

"Peace—incestuous bastard!" exclaimed he, grasping the infant by the throat with frantic violence.

"Ah, monster! you murder your child!" cried Laura, agonized with terror, and endeavouring to remove his distracted hand.

It was removed too late;—the child never breathed more.

The wretched mother sunk again upon her seat; her soul suspended between hope and despair, while her imploring eyes were rivetted on the face of the infant, which lay breathless on her knee.

The women hearing a confused noise, rushed into the room:—every means were used for the recovery of the child;—all were fruitless.

When it became certain that there was no hope, Laura, yielding to despair, clasped the dead infant to her bosom, crying, "O my child! my child! take thy miserable mother with thee to the grave!" and she directly fell senseless on the floor.

The child's body being removed, Laura was carried to her bed in a state of insensibility.

CHAPTER LXXXIX.

Notre repentir n'est pas tant un regret du mal que nous avons fait, qu'une crainte de celui qui nous en peut arriver. ROCHEFOUCAULT.[1]

WHEN it appeared that the child was irrecoverably gone, Zeluco's jealous phrenzy dwindled into personal fear, lest he should be called to account for the murder of the child. To the attendants, therefore, he made a great display of concern for the child's death, and still more for the consequences it might have on the health of his beloved wife. And when Signora Sporza returned, he took care to meet her, and informed her, before the nurse and other domestics, with an air of infinite sorrow, That the dear infant had been seized on a sudden in a most unexpected manner with convulsions while he was in his mother's arms; and that, in spite of all the means which could be used to save his life, the poor child had expired; on which Laura had immediately fainted, and nothing but his concern for her had prevented him from being in the same state; that she still continued very much disturbed, for which reason it was highly proper to keep her quiet and secluded from all company; for the sight of any body, or asking her questions in her present situation, might have very bad consequences.

Signora Sporza did not listen to this representation without shewing symptoms of impatience; and when he finished, she made no answer, but that she must immediately see her friend.

"You cannot think of it at present, my dear Madam," said Zeluco.

"I must see my friend immediately," said she, moving towards the apartment in which Laura was.

"Good Heavens!" cried he, stepping between her and the door, "you would not intrude upon her sorrow at such a moment?"

"She never thought my visits intrusion," replied Signora Sporza; "I must see her, Sir.—Allow me to pass."

Zeluco was apprehensive that Laura would immediately accuse him of the child's death, or allow some expression to fall from her that would unfold the manner of it; he was very desirous therefore that no person should be admitted to her till he himself had tried to persuade her that the infant's death was accidental; or, if he failed in that, he hoped he should, by expressing great grief and contrition for the involuntary movement his hand had made, be able to prevail on Laura to promise never to mention what she had seen. Had he once obtained such a promise, he knew that he should be safe, being well acquainted with her inviolable attachment to her word. He strove therefore by every argument he could devise to prevail on Signora Sporza to postpone her visit; but all his arguments were lost on her. Signora Sporza's impatience to see her friend augmented in proportion to the earnestness he shewed to prevent it; she became louder and more violent in her manner, and Zeluco was obliged to yield the point, informing her at the same time, that he was much afraid that Laura's senses were disturbed by the shock of such an unexpected accident.

Zeluco did not know when he made this assertion that it was true; he even dreaded that it was not; but he threw it out, that less stress might be laid on any expression which, in the agony of grief, might fall from Laura. The disturbance of Laura's senses, which he asserted at random, had in reality taken place.

Sometime after her being carried to bed, as was mentioned, she shewed signs of life, but of no distinct recollection; after remaining a few minutes in this state, she relapsed into a complete stupor, from which, after some interval, she recovered as before, having only a confused impression that something dreadful had happened, but without being able to recover her scattered senses so far as to remember what it was.

When Signora Sporza came to the door of Laura's bed-chamber, she heard her, in a wild and plaintive tone, saying, "Alas! where have I been? What has happened? Can no body tell? Do all your brains turn round, do your hearts fail, like mine?" She then fell back into her former stupor.

While she lay in this state, the attendants informed Signora Sporza, that their mistress repeated nearly the same expressions as often as she recovered from those fits of fainting.

Signora Sporza seated herself at Laura's bed-side, with her eyes fixed on her face, and watching all her movements. As soon as she perceived her recovering, she took hold of her hand, and addressing her in the most soothing and affectionate tone of voice, "How do you do, my lovely friend?" said she.

Laura stared her wildly in the face for some time without speaking, and then cried, "O! is it you? Are you come at last?"—"Yes, my dear, I am come," replied Signora Sporza.—"But do you know," said Laura, "what has happened?"—"I am very sorry," replied Signora Sporza, "for what has happened."—"Pray, tell me," cried Laura, "what it is? None of them will tell me; but I am sure it is something very sad; for see, they all look sad and mournful, and you are sorrowful too, and my poor heart is sad, although I know not wherefore—but my head turns so!——"

Madame de Seidlits, by the indiscretion of a servant, had been told of the infant's death, with the additional circumstance that Laura herself was dying.

Half frantic at the intelligence, she hurried from her own house to that of Zeluco, and without listening to the accounts he endeavoured to give her, or regarding the opposition that was made to her appearance suddenly before her daughter, she rushed into her bedchamber, exclaiming, "My child! my child! where is my child?"

At this expression Laura started, sat up in the bed, and seemed in some degree to recover her recollection; with one hand opposing her mother's embrace, while with a solemn tone of voice and sternness of regard, most unlike her natural sweetness, she pronounced, "*My* child is gone for ever!—the fiend grasped him;" after which she screamed and fell back again insensible on the pillow. When she recovered, she uttered many expressions seemingly incoherent, but which bore some relation to the act which had produced her disorder. Had any person been witness to the child's murder, he would easily have perceived that Laura's most incoherent expression glanced at that deed; but as nobody had, all imagined they were quite unmeaning, and proceeding from the disorder which the child's unexpected death had produced.

Madame de Seidlits having recovered in some degree the first shock she felt on perceiving the melancholy state in which her daughter was, summoned all her fortitude, that she might be enabled to assist Signora Sporza in soothing, supporting, and comforting Laura.

A Physician having arrived, was, according to the orders given by Zeluco, introduced to his apartment before he was permitted to see Laura. Zeluco, with ostentatious sorrow, told him of the child's being suddenly carried off by a convulsion fit; that there was reason to apprehend this sad event had disturbed the senses of his wife, as she had been talking extravagantly ever since, did not know her intimate acquaintance, and was terrified at the sight of her best friends. Having thus prepared the Physician, he allowed him to visit Laura.

She was just recovered from a fit of stupor when he was introduced. On his addressing her, she raised her head from the pillow, and looked very earnestly at him, but made no answer to his questions; on his proposing to retire, she said with a timid voice, "I beg, my good Sir, that you will not permit the wicked fiend to come near me."

The Physician being now confirmed in the belief of what Zeluco had told him, ordered her to be blooded, to be kept very quiet, and not to be disturbed with questions, or in any way encouraged to speak, for it was too evident that her mind was disturbed; at the same time he gave Madame de Seidlits and Signora Sporza great reason to hope, that with care she would be in a short time restored to her perfect health.

Although Zeluco had reason to be pleased with the first part of the Physician's declaration, he was alarmed at the last. While Laura remained in the present state, little stress could be laid on what she said; but should she recover, whatever account she gave, he well knew, would carry complete conviction to the minds of all who knew her. He could not indeed accuse himself of a predetermined intention of murdering the child; but he had great reason for remorse and self-condemnation, when he reflected that the child's death was occasioned by the propensity he betrayed in his infancy, and had indulged ever since, of giving way to every impulse of passion. In this hour of reflexion, among the many stinging recollections which intruded themselves on his memory, he could not exclude the remonstrance of his tutor, when he himself, yet a child, had, in a fit of groundless passion, squeezed his sparrow to death; that remonstrance now appeared to his alarmed conscience in the light of a prophecy: "Had I paid more regard," said he to himself, "to what that worthy man then, and on other occasions, told me, I should not now have reason to dread the consequences of this cursed accident."

Yet, whatever remorse Zeluco felt for various and accumulated instances of wickedness, of which his conscience accused him, what chiefly kept his mind on the rack at present was, a fear that those allusive expressions, which constantly dropt from Laura, might lead to a suspicion of the fact which he wished so much to conceal; for however mysterious or incoherent they might appear to others, they were so clear and connected to him, that he received a fresh alarm as often as any of them were repeated; and whatever he hoped, he was by no means certain, that when Laura recovered, she would not relate the fact as it really happened, and accuse him publicly; for these reasons he fervently wished that she might die of her present illness, or remain distracted.

The continual anxiety he had for his own safety suspended the ripening of a certain plan which before occupied his thoughts for the destruction of Seidlits, who was now daily expected. His whole attention was directed towards Laura; for, although he never ventured to appear in her sight, yet he took care to have every word reported to him that fell from her lips; and he was kept in continual alarm at the import of her expressions.

CHAPTER XC.

Him shall the fury passions tear,
 The vultures of the mind,
Disdainful Anger, pallid Fear,
 And Shame that sculks behind;

* * * *

Or Jealousy, with rankled tooth,
 That inly gnaws the heart;
  And Envy wan, and faded Care,
  Grim-visag'd comfortless Despair,
 And Sorrow's piercing dart.   GRAY.[1]

ABOUT this time Carlostein and Seidlits returned from their excursion; they went directly to the house of Madame de Seidlits, and had the first account of the child's death and Laura's indisposition from her maid; Madame de Seidlits herself being then in bed, indisposed with the watching and fatigue which she had undergone. The two friends were equally shocked at this affecting narrative; they spoke of calling at Signora Sporza's, but were informed that she slept constantly at the house of Zeluco, and was hardly ever a moment from her bed-side. Captain Seidlits then proposed to go directly there, whither Carlostein thought he could not with propriety accompany him; but, overwhelmed with the deepest sorrow, went to his lodging, there to wait for the return of his friend.

Zeluco received Seidlits with all the appearance of affliction. "Alas! my friend," cried he, "we have lost your dear little nephew; he was cut off by convulsions in the arms of his mother. I am told by physicians, that such accidents are not uncommon among infants. I leave you to judge of his poor mother's situation; she has been in a most disordered state of mind ever since; and she seems to be always worse after seeing any of her old acquaintance."

To all this Seidlits made little or no answer; but a woman who had the particular care of Laura coming out of her bed-chamber, and reporting that she was more composed than usual, he desired to be admitted to see her.

"I fear it will increase her uneasiness," said Zeluco.

"I am convinced it will give her pleasure," said Seidlits; "for she had always pleasure in seeing me."

"Really!" said Zeluco, looking fiercely at Seidlits, for a movement of jealousy threw him off his guard.

"I have every reason to think so," resumed Seidlits naturally, and without observing how Zeluco was affected.

"The Doctor must determine," said Laura's nurse, pointing to the Physician who entered the room.

The case being stated to him, "Let her brother's name be mentioned to her," said he, "before he appears, and we will observe how she is affected."

Zeluco did not object to the experiment; he thought something might fall from Laura, on mentioning or seeing Seidlits, which would betray the intimacy that, as he suspected, had been between them.

The Physician conducted Seidlits to Laura's bed-chamber. Zeluco stood at the door, which he kept a-jar for the purpose of listening.

Laura sat up in the bed, propped with pillows; Signora Sporza near her. The Physician whispered to Signora Sporza, that Captain Seidlits was arrived, and in the house; and he then said aloud to her, "Your friend Captain Seidlits is safely arrived at Naples."

"I am most happy to hear it," said she, looking at Laura, who took no notice.

"Did you not hear, my dear," said Signora Sporza, addressing Laura—"Did you not hear what the Doctor said?"

"No;" replied Laura.

"He said your brother Captain Seidlits is returned."

"Yes—" said Laura, without any emotion.

"O merciful Virgin!" cried Signora Sporza, bursting into tears, "her sweet senses are gone;—she knows not what I say."

What Laura heard, it appeared, made much less impression on her mind than what she saw; for she no sooner beheld Signora Sporza in tears, than she took hold of her hand, and with a look and tone of contrition, said, "Woe is me! I fear I have offended you; truly, I meant it not."

"I know you did not, my angel," said Signora Sporza; "but surely you remember Captain Seidlits."

"Seidlits!" said Laura.

"Yes, my sweet friend, your brother," rejoined Signora Sporza.

"My brother!" repeated Laura, with a vacant stare—"Where is my brother?"

"Here is your brother," said Captain Seidlits, who, concealed by a skreen, had with impatience heard the conversation, and being no longer able to restrain his emotion, broke forth in this imprudent manner.

Laura screamed, and hid her face under the bed-cloaths at his sudden appearance; "My beloved Sister," said Seidlits, "do you not know me?" Signora Sporza and the Physician continuing to assure her that it was her brother, she raised her head, and looked with caution and an appearance of terror at Seidlits; she threw her eyes also around the room, as if she suspected that some other person was in it.

"There is nobody present but your friends, my love," said Signora Sporza.

"I was afraid the wicked fiend had returned," said Laura.

"There is no wicked fiend here, my love," said Signora Sporza. "This is your brother; you know him, do you not?"

"Surely you do, my dear," said Seidlits, with a broken voice.

Laura then looked more attentively at him, then throwing her eyes on Signora Sporza, she pointed, with a smile, to Seidlits.

"Yes, my angel," said Signora Sporza, "that is your brother."

Laura made no answer, but continued to look with complacency on Seidlits.

The name of Brother affected her not; but seeing him seemed to give her an agreeable impression, without her being able to recollect his connexion with herself; yet when addressing her in the most affectionate terms he held forth his hand to her, she gave him hers, and displayed not only evident marks of satisfaction while he remained, but also of uneasiness when he proposed to withdraw.[2]

Signora Sporza attended the Captain out of the room, and Zeluco conducted both into an adjoining apartment.

"How strange," said Zeluco, "that she was no way affected when told that you were come?"

Seidlits made no answer, but wiped his eyes.

"Yet she seemed pleased at seeing you," continued Zeluco.

Seidlits was absorbed in thought, and could not speak for some time; he at length said, addressing himself to Signora Sporza, "She seemed in terror at first;—she certainly took me for some other person.—What did she mean by the wicked fiend?"

Zeluco anticipated the answer, saying, "There is no knowing what she means,—her expressions are so extravagant,—she probably has no meaning;—the severe shock she received by the sudden death of the dear child, has entirely deranged her memory and judgment; only conceive a woman of her great sensibility to see her child expire in her arms without any visible cause! for although the Physician declares he has known many instances of infants carried off in the same sudden manner, yet her delicate constitution could not stand it;—but, thank Heaven! she is better than she was; and the Physician still hopes she will recover entirely."

During this recital, Signora Sporza preserved a gloomy silence, but at one time shook her head in a manner which struck terror into the heart of Zeluco, and raised suspicions in the mind of Seidlits.

When he went to his lodgings he found Mr. N—— with Carlostein. It was not without difficulty and many interruptions that he gave them an account of Laura's situation. They were all so much affected that little conversation passed between them, and Seidlits retired without communicating even to Carlostein the doubts which he had on his mind.

When he called next morning to know how his sister was, he found an opportunity of speaking with Signora Sporza by herself. "My dear Madam," said he, "I beg you will let me know your real sentiments of this melancholy affair. I fear you conceal something."

"I know nothing," replied she, "which I will not communicate to you.—I do not know what to think.—I left your sister and the child well; in a few hours I returned, and the child was dead, and your lovely sister thus; I then got the same account which you have heard.—We must take patience.—The Physician is an honest man, and your sister grows a little better. I never quit her;—we must have patience." Zeluco entering the room, prevented any farther conversation.

Laura seemed gradually and uniformly to grow better from the time that Seidlits arrived; but she recovered her bodily strength and looks in a greater proportion than she did her memory and judgment.

Carlostein meanwhile remained in the most agonizing state of suspence; his spirits rose or fell according to the accounts he received of her state of health from the Physician, from Signora Sporza, and from his friend Seidlits, he was continually going from the one to the other; and when they were all engaged at the same time with Laura, he walked in sight of the house watching till one of them came out, that he might receive fresh intelligence on the only subject on which he could think or converse.

CHAPTER XCI.

> O, it is monstrous!
> Methought the billows spoke, and told me of it;
> The winds did sing it to me. SHAKESPEARE.[1]

THE death of the child, the disorder of Laura, with the fears which oppressed the mind of Zeluco, lest the immediate cause of both should be suspected from the mysterious expressions of Laura, had so much engrossed his time, that it was not in his power to bestow much of his company on Nerina; he well knew that all the display of sorrow he made would be considered as mere grimace,[2] and would even strengthen the suspicions which his personal safety rendered it so necessary for him to extinguish, if he were known to visit her at the very time he was affecting so much grief on account of the child's death and his wife's disorder. He therefore visited Nerina very seldom, and with the utmost secrecy.

This conduct, though prudent and expedient in Zeluco's situation, was highly offensive to Nerina, and all the apologies and explanations he was able to make could not persuade her to view it in any other light.

It is true, she was not acquainted with the chief reason he had for observing this line of conduct; for although he had informed Nerina of the child's sudden death, and the effect it had produced on Laura, he was of too reserved and cautious a temper to entrust her with the original cause of both, which constantly preyed upon his mind, and filled him with increasing inquietude.

In one of his secret visits to her, she imputed the dejection of spirits which arose from those painful reflections, to grief for the death of his child; and considering this as an insult to her, she could not refrain from displaying her ill-humour.

"I cannot help thinking you one of the most fortunate men living," said she to him.

"In what?" said he, a little surprised at the observation.

"Why, in getting so cleverly rid of a bastard," replied she, "who would have cut off great part of your fortune from your own children, if ever you have any."

To this Zeluco making no reply, she proceeded: "But although you have been so providentially freed from one, it would be wise in you to be a little more watchful in future; you may not get so quickly rid of the next."

At this observation he fell into a fit of swearing.

"I am not surprised at your ill-humour," continued she; "it is to be sure a little provoking to have a wife who pretends to have lost her senses, and a brother-in-law so disagreeable to you, and so very agreeable to her, constantly at her bed-side."

"Pretends," cried Zeluco: "can you conceive it is pretence?"

"Nay," replied Nerina, "you ought to be the best judge of your wife's sensibility; but one cannot help thinking it a little extraordinary that she should be so much affected with a loss which she can so readily supply."

Zeluco poured fresh execrations on Laura and her brother, wishing he knew how to get quit of both.

"Contrive only to free yourself from *her*," said Nerina, "and you will be no longer troubled with *him*."

"I shall never be freed from her," said he peevishly; "she grows better instead of worse."

"Do not despair," cried Nerina, "she may depart when it is least expected."

"No.—She grows better, I tell you," said Zeluco; "there is no chance of her departure now."

"There is one chance however," said Nerina.

"What is that?" said Zeluco eagerly.

"She may be snapt off in such a fit as the child was," said Nerina.

At this random expression, the alarmed heart of Zeluco shrunk; he became pale as ashes, and staring wildly, in a voice half suppressed, he uttered, "What do you mean?"

"Mean!" said she, surprised at his emotion; "What do *you* mean?—What in the name of wonder disturbs you?—Gracious heaven, how pale you are!—I do not know what I said.—What can be the matter with you?"

"I grew sick all of a sudden," said he, recovering his presence of mind, "but it is passing away already."

"I hope it was nothing which I said that affected you so."

"No; not in the least," replied Zeluco, forcing a smile; "I did not observe what you said:—I was thinking of something else;—but I have been subject of late to sickish qualms which invade me suddenly, and make me look very pale."

"You never mentioned this to me before," said Nerina.

"No assuredly," said Zeluco; "I hate to mention it to any body, or even to think of it.—Let us talk of something else."

The usual consequences of vice was strongly felt by this unhappy man; though naturally bold and daring, the conscious guilt which hung upon his mind unmanned him to such a degree, that he was appalled at every accidental expression; and the constant uneasiness which this occasioned suggested fresh crimes to free him from the effects of the former.

In spite of all his endeavours against them he often fell into fits of musing while he remained with Nerina; when she accused him of this, and inquired into the cause of his dejection, he imputed it to a return of sickness; and on her stating this as a mere pretext to conceal the true cause, "Why then," said he, by way of pleasing her, and to prevent her farther inquiries, "if you will have the truth, I am embarrassed with a wife, which puts it out of my power to devote my whole time and attention to her on whom my heart is fixed."

"In her present situation," said Nerina, "if your wife really is in the state you seem to think, it were better for the woman herself that she were dead."

"That may be," said Zeluco; "but she will not die a minute the sooner for that."

"What is the Physician's opinion?" resumed Nerina.

"It is impossible to know," replied Zeluco; "those fellows never give their real opinion."

"I have no notion of employing a Physician who will not give what opinion, and also what medicines are most expedient," said Nerina.

To this strange speech Zeluco made no answer.

"What medicines *does* he give her?" resumed she.

"Upon my soul I never asked," said Zeluco.

"Because," resumed Nerina, "I believe they give laudanum in such cases: I happened to know this by a singular accident enough; an acquaintance of mine was affected in the same way; she was ordered by a physician a certain number of drops every night; her maid, by mistake, gave a whole phial full, and she died next morning in the pleasantest way imaginable; her relations made a rout about it at first, but on calm reflection they were satisfied that in the patient's situation it was the luckiest accident that could have befallen her."

Zeluco, without seeming to understand the import of this story, replied coldly, "I shall leave the Physician to treat his patient as he pleases."

The constant terror under which Zeluco was, lest Laura, whether intentionally or not, should say any thing which might create suspicion against himself, was sufficient, independent of his absurd jealousy, to have converted his indifference for her into a rancorous hatred. He now wished for nothing more eagerly than her death, and the hint thrown out by Nerina was not lost on him; but as yet undetermined whether he should adopt it or not, he resolved at all events to act without a confident.

CHAPTER XCII.

——Animum pictura pascit inani,
Multa gemens——
Dum stupet, obtutuque hæret defixus in uno. Virg.[1]

In the mean time Laura seemed somewhat better; she had been free from lethargic stupor and faintings for a considerable interval, but still continued languid and dejected, and was in general silent: sometimes she shed tears, and without any obvious cause; at other times she seemed tolerably cheerful, particularly when her brother entered her room; her bodily health upon the whole was greatly better, but her memory and understanding continued impaired: she never inquired for any body, nor seemed to recollect that they existed till they appeared before her, on which it was evident whom she preferred: when she spoke, it was always in short and unconnected sentences.

Madame de Seidlits's indisposition confined her almost constantly to her chamber, so that Signora Sporza, Captain Seidlits, and her maids, were the only persons besides the Physician whom Laura saw.

One morning after Zeluco had rode out, Signora Sporza and Seidlits, by the Physician's permission, conducted Laura from her own apartment to a higher chamber, from whence there was a very commanding prospect. She sat for some time at the window, looking with complacency at the beautiful and varied scenery before her eyes, while Seidlits pointed out the particular objects. Both he and Signora Sporza were delighted with the composure of mind which Laura retained on this occasion.

She then rose and walked about the room, till a picture which hung on the wall engaged her attention: the subject was the Massacre of the Innocents.[2]—The instant she perceived it, she started and betrayed great emotion, but her eyes soon were rivetted on one particular group; it consisted of a mother struggling with a fierce soldier, who with one hand aimed a poniard at her infant, while with the other he grasped the child by the throat.

When Signora Sporza perceived what peculiarly engrossed Laura's attention, she endeavoured to remove her from the picture: it was not in her power. Laura was fascinated to the spot; she held her friend with a rigid grasp, while, with her face projected, her eyes devoured the group. "What is the meaning of this? what alarms you, my sister?" cried Seidlits.—Laura turned to him with a distracted glance, and then pointing with her finger to the assassin who grasped the child, she cried with a voice of wildness and terror,—"Look!—look!"—and being immediately seized with convulsions, she was in that state carried to bed.

The Physician prescribed some calming medicines, notwithstanding which the convulsions and spasms continued at intervals for near two hours, when they abated, and she fell into a slumber.

When Captain Seidlits understood that Laura was in this state, he had the curiosity to return to the room in which she was taken ill; and Signora Sporza, excited by the same curiosity, left her friend for a few minutes and followed him. She found Seidlits examining the picture; it happened by a singular coincidence, that the face of the assassinating soldier had some resemblance to that of Zeluco. Signora Sporza had not looked long at the picture till she observed it; "Almighty Providence," exclaimed she; "How is this?" and then she looked at Captain Seidlits.

"It is certainly so," said he; "I am quite of your opinion."

"What, you perceive a likeness?" resumed she.

"A most diabolic likeness," answered Seidlits.

"But the subject was what first attracted her notice," continued Signora Sporza.

"Which confirms my suspicions," said he, "that this accursed villain——" As Seidlits raised his voice, Signora Sporza, clapping her hand on his mouth, begged him to be more temperate. After some conversation, they agreed to the propriety of concealing their sentiments, till they could get more light into a matter so mysterious, and which gave birth to ideas so horrid; Captain Seidlits gave her his promise to take no step without acquainting her, and she assured him of all the assistance she could give in his endeavours to get at the truth.

But their mutual efforts to this purpose were suspended by the increasing danger of Laura; the slumber in which they left her did not continue long, she was restless, uneasy, and feverish in the night; the feverish symptoms augmented next day, she was delirious the whole of the following night, and was for three days in such imminent danger that all her attendants *dreaded*, and her husband *hoped*, that she would expire: but all at once, when she seemed at the height of danger, she fell into a profound calm and long continued sleep, at the end of which she awoke entirely free from fever, and with her memory and senses restored.

The joy of Signora Sporza and Captain Seidlits on this happy event was somewhat mitigated by the fear that Laura's memory being now returned, a recollection of the child's death, and the circumstances attending it, might produce a relapse; but whether it was the natural consequence of that languor to which the fever reduced Laura, or whatever else was the cause, certain it is that she bore the recollection of the scene which first occasioned her illness with diminished sensibility; her sorrow was accompanied with none of those violent effects, but seemed to be all at once mellowed into a calm uniform melancholy: and the Physician gave the most flattering hopes of the full restoration of her strength and spirits, desiring at the same time that nothing should be said during her convalescence which alluded to her child.

Laura herself perceived that every allusion of that nature was carefully avoided; but one day when Signora Sporza was with her alone, she asked, How her poor mother had borne the shock of the child's death; and put several other questions to Signora Sporza, respecting the interment of the infant; during the recital, which was given in consequence of those inquiries, she wept abundantly, but soon wiping away her tears, she said, "Why should I be grieved for my child? he has escaped many evils to which he must have been exposed had he lived; some of them of more importance than that of dying; but his future happiness is now secure."

Signora Sporza finding, to her great surprise and satisfaction, that she could speak with such serenity on this subject, took occasion some time after to ask Laura, What she thought gave occasion to the *convulsions* of which the infant died. From this question Laura perceived at once what account Zeluco had given of that transaction, and from Signora Sporza's manner, as well as from her subsequent inquiries, Laura also perceived that her friend had suspicions that his account was not exactly true. To these inquiries she answered, That it was impossible for her to tell what was the cause of such fits, but she had often heard that infants were liable to them from various causes; and by her manner she plainly shewed that she was not inclined to speak more fully on the subject. Laura knew that she was the only witness of the child's death, and although she had come to a resolution to take measures for being for ever separated from her husband, she was equally determined not to appear herself, or put it in the power of any other person to appear as his accuser.

During all the time that Laura was disordered Zeluco had kept out of her sight, on the pretence that he could not bear to see one so dear to him in that melancholy state; the real reason was, his dreading that she would discover symptoms of horror, and thereby give rise to suspicions which he was most solicitous to prevent.

As she was now, to his great sorrow, much better in her bodily health, and not at all disordered in other respects, he thought it would seem very singular for him to delay seeing her any longer; but being willing to sound her own inclination in the first place, he told the Physician he was impatient to see his beloved wife, but would not till he should know from him if he could with safety. The Physician mentioned this to Laura, who immediately declared that she could not as yet bear the company or conversation of any body, except that of her mother, who was now somewhat better, or of Signora Sporza; that even their's, when unusually prolonged, occasioned head-ach and feverishness; she begged, therefore, that no other, not even her brother, or husband, would think of visiting her till she was stronger.

Laura had added her brother, whom she had not seen since the picture scene, to render the exclusion of her husband the less extraordinary.

Ever since her mind had recovered its powers, Laura had been reflecting how she ought to proceed in order to obtain a separation from her husband with the least possible eclat or other disagreeable circumstance; having resolved to conceal her principal reason, she did not chuse to consult with her mother, brother, or Signora Sporza, till she had tried what effect an application to Zeluco himself would have.—What the Physician told her rendered her impatient to make this trial. Having written the following letter, therefore, she sent it to her husband, when she knew he was alone in his own apartment.

"To Signor Zeluco.

"You cannot be surprised, or sorry to be informed, that it is my unalterable resolution never to see you more.

"I am the only witness of the horrid deed.

"I have mentioned it to no mortal, nor ever shall, unless forced by your refusal to comply with my proposal, or by madness, which a sight of you might again drive me into.

"The plan of separation shall be proposed by me to my friends, and on a pretext which cannot affect you; all I require is your concurrence that it may take place without noise or difficulty.

"I demand no settlement,—but shall delay mentioning this affair to my relations till my mother's health is a little better established, which there is every appearance will be very soon.

"Do not think of turning me from my purpose; the attempt alone will involve you in trouble.

"I desire no answer but a simple assent, and shall ever pray that the mercy of Heaven may be extended to you.

LAURA SEIDLITS."

Zeluco was preparing to go abroad when he received this letter, he changed his purpose, and remained in his apartment the whole day.

He was at first so much exasperated, that he had thoughts of bursting into Laura's apartment, demanding an explanation of what she had written, with a view of intimidating her into silence, by threats of confining her for life as a distracted woman, if she dared to accuse him. But a very little reflexion convinced him of the danger such a measure would be attended with; besides, he saw that no colouring of his would efface the impression which her story, if she was forced to unfold it, must make on a public by no means disposed to think with partiality of him. Zeluco, therefore, determined on this occasion to bridle the impetuosity of his rage, and make both his pride and humour obey the dictates of prudence; he relinquished every openly violent measure, and sent the following answer to Laura:

"Although I understand not what some parts of your letter allude to, I agree to your proposal of separation; when you mention this matter to your relations, you will let them know that although this proceeds entirely from a piece of humour of your own, unsought by me, yet I am willing to give you a reasonable annuity for life."

Laura was greatly pleased with this answer; she was resolved to accept of no settlement from Zeluco, but thought it best to say nothing on that head, till she should remove from his house. She herself would have preferred returning to Germany, had she not feared it would be disagreeable to her mother, and had she not mistrusted her own heart, which she was conscious suggested that measure from partiality to Carlostein. The plan, therefore, which she resolved to adopt immediately after the separation was, to take refuge for some time at least in a convent at Naples, or perhaps at Rome or Florence, where she could board at a very moderate expence; and having determined to acquaint no mortal with the chief reason of this separation, she expected to meet with difficulty in convincing her mother of its propriety; and therefore she watched the advance of her health, that she might mention it at a time when she would suffer little from the uneasiness it would give her.

CHAPTER XCIII.

Me, me (adsum qui feci), in me convertite ferum. VIRG.[1]

CAPTAIN SEIDLITS informed his friend Carlostein of the effect which the sight of the picture had on Laura; also of his own and Signora Sporza's suspicions relating to the child's death and the mother's illness, which suspicions acquired new strength from the second illness of Laura, and the singular manner in which it had originated. While Laura continued in danger, the minds of her relations were so much agitated, that they could think of nothing else; but when the danger was over, and it appeared that the crisis of the fever had not only thrown off the bodily disease but also the mental disorder, Seidlits resumed his conferences with Carlostein respecting the mysterious circumstances which accompanied the child's death, and had occurred since; and Carlostein expressing a great desire to see the picture, Seidlits conducted him one day to the room in which it hung.

"There is the villain!" said Seidlits, pointing to the figure of the soldier with the poignard. "Observe with what fury he aims at the child."——Carlostein continued to examine the group with silent attention.

"It is true," resumed Seidlits, "that there was no wound on the body of my sister's infant."

"But observe," said Carlostein, "with what force the murderer *grasps* that child by the throat."

"Do you not see the resemblance which strikes Signora Sporza?" continued Seidlits, not having perceived the import of Carlostein's remark.

"Yes; I perceive something of that nature; not a great deal however," answered Carlostein, who already repented of the insinuation which had escaped him, for he wished not to strengthen his friend's suspicions without stronger evidence.

"The resemblance seems to me very evident," said Seidlits.

"Perhaps there is some resemblance," added Carlostein; "such things occur often enough."

"Do you not think it would strike the villain himself, were he to see it?" said Seidlits.

"I should think not," replied Carlostein, who dreaded the consequence of his friend's retaining that idea.

"Pray lend me your pencil," said Seidlits; "it *shall* strike him, by heaven! if he ever looks at it."

He immediately wrote over the figure of the soldier, the name of *Zeluco*.—"There," said he, "now, it will be impossible for him to mistake his representative."

Carlostein endeavoured to prevail upon his friend to obliterate what he had written; but finding him obstinate, he determined to get Signora Sporza to do it before there was any probability of Zeluco's entering that room.

As Carlostein and Seidlits walked out of the court, they met

Zeluco. Carlostein having received the pencil, still held it in his hand, but seeing his friend's eyes kindle at the approach of Zeluco, he whispered, "Pray, say nothing to him at present."—"I must give him a slight hint," replied Seidlits; and then said aloud to Zeluco, "We were examining the picture, Signor, which affected my sister so violently."

"What picture?" said Zeluco. "I know nothing of a picture."

Signora Sporza had concealed that incident carefully from him; having only informed him that Laura had relapsed suddenly, without mentioning the cause.

"By much the most interesting piece in your collection," replied Seidlits; "it had almost proved fatal to your wife: pray examine it carefully, and when we next meet, I shall be glad to know how you relish it." Having said this, Seidlits walked on, and Carlostein whispered Zeluco, "There is a name written *with this pencil* over the principal figure; if you wish for any further ecclaircissment, apply to me.—I shall be at home in less than an hour, and ready to give you whatever satisfaction you desire."

Carlostein was fully persuaded that the consequence of Zeluco's looking at the picture, with the style in which Seidlits had directed him to it, must be a personal quarrel between them; he knew that Laura dreaded nothing more than such an event, and well remembered with what earnestness she had intreated him, if he should ever see any appearance of that kind, to do every thing in his power to prevent it. She had once said, talking on that subject to Signora Sporza, that she would consider this as the greatest obligation that any person could confer upon her. He had accordingly endeavoured as much as he could to prevail on Seidlits to obliterate the name; he had resolved to write to Signora Sporza to do what Seidlits refused; and he had tried to prevent Seidlits from addressing Zeluco in the manner he did. Having failed in all, he saw no means of obviating a personal contest between the husband and brother of Laura, but by drawing the resentment of Zeluco from Seidlits to himself; this having struck him instantly, he whispered Zeluco as has been mentioned.

Carlostein had also another reason for being solicitous to prevent Seidlits from meeting Zeluco in the field; he knew the latter to be far more skilful and expert in the use of the small sword than his friend. He had often seen them fence together, and Zeluco had an evident superiority even when he did not exert his whole powers. Although Seidlits had been as fully convinced of this as his friend, which he was not, it would, on the present occasion, have had no weight with them. Pistols were out of the question, no such weapon being used in affairs of this nature in Italy. Carlostein imagined himself rather a more skilful fencer than Seidlits, though conscious of being by much inferior to Zeluco, who was accounted one of the best in the kingdom of Naples.

When the two friends had walked a little way after quitting Zeluco, Seidlits turning round to Carlostein, who followed him, said, "I shall certainly hear from him this afternoon or to-morrow."

"I dare swear," answered Carlostein, "he will take till to-morrow to consider in what manner he is to ask an explanation of the words which you addressed to him."

"I shall give him a very brief and clear explanation whenever he does," said Seidlits.

"Suppose," resumed Carlostein, "he should be able to explain to your satisfaction the circumstances which seem so dismally mysterious to us."

"I shall make an apology without hesitation," said Seidlits. "But you will *attend me* in case we do go out?"

"Of course," replied Carlostein. "If I remember, you are engaged to dinner at our minister's.—You go, I suppose?"

"I cannot do otherwise," said Seidlits; "but I will leave word with Targe to bring me any message."

"I am convinced you will have none before to-morrow," rejoined Carlostein; "and if no accommodation takes place, you will probably arrange matters for the following morning:—at all events, I shall have a post-chaise prepared to carry you directly to the ecclesiastical state."[2]

"Pray do," said Seidlits, "for I am confident I shall do his business for all his vaunted skill:—there is some difference between a foil and a sword. Adieu, I must dress for dinner.—You dine with Mr. N——, do you not?"

"I do," replied Carlostein; "but we shall meet in the evening." They separated.

Zeluco had observed something fierce and menacing in the countenances both of Carlostein and Seidlits; he was much more surprised at this in the former than in the latter, because Carlostein and he had always been apparently, at least, on the most friendly footing. He could not comprehend the import of what was said by either. On going up stairs, he demanded of one of Laura's maids, in what room her mistress was when she was last taken ill. On entering the room, he threw his eyes in a cursory manner over the pictures, but the moment he perceived the massacre of the innocents, his heart shrunk within him, and he was convinced that this must be the piece in question; with a trembling step he approached nearer to the picture, and having distinguished the soldier grasping the neck of the child, he started back, as if the poignard had been aimed at his own breast:—after a pause, he advanced again, forcing his averted eyes once more on the picture, and with horror and dismay observed his own name inscribed over the head of the soldier.

Perplexed, confounded, and terrified, he shrunk down upon a chair, and as soon as he was able to walk, he stole down stairs, and shut himself up in his own apartment.

He had promised to pass that evening with Nerina, but finding himself in a state of such perturbation, quite undetermined what measures to adopt, not daring to inform her or any other person of the cause of his perplexity; he sent a verbal message by the servant usually employed by them, importing, That he was taken suddenly ill, and therefore could not possibly wait on her at the appointed time; but if he found himself better, he should have that pleasure the following evening.

Having dismissed the footman with this message, he continued in painful reflexion on these extraordinary incidents; he could no longer doubt of both Seidlits and Carlostein's having strong suspicions of his being the cause of the child's death and Laura's illness: he was impressed also with the notion that those suspicions were conveyed to them by Laura, either designedly, when she recovered her memory, or undesignedly, during the ravings of her disorder: in either case she was the object of his undistinguishing vengeance.

His former plan of treating her as a mad woman, he saw would not be of any use now, when, to his infinite mortification, she was perfectly recovered. He felt the necessity under which he was to demand an explanation of Seidlits and Carlostein. As the expressions which Carlostein had whispered were the most direct and pointed, he resolved to begin with him. Yet should the effect of this be a duel, he plainly saw, that by attracting the public attention, and exciting inquiries, it would produce a great many of those consequences he so anxiously wished to prevent.

In this state of hesitation and direful perplexity, how often did this wretched man wish for a friend to whom he could with safety unbosom himself, and from whom he might receive counsel and consolation? but having in the whole course of his life been the friend of no man, he well knew that no man was his friend. He could hardly meet an eye even in his own family, which he did not suspect of looking on him with aversion, either from love for Laura, or direct hatred for him.

After weighing all the difficulties and dangers, a great choice of which presented themselves to his mind, he could form no fixed plan of future conduct, but in the meantime thought himself absolutely bound without farther hesitation to go and talk to Carlostein.

In all cases where he was not disturbed by conscience, which makes cowards of us all,[3] Zeluco had less personal fear than most people; but as he was equally devoid of principle, his notions on the subject of duelling were somewhat singular.

One of his maxims was, that a man who injured another might, consistent with good sense, and ought, from a regard to his own character, to fight the person he had injured, the moment he was required; but he thought it in the highest degree silly and absurd in the injured person to take such a dangerous and precarious method of obtaining reparation; justice and common sense would dictate, he imagined, some more certain plan of vengeance, except indeed the injury was known to the public, or of a nature which admitted of no delay. In such cases, a regard to the world's opinion superseded every other consideration. His present business with Carlostein he considered in this last class; he had no doubt of Carlostein's having communicated to Seidlits and to others what he had whispered to himself: therefore, notwithstanding that he considered himself as the injured person, not the injurer, he thought it incumbent on him to demand an explanation in the usual mode; being determined however not to bring matters to the last extremity, if he could find any plausible means of avoiding it; not that he feared the issue of the duel, being too confident in his own skill to harbour any doubt; but merely because he wished, if possible, to avoid every measure which might tend to make an eclat, or lead to inquiries into the cause of the quarrel.

CHAPTER XCIV.

What stronger breast-plate than a heart untainted?
Thrice is he arm'd that has his quarrel just,
And he but naked, though lock'd up in steel,
Whose conscience with injustice is corrupted.

SHAKESPEARE.[1]

ZELUCO found Carlostein, as he expected, alone. "You will not be surprised at seeing me, Sir, after your late behaviour," said Zeluco.

"I am not surprised," replied Carlostein.

"You promised me an explanation," added Zeluco.

"Propose your difficulty," rejoined Carlostein, "and you'll find me as good as my word."

"I was desired to examine a picture," said Zeluco, fiercely.

"Which I presume you have done," added Carlostein, with calmness.

"I *have*," answered Zeluco; "and I find somebody has had the insolence to inscribe my name over one of the figures."

"You could not miss it," said Carlostein; "it was very distinctly written with this pencil;" taking the pencil out of his pocket;—"but there was no insolence intended."

"What was intended then?" said Zeluco, in somewhat of a milder tone, for he began to imagine that Carlostein meant to explain it in a friendly or jocular manner.

"It was intended," replied Carlostein, in a sedate and solemn accent, "to signify the conformity of character and conduct between you and a murderer."

This answer, being rather unexpected, disconcerted Zeluco a little; but recovering himself, he said, "You can have but one meaning by such behaviour, Sir; I expect you will meet me to-morrow morning."

"Wherever you are pleased to appoint," said Carlostein.

After some farther conversation, they agreed to meet at a remote spot which happened to be near the villa where Nerina dwelt, and at an early hour; each to be attended by a friend.

"I presume," said Zeluco, "Captain Seidlits will accompany you."

"He is the very last man I should think of on this occasion; neither Captain Seidlits, nor any other person, except the gentleman who *is* to attend me, shall know of what has passed between us; for this I pledge my honour." As Carlostein pronounced the last sentence, he looked at Zeluco as if he expected an assurance to the same purpose from him.

"None but a coward would act otherwise," said Zeluco.

"It is well," said Carlostein. "Now, Signor, your weapon?"

"The sword, unquestionably," replied Zeluco.

"Although you are the challenger, and I am not ignorant of your dexterity at that particular weapon, I agree," said Carlostein.

"If you have any objection to the weapon of a gentleman, you should have thought of it before you insulted one," said Zeluco.

"I have told you," said Carlostein, "that I agree."

Immediately on their separating, Carlostein informed Mr. N—— of all that had passed; and asked the favour of his accompanying him to the place of rendezvous.

Mr. N—— accepted the invitation, after having expressed his admiration of the generous conduct of Carlostein; for he plainly perceived, notwithstanding Carlostein's having passed over that circumstance, that he had provoked the quarrel to prevent Seidlits from being engaged in it. Carlostein begged that he would let nothing escape him, in case of his meeting Seidlits, that could give him any suspicion of what was intended. Mr. N—— assured him he would be on his guard. "But I am afraid," added he, "that, by your eagerness to prevent Laura from the danger of losing a brother, you expose her to a misfortune which she will feel with still severer anguish."

Carlostein made no other answer to this observation of Mr. N——'s, than a gentle inclination of the head.

The generous friendship of Mr. N—— for Carlostein was increased, and not diminished, by the great regard which he had long observed Laura had for him. What gave him most uneasiness in the business of the following morning was, the fear of any fatal accident happening to Carlostein, which, although he should regret on his own account, he was of a character to regret doubly on account of the affliction it would occasion to Laura.

When Carlostein met Seidlits in the evening, he told him, That he had as yet heard nothing from Zeluco.

Carlostein answered, That he was convinced there would be no message till next day; "Indeed," added he, "I think you had best keep out of his way for this evening; let him digest what he has already got, before you give him any new provocation."

"If a sight of me disturbs his digestion," said Seidlits, "he must keep out of my way, for I shall certainly take no pains to keep out of his; nor will I circumscribe my walks or visits on account of any man alive."

"I only meant for this evening," rejoined Carlostein.

"Well," interrupted Seidlits, "if he wishes not to meet me this evening, he had best not appear at the Corso;[2] for I am engaged with some company there about this time, and shall go directly; perhaps you will go with me."—Carlostein excused himself, after begging of his friend to return soon to their lodgings. He was particularly solicitous to prevent Seidlits from meeting with Zeluco that evening, foreseeing that it might entirely defeat the plan he had already settled for the next morning.

In the mean while, Zeluco, wishing to conceal the source of this dispute as long as possible, did not chuse to apply to any person acquainted with Seidlits or Laura to accompany him next morning, lest they should make inquiries which he might not chuse to answer; he therefore waited on Bertram the Genevois, and as an old brother officer, and a person of whose gallant spirit he had an high opinion, begged he would accompany him the following morning on an affair of honour with a foreign officer, who, he said, had insulted him.

Bertram hesitated, and expressed a desire of knowing the particulars of the quarrel; "Is there no possibility," said he, "of accommodating the affair?"

Zeluco assured him he had been insulted in such a manner as no gentleman could bear, without a very ample apology; and then, to prevent his insisting on knowing the particulars, added, "If my antagonist agrees to make such an apology as you shall think sufficient, I assure you that it shall satisfy me."

Bertram then consented, in the hope that it would be in his power to bring the affair to an amicable termination. On being informed of the place, he recollected it perfectly, having frequently taken notice of it during the various excursions which he had made since his arrival at Naples; and he promised to call on Zeluco precisely at the hour appointed.

When Zeluco returned home he found the following letter from Nerina:

"Merciful Heaven! what is the matter with you? What am I to think of a verbal message of such cruel import? Do you not know how my soul doats on you? Do you not know how miserably I pass the lingering moments which cruel fate obliges me to spend out of your company?—Or, are you so ill that you cannot write?—Ah! let me not palliate your conduct by a supposition which would render me more wretched than even your neglect. No; let me be blest in the certainty of your recovery; and I will endeavour to support whatever other misfortune may befal me. Let me know by the bearer at what hour I may expect you to-morrow. But I earnestly intreat, that no consideration, which solely regards me, may induce you to venture out sooner than it can be done with safety to your health; that I may not purchase a transient happiness at the price of a whole life of despair. Alas! why am I not permitted to tend you, to watch you through the sleepless night, and endeavour to cheer the gloom of sickness? that were happiness indeed, when compared to the tortures of absence and uncertainty. Write, or rather let your valet write, a short line to the wretched

"Nerina."

Zeluco was himself a great dissembler, exceedingly profuse in compliments and professions of attachment, naturally suspicious, and generally acute in discovering the concealed motives and designs of others; yet the cajoleries of this woman lulled his usual diffidence, and his penetration was the dupe of his vanity.

Had he seen such a letter as this from any woman to another man, he would have been instantly convinced that the artful effusion was dictated by affected, not real, passion; and he would have considered it as weakness and vanity in any man to be imposed upon by it for a moment; yet such is the fascination of self-love, that he thought the same sentiments sincere and natural when he was himself their object, that he would have considered as extravagant and deceitful, had they been addressed to another man. His answer was couched in the following words:

"My dearest Nerina,

"Make yourself easy—I am somewhat better already. Your affectionate letter has contributed to my recovery. When my servant left me, I could not write without pain; but had I thought of the uneasiness which the omission would give you, I should not have permitted him to return without a letter. I may possibly have it in my power to wait on you to-morrow at dinner, certainly not sooner; at any rate you will hear from me, and you need not expect me, nor send any message till then.

"I remain most affectionately,

"Yours, *&c. &c.*"

CHAPTER XCV.

——quo modo adolescentulus
Meretricum ingenia et mores posset noscere:
Mature ut cum cognorit, perpetuo oderit.

TERENT.[1]

IMMEDIATELY after engaging Bertram to accompany him to the field, Zeluco took precautions to insure his own escape out of the kingdom of Naples, in case it should be necessary; he next employed himself in burning certain papers, in arranging others; and having prepared whatever he thought necessary, and given orders to his servant at what hour to call him in the morning, he went to bed in the hope of being refreshed by sleep before his meeting with Carlostein; but such a tempest of distracting thoughts rushed on his mind as totally deprived him of repose. The violent impression which the sight of the painted murderer of a child had made on Laura, with which he thought even her maids were acquainted, was sufficient to create a pretty general suspicion of the real fact. What had been written to him by Laura, strongly hinted by Seidlits, and directly asserted by Carlostein, were evidences that they all believed him to be accessary to the death of the child. And he often cursed the unlucky incidents by which, while he was projecting a scheme of secure revenge against his wife and her brother, he found himself unavoidably engaged in a contest, on equal terms, with a third person, against whom he never before had harboured any enmity. In the event of his killing Carlostein, of which he had little doubt, it struck him that Laura, or perhaps her brother, might during his absence mention such circumstances relative to the child's death, as would give the public an impression against him, which they themselves, should they be so inclined afterwards, might not be able to efface.

This idea prompted him to rise and to write a letter addressed to Laura, in which he cautioned her in general terms not to allow any expression to escape her which might injure him during his temporary absence; and advising her to admonish her brother to the same effect; for that any thing of that nature would prove ruinous to themselves, and would most materially injure her mother. This letter he sealed and put into his pocket, intending to send it to her from the field, in case it should be necessary after his business with Carlostein was over.

The picture and the inscription came next into his recollection; he had already locked the door of the room, and put the key into his escritoire; but now, all the family being asleep, he stole again to the room, unfixed the picture from the wall, brought it into his own bedchamber, and burnt it to ashes.

He threw himself again into his bed, but with as little success as before; a retrospect of his past life, which obtruded itself upon his mind in spite of all his endeavours to exclude it, and the dread of the world's soon reviewing it in the same light that he himself did, with a confused prospect of consequences which he dreaded without knowing how to prevent, banished sleep from his pillow. He rose, and walked with precipitation about his chamber, as if he could have dissipated the uneasiness of his mind by the agitation of his body. Nerina's letter lay on the table—he read it once more, and with redoubled complacency.—Convinced of the sincerity of *her* attachment, he could not flatter himself with the friendship of another person on earth:—in moments of difficulty and distress, it is natural for the most arrogant and stubborn of the human race to wish for the support of friendship and of love, however powerless the person is in whose breast they reside. There was yet an interval of two or three hours to the time at which Bertram was to call for him. In the state of anxiety and impatience in which Zeluco was, it appeared an age.

> With what a leaden and retarding weight
> Does expectation load the wings of time?[2]

This fine observation of the poet is not only highly applicable where he places it, but is also just when the mind is agitated with the thoughts of any important event which we know to be unavoidable, and have no hopes of tranquillity till it has taken place. Zeluco had sometimes found that Nerina had the art of unloading the wings of time; and being seized with an irresistible desire of passing the interval till he should meet Carlostein with her, he ordered his horses to be got ready, and wrote the following note directed to Bertram:

"Dear Bertram,

"I have ordered two horses to be ready, one for you, the other for the servant, who will deliver you this, and then accompany you to the appointed place, where you will find me waiting your arrival. I will then inform you why I set out before you.

"I am your assured friend,

"and obliged servant,

"Zeluco."

Having given the necessary directions to the servant who waited for Bertram, he set out, attended by another servant, for the habitation of Nerina, where he arrived a little after day-break.

Confident of a cordial welcome at all hours, he entered without knocking, by the means of a key which he kept for that purpose. Being obliged to pass through the parlour in his way to the bed-chamber of Nerina, he was somewhat surprised to find her maid up at so early an hour. The maid was still more surprised at seeing him. He asked how her mistress was, and without waiting for her answer, walked towards Nerina's chamber.

"Maria Virgine!" cried the maid, running between him and the door.

"What is the matter?" said Zeluco.

"Lord, Sir!" cried the maid, "you cannot see my mistress at present."

"Why not?"

"Dear Sir," replied the maid, "only stay in the parlour, till I acquaint my mistress that you are here."

"Psha!" said Zeluco, pushing her aside.

"O Lord, Sir!" cried the maid, taking hold of his coat, "you will terrify my mistress out of her senses, if you go in to her at this unseasonable hour."

"Get along;" said Zeluco, shaking her from him.

"My mistress is indisposed, Sir; she is extremely ill," said the maid.

"Ill!" cried Zeluco.

"Yes," said the maid; "she has been exceedingly ill these two days."

"She did not mention that in the letter I received from her yesterday."

"No! that is very odd, indeed," cried the maid, "but she has forgot it; for you know my mistress sometimes has but an indifferent memory. Pray, Sir, be so obliging as to return to the parlour, till I inform my mistress that you are come; when I have informed her, I dare swear she will be very happy to see you. But——"

"Peace, babler," cried Zeluco, pushing her aside, and walking through the passage towards Nerina's bed-chamber.

"Pray, Signor Zeluco, stay in the parlour; indeed, Signor Zeluco, you'll frighten my mistress,—dear Signor Zeluco,—I protest, Signor Zeluco," following him through the passage, and raising her voice louder and louder; but perceiving him pushing with violence at the door of the bed-chamber, she screamed, "O, my poor mistress will be murdered," and immediately the voice of Nerina was heard from within, shrieking and crying out, "murder! rape! murder! villain! monster, be gone!"

Zeluco drew his sword, drove the door open with a violent kick of his foot, and, to his utter astonishment, saw a man, half-dressed, standing by the bed of Nerina.

"What is your business here, scoundrel?" cried Zeluco, furious with rage, and making a push at him with his sword.

The fellow very dexterously put the sword aside with one hand, plunged a stiletto into the bowels of Zeluco with the other, and made his escape.

Zeluco fell to the ground.

Nerina, who had continued screaming from the bed, seeing Zeluco fall, sprang up, exclaiming, "Oh, the villain has murdered my dear Lord," kneeling down by him, and offering her aid.

"Be gone, perfidious wretch!" said Zeluco, with a faint voice.

With loud lamentations she took all the saints of heaven, with the angels and blessed martyrs, to witness that she was innocent as the chaste Susanna,[3] or the Holy Virgin herself, for that the villain had concealed himself in her chamber, with an intention to rob or murder her; and that being awaked by the voice of her maid in the passage, she had perceived him for the first time, and instantly cried out.

Zeluco, without seeming to regard her, desired the maid to call in his own servant.

As soon as with his assistance he was placed on the bed, a message was dispatched to Naples for surgeons.

The man who stabbed Zeluco, we had not occasion to mention before, although he was an old acquaintance of Nerina's. He was originally a rope-dancer;[4] she had first seen him at Venice, where he was greatly admired for his shape, strength, and agility. She found means to prevail on him to quit his profession, and attach himself entirely to her service; he had come with her first to Rome, where he attended her as a servant out of livery, and afterwards accompanied her to Naples. Zeluco soon after his connexion with Nerina, saw something in this man's appearance which he did not relish; and he gave her a hint to that effect. Nerina instantly dismissed him with such an air of indifference as dissipated certain ideas which began to arise in the suspicious mind of Zeluco. The dismission however was of little importance; the man remained secretly at Naples, and was admitted to the bed-chamber of Nerina when she thought herself secure of not being visited by Zeluco: those interviews were unknown to all the servants except Nerina's confidential maid, who was actually sitting up for the purpose of letting him out before the other servants should get up, when Zeluco entered so unexpectedly.

When Nerina heard the voice of her maid, she comprehended the reasons of her noisy remonstrances, and perceiving that Zeluco was breaking into the room, she instantly formed a resolution worthy of her abandoned character: she screamed and accused her paramour of violence, with a view to convince Zeluco of her own innocence, and instigate him to put the man to death as a housebreaker. The scene however took a different turn, and Zeluco saw the whole in a true point of view.

When the person who was sent to Naples for the surgeons was returning, he met Bertram, who had just mounted his horse, and, accompanied by the other servant, was going to the rendezvous: this person knowing Zeluco's servant, informed him of the misfortune which had happened to his master. Bertram desired to be conducted as fast as possible to the house where Zeluco lay.

They overtook Carlostein and Mr. N——, who were riding to the appointed place. Bertram informed Mr. N—— of what he had just heard, and they all rode to the dwelling of Nerina.

Carlostein and Mr. N—— remained in the parlour, while Bertram introduced the surgeon and his assistant into the room in which Zeluco was. He stretched forth his hand to Bertram, saying, "I am glad to see you; when my wound has been examined, I wish to have some conversation with you. In the mean time," added he, pointing to Nerina, "let that woman be secured and kept separate from her maid; she is the cause of what has happened."

Zeluco had kept his own servant by him from the time he received the wound till Bertram with the others arrived; Nerina had also remained constantly in the room, and had often renewed her lamentations. Zeluco took no other notice of her, than by begging of her not to make a noise, for he was in great pain. His eyes were now open to her true character, and she attempted in vain to deceive him any more; yet he explained himself only by keeping a steady silence till Bertram came.

A more unpleasant party than this must have been, can hardly be conceived, consisting of Zeluco lying wounded on the bed of Nerina; Nerina herself in the most agonizing state of suspense. The servant of Zeluco was the only person of the company tolerably at his ease, and *he* was rather anxious that his master should die, that he might be relieved from a troublesome attendance; and that Nerina, whom he heartily hated, might be hanged.

But when she heard herself so plainly accused by Zeluco, in the directions he addressed to Bertram, she began to vindicate her innocence with all that violence of vociferation which so often attends guilt. Being forced out of the room by the company, she and her maid were secured in separate chambers.

Zeluco suffered great pain while the state of his wound was examined; after dressing it, however, the surgeon gave him hopes of recovery, but declared it necessary that he should be kept quiet, which, as he found himself easier and inclined to sleep after the dressing, Zeluco agreed to. He earnestly begged of Bertram not to leave the house, who assuring him he had no such intentions, they all left the room except one servant.

Bertram then joined Mr. N—— and Carlostein in the parlour, with the surgeon, who was the same that had formerly attended Zeluco. He spoke more dubiously of his recovery to these gentlemen than he had done to the patient himself; and leaving an assistant to be at hand in case of accidents, he set out for Naples, promising to return in the morning.

Bertram, with a frankness which belonged to his character, and which was encouraged by the appearance and manners of Carlostein, informed him by what accident he himself came there, and of the whole of his connexion with Zeluco; he expressed a desire of knowing what was the origin of their quarrel, for he understood that Carlostein was the person Zeluco was to have met, had he not been prevented by the accident just mentioned.

Carlostein refrained from mentioning the real source of the quarrel, saying, it was an unlucky business, of a delicate nature, which he was not at liberty to reveal, expressing at the same time a humane concern for the condition of Zeluco, and the highest esteem for Bertram, with whose character Mr. N—— had acquainted him.

Carlostein and Mr. N—— were still conversing with Bertram, when the officers of justice arrived. Zeluco being acquainted with this, desired to see them; in the bitterest terms he accused Nerina of being an accomplice of the fellow who had stabbed him; declared that he recollected this man to be the same whom she had brought to Naples in her service, and had dismissed at his request. Nerina did not suspect that Zeluco had recognized this man; she therefore denied that she had ever seen him; but the maid, who was examined apart, acknowledged that he was the person who had formerly been in Nerina's service, and with whom she had been connected ever since. They were both carried to prison.

CHAPTER XCVI.

Carlostein visits Zeluco.

Zeluco having demanded of Bertram whether he had heard any thing of the gentleman whom he was to have met, Bertram informed him that Carlostein was then in the house, and of his humane behaviour ever since he had heard of the unlucky accident.

Zeluco expressing a desire to speak with him alone, Carlostein was introduced.

"It is doubtful, Signor," said Zeluco, "when, or if ever, it will be in my power to meet you in the way we had agreed upon; but it would be satisfactory to me in the mean time to know whether you and Captain Seidlits received from my wife the impressions which both of you seem to entertain."

Carlostein replied, That both he and Seidlits had received the impressions he alluded to from certain circumstances they had themselves observed, without their having been pointed out by any third person whatever; that as for his own part, he had never once seen Laura since her being first taken ill, and that he knew she had been at great pains, both before and since her illness, to make her brother believe that she had lived on the best terms with her husband, and seemed extremely unhappy when she perceived that Captain Seidlits suspected the contrary, and had endeavoured by every means to convince him that his suspicion was ill founded.

Zeluco seemed satisfied with this explanation; "I have a curiosity to know also," said he, "if you have no objection, what was your inducement to draw upon yourself a quarrel which Captain Seidlits was sufficiently eager to make his own?"

"As you say this will afford you satisfaction, Signor," replied Carlostein, "I shall not scruple to tell you that when I heard Captain Seidlits express himself in the manner he did to you at your last meeting, I thought it probably would produce a quarrel between you, which might end fatally to one or other; whichever fell, the consequence would be unfortunate for Madame de Seidlits and her daughter; the former must lose a son-in-law, and the latter a brother or husband; whereas my being your antagonist could not have such ill consequences; if the chance went against me, they would be deprived of no such near relation; and even in the event of your falling by my sword, they would be involved in less trouble than if you should owe your death to their nearest relation."

"It is impossible not to admire your conduct, Sir," said Zeluco; "you must take a prodigious interest in those two ladies."

"There are no two persons on earth, Signor, for whom I have a greater regard; their virtues command the esteem of all who have the honour of knowing them; but independent of my friendship for them, I will confess to you, that another consideration had weight with me; I am indebted for my own life to the gallantry of Captain Seidlits; I was desirous therefore of seizing, without his knowledge, a chance of repaying what I owed him, by taking the consequences, whatever they might be, of a meeting with you."

"Captain Seidlits is much to be envied," said Zeluco, with a sigh, "in having such a friend;—perhaps," continued he, after a pause, "it may yet be in my power to convince both you and your friend, that what you have mistaken in my conduct was intirely owing to the malice and base suggestions of the accursed woman who is carried to prison, and who, I trust, will meet the fate she so well deserves."

To this Carlostein made no reply; but the Physician, who had also been sent for to visit Zeluco, arriving, put an end to their discourse.

The Physician had not met the Surgeon, and of course could have no just notion of the degree of danger in which Zeluco was; but finding him pretty free from fever, he ventured to pronounce still more favourably of the case than the Surgeon had done; and, after giving some general directions, took his leave.

Bertram remained at Zeluco's earnest request, and by his orders had the direction of every thing in the family; for the house, and all within it, was the property of Zeluco, except the wearing apparel of Nerina, which she had been permitted to pack up; and what she did not take with her was left under the care of a maid in whom she placed confidence.

Carlostein and Mr. N—— returned to Naples after hearing the opinion of the Physician.

Carlostein gave his friend Seidlits an account of the whole affair; stating it in such a manner, however, that his intended meeting with Zeluco appeared to have been owing to a fortuitous rencounter with him the preceding evening, in which Zeluco had directly challenged him. Seidlits seemed displeased at his friend for concealing this.—"How could I, my dear Seidlits," said Carlostein, "shuffle over on you the answer of a challenge directly addressed to myself?—Would you have acted so?"

"Well," said Seidlits, recovering his good humour, "although, from certain circumstances which I now recollect, I still suspect that some fraudulent practices have taken place on this occasion, yet I shall take no farther notice of them; since, however," added he, smiling, "you tried to rob me of a small sprig of laurel, I rejoice that it has missed your head as well as mine."

They then informed Signora Sporza of all that had happened, leaving it to her to mention it to Madame de Seidlits, when she found a fit opportunity; but they all agreed to keep it concealed from Laura, till the fate of Zeluco should be more fully ascertained.

Zeluco continued tolerably easy till towards midnight, when the pain of his wound became very severe; amidst his groans he poured forth horrid imprecations against Nerina.

The assistant Surgeon, who had been left to attend him, finding that the fomentations and other means which he used to relieve the pain failed, spoke of sending to Naples for some laudanum, a few drops of which, he said, might be of service.

Zeluco hearing him give orders for that purpose, told the Surgeon to search one of his pockets, where he found a phial full of that drug.—Zeluco having secretly provided himself with it, soon after a conversation with Nerina, which has been already mentioned.—Whether he would ever have used it for the purpose to which she meant to prompt him, can never be known, for the most profligate of mankind often shrink from executing the crimes which they have in speculation.

The Surgeon administered a dose of this medicine, which abated the pain, and gave him some hours rest.

CHAPTER XCVII.

> What nothing earthly gives, or can destroy,
> The soul's calm sun-shine, and the heart-felt joy,
> Is virtue's prize. Pope.[1]

The following morning early, Bertram understanding that Zeluco was awake, entered his room to inquire how he was. Being then pretty easy and refreshed by sleep, he begged that Bertram would sit by his bed-side; and as the story of Antonio had made some impression on him, he began to make more inquiry concerning him; after a few questions, he said to Bertram, "On the whole, I perceive that this Savoyard has put you to a considerable deal of expence, as well as trouble."

"I have already been amply repaid," said Bertram; "but I still expect an additional recompence."

"I understood the fellow *had nothing*," said Zeluco.

"He has both a father and a mother," replied Bertram, "very honest people as I have been told; they live at Chamberry, which is in my way home to Geneva; the poor old couple have been miserable on account of their son's misfortune. I shall have the pleasure of restoring him to them;—only think, Signor, what satisfaction I shall have—their old hearts will be ready to burst with joy.—I often anticipate in my imagination, the scene of their first meeting;—why, Signor, a single scene of that kind is worth all the five acts of dull selfish life."

"You enter into these people's happiness as if it were your own," said Zeluco.

"A great part of it will be my own," said Bertram; "I question if any of the three will be much happier than myself. You must have often felt, Signor, what a pleasing sensation being the author of happiness conveys to the heart."

Zeluco seemed distressed, and made no reply.

"I fear your wound gives you pain," said Bertram.

"Not at all," said Zeluco; "and this is the only recompence you expect?"

"It is all I would accept of from man," replied Bertram; "the consciousness of a good action is delightful when performed and is also a source of pleasing recollection through life. Would to God I had more of them to boast of! being conscious of but few, makes me perhaps too vain of this."

"You have reason to be vain indeed," said Zeluco.

"I am certain at least," rejoined Bertram, "that I should have been lower in my own eyes had I acted otherwise:—yet I make no doubt but you, and many others, would have done the same thing with less hesitation than I shewed."

Zeluco groaned.

"I am heartily sorry to see you in so much pain," said Bertram; "shall I call the Surgeon?"

"No, no," cried Zeluco; "the Surgeon cannot relieve me."

"I fear talking does you harm; I'll leave——"

"Pray stay," said Zeluco; "I shall be worse when you go.—Tell me, my friend, what fortune have you?"

Bertram named a very moderate sum.

"And with this you are happy!" exclaimed Zeluco.

"With this I am contented," replied Bertram; "and I am happy in many other particulars;—riches cannot give happiness."

"I'll be sworn they cannot," said Zeluco; "yet I am surprised that you, who have been abroad in the world, and have seen extensive scenes of life, could be contented with so little."

"Perhaps," replied Bertram, "the circumstance you mention has contributed to it; for, limited as my circumstances always were, I saw multitudes of my fellow-creatures, in every country where I have been, much poorer than myself; but what had more influence than any thing in keeping me from discontent was the remembrance of a maxim often repeated to me by my excellent father."

"What is that maxim?" said Zeluco.

" 'When you are disposed to be vain of your mental acquirements, Bertram,' said he, 'look up to those who are more accomplished than yourself, that you may be fired with emulation. But when you feel dissatisfied with your circumstances, look down on those beneath you, that you may learn contentment.' "

"But even of the small pittance you mention," said Zeluco, "you allowed a considerable proportion to your father."

"For that I can claim no merit," said Bertram; "it is only a proof that I am not a monster.—Ingratitude to a parent is the height of profligacy, including almost every kind of wickedness."

Zeluco started as if he had been stung by a serpent; the recollection of his own behaviour to his mother rushed on his mind with all the bitterness of remorse.

"I really am grieved, Signor," said Bertram, in a sympathising tone of voice, "to see you suffer so much."

"I do indeed suffer," said Zeluco, after a long and painful pause.

"I am sincerely sorry for it," resumed Bertram; "I wish I knew what would give you relief;—but the medical people will be here soon;—they perhaps——"

"No, no," interrupted Zeluco, "they cannot relieve me."

"I hope, my good Sir," continued Bertram, taking him by the hand, "that after the next dressing your wound will become easier."

"My wound *is* easier," said Zeluco with a voice of anguish; "but I have deeper wounds which their skill cannot reach."

"Alas!" said Bertram; "some mental affliction; the loss of some dear friend perhaps, cut off by a similar but more fatal accident than what has now befallen you.—Have patience, my good Sir," continued he, "reflection, and the soothing hand of time——"

"I tell you," interrupted Zeluco, in the accent of despair, "that I never had a friend; that time developes fresh sources of sorrow to me; and reflection drives me to madness."

Bertram, being greatly shocked, made no reply; and Zeluco, after a considerable interval, having recollected himself, said, with apparent composure, "I have been feverish and restless; I know not what I say; but the pain seems now to abate, and I feel myself drowsy. Pray, my good friend, leave me;—perhaps I may get a little sleep before the Surgeon arrives."

When Zeluco found himself alone—"Happy man!" said he, with a deep sigh, "who can look back with pleasure and self-approbation, and forward with tranquillity and hope.—What false estimates are formed by mankind! This Bertram they will consider as an unfortunate man, yet he has never been unhappy, and has found many sources of enjoyment unknown to me. I have been reckoned remarkably fortunate, although I have never known what happiness is.—His life has been devoted to duty, and mine to enjoyment; yet it is evident he has had more enjoyment in his pursuit than I ever had in mine; I begin to think that pleasure is most frequently found while we are on some more worthy pursuit, and missed by those who are in search of nothing else.—O fool! fool! to sacrifice the permanent rewards of virtue, without enjoying the only allurement of vice. After having passed my life hitherto in disquietude, I am now stretched on a bed of danger, without a friend, or one person I can trust, except this stranger, Bertram, on whom I have no claim but that of humanity and benevolence, which I myself have so little practised."

After these general reflexions on his past conduct, when he turned his thoughts to Laura, all his former causes of suspicion appeared in their native weakness; for anguish, languor, and humbled pride, presented her conduct in a more candid point of view, untinged by the medium of jealousy, and stripped of the glosses of Nerina. "Ah, that perfidious and accursed woman!" exclaimed he, endeavouring to relieve the anguish of his own conscience, by throwing the greater part of the guilt upon another; "I should never have behaved as I did to the most virtuous of women had I not been instigated by a dæmon."

In reflexions of this kind, and in resolutions of altering his system of life, Zeluco passed the time till the Surgeon arrived to dress his wound. Upon this second examination, the Surgeon was confirmed in the opinion he had formed at the first, that the wound was mortal; he thought proper to tell Zeluco, however, that it looked as well as he expected, and added other expressions of an encouraging nature.

When he returned to the parlour, he found Carlostein with Bertram, and immediately after Father Mulo also arrived.

The Surgeon then fairly told them, that although he had said nothing to his patient which would depress his spirits, yet he had now little or no hopes of his recovery.

"If that is your real opinion," said Father Mulo, "why did you not inform the unhappy gentleman of the danger he is in?"

"Because it is my business, Father," replied the Surgeon, "to cure him, if it is possible, and not to diminish the very small chance of his recovery by disagreeable news."

"You acted otherwise when you attended him formerly," replied Father Mulo; "for you then made him believe he was in more danger than was really the case."

"That is a remark, my reverend Father," said the Surgeon, "which I hardly could have expected from you; yet you are too learned in your profession not to know the *use of terror* in rendering mankind obedient. At the time you allude to, it was expedient to give this gentleman a strong idea of his danger, that he might submit to the regimen necessary for his cure; but at present it would disquiet him without being of any manner of use."

"Why, Sir," rejoined the Monk, "it may be of the greatest use."

"In my humble opinion," said the Surgeon, "it cannot be of the least, as I dare say those gentlemen will acknowledge when I declare, I do not think it possible he can live above two, or at most three days."

"Jesus Maria!" cried the Father, turning up his eyes; "why, for that very reason, Sir, it is your indispensable duty, on such an occasion, to tell him the truth."

"There is no cause for being in a heat, Father," said the Surgeon, bowing; "but I cannot think it consistent with *politeness* to tell a gentleman a disagreeable and unnecessary truth on *any* occasion.—I will refer it to this gentleman," continued he, addressing himself to Carlostein, who he knew had been at Paris, "whether in France such a thing would not be considered as quite unpardonable?"

"How it would be considered in France is very little to the purpose," said Father Mulo; "the important point is, how it will be considered in the other world, where the manner of thinking is very different from what it is in France."

"That is saying a severer thing of the other world than I should have expected from a man of your cloth," said the Surgeon.

"Will you, or will you not go directly and acquaint your patient of his danger?" said Father Mulo.

"You cannot possibly imagine, my good Father," replied the Surgeon, "that I will behave so *unpolitely* to a gentleman, especially when he is on the point of leaving the world."

"Why, Sir," rejoined the Father warmly, "by concealing his danger from him he may die without confession, and his soul of course will be lost for ever."

"As for his soul, and whether it shall be lost or saved, that is his affair, or your's if you please, my good Father; but it is mine not to deviate from the laws *of good-breeding* and *politeness.*" So saying, with a low bow to the company, he stepped into his carriage, and drove to Naples.

CHAPTER XCVIII.

Thou canst enter the dark cell
Where the vulture conscience slumbers,
And unarm'd by charming spell,
Or magic numbers,
Canst rouse her from her formidable sleep,
And bid her dart her raging talons deep.

MASON.[1]

ON his departure, Father Mulo shewed great impatience to be introduced into Zeluco's bed-chamber, and to acquaint him with the dangerous state he was in, that every ceremony requisite for his salvation might be performed without loss of time. Captain Seidlits and Bertram being Protestants, and thinking that the intended ceremony of confession would not do so much good as the Monk's abrupt manner of communicating the immediate necessity of it would do harm, endeavoured to persuade him to defer it a little, as Zeluco seemed disposed to sleep when the Surgeon left him. While they disputed the point, the Physician arrived; he had met with the Surgeon, who had informed him that there was now a certainty of the bowels being pierced in such a manner as to leave very little or no hopes of the patient's recovery.

It was the opinion of all present, that this information would come with more propriety from him than from Father Mulo: out of tenderness to the unhappy man, therefore, he was desired to convey it.

With whatever delicacy the annunciation was made by the Physician, it seemed greatly to shock the patient, for till that moment he had little doubt of his surviving. He immediately renewed all his curses and imprecations against Nerina, with such violence, that the Physician thought proper to withdraw. What repelled the Doctor attracted the Monk. Father Mulo entered, and began an exhortation which had by no means the same soporific effect on Zeluco with the former, of which we have made mention, but seemed on the contrary to throw him almost into convulsions. "You see, my worthy Father," said Bertram, "that he is in too much pain to listen to your admonitions at present; you had best leave him a little, and perhaps, after he has recovered the shock he has just received, he will be able to profit by your kind intentions."

After Father Mulo had been with difficulty removed, Zeluco desired to see the Physician again, of whom he inquired once more if there absolutely was no hope of his recovery. The Physician expressed much uneasiness at being obliged to confirm the opinion which he had already given; adding, that although the wound, from the different functions of the parts injured, was not so *immediately* mortal, yet he feared it would prove as *certainly* so as if the poignard had pierced his heart. Zeluco then asked, how long the Physician thought he could live? to which the other answered, There was reason to believe he could not suffer above two or three days longer.

Zeluco made no answer, and continued several hours without speaking a word to any body, but sometimes muttered indistinct sentences to himself, and shewed marks of impatience when any discourse was addressed to him. He at length inquired whether Captain Seidlits had been to call for him, and expressed a desire of seeing him. The Captain, who was just taking his horse to go to Naples, immediately returned, and was introduced to Zeluco's bed-chamber, every other person being requested to retire. Zeluco then addressed him to the following effect:

"Amidst many sources of regret, none affects me so sensibly, Sir, as my behaviour to your sister. Prompted by headstrong passion, I used every means I could devise, some of them not justifiable, to prevail on her to consent to a marriage to which I plainly saw she had a rooted dislike. When, by the continuation of my artifices, and the persuasion of her mother, she gave a reluctant consent, it might have been expected that, happy in the attainment of my wishes, I should have behaved with kindness and affection to her, however difficult it was for her to behave in the same manner towards me. The fact was otherwise: had *I* conducted myself with half the good nature to the wife I really esteemed, and even admired, that *she* did to the husband she disliked, I should not feel the remorse I now do. On recalling to my memory the whole of her conduct, I cannot charge her with a single impropriety; but in spite of her most blameless conduct, I plainly saw she did not love me; every duty of a wife which was in her power, she fulfilled; her affection it was impossible for her to place upon me, and this I had the injustice to consider as an injury. I indulged groundless suspicions, which were cherished, and new ones of the most profligate nature were suggested by a devil in the shape of a woman, who, by the wickedest artifices, entangled my affections, stimulated my passions into madness, and was the cause of even involuntary crimes. I earnestly hope she will be brought to the punishment her guilt and perfidy deserve. I earnestly hope—but let me drive her from my thoughts,—let no more time be lost, but let me at length make all the expiation in my power.

"I was willing that you should know, Sir, that these were my sentiments, which at a proper time you will communicate to the most virtuous and deserving of women."

Seidlits was affected. The wretched condition to which he saw the man reduced, had long since dissipated all his animosity; with a sympathising accent which was not very usual to him, and a sincerity which never forsook him, he expressed wishes for his recovery. Zeluco shook his head as if he thought that entirely out of the question, and Seidlits withdrew.

Zeluco then directed Bertram to send to Naples for his lawyer, who arrived in a short time, and received orders regarding his last will and deed, which were executed in due form, and signed by Zeluco the following morning, in the presence of certain persons who came from Naples at his request for that purpose.

CHAPTER XCIX.

Hail, piety! triumphant goodness, hail!
Hail, O prevailing, ever O prevail!
At thine entreaty, justice leaves to frown,
And wrath appeasing lays the thunder down;
The tender heart of yearning mercy burns.

PARNELL.[1]

THE following day Laura was informed for the first time of her husband's being wounded, and that he was thought to be in danger. She was much more shocked at the intelligence than Signora Sporza who communicated it thought she had reason to be. Signora Sporza proceeded to inform her of the particulars,—on what occasion the accident had happened, and at what place her husband was then lying; those circumstances made no alteration in the feelings of Laura. "May heaven in mercy," cried she, "prolong his life till he is better prepared for death! O how dreadful for him to be hurried into eternity now!" Signora Sporza insinuated something regarding the wretched prospect which Laura would have before her with such a husband, in case of his recovery. "Ah!" cried Laura, "is my temporal wretchedness to be put in the scale against his eternal misery? Almighty God, have compassion upon him!" exclaimed she, leaving Signora Sporza, and retiring to her bed-chamber, where she immediately fell upon her knees before a crucifix, and, every selfish consideration being annihilated in her breast, with all the sincerity of the most sublime piety, she poured forth her prayers to the fountain of mercy, that the life of her husband might be preserved, and that heaven might inspire him with repentance, and extend mercy to him.

Returning to the room where her mother now was with Signora Sporza, she inquired for her brother, and was told he had gone early the same morning to see Zeluco.—"Has my brother sent no message since?" said Laura. Madame de Seidlits and Signora Sporza looked at each other as if they hesitated what answer they should give. "I perceive you *have* heard from him," cried Laura. "Pray tell me how it is with the unfortunate man? Alas, I fear he is worse."

"It is surprising," said Signora Sporza, "that you shew so much concern for one, who, had this not happened, might have been the cause of your brother's or your friend Carlostein's death."

"Heaven be praised, they are both alive, and well," cried Laura, "whereas this unhappy man is—— Ah, tell me how he is? What account have you received from my brother?"—"The account is not favourable, my dear," said Madame de Seidlits. "Alas, he is gone," cried Laura. "Merciful heaven! has he been hurried off so suddenly?"—"Shew her the Captain's letter," said Madame de Seidlits. Signora Sporza then gave Laura a letter which she had received from Captain Seidlits a little before she informed Laura of what had befallen her husband, but which she abstained from shewing her upon seeing her so much affected. The letter was in the following words:

"Dear Madam,

"The surgeons in the presence of the physician have just examined the wound; their opinions are the same as before, notwithstanding some of the attendants had begun to entertain hopes of a favourable turn, on account of his being a great deal easier for these two hours than he has ever been since he received the wound; he seems very weak and languid; he sometimes mentions my sister, and once inquired if she was in the house, but in a manner as if he wished rather than expected it: on being told she was not—'How could I imagine she would?' said he. 'Why should she think of a wretch like me?' I own I am affected at the dismal condition of this poor man. Yet it were highly improper that Laura should see him; it would be disagreeable to her, and might have very bad effects on her health; I imagine it would be right, however, to let her know in general what has happened, and the danger in which he is. You will consult with Madame de Seidlits on this subject. I shall probably not leave this place till the evening.

"I am, &c. &c."

"I *will* go and see him," cried Laura, as soon as she had perused the letter. Madame de Seidlits and Signora Sporza endeavouring to dissuade her—"I conjure you, my dear mother," said she, "as you value the future peace of my mind, do not oppose me. My sincere sympathy may comfort him in this sad hour of——. Pray, do not oppose my inclination. Indeed, I must go." Fearing that stronger opposition might have worse consequences than the interview they dreaded, the carriage was ordered, and Laura, with her mother, immediately proceeded to the house in which Zeluco lay.

Laura passed the whole time in which they were on the road, in ejaculations and fervent prayers to Heaven, to look with an eye of mercy and compassion on her wretched husband.

When they arrived, Captain Seidlits came to the door of the carriage,—"O brother, how is he?" cried Laura. Seidlits shook his head, and was silent. "Ah, miserable man," exclaimed she, "he is gone!"—"It is but a few minutes," said Seidlits, "since he breathed his last."—"All-merciful God, have compassion on his soul!" cried Laura.

Madame de Seidlits then ordered the coach to return with them to Naples. Laura passed the interval of her return in the same manner she had done when going; and being arrived at Naples, she intreated her mother, instead of driving directly home, to stop at the church in which they usually heard mass, and there kneeling before the altar, she spent some time in mental prayer for the soul of her husband.

After which, she sent for the priest, and directed that a certain number of masses might be performed for the same pious purpose.

Any person, ignorant of the real case, would naturally have imagined that Laura had been the happiest of women in her marriage; for no woman deprived suddenly of the husband of her heart, was ever touched with more sincere anguish for her own misfortune, than the compassionate and benevolent breast of Laura was with generous solicitude for the eternal welfare of the husband who had used her so ill, and whom she had during his life detested.

When the last will of Zeluco came to be examined, which it was soon after his death, in the presence of two of the magistrates of Naples, of Captain Seidlits, Bertram, and others, it appeared that he had left his paternal estate in Sicily to a distant relation, who was his natural heir; and the rest of his fortune, which was of much greater value, to his widow, burdened with a few legacies, of which the principal was one of two thousand pistoles[2] to Bertram, and another of one thousand to Captain Seidlits.

The relation of Zeluco, to whom he left the estate, had always been neglected by him, and had not the least expectation of the good fortune which now befel him. On his arrival at Naples, Laura, having heard him spoken of as a man of worth, and that he had a family of children, made a considerable present in ready money to each of his children. She desired this gentleman also to give her a list of such of her husband's relations as were in bad circumstances; she had often made the same request to Zeluco with a view to assist them, but he had always evaded it, and shewed so much ill humour every time she made the request, that she never had been able to put her good intentions towards those people in execution. The legacy to Bertram was immediately paid, to which Laura made a considerable addition, and he soon after set out with Antonio for Geneva, esteemed and loved by all who had known him.

Laura also used her interest to have Nerina treated with lenity while she was detained in confinement; and as it was clear that she was not directly accessary to the murder of Zeluco, she used her influence to soften the minds of the judges, who were violently prejudiced against Nerina, so that she was at last liberated, and immediately after left Naples.

CHAPTER C.

The Conclusion.

Captain Seidlits's leave of absence was now nearly expired; he had often expressed his wishes that Madame de Seidlits and Laura would return to Germany with him; and urged, among other reasons, that it was expedient for his sister's health, and the tranquillity of her mind, that she were removed from a place where so many objects would awaken painful recollections; asserting, at the same time, that his mother-in-law and sister would now live much more happily in Germany than at Naples.

Signora Sporza had mentioned to Captain Seidlits her opinion that Carlostein was enamoured of his sister; but from a delicacy natural to the sex, she gave no hint concerning what she was as fully persuaded of, namely, Laura's partiality for him. Seidlits readily believed what he wished to be true, and the high idea he had of his friend, left him no doubt that their love was mutual.

Although Signora Sporza had communicated only one half of her opinion on this subject to the Captain, she unfolded the whole to Madame de Seidlits, who embraced the idea with great satisfaction; and the proposal of returning to Berlin became more agreeable to her from that moment.

It is probable that Laura relished the plan of ultimately settling in Germany fully as much as her mother; but she was solicitous to see certain distant relations of Zeluco established in a manner which he had pointed out, and in which she wished to assist them; the arrangements she had made for this purpose could not be effectual without her presence; nor could they be properly finished in the short interval that remained before her brother would be under the necessity of leaving Naples.

In the mean time Carlostein received a letter from the Prussian Minister at Berlin, acquainting him that he was nominated by the King to an office at Court which had just become vacant; and hinting that he would pay his court in a manner very acceptable to his Majesty, by returning immediately with his friend Seidlits, without waiting for the expiration of his own leave of absence.

The pleasure which Carlostein would have felt from the knowledge of this mark of his sovereign's favour, did not prevent the hint with which it was accompanied from distressing him greatly. His passion for Laura, and his admiration of her conduct, were higher now than ever; and she continued to behave to him with every proper mark of confidence and esteem. But he plainly perceived that the death of Zeluco, and the circumstances attending it, had made a strong impression upon her, and had put her into a frame of mind which ill accorded with the subject that engrossed his. He therefore abstained from any direct declaration of his sentiments to her, and it is probable would not have ventured on any thing of that nature so soon, had it not been for this letter from Berlin; but he could not think of leaving Naples in the same undecided state, with regard to what he considered as the most important object of his life.

Without mentioning the contents of the Minister's letter even to his friend Seidlits therefore, he watched an opportunity of speaking to Laura alone; and then in the warmest language of respectful love he declared his admiration of her virtues, the sincerity of his passion, and the supreme wish of his heart.

The whole of Carlostein's conduct left no doubt of his sincerity in the mind of Laura, yet she shewed some surprise at the precipitancy of these declarations.—"I would have waited," continued Carlostein, "for opportunities of giving stronger proofs than have hitherto been in my power of my attachment, before I had ventured to mention the honour and happiness to which I aspire, had I not received intelligence by yesterday's post, which fills my heart with ten thousand disquietudes."

"Intelligence!" cried Laura.

"Of the most cruel import," said Carlostein; "which threatens to tear me, when I least expected, from all my soul holds dear."

"What do you mean?" interrupted she, with an alarmed voice, and becoming instantly pale; "pray, explain yourself."

Carlostein then gave her the Minister's letter, which she took with an unsteady hand.

Having perused it, she said, "I see nothing here but good news; his Majesty I find has done you the honour to appoint you to an office near his person."

Carlostein pointed to the passage which hinted that the King expected him to return with Captain Seidlits, and renewing his addresses, declared, That his happiness depended on her; that if he could flatter himself with the hope of her favour, he would immediately write to the Minister in such terms as he had no doubt would procure him his Majesty's approbation of his prolonging his stay at Naples; that no consideration could prevail on——

Laura interrupted him, desiring that he would not insist on a subject which she thought unbecoming her, as she was then situated, to listen to, adding, That she would not attempt to conceal the sentiments of esteem which she had always felt for him; she acknowledged that she valued his good opinion and friendship above that of any other man; that with respect to the Minister's letter, she believed that such a hint as it contained, coming from a king or minister, was generally thought equivalent to a command; that he certainly could not consider it in any other light, and must act accordingly; that, independent of the Minister's letter, she imagined there were considerations which might determine him not to remain longer at Naples, and would oblige her not to receive his visits after the departure of her brother.

Carlostein seemed uneasy, and remained for some time silent after this declaration; but recollecting himself, he said, "Your brother, I believe, is not entirely without hopes that Madame de Seidlits may be persuaded to leave this country, and return immediately with him to Germany."

"My mother is so good as to assure me," said Laura, "that she will never separate herself from me, and certain affairs which I think indispensable will detain me a long time after my brother's departure."

"A long time!" repeated Carlostein with an accent of sorrow.

"I shall think it a long time," said she, with a smile and a look which conveyed happiness to the heart of Carlostein; "for I do assure you," added she, "that there is nothing which I wish more sincerely than to return to my native country."

Carlostein being now more assured in the hopes which he could not help indulging, did not venture to urge her farther; for, however favourable to him her sentiments might be, he plainly perceived that Laura thought it indelicate to admit of his addresses so soon after the death of her husband.

Immediately after leaving her, he communicated the Minister's letter to his friend Seidlits, informing him at the same time that he would accompany him home.

The interval between this time and that of their departure, was spent almost entirely with Madame de Seidlits, Signora Sporza, and Laura; Mr. N—— was very frequently of the parties, every individual of the society having the highest esteem for that gentleman.

Carlostein earnestly wished to correspond with Laura after he should leave Naples. As she stood at a window apart from the rest of the company, he seized the occasion, and solicited her permission to write to her. Laura beckoned to her mother, who having joined them, she said, "The Baron, my dear Madam, proposes to write to *us*, which I dare say will be very agreeable to you, and will prevent our having so much reason to regret my brother's want of punctuality."

Madame de Seidlits, although she was convinced that the proposal was intended for Laura only, answered, That *they* should be happy to hear from him as often as his leisure permitted him to write.

The day immediately preceding the departure of Carlostein and Seidlits was to this society mournful, but not unhappy; the flow of the virtuous and tender affections of the heart, of benevolence, gratitude, friendship, and love, are never without enjoyment.

——Who that bears
A human bosom, hath not often felt
How dear are all those ties which bind our race
In gentleness together, and how sweet
Their force, let Fortune's wayward hand the while
Be kind or cruel?—— Akenside.[3]

Targe and Buchanan supped together tête-à-tête the same evening; they felt a mutual regard for each other, a mutual sorrow at the thought of separating, and they mutually agreed that the best way of disposing of sorrow is to wash it away with wine.

When the night was far advanced, Buchanan rose, shook his friend very cordially by the hand, saying, "As you are to be up so early in the morning, I will not keep you any longer from your bed. So, God bless you, my dear Duncan."

"Nay, God shall not bless me these three hours," said Targe; "for as I am to rise so early, I do not think it worth while to go to bed this night: so sit you down on your seat, George, and let us have a fresh bottle without farther ceremony."

Buchanan, not being in a humour to dispute a point of this kind, immediately complied, slapping Targe upon the shoulder, and singing the following line from an old Scottish song:

> He's the king of good fellows, and *wale** of auld men;[1]

and never made another offer of taking leave, till he saw Targe ready to set out with his master and Carlostein.

The latter wrote from the various towns of Italy and Germany in the course of their journey to Berlin, addressing his letters alternately to Madame de Seidlits and to Laura. Captain Seidlits, who was not in love, and hated letter-writing, was contented with occasionally adding a postscript of a few sentences to Carlostein's letters.

This correspondence continued with equal regularity after their arrival at Berlin; and Carlostein, who had repeatedly begged of Madame de Seidlits to let him know the exact time when she and Laura intended to leave Italy, at length wrote to her that he should be happy to return to Naples, merely that he might have the honour of accompanying them to Berlin, and earnestly intreated her to use her influence with Laura to consent to that measure; for which, he said, he was assured of the king's permission.

Madame de Seidlits could not give a satisfactory answer for a considerable time, because, although Laura herself was impatient to leave Naples, yet she had resolved to remain till she settled her affairs in such a manner as not to require her returning: this she accomplished at length, having at the same time gratified her own benevolent and generous disposition by doing, what she called, justice to the relations of Zeluco, in a degree far beyond their expectations; and so as to procure their fervent prayers for her happiness, and the admiration of all who were acquainted with her behaviour.

At the approach of summer, Madame de Seidlits gave Carlostein the joyful news, that Laura and she were immediately to set out on their return to Germany, and that they could not think of putting him to the inconveniency of coming so far as Naples, especially as his friend Mr. N—— being to return at the same time to England, had offered to accompany them the whole way to Berlin; that they had agreed to accept of his escort, however, no farther than to Milan, which did not lead him out of the route that at all events he would have taken. At Milan, Madame de Seidlits added, she had a friend who

* Wale or choice. [Moore's note.]

would accompany them to Dresden; and as they could not reach that city for a considerable time after the Prussian reviews were over, she hoped it would not be inconvenient to Carlostein to meet them there, at a time which she mentioned, from whence he might accompany them to Berlin.

When Madame de Seidlits, Laura, and Signora Sporza, attended by Mr. N——, arrived at the inn at Milan, they were greatly surprised to find Carlostein and Captain Seidlits ready to hand them out of the carriage. Carlostein had received his mother-in-law's letter during the reviews; his friend and he set out for Milan soon after, and arrived some time before the ladies.

The unexpected appearance of these two gentlemen certainly occasioned an agreeable sensation to the company just arrived; but it was too strong for the sensibility of Laura. She could not help being a good deal agitated, the consciousness of which increased her confusion; every body observed the manner in which she was affected, and all had the delicacy to impute it to the fatigue of the journey. Laura soon recovered her usual serenity, and the whole party spent a few very happy weeks at Milan; during which Mr. N—— received a letter from the Earl his father, informing him that Miss Warren had consented to give her hand to his friend Steele, to the infinite satisfaction of old Mr. Transfer and Mrs. Steele, as well as that of Lady Elizabeth and the Earl himself; and that the nuptial ceremony was delayed till Mr. N——'s arrival in England, all parties being desirous that he should be present on that happy occasion.

This intelligence afforded much pleasure to Mr. N——, who had great good-will towards Steele, a very high esteem for Miss Warren, and was besides of a frame of mind which takes delight in the happiness of others. With this charming disposition Mr. N—— must have been highly gratified in the contemplation of the company he was then in, every individual of which was in a state of felicity.

Signora Sporza, who loved Laura with an affection little inferior to that of her mother, could not conceal her joy in the persuasion she had of the approaching happiness of her young friend; for it was now obvious that her marriage with Carlostein would take place soon after their arrival at Berlin. Captain Seidlits was delighted with the idea of his beloved sister's being united to the man whom of all mankind he loved and esteemed the most. The satisfaction of Madame de Seidlits, it may be easily supposed, was equal to both theirs. Laura and

Carlostein saw in each other all that their imaginations conceived as amiable; and they beheld in the faces of their surrounding friends a generous joy at the prospect of their felicity, and an impatience to see them speedily united.

It would have been difficult for Mr. N—— to have resisted the importunities of his friends and his own inclination, to accompany them to Berlin, had he not received the letter above mentioned from his father; this determined him to follow the plan he had formed on leaving Naples.

After expressing hopes of meeting again in Germany, or perhaps in England, Mr. N—— took a most affectionate leave of a company he so greatly esteemed, carrying with him the friendship and best wishes of every person in it. The ladies, escorted by Carlostein and Captain Seidlits, set out for Berlin on the same day that Mr. N—— took his route for Geneva, where he proposed to pass a few days with Bertram, and endeavour, if possible, to prevail on him to accompany him to England.

On his arrival at Turin, where he stopped only one night, he wrote an answer to his father's letter, the conclusion of which was in the following terms:

"I AM every day more confirmed in the truth of what you, my dear Sir, took so much pains to impress early on my mind, That misery is inseparable from vice, and that the concurrence of every fortunate circumstance cannot produce happiness, or even tranquillity, independent of conscious integrity.

"Had I harboured doubts on this head, the fate of a person with whom I had some acquaintance at Naples, would have served to dissipate them; the particulars of this wretched man's story I will communicate to you at more leisure. I need only mention at present, that with every advantage of person, birth, and fortune, and united by marriage to the most beautiful and accomplished woman I ever had the happiness of knowing, he was miserable through the whole of his life, entirely owing to the selfishness and depravity of his heart. I am equally convinced that it is not in the power of external circumstances to render that man, who is in possession of integrity and the blessing of an applauding conscience, so wretched as the person above alluded to often was in the midst of prosperity and apparent happiness. An acquaintance I lately formed with another person, a citizen of Geneva, of a character the reverse of the former, and who I am not without hopes of presenting to you at my return, tends to confirm this opinion, and to convince me that the Poet is right in declaring,

> "The broadest mirth unfeeling Folly wears,
> Less pleasing far than Virtue's very tears."[2]

THE END.

NOTES

title page: But why must those be thought to *'scape*, that feel / Those Rods of Scorpions, and those Whips of Steel / Which *Conscience* shakes, when she with Rage controuls, / And spreads amazing Terrors through their Souls? / Not sharp Revenge, nor *Hell* itself can find / A fiercer Torment than a *Guilty* Mind, / Which Day and Night doth dreadfully accuse. (Juvenal, Satire 13, lines 192-198. Translated by Thomas Creech for John Dryden's 1693 edition of translations of Juvenal.)

CHAPTER II

1 *epigraph* (p. 4): Alexander Pope, "Epistle to a Lady: Of the Characters of Women" (1735), lines 243-244.

2 *torpedo* (p. 5): An electric eel.

3 *Neapolitan dominions* (p. 5): As a Sicilian, Zeluco would naturally look to the Neapolitan service; for most of the eighteenth century, Sicily and Naples were ruled together by a Spanish Bourbon king.

4 *Tantalus* (p. 6): According to Greek mythology, Tantalus offered his son as food for the gods and was punished by being condemned to stand in a pool that receded whenever he attempted to drink, and below a fruit tree, the branches of which pulled away whenever he attempted to eat.

5 *Palermo* (p. 6): The capital city of Sicily.

CHAPTER III

1 *epigraph* (p. 8): Pope, "Epistle to a Lady: Of the Characters of Women," lines 163-164.

2 *Ægis of Minerva* (p. 8): Minerva was the goddess of wisdom; she supposedly wore the head of Medusa in the centre of her breastplate, or aegis, thereby repelling would-be suitors. Milton used Minerva's aegis as a symbol of chastity in his masque *Comus* (1634).

3 *eclat* (p. 10): A scandal or sensation.

CHAPTER IV

1 *mind in his visage* (p. 11): Shakespeare, *Othello* I.iii.252; Desdemona, justifying her love for Othello, proclaims that she "saw Othello's visage in his mind."

2 *a complaint which debarred him equally from pleasure and amusement* (p. 11): Presumably a venereal disease.

3 *How sharper than a serpent's tooth...* (p. 13): Shakespeare, *King Lear* I.iv.204-205.

CHAPTER V

1 *epigraph* (p. 14): Ovid, *Heroides*, Epistle II (Phyllis to Demophoon), lines 63-64: There is no glory in deceiving a credulous girl.

2 *sequin* (p. 15): A gold coin; from a French adaptation of the Italian word "zecchino."

3 *St. Rosolia* (p. 15): The Mother Church; St. Rosalia, a twelfth-century hermit, is the patron saint of Palermo. Moore's spelling, Rosolia, is a very unusual variant, although—perhaps not coincidentally—it is also the spelling that Matthew Lewis uses in *The Monk* (1796), in which St. Rosolia is the "patroness" of the innocent and doomed heroine Agnes.

CHAPTER VI

1 *Naples, Jerusalem, and the Two Sicilies* (p. 18): The Kingdom of the Two Sicilies was made up of Sicily itself and the Neapolitan dominions. The king at the time was Ferdinand IV (1751-1825), a Bourbon monarch, whose father was King of Spain and whose wife was the daughter of the Empress Maria Theresa.

CHAPTER VIII

1 *Hussars in the Emperor's service* (p. 25): A hussar is a member of a cavalry unit; the Emperor is Joseph II, who ruled the Holy Roman Empire, which at that time included much of central Europe, between 1765 and 1790.

CHAPTER IX

1 *epigraph* (p. 27): François, Duc de la Rochefoucauld, *Reflections; or, Sentences and Moral Maxims*. Maxim 174 (1665 edition): Natural ferocity makes fewer people cruel than does self-love. All further references are to the numbering of the 1665 edition, with a note indicating if the maxim was renumbered in later editions.

CHAPTER X

1 *Hispaniola* (p. 33): The large island southeast of Cuba containing the Dominican Republic and Haiti; in this period, colonial rule was split between France and Spain.

2 *. . . after he had gained her heart* (p. 34): This tactic was also used by Valmont, the seductive anti-hero of Choderlos de Laclos' 1782 novel *Les Liaisons Dangereuses*.

CHAPTER XI

1 *epigraph* (p. 35): Jean de la Fontaine, *Fables* (1671), Book VIII, number 6, "Women and the Secret," lines 1-4: Nothing weighs as heavily as a secret;

it is difficult for women to carry it far. And I even know a number of men who are women in this respect.

2 *first favour . . . last* (p. 36): The "last favour" a woman could grant was sexual intercourse.

3 *dark lanthorn* (p. 37): A lantern with a single opening that could be covered, hiding the light.

CHAPTER XII

1 *mummery* (p. 41): Foolish pretense or playacting.

CHAPTER XIII

1 *epigraph* (p. 42): La Rochefoucauld, Maxim 306: One hardly finds anybody who is ungrateful when one is able to do favours.

2 *Fame, wealth, and honour . . .* (p. 44): Alexander Pope, "Eloisa to Abelard" (1717), line 80.

CHAPTER XIV

1 *epigraph* (p. 44): Tacitus, *Agricola*, Book I, par. 42: It is human nature to hate those you have injured.

2 *Caligula and Nero* (p. 48): Caligula was emperor of Rome from 37-41 A.D.; Nero, Caligula's nephew, ruled from 54-68. Both were notorious for their cruelty and depravity.

CHAPTER XV

1 *epigraph* (p. 49): Shakespeare, *Measure for Measure*, II.ii.141-149.

2 *capuchin* (p. 50): A name given to priests in the Franciscan order, derived from the distinctive hood that they wear.

3 *Honny* (p. 50): Honey; an endearment intended to suggest the speaker's Irish accent, as is the colloquial use of "after" in the previous sentence.

4 *snug birth* (p. 51): That is, in this context, a berth or bed.

5 *b——de* (p. 51): Presumably "backside."

CHAPTER XVI

1 *coup de main* (p. 53): A sudden, unexpected attack.

CHAPTER XVII

1 *quantity of blood he lost . . .* (p. 56): Bleeding a patient as a treatment for physical or mental disorder was standard medical practice in the eighteenth century.

2 *wormwood* (p. 57): A bitter herb, used both medicinally and as an insect or pest repellent.

CHAPTER XVIII

1 *epigraph* (p. 58): Helen Maria Williams, "Poem on the Bill Lately Passed for Regulating the Slave-Trade" (1788), 149-152.

2 . . . *happier than the common labourers in England* (p. 59): Debates about the morality of the slave trade and the slave economies of the West Indies became increasingly vehement during the second half of the eighteenth century. There was a strong abolitionist movement, but there were also loud voices—especially among the West Indian planters—arguing the pro-slavery position along the lines sketched out here by Zeluco.

3 . . . *that you English are a most lugubrious race* . . . (p. 59): The idea that the English were a peculiarly melancholy people was an eighteenth-century commonplace. For a representative expression of this idea, see Mme de Staël's essay "De la plaisanterie anglaise" (1800), in which she argues that even the comic writers in England are marked by their nation's gravity and melancholy.

4 *the slave trade is authorized by the Bible* (p. 60): Eighteenth-century defenders of slavery frequently appealed to the Bible for justification, referring both to the frequent allusions to slavery as a practice in the Old Testament and to specific passages such as Noah's curse of Ham (Genesis 9:20-25).

5 *Blessed are the merciful* (p. 60): The first two lines are from the Sermon on the Mount (5:7 and 7:12); the third is Matthew 11:28.

CHAPTER XXI

1 *although unjustly accused of Judaism* . . . (p. 76): Laws were passed at the end of the fifteenth century expelling the Jewish population from Spain (1492) and Portugal (1497). Those who converted to Christianity and remained in the country were subject to suspicion and persecution, even long after the expulsion; legal distinctions between the descendants of Jewish converts and "old Christians" were not lifted until 1772.

CHAPTER XXII

1 *epigraph* (p. 78): Samuel Butler, *Hudibras*, Part One (1663), Canto I, lines 213-214 (the original reads "they" rather than "he.")

2 *challenge him honourably* (p. 81): That is, to issue a formal challenge to a duel. Although such a duel would have been seen as more "honourable" than the assassination that the Portuguese merchant presumably has in mind, a man who killed an opponent in a duel would still, under English law, be charged with murder.

3 *Pater Noster* . . . *Rosary* (p. 83): The Lord's Prayer, the Hail Mary, and the Creed, or statement of faith. A rosary is a string of beads used to count prayers.

4 *gospel of St. Matthew* (p. 83): Again, the reference is to the Sermon on the Mount.

CHAPTER XXIII

1 *epigraph* (p. 84): Pope, *Essay on Man* (1733-34), Epistle IV, lines 185-188.

CHAPTER XXIV

1 *epigraph* (p. 85): Pope, "Epistle to a Lady: Of the Characters of Women," line 30.

2 *never dined but with a club of their countrymen* (p. 88): The supposed tendency of English travelers on the Grand Tour to resist mixing with the inhabitants of the country in which they were living was the subject of some disapproving commentary at the time; see, for example, a letter by Lord Chesterfield to his son (Sept. 12, 1749) in which he mocks xenophobic English travelers and advises the young man to avoid them. Moore himself commented approvingly in his account of his travels in Italy that his pupil, the young Duke of Hamilton, spent his evenings at *conversazioni* in the company of "almost all" of those "of a certain rank in Rome" (*A View of Society and Manners in Italy*, 2 vols, 1787 [4th ed.], 1: 383).

3 *Basta!* (p. 89): Enough!

CHAPTER XXV

1 *epigraph* (p. 91): Ovid, *Tristia*, Book I, Elegy 5, line 4: Worthy of a happier, not better, husband.

CHAPTER XXVI

1 *epigraph* (p. 96): La Rochefoucauld, Maxim 296 (later renumbered as 56 in the first supplement): We enjoy discerning the characters of others, but we don't like others to discern ours.

2 *cousin-german* (p. 96): First cousin.

3 *Campagna Felice* (p. 96): The countryside around Naples.

CHAPTER XXVII

1 *epigraph* (p. 100): Jean de La Bruyère, *Les Caractères* (1688), "Des Jugements" (Chapter 12): Physiognomy is not a rule that allows us to judge people, but it can serve as a basis for conjecture.

CHAPTER XXVIII

1 *epigraph* (p. 102): Ovid, *Metamorphoses*, Book IX, line 456: She did not at first understand this fire.

2 *Frederic* (p. 103): Frederick II ("the Great") of Prussia (1712-1786); the War of the Bavarian Succession took place in 1778-79 and was mainly a territorial skirmish between Austria and Prussia.

3 *Le Brun's picture of the family of Darius* . . . (p. 104): Charles Le Brun (1619-1690) was a painter patronized by the French court under Louis XIV. "The Family of Darius before Alexander" depicts Alexander the Great's triumph over the Persian emperor.

4 *A violet in the youth* . . . (p. 104): Shakespeare. [Moore's note.] The lines are from *Hamlet* I.iii.7-10.

CHAPTER XXIX

1 *epigraph* (p. 105): Horace, *Odes*, Book III, Ode 10, lines 11-12: You are not Penelope, distant with suitors and born to Etruscan parents.

2 *a country where a free system of gallantry prevails* . . . (p. 106): British writers of this period tended to be scandalized by what they perceived as the looser Italian sexual manners. In particular, the custom of aristocratic married women having a regular escort—the cicisbeo or cavalier servente—was seen as implying an un-English degree of license in female behaviour.

3 *Montaigne has said* . . . (p. 108): Essais de Montaigne, livre II. chap. xi. [Moore's note.] Michel de Montaigne, *Essays*, Book 2, chapter 9, "Of Cruelty": I fear that nature herself has given man an instinct for inhumanity.

CHAPTER XXX

1 *L'amour propre* . . . (p. 109): La Rochefoucauld, Maxim 157 (renumbered as 28 in the first supplement): Self-love prevents him whom we flatter from ever being him who flatters us most.

CHAPTER XXXI

1 *epigraph* (p. 111): Juvenal, Satire 13, lines 239-240: It is generally the nature of evildoers to be fickle and unreliable.

CHAPTER XXXII

1 . . . *self-interest would be found at the bottom of the crucible* (p. 114): A philosophical position associated most strongly with the thought of Thomas Hobbes (1588-1679) and Bernard Mandeville (1670-1733); the belief that self-interest lay at the bottom of all human actions was, however, vigorously attacked by many of the Scottish Enlightenment thinkers whose ideas underlie Moore's work.

CHAPTER XXXIV

1 *epigraph* (p. 120): La Rochefoucauld, Maxim 374: If we think we love a mistress for her own sake, we're deceiving ourselves.

CHAPTER XXXV

1 *epigraph* (p. 125): Virgil, *Aeneid*, Book I, lines 657-658: "[Venus] new counsels tries, and new designs prepares" (in Dryden's 1697 translation).

CHAPTER XXXVI

1 *epigraph* (p. 128): James Thomson, *The Castle of Indolence* (1748), stanza 69.

2 *Epicuri de grege porcus* (p. 129): One of the hogs of Epicurus. Horace, *Epistles* Book I, no. 4. The phrase is used proverbially to mean an exquisite banquet; in the original context, Horace is describing his own well-fed contentment.

3 *culverin* (p. 130): A light cannon.

CHAPTER XXXVII

1 *epigraph* (p. 132): Samuel Butler, *Hudibras*, Part One, Canto I, lines 157-162

CHAPTER XXXVIII

1 *epigraph* (p. 135): Samuel Butler, *Hudibras*, Part Three (1680), Canto II, lines 447-452.

2 *Transubstantiation* (p. 135): The belief that the bread and wine of the communion service actually become, rather than merely symbolize, the body and blood of Christ. The belief in Transubstantiation is one of the major doctrinal points differentiating Catholicism from Protestantism.

3 *Koningsburg* (p. 137): More usually Königsberg; the capital of East Prussia (now the Russian city Kaliningrad). In the eighteenth century, it was one of the major German university towns.

4 *Massacre of St. Bartholomy . . . Duke of Alva* (p. 139): The St. Bartholomew's Day Massacre (24 August 1572) was a series of attacks by Catholic mobs on French Protestants. The violence was believed to have been orchestrated by the government (possibly even by the queen, Catherine de Medici). Estimates of the numbers killed vary wildly, but nationwide, tens of thousands died. The Duke of Alva (1508-1582) was sent, in 1567, by Philip II of Spain (1527-1598) to crush Protestant resistance in the Spanish-controlled Netherlands. His harsh governorship—he supposedly boasted of being responsible for eighteen thousand executions—made him one of the most hated figures in Protestant Europe. Philip himself was notorious in England both as the consort—briefly—of the Catholic queen Mary and as one of the major threats to Mary's Protestant successor Elizabeth. The defeat of the Spanish Armada, which was launched against England in 1588, and the subsequent destruction of many of the retreating ships during a storm, was seen by Protestants as a providential defeat of Philip's Catholicism.

5 *nescire malum est* (p. 140): Horace, *Satires* 2: 6, line 73: It is bad not to know it.

CHAPTER XXXIX

1 *epigraph* (p. 142): Virgil, *The Aeneid*, Book VI, line 332: "Revolving anxious thoughts within his breast" (Dryden).

2 *Hochkirchen* (p. 142): A 1758 battle in which the Prussians, under Frederick the Great, were defeated by the Austrians; Leopold von Daun (1705-1766) was the Austrian commander.

3 *you shall educate your daughters in your way of thinking, as our sons shall be educated in mine* (p. 145): This was the compromise famously proposed in Samuel Richardson's *Sir Charles Grandison* (1753-54), in which the staunchly Protestant Sir Charles attempts (unsuccessfully) to arrange a marriage with an Italian Catholic.

4 *Keith* (p. 146): James Keith (1696-1758) was a Scottish soldier who became a field marshal in the Prussian service; he was killed at the Battle of Hochkirch.

5 *Prince Francis of Brunswic* (p. 146): The brother of the Prussian queen.

CHAPTER XL

1 *epigraph* (p. 147): James Beattie, *The Minstrel; or, The Progress of Genius* (1771), Book I, Stanza 29. The original reads "I," not "man," in the first line.

2 *short war respecting the succession of Bavaria* (p. 147): See note 2 to Chapter XXVIII, p. 103.

3 *il n'y a que la mort . . .* (p. 148): Only death is certain, and yet we act as if it were the one thing that were uncertain. The maxim does not in fact appear in collections of La Rochefoucauld's work, although it is attributed to him (without a specific source) in some nineteenth-century dictionaries of quotations. It is, however, included in a volume that brings together several French aphorists of the period: *Reflexions ou Sentences et Maximes Morales de Monsieur de la Rochefoucault* [sic], *Maximes de Madame la Marquise de Sablé, Pensées Diverses de M.L.D et les Maximes Chretiennes de M. ***** (Amsterdam, 1712). It is there listed as number 51 of M.L.D.'s *Pensées Diverses*.

4 *mother-in-law* (p. 149): That is, his stepmother (a common usage at the time).

CHAPTER XLI

1 *epigraph* (p. 150): La Rochefoucauld, Maxim 257: Gravity is a mysterious way of carrying the body, intended to hide faults of the mind.

2 *Balaam the son of Beor* (p. 152): Numbers 23:5-10.

CHAPTER XLII

1 *epigraph* (p. 153): John Milton, *Paradise Lost* (1667), Book IX, lines 510-516.

CHAPTER XLIII

1 *epigraph* (p. 155): La Rochefoucauld, Maxim 69: If there is a love that is pure and unmixed with our other passions, it is hidden at the very bottom of our hearts, and we are ignorant of it ourselves.

2 *Magdeburg* (p. 156): Potsdam was the main residence of Frederick the Great; Magdeburg was another city in the Prussian territories.

CHAPTER XLIV

1 *servant out of livery* (p. 157): That is, a servant who did not wear a special outfit marking his servitude. Generally, lower-ranking servants, such as footmen, would wear livery, while a valet or personal attendant would not.

2 *Mr. Bronze* (p. 158): Bronze, at the time, was a slang term for impudence or excessive self-assurance.

3 *intaglios* (p. 158): A stone or other hard material engraved with a design.

4 *whether it was painted by Guido or by Rheni, he could not recollect* (p. 159): Guido Reni (1575-1642), an Italian baroque artist, was born in Bologna and painted a number of Madonnas, several of which are still displayed in his home city. The painting Moore has in mind may be "The Madonna and Child in Glory and the Patron Saints" (now owned by the Pinacoteca Nazionale di Bologna), which Moore had seen during his own visit to Bologna.

5 *bon mot* (p. 159): A joke or witticism.

6 *haberdashing* (p. 159): Selling miscellaneous small goods.

7 *Vultus nimium lubricus aspici* (p. 160): Horace, *Odes*, Book I, Ode 19 ("To Glycera"): I gaze at the shining beauty of her face.

8 *Hinc illæ lachrymæ* (p. 160): Terence, *Andria*, I. 126: Hence these tears.

9 *Her mother did so before her* (p. 161): An adaptation of the refrain of a song published in a number of late eighteenth-century songbooks, in which a flirtatious girl plans her romantic conquests, concluding each stanza with the line "My mother did so before me." (See, for example, *The Scots Nightingale; or, Edinburgh Vocal Miscellany* [1778], 17-18.)

10 *Quo semel . . . Testa diu* (p. 161): Horace, *Epistles*, Book I, number 2, lines 69-70. A jar retains for a very long time the odour of whatever it first held.

11 *Heu, quoties fidem mutatosque Deos flebit* (p. 161): Horace, *Odes*, Book I, Ode 5, lines 5-6 ("To Pyrrha"): Ah! He will frequently lament his faith and altered Gods.

12 *Quid enim ratione timemus aut cupimus* (p. 161): Juvenal, Satire X, line 4: What do we reasonably fear or desire?

CHAPTER XLV

1 *epigraph* (p. 163): La Rochefoucauld, Maxim 218: Hypocrisy is the homage that vice pays to virtue.
2 *The God of Hell . . . get himself a wife* (p. 163): A reference to the myth of Hades, Greek god of the underworld, who forcibly abducted Persephone and made her his queen.
3 *Mount Vesuvius* (p. 166): Vesuvius, the volcano that destroyed Pompeii in 79 A.D., had become active again in the mid-17th century, following a few hundred years of quiescence. Despite—or because of—a number of eruptions in the later eighteenth century, including one in 1779 and another in 1794, it was a major tourist site during this period. (See Appendix B.)
4 *Portici* (p. 166): A town on the Bay of Naples at the foot of Mount Vesuvius.

CHAPTER XLVI

1 *epigraph* (p. 166): *Paradise Lost*, Book IX, lines 171-172.
2 *St. Januarius* (p. 169): The patron saint of Naples (died c. 305); his dried blood, preserved in a glass phial, is supposed to liquefy when brought out annually on his feast day. Moore provides an amused, sceptical eyewitness account of the supposed miracle in his account of his tour of Italy.
3 *St. Dominic* (p. 169): A Spanish saint (c. 1170-1221), founder of the Dominican order of monks.
4 *hallooing* (p. 169): "Hollowing" in the first edition; emended to "hallooing" in later editions.
5 *ad ogni uccello suo nido è bello* (p. 170): Proverbial; each bird finds its own nest beautiful.
6 *broken on the wheel* (p. 170): A form of judicial torture in which the criminal is bound to the spokes of a wheel while his limbs are broken by blows from the executioner.

CHAPTER XLVII

1 *a Physician and Surgeon* (p. 172): In the eighteenth century, physicians received formal medical training in a university and would have been of different and higher status than surgeons, who learned their practical skills through apprenticeships outside the traditional university system.
2 *Lascia far' a Sant' Antonio* (p. 172): Leave it to Saint Anthony.
3 *secundem artem* (p. 173): According to accepted practice.
4 *Benè repondisti* (p. 173): Well said.
5 *a Russian fleet in the Mediterranean* (p. 173): Most likely an allusion to the attempts by Turkey to enlist the support of various European powers to keep the Russian fleet out of the Mediterranean during the Russo-Turkish war of 1787-91. (See *The Annual Register* for 1788, pp. 23-24, 32-33, 58-63).

6 *vi prego di scusarmi* (p. 173): Please excuse me, Sir.
7 *A fe di Dio . . . non m'è venuto mai in pensiero* (p. 173): By God, Sir, that never came into my thought.
8 *ptisan* (p. 173): An obsolete spelling of tisane, a medicinal, usually herbal, drink.

CHAPTER XLVIII

1 *eleve* (p. 176): Student.

CHAPTER XLIX

1 *epigraph* (p. 178): Horace, Satire X, line 10: Do not tire the ear with a weight of words.
2 *Lamentations of Jeremiah* (p. 179): One of the books of the Old Testament; it contains what is said to be the lament of the prophet Jeremiah on the destruction of the temple in Jerusalem.
3 *lachrymæ Christi* (p. 181): Literally, the tears of Christ; a wine that is native to the Naples region and made from grapes grown along the slopes of Mount Vesuvius.
4 *Prometheus . . . vulture* (p. 183): In classical mythology, the Titan who brought fire to mankind and who was then punished by being chained to a rock, where he suffered the daily torment of having his liver torn out and eaten by an eagle or (in some versions) a vulture.

CHAPTER L

1 *epigraph* (p. 184): La Rochefoucauld, Maxim 115: It is as easy to deceive oneself without realizing it as it is difficult to deceive others without their noticing it.

CHAPTER LI

1 *epigraph* (p. 187): La Rochefoucauld, Maxim 443: The most violent passions sometimes allow us respite, but vanity torments us constantly.

CHAPTER LII

1 *epigraph* (p. 192): Pope, "Epistle to a Lady: Of the Characters of Women," lines 277-278.

CHAPTER LIII

1 *epigraph* (p. 195): Ovid, *Metamorphoses*, Book VIII, line 508: Now piety and a mother's name shatter my soul.

CHAPTER LIV

1 *epigraph* (p. 199): Virgil, *The Aeneid*, Book X, lines 812: "In rash attempts, beyond thy tender age, / Betray'd by pious love" (Dryden).

CHAPTER LV

1 *epigraph* (p. 203): Pope, *The Dunciad* (1744), Book IV, line 321. The original reads "All classic learning lost…"

2 *Pantheon . . . St. Peter's* (p. 204): The Pantheon, a classical temple dedicated to all the gods, and St. Peter's Basilica, the Vatican cathedral, are two of the major tourist sites in Rome and would have been highlights for Englishmen on the Grand Tour.

3 *ounces* (p. 204): A coin, either silver or gold, used in the Sicilian territories in the later eighteenth and early nineteenth centuries.

4 *Tivoli, Frescatio, and other places . . .* (p. 206): Tivoli, Frascati, and Albano are all scenic towns outside Rome; they were popular rural retreats for visitors to Rome in the eighteenth century. (See Appendix B.)

CHAPTER LVI

1 *parterres* (p. 209): An area of ornamental flower beds in a formal garden.

2 *Piccadilly* (p. 209): A street in central London that included both residential and commercial developments.

3 *Lombard-street* (p. 209): One of the main commercial streets in the City of London.

4 *Piazzas* (p. 209): Used here not in the more usual sense of an open square but in the now obsolete sense of a covered walkway in front of a building.

5 *rotunda* (p. 210): A circular building; in this case, a summerhouse.

6 *Venus or Vulcan* (p. 210): Venus was the Roman goddess of love and beauty; Vulcan, her husband, was the lame and ugly god of metal-working.

7 *Mars . . . Neptune* (p. 211): Mars, the Roman god of war, would have been depicted clad in a tunic, which Transfer reads as a Highlander's kilt; likewise, he misreads the trident that is one of the traditional attributes of Neptune, god of the ocean, as a pitchfork.

CHAPTER LVII

1 *epigraph* (p. 214): Horace, *The Art of Poetry*, line 162: He amuses himself with his horse and dogs.

2 *procure him a cornetcy of dragoons* (p. 215): A lower-level commission in a cavalry regiment. It was usual eighteenth-century practice to purchase military commissions.

3 *curate* (p. 216): A clergyman hired to assist a more senior minister. Steele anticipates being given a living—that is, the charge of a parish and the income arising from tithes and from certain rents and fees—and then hiring a substitute to do the actual preaching. One of the frequent complaints about the eighteenth-century church was that ministers were

deputizing their responsibilities to underpaid curates, as Steele matter-of-factly plans to do.

4 *dubbed* (p. 217): Invested with an honour or title; slightly mocking in this context.

CHAPTER LVIII

1 *epigraph* (p. 217): Horace, *The Art of Poetry*, line 196: It should favour the good and give friendly counsel.

CHAPTER LIX

1 *epigraph* (p. 220): Matthew Prior, *Alma: or, The Progress of the Mind* (1718), Canto I, lines 319-320.

CHAPTER LX

1 *epigraph* (p. 224): Jean de la Bruyère, *Les Caractères*, "Du cœur" (Chapter 4). To regret the absence of a loved one is pleasant compared to living with a person one hates.

CHAPTER LXI

1 *son-in-law* (p. 227): That is, her stepson.

2 *Cardinal Bernis* (p. 228): François-Joachim de Pierre de Bernis (1715-1794) was the French ambassador to Rome in the 1770s and 1780s. Moore attended one of his assemblies and was much impressed by him; see Appendix B.

3 *war between France and Great Britain* (p. 229): Presumably the Seven Years' War (1756-1763), although France and Britain also fought against each other during the American War of Independence.

CHAPTER LXII

1 *A vous ma sœur* (p. 232): For you, sister.

2 *Volontiers, frere* (p. 232): Willingly, brother.

3 *virtù* (p. 233): In this context, works of art, antiquities or other subjects of connoisseurship.

4 *Ciceroné* (p. 233): A hired tourist guide.

5 *Herculaneum and Pompeia* (p. 233): The ruins of Herculaneum and Pompeii were first discovered in 1738 and 1748 respectively; more or less haphazard excavations were carried out throughout the century.

6 *firelock and bayonet* (p. 233): A firelock is a type of musket and was standard equipment for an eighteenth-century foot soldier; a bayonet was often attached to the firelock for use in hand-to-hand combat.

CHAPTER LXIII

1 *epigraph* (p. 234): Ovid, *Metamorphoses*, Book XIV, lines 108-109: whose right hand has used the sword and whose piety is shown by the flame.

2 *Duncan Targe* (p. 234): A targe is a small shield.

3 *condescension* (p. 234): Courtesy to a social inferior; in this context, it did not have the negative connotations it does today.

4 *surety* (p. 234): That is, he promised to be liable for his relative's debts in the event of default.

5 *rebellion broke out in the year 1745* (p. 235): The last major Jacobite uprising, in which Charles Edward Stuart ("Bonnie Prince Charlie") attempted to reclaim the British throne for his father. The uprising was decisively defeated at the Battle of Culloden, near Inverness, on 16 April 1746.

CHAPTER LXIV

1 *epigraph* (p. 237): Oliver Goldsmith, "The Traveller" (1764), lines 203-208.

2 *hotch potch and minched collops* (p. 237): Hotch potch is a type of stew, usually made with lamb or mutton; minched collops are minced meat.

3 *songs of Lochaber, Gilderoy . . . Flowers of the Forest* (p. 237): All popular Scottish songs, much reprinted in song books of the day.

4 *Covenanters . . . remembered with horror in that part of the country* (p. 237): The Covenanters were radical Protestants who rejected any sort of government authority over religion. They were severely persecuted in the later seventeenth century, especially in their southwestern strongholds.

5 *neighbouring university* (p. 237): The "neighbouring university" in the west of Scotland would be Glasgow, at which Moore himself studied.

6 *Castle of St. Elmo . . . Holyrood House* (p. 238): The Castle of St. Elmo is a major fortification in Naples; Edinburgh's castle, built on a hill, dominates the city and offers panoramic views of it. Holyrood was the palace of the Scottish kings, while the palace of Caserta, which was designed as a major showpiece and was still under construction when Moore himself visited it, was the seat of the later Neapolitan kings. (See Appendix B.)

7 *. . . live like a private person in Italy* (p. 238): A reference to Charles Edward Stuart, then living in exile in Italy; Moore and the Duke of Hamilton saw—but did not meet—him during their tour.

8 *. . . limitations made at the Revolution* (p. 238): The so-called Glorious Revolution of 1688, in which the Catholic monarch James II and VII was deposed by Parliament in favour of his Protestant daughter Mary and her husband William of Orange. James and his wife and son took refuge in France, as Buchanan later notes.

9 *king James and his descendants* (p. 238): Targe, in this case, would not be referring to either of the English kings named James but rather to the

exiled son of James II, who was considered by his supporters to be the rightful James III. He was the father of Charles Edward Stuart.

10 *iniquity of fathers upon their children* (p. 240): Numbers 14:18.

11 *"The Land of Cakes"* (p. 240): A name for Scotland; it alludes to the use of oatcakes, rather than bread, as a staple food.

12 *perfect garden* (p. 241): A phrase applied to Naples in at least one guidebook of the period (Henry Swinburne, *Travels in the Two Sicilies* [1783-85], 20). By way of contrast, travellers in Scotland—most famously, perhaps, Samuel Johnson—tended to focus on the country's barrenness.

13 *the Union* (p. 241): The Union of the Parliaments of Scotland and England in 1707.

14 *pas* (p. 242): That is, take precedence over.

15 *George Buchanan* (p. 242): George Buchanan (1506-1582) was perhaps the most distinguished scholar of the sixteenth-century Scottish court; he was also an accomplished poet, though he wrote only Latin verse. He was the tutor of Mary Queen of Scots (and one of her half-brothers) as well as of Mary's son James. Initially an admirer and supporter of the queen, Buchanan became one of her most bitter attackers following his conversion to Protestantism.

16 *Illa pharetratis est propria gloria Scotis . . .* (p. 243): The poem was written to celebrate the 1558 marriage of Mary Queen of Scots and the French Dauphin; an eighteenth-century English language version, *Mary Queen of Scots Dowary* (Edinburgh, 1711), translates the lines quoted here as follows:

> These Glories do the Valiant *Scots* commend
> To which no Rival Nation must pretend
> In hunting bravely they surround the woods
> And swimming with Address, divide the Floods
> Nor heat, nor cold, nor hunger them appall
> Their bodies are their Countries firmest wall
> Ther Love of fame is than of Life more great
> What once they promise is of fixed fate:
> None more the Rights of Friendship do regard
> And love the person, not his bright reward.
> By such like Arts when Bloody War was hurl'd
> With fatal Desolation throw the World
> And Nations did their antient Laws forgo
> Because the Victors needs would have it so
> The *Scots* alone their pristine Right enjoy'd
> And Liberty for which they Nobly Dy'd
> Here stopt the Gothick fury, here was crost
> The *Saxon* Brav'ries, and the *Danish* lust,
> And all th' efforts which *Normandy* could boast. (pp. 7-8)

17 *murderer of her husband* (p. 244): Mary Stuart's second husband, Henry Darnley, died when the house in which he was sleeping was blown up. She

was soon after abducted and, by her own account, forced into marriage with Lord Bothwell, who was suspected of being involved in Darnley's murder. Mary's enemies, at the time and since, accused her of colluding with her third husband in her second husband's death, charges that were vehemently contested by her supporters.

CHAPTER LXV

1 *epigraph* (p. 245): Virgil, *Aeneid* Book X, line 782: his eyes / He cast to heav'n, on Argos thinks and dies (Dryden).

2 *Gentleman and a gentleman-farmer* (p. 245): A lord's "gentleman" would be his valet, or personal attendant; a gentleman farmer would be either a small landowner who had income other than from farming or a farmer wealthy enough to hire others to work his land. Neither, of course, would be considered a gentleman in any strict sense of the term. Settling differences by boxing—as opposed to the sword—would be considered very ungentlemanly; Sir Walter Scott's short story "The Two Drovers" turns on this point.

3 *farrier* (p. 246): A specialist in caring for injuries to horses.

4 *give our own fish-guts to our own sea-mews* (p. 247): A Scottish proverb: give whatever benefits you have to disperse to those near at hand.

5 *met death with such serene and dignified courage* (p. 248): Mary Queen of Scots spent the last two decades of her life imprisoned in England; she was executed in 1587 for allegedly plotting to overthrow Elizabeth I. Accounts of her execution emphasize the serenity with which she met her death.

CHAPTER LXVI

1 *epigraph* (p. 249): Horace, *Odes*, Book I, Ode 33, lines 10-12: it pleases her to put unequal spirits under her bronze yoke.

CHAPTER LXVII

1 *epigraph* (p. 253): La Rochefoucauld, Maxim 70: There is no disguise that can hide love for long, nor that can feign it where it does not exist.

2 *Why did he not draw it?* (p. 255): By not drawing his sword, Carlostein would be implying that his opponent was not worthy of the usual gentlemanly courtesies of a proper duel.

3 *a mode of avenging injuries . . .* (p. 256): That is, assassination.

CHAPTER LXVIII

1 *epigraph* (p. 256): Ovid, *Tristia*, Book III, Elegy 7, lines 13-14: For nature gave you modesty and the rare gift of genius.

2 *Puzzoli . . . other ruins of that seat of ancient luxury* (p. 257): Pozzuoli is a town near Naples; Baia (or Baiae), which is across the Bay of Naples, was a resort town for the Roman emperors. The Ponte di Caligula is the

remnant of a Roman causeway; it takes its name from a famous exploit of the Emperor Caligula, who supposedly set up a pontoon bridge so that he could ride his horse across the bay. The Baths of Nero, in Baiae, were part of the usual tourist sites, as was a Roman-era ruin in Bacoli, near Baiae, that was traditionally (though wrongly) said to be the tomb of Agrippina, sister of Caligula and mother of Nero.

CHAPTER LXIX

1 *epigraph* (p. 261): Mark Akenside, "Ode: Against Suspicion" (1745), stanza 4.
2 *Trifles, light as air . . . as proofs of Holy Writ* (p. 262): *Othello*, III.iii.325-327.
3 *fine essenced mignon* (p. 264): A perfumed, delicate dandy.

CHAPTER LXX

1 *un homme fait exprès pour être cocu* (p. 265): Here is a man made especially to be cuckolded.

CHAPTER LXXI

1 *pretended* (p. 269): Claimed—there is no implication that he has merely invented the friendship.
2 *coast of Malabar* (p. 269): The southwestern coast of India.
3 *virtuoso* (p. 269): In this context, a scholar or antiquarian.

CHAPTER LXXII

1 *never write by the post to any but strangers* (p. 269): In the eighteenth century, the recipient would have paid the cost of delivery of anything sent by the public post.
2 *from Carlisle to Newcastle* (p. 271): The Firth of Clyde, the estuary where the Clyde River meets the sea, is near Glasgow; the Firth of Forth is near Edinburgh. The Antonine Wall, completed in 144 A.D. was built between them to keep the northern tribes out of Roman territories. Hadrian's Wall, built between 122 and 130 A.D. marked what was then the northern boundary of the Roman Empire in Britain and ran from Carlisle in the Northwest to Newcastle in the Northeast.
3 *David Rizzio* (p. 272): David Rizzio (c. 1533-1566) was an Italian musician and a favourite of Mary Queen of Scots, though much disliked by her courtiers. He was dragged from her private rooms at Holyrood and stabbed to death in the antechamber by a group of Scots nobles backed by Mary's husband Lord Darnley.
4 *Loch Lomond* (p. 272): Loch Lomond is a famously beautiful lake north of Glasgow.
5 *not quite so sublime as Edinburgh* (p. 272): Freestone is a soft stone—usually sandstone or limestone—that can easily be carved. The height of

Edinburgh buildings was much commented upon by eighteenth-century visitors to the city.

6 *show and gewgawry* (p. 272): Gawdy or paltry ornamentation.

7 *Selkirk* (p. 273): A small town in the Scottish Borders.

8 *St. Andrew's Day* (p. 273): St. Andrew, one of the twelve Apostles, is the patron saint of Scotland; his feast day, November 30, was a traditional day of celebration.

9 *nemo me impune lacessit* (p. 274): No man harms me with impunity.

10 *Enrick* (p. 274): The River Enrick runs through Glen Urquhart in the Scottish Highlands.

CHAPTER LXXIII

1 *che . . . Engliterr* (p. 274): The writer's misspellings of chez le ("at the residence of") and Angleterre.

2 *Dowfiness* (p. 275): That is, the dauphiness (or dauphine), the wife of the heir to the French throne. The last pre-Revolutionary dauphine was Marie Antoinette (1755-1793), who became queen in 1774, suggesting a slightly earlier date for the action of the novel than some of the book's other references to current events (such as the mention of the Russian fleet going into the Mediterranean), which imply a date closer to the time of writing.

3 *"the gray mare is the better horse"* (p. 275): Proverbial: the woman is superior to her husband.

4 *something like a leek* (p. 275): The reference is to the Salic law, according to which a woman could not inherit the French throne as queen in her own right.

5 *bull* (p. 275): An Irish bull is a paradoxical or self-contradictory statement.

6 *Parlivoos* (p. 276): Parlez-vous (do you speak…?): slang for a Frenchman.

7 *man-midwife* (p. 276): The development, around this time, of obstetrics as a medical speciality, replacing traditional midwifery, was very controversial, and the so-called "men-midwives" were a frequent target of mockery and satire.

8 *cortillong* (p. 276): That is, a cotillion, an elaborate, formal dance originating in France but increasingly popular in England during the eighteenth century.

9 *Jangdarms* (p. 276): Gendarmes; at this time, members of a military police unit. The Horse Guards are a British military unit whose responsibilities include protecting the monarch.

10 *Tower of London* (p. 277): St. Paul's Cathedral, the Monument (a freestanding stone column built to commemorate the Great Fire of 1666) and the lions and other wild animals held (until the nineteenth century) in the menagerie at the Tower of London were all among the major tourist sights of London during this period.

11 *pappy mashee* (p. 277): Papier-mâché, which was often used for decorative objects, such as tobacco boxes, at the time.

CHAPTER LXXV

1 *Belvidere Apollo* (p. 281): A Greek statue of Apollo, now on display in the Vatican. It was considered by many eighteenth-century commentators to epitomize perfect masculine beauty.

2 *ami du voyage* (p. 282): Travel companion.

CHAPTER LXXVI

1 (p. 284): Anna Laetitia Barbauld's edition for *The British Novelists* (1810, 1820) cuts this repetition and reads as follows: "Distressing, however, as his ill-temper was, it did not seem so dreadful, as was already observed, in the eyes of his wife, as the returns of fondness with which he was occasionally seized."

CHAPTER LXXVII

1 *epigraph* (p. 284): Virgil, *The Aeneid*, Book XI, lines 340-341: "Noble his mother was, and near the throne; / But, what his father's parentage, unknown" (Dryden).

CHAPTER LXXVIII

1 *epigraph* (p. 287): La Rochefoucauld, Maxim 324: There is more self-love than love in jealousy.

2 *albeit, unused to the blushing mood* (p. 288): A paraphrase of *Othello* V.ii.345: "Albeit unused to the melting mood."

3 *two Calabrias* (p. 289): Calabria is the Italian region extending south of Naples towards Sicily.

4 *Casserta* (p. 290): That is, Caserta Vecchia, the town just outside Naples that was the site of the grand palace of Caserta.

CHAPTER LXXX

1 *epigraph* (p. 295): Horace, *Odes*, Book I, Ode 5, lines 12-13: Unhappy those yet untried admirers for whom you shine.

CHAPTER LXXXII

1 *epigraph* (p. 301): Pope, "Epistle to a Lady: Of the Characters of Women," lines 47-48.

CHAPTER LXXXIII

1 *epigraph* (p. 303): Virgil, *The Aeneid*, Book XI, line 337: "who grudged, long since, / The rising glories" (Dryden).

CHAPTER LXXXIV

1 *separation upon proper terms* (p. 308): That is, since a formal divorce was impossible, she would be ensured a proper financial settlement in a private, quasi-legal arrangement.

CHAPTER LXXXV

1 *episode* (p. 310): John Dryden, "Sigismonda and Guiscardo," in *Fables Ancient and Modern* (1700), lines 256-258.

2 *Pausilippo* (p. 310): A mountain just outside Naples; it is the location of the supposed tomb of Virgil, another popular tourist site. (See Appendix B).

CHAPTER LXXXVI

1 *epigraph* (p. 312): *Hamlet* III.ii.75-81.

2 *Whatsoever a man soweth that shall he reap* (p. 316): Galatians 6:7.

CHAPTER LXXXVII

1 *epigraph* (p. 319): James Thomson, *The Seasons* (1730), "Summer," lines 1635-1645. (Moore omits the line "Boastless, as now descends the silent dew," which follows "Diffusing kind beneficence around" in the original.)

CHAPTER LXXXVIII

1 *epigraph* (p. 324): Tacitus, *Annals*, Book IV, par. 71: Though slow in considering matters, when driven to act, he joined harsh words with terrible deeds. (Moore changes the tense of the original.)

2 *additional strength from the commands of Nerina* (p. 324): Barbauld's edition adds the following paragraph at this point: "As the transactions of his past life often presented themselves to Zeluco's mind in painful review, it is probable, that the suspicions which, with a vindictive spirit, he had formerly raised in the breast of the Portuguese, now afforded him no very agreeable reflection; and the anguish which Zeluco himself felt, from the idea of his not being the father of Laura's child, seems a just retribution for the thorns which, on a similar occasion, he had planted in the breast of another."

CHAPTER LXXXIX

1 *epigraph* (p. 327): La Rochefoucauld, Maxim 180. Our penitence is not so much regret for the wrong that we have done as it is fear for that which might befall us.

CHAPTER XC

1 *epigraph* (p. 331): Thomas Gray, "Ode on a Distant Prospect of Eton College" (1747), lines 61-70.

2 (p. 333): The Author has been informed that this distinction between the effect of audible and of visible objects, has been criticized as unnatural. He is convinced, however, that he has observed it in people in the state of mind in which Laura is here represented, and in tracing it, he endeavoured to copy faithfully from nature. Not to recur to the trite, though true, remark of,

> Segnius irritant animos demissa per aurem
> Quam quae sunt oculis subjecta fidelibus;

I conceive that the eye may continue to do its office of conveying intelligence to the mind, long after the latter has ceased to derive any information from words. The communication in the first case is natural and immediate. The set-end requires the intervention of a medium. [Moore's note.] The quotation is from Horace's *Art of Poetry*: Our minds are less affected by what we hear than by what we see with our own eyes (180-181). The footnote was not included in the 1789 edition; it first appeared in the third edition (1790).

CHAPTER XCI

1 *epigraph* (p. 335): Shakespeare, *The Tempest*, III.iii.95-97.
2 *mere grimace* (p. 335): That is, as hypocritical pretence.

CHAPTER XCII

1 *epigraph* (p. 338): Virgil, *The Aeneid*, Book I, lines 464-465, 495: "And with an empty picture fed his mind … His eyes / Fix'd on the walls with wonder and surprise" (Dryden).
2 *Massacre of the Innocents* (p. 339): The murder of all the children in Bethlehem under the age of two, ordered by King Herod in an attempt to kill the newborn Jesus (see Matthew 2:16). It was a much-painted subject; Moore would probably have seen the version by Guido Reni (painted 1611) in Bologna, in which two soldiers brandishing daggers attack infants, although neither is shown grasping the throats of the children in question. Charles Le Brun's 1647 painting of the subject shows a soldier with his hand on a child's throat, although he does not hold a poignard; a famous version by Nicholas Poussin (1630-31) shows a soldier with his foot on the throat of a child that he is apparently about to decapitate with a sword.

CHAPTER XCIII

1 *epigraph* (p. 343): Virgil, *The Aeneid*, Book IX, line 427: "'Me! me!' he cried—'turn all your swords alone / On me'" (Dryden).

2 *ecclesiastical state* (p. 346): The Vatican. If Seidlits killed a man in a duel, he would have to flee the legal authorities of the Kingdom of Naples.
3 *conscience, which makes cowards of us all* (p. 348): *Hamlet* III.i.83.

CHAPTER XCIV

1 *epigraph* (p. 349): Shakespeare, *King Henry VI, Part 2*, III.ii.234-237.
2 *Corso* (p. 351): Generally, a street; in this case, a fashionable promenade.

CHAPTER XCV

1 *epigraph* (p. 353): Terence, *The Eunuch*, V. iv (lines 931-933): a means by which a young man can learn the customs and manners of prostitutes, so that afterwards he will always despise them.
2 (p. 354): The lines are from William Mason, *Elfrida: A Dramatic Poem* (1752).
3 *chaste Susanna* (p. 356): In the Book of Daniel, a young woman is observed while bathing by two lecherous judges who attempt to coerce her into having sex; when she refuses to give in, they accuse her of adultery, but she is triumphantly vindicated in a trial.
4 *rope-dancer* (p. 357): An acrobat.

CHAPTER XCVII

1 *epigraph* (p. 362): Pope, *Essay on Man*, Epistle IV, lines 167-169.

CHAPTER XCVIII

1 *epigraph* (p. 367): William Mason, *Caractacus: A Dramatic Poem* (1759).

CHAPTER XCIX

1 *epigraph* (p. 369): Thomas Parnell, "Deborah," lines 367-371. (Published 1758 in *Posthumous Works*).
2 *pistoles* (p. 372): A gold coin.
3 *Akenside* (p. 376): Mark Akenside, *The Pleasures of the Imagination* (1744), Book II, lines 609-614.

CHAPTER C

1 *He's the king of good fellows, and wale of auld men* (p. 377): The song is called "Auld Rob Morris"; it was included in Allan Ramsay's *Tea-Table Miscellany* (1724) and frequently reprinted thereafter.
2 *The broadest mirth . . .* (p. 380): Alexander Pope, *An Essay on Man*, Epistle I, lines 314-315.

APPENDIX A:

Anna Laetitia Barbauld and Mary Wollstonecraft on *Zeluco*

1. From Anna Laetitia Barbauld, ed. *Zeluco. The British Novelists*, vol. 34 (London, 1820), i-vii.

Among modern novels of English growth, few possess greater excellence than *Zeluco* [….] The novel of *Zeluco* [...] is one of the most entertaining we possess, from the real knowledge of the world which it displays, and the humour and spirit of the dialogue. It also excites no small degree of interest. The scene is laid in Italy, and the familiarity of the author with foreign manners enabled him to diversify his productions with descriptions and characters beyond the range of our own domestic society. This work is formed on the singular plan of presenting a hero of the story, if hero he may be called, who is a finished model of depravity. Zeluco is painted as radically vicious, without the intermixture of any one good quality; but if the perfectly virtuous character is to be considered, for so we are sometimes told, as out of nature, "a faultless monster, whom the world ne'er saw," it is to be hoped a perfectly vicious character is at least as extraordinary a production. There is no degree of atrocity to which human nature may not arrive from time and circumstances; want and misery harden the heart as well as the features; but it is scarcely conceivable that a youth coming into life with every advantage of fortune and person and abilities, should never feel his heart expand, amongst his youthful companions, into some kindly feeling, bearing at least the semblance of benevolence. The whole character has a darker tinge of villainy than is usually found in this country: it is drawn with great strength, and proceeds in a regular progress of depravity, from his squeezing the sparrow to death when a child, to the incident of the deadly grasp which he gives his own child; a circumstance of horror new and truly tragical. It reaches, like the character of Satan, the sublime of guilt. The attachment between the wife and the lover is managed with great delicacy; yet if she preserves her virtue, it may be said to be *heureusement*: and amiable and excellent as they both are, it may admit of a doubt how far it is favourable to good morals to interest the reader in a passion for a married woman, however unhappily she may be yoked. The character of Signora Sporza is drawn with spirit; it is quite a foreign one. The conversation-pieces abound in humour, and show that intimate knowledge of real life and characters which mere sentimental novels are generally deficient in. The quarrel between the two Scotchmen about the character of their queen Mary is infinitely amusing; and while it touches the national character and national partialities with the hand of a friend, it at the same time exhibits them in a light truly comic. Father Mulo is amusing; and there is a good deal of light humour in the story of Rosolia, or rather in the manner of telling it. Much knowledge of the world and good sense are exhibited in the dialogues between the hot-headed young protestant divine and the colonel, whose wife he insists upon converting: the death-bed of the latter is affecting, and exhibits views of piety if not vivid, at least calm and rational. It must by no means be forgotten that, to the honour of the author, there is a great deal of forcible reasoning against the slave-trade; and there is no stroke in Sterne of a finer pathos than the answer of the dying Hanno, when he was told that his cruel master would broil in hell to all eternity,—"I hope he will not suffer so long." The young may melt into tears at *Julia Mandeville* and the *Man of Feeling*; the romantic will love to shudder at *Udolpho*; but those of mature age, who know what human nature is, will take up again and again Dr. Moore's *Zeluco*.

2. Mary Wollstonecraft, review of *Zeluco* in *The Analytical Review*, vol. 5 (1789), 99-102. (All long quotations from the book included in the review have been omitted.)

The involuntary homage which every human being pays to virtue, when not under the immediate influence of a particular passion, has often been remarked, and it may be mentioned as a striking instance, that the productions of men of abilities have not had their wonted effect, when they have attempted to render the history of a decided villain interesting. Humanity binds the whole family on earth together by the same sympathies; and when not warped by some mean motive, we are unwilling to become acquainted with a heart we instinctively despise; besides, in the character of a villain, there is so much deformity and want of order, that the contemplation of it fatigues, while it raises disgust in the mind. From the vicious hero of a tale, the reader turns to the episodes, for who would watch the ravages of a pestilence, if not impelled by anxious concern for the fate of those within its reach: attention and interest thus divided become weak, and want that enthusiastic vital warmth, which makes the heart fix a conviction in the understanding. But if it is granted that the history of a depraved selfish being cannot be a finished production, yet it may be a very useful one, and convey a forcible unbroken moral, the decided result of reason and feeling. Aware of this difficulty, the author has given a second title to his book, and a short account of his design, in the first chapter, which we shall transcribe [....]

The author never loses sight of his design, and by that means preserves a unity in the whole; which the detached episodes, and long discussions of important subjects, abruptly introduced, would otherwise destroy. In the character of Zeluco, there are some masterly touches, and his anxious restless hours, pourtrays in lively colours, the misery which vice naturally produces:—while in the various interspersed views of life, the virtues of many individuals, are ingeniously contrasted with the bloated monster, who stands forward in the foreground.

After pointing out the purport of the work, we shall not attempt to abridge the incidents which give it force; but only mention the parts we were most struck with, and select two extracts. Though we have observed throughout that discrimination of character, which is the result of a sound understanding, yet we think a few are overcharged or rather caricatured. We now proceed to point out a few striking passages. The remonstrance of an old officer, on the treatment of soldiers.—Remarks on the slave trade.—A Portuguese character.—The conduct and conversation of a physician.—The character of an Italian lady.—The conduct of two monks, and of a protestant clergyman.—Bertram's system of morality. [....]

This respectable publication, for which the public are indebted to the ingenious Dr. Moore, author of travels in France, Italy, &c. will afford many striking lessons to youth; and they will here find the purest morality, levelled to their understandings, enforced by familiar arguments and forcible examples; we therefore warmly recommend it to their attentive perusal, instead of the insignificant sentimental productions, which the press teems with, under the form of novels. Sound principles are here inculcated, and fixed on a simple steady basis, on reason rather than transient feelings; virtue is taught, but not in that romantic style, which too often borders on vice—or requires more sense to discriminate the nice distinctions, than can be expected from an inexperienced reader.

To give a more compleat specimen of the work, we had intended to insert Bertram's System of Morality, but for want of room, are obliged to defer it to our next number.

APPENDIX B:

John Moore on Italy[1]

1. On Guido Reni and the art of Bologna (1: 310-312).

Next to Rome itself, there is, perhaps, no town in the world so rich in paintings as Bologna. The churches and palaces, besides many admired pieces by other masters, are full of the works of the great masters who were natives of this city. I must not lead you among those master-pieces; it is not for so poor a judge as I am to point the peculiar excellencies of the Caraccis, Dominichino, Albano, or compare the energy of Guercino's pencil with the grace of Guido's. With regard to the last, I shall venture to say, that the graceful air of his young men, the elegant forms, and mild persuasive devotion, of his Madonas; the art with which, to all the inviting loveliness of female features, he joins all the gentleness and modesty which belong to the female character, are the peculiar excellencies of this charming painter.

It requires no knowledge in the art of painting, no connoisseurship, to discover those beauties in the works of Guido; all who have eyes, and a heart, must see and feel them. But the picture more admired than all the rest, and considered, by the judges, as his master-piece, owes its eminence to a different kind of merit; it can claim none from any of the circumstances above enumerated. The piece I mean is in the Sampieri palace, and distinguished by a silk curtain, which hangs before it. The subject is, the Repentance of St. Peter, and consists of two figures, that of the Saint who weeps, and a young apostle who endeavours to comfort him. The only picture at Bologna, which can dispute celebrity with this, is that of St. Cecilia, in the church of St. Georgio in Monte. This picture is greatly praised by Mr. Addison, and is reckoned one of Raphael's capital pieces. If I had nothing else to convince me that I had no judgment in painting, this would be sufficient. I have examined it over and over with great attention, and a real desire of discovering its superlative merit; and I have the mortification to find, that I cannot

---

1 All excerpts are taken from the 1781 first edition of *A View of Society and Manners in Italy*.

perceive it.—After this confession, I presume you will not desire to hear any thing farther from me on the subject of painting.

2. On Mount Vesuvius (2: 204-216)

I have made two visits to Mount Vesuvius, the first in company with your acquaintance Mr. N———t. Leaving the carriage at Herculaneum, we mounted mules, and were attended by three men, whose business it is to accompany strangers up the mountain. Being arrived at a hermitage, called Il Salvatore, we found the road so broken and rough, that we thought proper to leave the mules at that place, which is inhabited by a French hermit. The poor man must have a very bad opinion of mankind, to choose the mouth of Mount Vesuvius for his nearest neighbour, in preference to their society. From the hermitage we walked over various fields of lava, which have burst out at different periods. These seemed to be perfectly well known to our guides, who mentioned their different dates as we passed. The latest appeared, before we left Rome, about two months ago; it was, however, but inconsiderable in comparison of other eruptions, there having been no bursting of the crater, or of the side of the mountain, as in the eruption of 1767, so well described by Sir William Hamilton; but only a boiling over of lava from the mouth of the volcano, and that not in excessive quantity; for it had done no damage to the vineyards or cultivated parts of the mountain, having reached no farther than the old black lava on which soil had not as yet been formed. I was surprised to see this lava of the last eruption still smoking, and in some places, where a considerable quantity was confined in a kind of deep path like a dry ditch, and shaded from the light of the Sun, it appeared of a glowing red colour. In other places, notwithstanding its being perfectly black and solid, it still retained such a degree of heat, that we could not stand upon it for any considerable time, but were obliged very frequently to step on the ground, or on older lava, to cool our feet. We had advanced a good way on a large piece of the latest lava, which was perfectly black and hard, and seemed cooler than the rest; while from this we looked at a stream of liquid lava, which flowed sluggishly along a hollow way at some distance. I accidentally threw my eyes below my feet, and perceived something, which mightily discomposed my contemplations. This was a small stream of the same matter, gliding to one side from beneath the black crust on which we stood. The idea of this crust giving way, and our sinking into the glowing liquid which it covered, made us shift our ground with great precipitation; which one of our guides observing, he called out, "Animo, animo, Signori;" and immediately jumped on the incrustation we had abandoned, and danced above it, to shew that it was sufficiently strong, and that we had no reason to be afraid. We afterwards threw large stones of the heaviest kind we could find, into this rivulet, on whose surface they floated like cork in water; and on thrusting a stick into the stream, it required a considerable exertion of strength to make it enter. About this time the day began to overcast; this destroyed our hopes of enjoying the view from the top of the mountain, and we were not tempted to ascend any farther.

Some time after, I went to the summit with another party;—but I think it fair to inform you, that I have nothing new to say on the subject of volcanos, nor any philosophical remarks to make upon lavas [....]

Those who wish to view Mount Vesuvius to the greatest advantage, must begin their expedition in the evening; and the darker the succeeding night happens to be, so much the better. By the time our company had arrived at the top of the mountain, there was hardly any other light than that which issued by interrupted flashes from the volcano.

Exclusive of those periods when there are actual eruptions, the appearance and quantity of what issues from the mountain are very various; sometimes, for a long space of time together, it seems in a state of almost perfect tranquillity; nothing but a small quantity of smoke ascending from the volcano, as if that vast magazine of fuel, which has kept it alive for so many ages, was at last exhausted, and nothing remained but the dying embers; then, perhaps, when least expected, the cloud of smoke thickens, and is intermixed with flame; at other times, quantities of pumice stone and ashes are thrown up with a kind of hissing noise. For near a week the mountain has been more turbulent than it has been since the small eruption, or rather boiling over of lava, which took place about two months ago; and while we remained at the top, the explosions were of sufficient importance to satisfy our curiosity to the utmost. They appeared much more considerable there than we had imagined while at a greater distance; each of them was preceded by a noise like thunder within the mountain; a column of thick black smoke then issued out with great rapidity, followed by a blaze of flame; and immediately after, a shower of cinders and ashes, or red hot stones, were thrown into the sky. This was succeeded by a calm of a few minutes, during which nothing much issued but a moderate quantity of smoke and flame, which gradually increased, and terminated in thunder and explosion as before. These accesses and intervals continued with varied force while we remained.

When we first arrived, our guides placed us at a reasonable distance from the mouth of the volcano, and on the side from which the wind came, so that we were no way incommoded by the smoke. In this situation the wind also bore to the opposite side the cinders, ashes, and other fiery substances, which were thrown up; and we ran no danger of being hurt, except when the explosion was very violent, and when red hot stones, and such heavy substances, were thrown like sky-rockets, with a great noise and prodigious force, into the air; and even these make such a flaming appearance, and take so much time in descending, that they are easily avoided [....]

After having remained some time at the place where they were posted by the guides, our company grew bolder, as they became more familiarised to the object. Some made the circuit of the volcano, and by that means increased the risque of being wounded by the stones thrown out. Your young friend Jack was a good deal hurt by a fall, as he ran to avoid a large portion of some fiery substance, which seemed to be falling directly on his head.

Considering the rash and frolicsome disposition of some who visit this mountain, it is very remarkable that so few fatal accidents happen. I have heard of young English gentlemen betting, who should venture farthest, or remain longest, near the mouth of the Volcano. A very dreadful event had nearly taken place while our company remained. The bank, if it may be so called, on which some of them had stood when they looked into the Volcano, actually fell in before we left the summit of the mountain. This made an impression on all present, and inclined them to abandon so treacherous a neighbourhood. The steep hill of dross and cinders, which we had found it so difficult to ascend, we descended in a twinkling; but, as the night was uncommonly dark, we had much trouble in passing over the rough valley between that and the Hermitage, near which the mules waited. I ought to be ashamed, however, to mention the fatigue of this expedition; for two ladies, natives of Geneva, formed part of the company. One of them, big with child, accompanied her husband as far as the Hermitage, and was then with difficulty persuaded to go back; the other actually went to the summit, and returned with the rest of the company.

3. On Tourist Sites near Naples (2: 290-300)

The tomb of Virgil is on the mountain of Pausilippo, a little above the grotto of that name; you ascend to it by a narrow path which runs through a vineyard; it is overgrown with ivy leaves and shaded with branches, shrubs, and bushes; an ancient bay-tree, with infinite propriety, overhangs it. Many a solitary walk have I taken to this place. The earth, which contains his ashes, we expect to find clothed in the brightest verdure. Viewed from the magic spot, the objects which adorn the bay become doubly interesting. The Poet's verses are here recollected with additional pleasure; the verses of Virgil are interwoven in our minds with a thousand interesting ideas, with the memory of our boyish years, or the sportive scenes of childhood, of our earliest friends and companions, many of whom are now dead; and those who still live, and for whom we retain the first impression of affection, are at such a distance as renders the hopes of seeing them again very uncertain. No wonder, therefore, when in a contemplative mood, that our steps are often directed to a spot so well calculated to create and cherish sentiments congenial with the state of our mind. But then comes an antiquarian, who with his odious doubts, disturbs the pleasing source of our enjoyment; and from the fair and delightful fields of fancy, conveys us in a moment to a dark, barren, and comfortless desert;—he *doubts*, whether this be the real place where the ashes of Virgil were deposited; and tells us an unsatisfactory story about the other side of the bay, and that he is rather inclined to believe that the Poet was buried somewhere there, without fixing on any particular spot.

Would to heaven those doubters would keep their minds to themselves, and not ruffle the tranquillity of believers!

But, after all, why should not this be the real tomb of Virgil? Why should the enthusiasts, who delight in pilgrimages to this spot, be deprived of that pleasure? Why should the Poet's ghost be allowed to wander along the dreary banks of Styx, till the antiquarians erect a cenotaph in his honour? Even they acknowledge that he was buried on this bay, and near Naples; and tradition has fixed on this spot, which, exclusive of other presumptions, is a much stronger evidence in its favour than their vague conjectures against it [....]

The town of Puzzoli, and its environs, present such a number of objects, worthy of the attention of the antiquarian, the natural philosopher, and the classic scholar, that to describe all with the minuteness they deserve, would fill volumes.

The Temple of Jupiter Serapis at Puzzoli, is accounted a very interesting monument of antiquity; being quite different from the Roman and Greek temples, and built in the manner of the Asiatics, probably by the Egyptian and Asiatic merchants settled at Puzzoli, which was the great emporium of Italy, until the Romans built Ostia and Antium [....]

The bay between Puzzoli and Baia is about a league in breadth. In crossing this in a boat, you see the ruins called Ponte di Caligula, from their being thought the remains of a bridge which Caligula attempted to build across. They are by others, with more probability, thought to be the ruins of a mole built with arches. Having passed over this gulph, a new field of curiosities presents itself. The baths and prisons of Nero, the tomb of Agrippina, the temples of Venus, of Diana, and of Mercury, and the ruins of the ancient city of Cumæ; but no vestiges now remain of many of those magnificent villas which adorned this luxurious coast, nor even of the town of Baia. The whole of this beauteous bay, formerly the seat of pleasure, and, at one period, the most populous spot in Italy, is now very thinly inhabited; and the contrast is still stronger between the antient opulence and present poverty, than between the numbers of its antient and present inhabitants. It must be acknowledged, that we can hardly look around us, in any part of this world, without perceiving objects which, to a contemplative mind, convey reflections on the instability of grandeur, and the sad vicissitudes and reverses to which human affairs are liable; but *here* those objects are so numerous, and so striking, that they must make an impression on the most careless passenger.

4. On Caserta (2: 301-305)

The palace at Casserta was begun in the year 1750, after a plan of Vanvitelli; the work is now carried on under the direction of his son. While the present King of Spain remained at Naples, there were generally about two thousand workmen employed; at present there are about five hundred. It will be finished in a few years, and will then, unquestionably, be one of the most spacious and magnificent palaces in Europe. It has been said, that London is too large a capital for the island of Great Britain; and it has been compared to a turgid head placed on an emaciated body. The palace of Casserta also seems out of proportion with the revenues of this kingdom. it is not, properly speaking, a head too large for the body; but rather an ornament, by much too expensive and bulky for either head or body. This palace is situated about sixteen miles north from Naples, on the plain where ancient Capua stood. It was thought prudent to found a building, on which such sums of money were to be lavished, at a considerable distance from Mount Vesuvius [....]

Among the workmen employed in finishing this palace and the gardens, there are one hundred and fifty Africans; for as the King of Naples is constantly at war with the Barbary States, he always has a number of their sailors prisoners, all of whom are immediately employed as slaves in the gallies, or at some public work. There are present at Casserta, about the same number of Christian slaves; all of these have been condemned to this servitude for some crime, some of them for the greatest of all crimes; they are, however, better clothed and fed than the Africans. This is done, no doubt, in honour of the Christian religion, and to demonstrate that Christians, even after they have been found guilty of the blackest crimes, are worthier men, and more deserving of lenity, than Mahometan prisoners, however innocent they may be in all *other* respects.

5. On the Neapolitan character (2: 314-317)

[Classical authors] tell us, the very air in this part of Italy is repugnant to that kind of constitution, and that turn of mind, of which it would be peculiarly happy for nuns to be possessed. Propertius intreats his Cynthia not to remain too long on a shore which he seems to think dangerous to the chastest maiden [....] Martial asserts, that a woman who came hither as chaste as Penelope, if she remained any time, would depart as licentious and depraved as Helen [....] I have certainly met with ladies, after they had resided some time at Naples, who, in point of character and constitution, were thought to have a much stronger resemblance to Helen than to Penelope; but as I have no great faith in the sudden operation of physical causes in matters of this kind, I never doubted of those ladies having carried the same disposition to Naples that they brought from it. Though there are not wanting those who affirm, that the influence of this seducing climate is evident *now* in as strong a degree as it is described to have been anciently; that it pervades people of all ranks and conditions, and that in the convents themselves;

> Even there where frozen chastity retires,
> Love finds an altar for forbidden fires.

Others, who carry their researches still deeper, and pretend to have a distinct knowledge of the effect of aliment through all its changes on the human constitution, think, that the amorous disposition, imputed to Neapolitans, is only in part owing to their voluptuous climate, but in a far greater degree to the hot, sulphureous nature of their soil, which those profound naturalists declare communicates its fiery qualities to the juices of vegetables; thence they are conveyed to the animals who feed on them, and particularly to man, whose nourishment consisting both of animal and vegetable food, he must have in his veins a double dose of the stimulating particles in question. No wonder, therefore, say those nice investigators of cause and effect, that the inhabitants of this country are more given to amorous indulgencies, than those who are favoured with a chaster soil and a colder climate.

For my own part, I must acknowledge, that I have seen nothing, since I came to Naples, to justify the general imputations above mentioned, or to support this very ingenious theory. On the contrary, there are circumstances from which the opposers of this system draw very different conclusions; for every system of philosophy, like every Minister of Great Britain, has an opposition. The gentlemen in opposition to the voluptuous influence of this climate, and the fiery effects of this soil, undermine the foundation of their antagonists' theory, by asserting, that, so far from being of a warmer complexion than their neighbours, the Neapolitans are of colder constitutions, or more philosophic in the command of their passions, than any people in Europe. Do not the lower class of men, say they, strip themselves before the houses which front the bay, and bathe in the sea without the smallest ceremony? Are not numbers of those stout, athletic figures, during the heat of the day, seen walking and sporting on the shore perfectly naked; and with no more idea of shame, than Adam felt in his state of innocence; while the ladies from their coaches, and the servant-maids and young girls, who pass along, contemplate this singular spectacle with as little apparent emotion as the ladies in Hyde Park behold a review of the horse-guards?

6. On Tivoli, Albano, Frescati, and Scotland (2: 337-343)

The grand scale on which the beauties of nature appear in Switzerland and the Alps, has been considered by some, as too vast for the pencil; but among the sweet hills and vallies of Italy, her features are brought nearer the eye, are fully seen and understood, and appear in all the bloom of rural loveliness. Tivoli, Albano, and Frescati, therefore, are the favourite abodes of the landscape-painters who travel to this country for improvement; and in the opinion of some, those delightful villages furnish studies better suited to the powers of their art, than even Switzerland itself. Nothing can surpass the admirable assemblage of hills, meadows, lakes, cascades, gardens, ruins, groves, and terraces, which charm the eye, as you wander among the shades of Frescati and Albano, which appear in new beauty as they are viewed from different points, and captivate the beholder with endless variety [....]

The most commanding view is from the garden of a convent of Capucins, at no great distance from Albano. Directly before you is the lake, with the mountains and woods which surround it, and the castle of Gondolfo; on one hand is Frescati with all its villas; on the other, the towns of Albano, La Riccia, and Gensano; beyond these you have an uninterrupted view of the Campagna, with St. Peter's church and the city of Rome in the middle; the whole prospect being bounded by the hills of Tivoli, the Apennines, and the Mediterranean.

While we contemplated all these objects with pleasure and admiration, an English gentleman of the party said to Mr. B——, "There is not a prospect equal to this in all France or Germany, and not many superior even in England." "That I well believe," replied the Caledonian; "but if I had you in Scotland, I could shew you several with which this is by no means to be compared." "Indeed! Pray in what part of Scotland are they to be seen?" "I presume you never was at the castle of Edinburgh, Sir?" "Never." "Or at Stirling?" "Never." "Did you ever see Loch Lomond, Sir?" "I never did." "I suppose I need not ask, whether you have ever been in Aberdeenshire, or the Highlands, or——" "I must confess once for all," interrupted the Englishman, "that I have the misfortune never to have seen any part of Scotland." "Then I am not surprised," said the Scot, taking a large pinch of snuff, "that you think this the finest view you ever saw." "I presume you think those in Scotland a great deal finer?" "A very great deal indeed, Sir; why that lake, for example, is a pretty thing enough; I dare swear, many an English nobleman would give a good deal to have such another before his house; but Loch Lomond is thirty miles in length, Sir! there are above twenty islands in it, Sir! that is a lake for you. As for their desert of a Campagna, as they call it, no man who has eyes in his head, Sir, will compare it to the fertile valley of Stirling, with the Forth, the most beautiful river in Europe, twining through it." "Do you really in your conscience imagine," said the Englishman, "that the Forth is a finer river than the Thames?" "The Thames!" exclaimed the North Briton, "Why, my dear Sir, the Thames at London is a mere gutter, in comparison of the Firth of Forth at Edinburgh." "I suppose then," said the Englishman, recovering himself, "you do not approve of the view from Windsor Castle?" "I ask your pardon," replied the other; "I approve of it very much; it is an exceeding pretty kind of prospect; the country appears from it as agreeable to the sight as any plain flat country, crowded with trees, and intersected by enclosures, can well do; but I own I am of opinion, that mere fertile fields, woods, rivers, and meadows, can never, of themselves, perfectly satisfy the eye." "You imagine, no doubt," said the Englishman, "that a few heath-covered mountains and rocks embellish a country very much?" "I am precisely of that opinion," said the Scot; "and you will as soon convince me that a woman may be completely beautiful with fine eyes, good teeth, and a fair complexion, though she should not have a *nose* on her face, as that a landscape, or country, can be completely beautiful without a mountain." "Well, but here are mountains enough," resumed the other; "look around you." "Mountains!" cried the Caledonian, "very pretty mountains, truly! They call that Castel Gondolfo of theirs a castle too, and a palace, forsooth! but does that make it a residence fit for a Prince?" "Why, upon my word, I do not think it much amiss," said the other; "it looks full as well as the palace of St. James's." "The palace of St. James's," exclaimed the Scot, "is a scandal to the nation; it is both a shame and a sin, that so great a monarch as the King of Scotland, England, and Ireland, with his Royal consort, and their large family of small children, should live in a shabby old cloister, hardly good enough for monks. The palace of Holyrood-house, indeed, is a residence meet for a king."

www.ingramcontent.com/pod-product-compliance
Lightning Source LLC
Chambersburg PA
CBHW011657010726
47500CB00005B/1298
9781934555514